TO FIND CORA

Cora has run off with anot[...] the loss. It makes him so crazy, he starts searching everywhere for Cora. The memory of her long, flowing black hair and alabaster skin haunts him. Eventually Joe gets a lead in Frigate, Oklahoma. A couple, the woman matching Cora's description, has been seen occasionally coming into town. Joe drives out to a barren, desolate farmhouse, and is convinced at first that the woman coming to the door is his Cora. But Joe has found Viola instead, and a wreck of a man named Hall. They inhabit their own particular hell, and have no intention of letting Joe leave them. But Joe doesn't care—all he wants is his Cora.

LIKE MINK, LIKE MURDER

Sam Baynard has been out of prison for over a year, clean of his former crime partners. He's a milkman now, working for the Gorten Milk Company, in love with a sweet girl named Lois, but still dogged by the cynical Lt. Lantis. Then Elva shows up. Sam had been obsessed with Elva, but she'd been Collie's girl, and Collie was the boss. Oh sure, she'd tempted him, but she'd never delivered. And now she is back, back with new promises. But so is Collie, back with a new plan. Sam thought he could go straight, but between Elva's charms, Collie's threats and the heat from Lantis, Lois and her safe world just haven't got a chance.

BODY AND PASSION

Jeff Taylor is being framed for murder by ambitious Assistant D.A. Ben Young, when all he really wants to do is get out of the rackets. One night he takes Young up to his cabin for a showdown. But in the ensuing fight, fire breaks out. Only one man gets out alive, and he is so badly burned as to be unrecognizable. Worse, when he finally regains consciousness, he no longer has any memory of who he is. Ben Young's powerful parents and cold-hearted wife are convinced he is Ben. Taylor's conniving wife and shifty partner are convinced he's Jeff. Both sides want more from him than he can give. And the answer to his identity may just end in murder.

TO FIND CORA

LIKE MINK LIKE MURDER

BODY AND PASSION

HARRY WHITTINGTON
INTRODUCTION BY DAVID LAURENCE WILSON

STARK HOUSE

Stark House Press • Eureka California

TO FIND CORA / LIKE MINK LIKE MURDER / BODY AND PASSION

Published by Stark House Press
1315 H Street, Eureka, CA 95503, USA
griffinskye3@sbcglobal.net
WWW.STARKHOUSEPRESS.COM

ISBN: 1-933586-25-7

Cover design and layout by Mark Shepard, WWW.SHEPGRAPHICS.COM
Proofreading by Rick Ollerman and David L. Wilson

REPRINT EDITION

HARRY AND HIS BASTARD CHILDREN

BY DAVID LAURENCE WILSON

"It was a lot of leg work. That was what it amounted to. You saw a lot of people, and you asked a lot of questions, and you got a few answers. Most of it was confusion. But you kept moving, and you kept asking questions until the confusion straightened itself out and was as clear as a jigsaw puzzle once you supplied the missing piece." HARRY WHITTINGTON, 1951

You learn it early. There's never enough. Not enough of anything. It's not just the survival of the fittest, it's the survival of the acquisitive, the squirrel with the most nuts.

A performer finishes a second encore and gets a seven minute shower before he signs autographs, poses for pictures, shares an anecdote or a drink. The audience can never get enough.

A writer never has enough for the readers, either. When the Great Writer dies his last effort ought to be an unpublished novel or short story. That's the way a writer likes to go out, with the last story finished.

It's like an athlete going out a winner, an actor with one last movie in the can, like Vincent Price or Edward G. Robinson in a death scene.

A reader has a lot of choices when he is introduced to a new writer, though this sea of print is always finite. One day the scales move, and there are fewer of the books to find and read.

Some of those books are so rare that you're never going to find them, volumes rumored but never sighted. Maybe you can find them on the writer's own bookshelf. Maybe he doesn't have a copy either. Was it really published?

It's the thrill of the hunt. Somewhere, it waits: the smell of paper.

□   □   □

Here, among the dust and the detours, is one of those novels that has been waiting, a "new" Harry Whittington novel originally published in 1957. It is a Whittington that no one has read in its original form. No one living.

Whittington was among the greatest of suspense writers. In 1957, at the height of his powers, he was writing classic noir melodramas like *Fires That Destroy* (1951), *The Woman is Mine* (1954) and *Brute in Brass* (1956) for Fawcett's Gold Medal line of original paperbacks. With a little color and a few observations he wrote about ordinary people in fantastic situations. Harry was a gifted and passionate working class writer who was ascending to the title, "King of the Paperbacks." His books looked good at a bus station or a newsstand, the rack beside a cigar store.

It was a one-man production line. He wrote as if the craft of writing were an exercise in how quickly he could type the words. Deep, three-fingered meditation. Sometimes he wrote with more emotion than plausibility, a tricky stream of consciousness. He had the fastest typewriter in the south. He made the most incredible plots seem believable.

Whittington was a writer of intense, compulsively paced action. He'd begin with a simple, compelling premise and he'd top it again and again, putting his heroes into extravagant new forms of jeopardy. The stories built to moments of great danger and passion and they ended abruptly, as if his readers had suddenly awakened.

Harry was published in the last days of pulps, in hardback, paperback, in digests and men's magazines. His writing was derivative of the dark, cheap world of film noir. He was recreating the form in prose. Harry depended on volume. Ultimately, none of his markets gave him enough income to maintain his career.

Like Mink, Like Murder was one of the stories that didn't sell, at least not in the U.S., and not in its original state, as it left Harry's typewriter. As *Mink* it sold to the French publisher, Gallimard, where it became part of the Serie Noire, the classic French run of American crime novels featuring authors like Jonathan Latimer, David Goodis and Paul Cain. Day Keene and Gil Brewer, Harry's St. Petersburg neighbors and colleagues, were also among the writers published by Gallimard.

You couldn't tell much from the title, *Mink*, and the French title, *T'as Des Visions!* translated to "You Have Visions!" Colloquially it meant "You're Seeing Things!"

Was this a crime novel or a piece of natural history? The title "You Have Visons" seemed like more of an attempt to describe my stumbling effort to find an English manuscript than it described an actual book.

◻   ◻   ◻

You could say that the lucky break that lead to this first American edition of *Like Mink, Like Murder* — the fourth version of this story — came when Harry's son found the manuscript among his father's paperbacks. That would be the easy explanation and in a general sense, it would be true.

The incubation period was quite a bit longer, however. In 1983 I was writing for a magazine called *Mystery* and I spent the Fall touring the U.S. in a van with curtains and a homemade bed, visiting crime writers from one coast to the other. One of them was Talmage Powell, who had once collaborated with Whittington. Powell spoke about the recent deaths of the pulp writers Robert Turner and Gil Brewer.

I'd been studying and interviewing crime writers, starting with the hardback and pulp writers, but I was still unfamiliar with the writers of original paperbacks. I wasn't familiar with Harry's work, so I turned west at Daytona Beach and never made it to Tampa and St. Petersburg, where Powell and Whittington, Brewer, Al James, Day Keene and Jack Kerouac had all lived.

It left me with a certain sense of guilt, not trying to contact Whittington, because later I grew to love his writing. It was at a moment when a little more encouragement might have sent Harry back to crime fiction for one last hurrah. It might have pulled him away from his successful historical fictions, as Ashley Carter.

Later I had a chance to write about Harry's western novels for an encyclopedia, a short essay that became long and ultimately appeared as "Tough Luck: The Life and Art of Harry Whittington" in the first Stark House collection of Harry's fiction. I had begun my research by seeking any and all information I could find on the author.

Whittington's resurgence began in 1987 with a series of reprints from Black Lizard Books: *Fires That Destroy* (1951), *Forgive Me, Killer* (*Brute in Brass*, 1954), *Web of Murder* (1958), *A Moment to Prey* (*Backwoods Tramp*, 1959), *A Ticket to Hell* (1959) and *The Devil Wears Wings* (1960). Harry's own essay in the book, "I Remember It Well," was based upon remarks he had made in several lectures.

Harry's remarks seemed to cry out for greater explanation, particularly when he noted 39 additional books, unidentified and written under pseudonyms: "I signed, in 1964, to do a 60,000-word novel a month for a publisher under his house names," Harry wrote. "I was paid $1000. On the first of each month, I wrote one of these novels a month for 39 months." For most of us, this was the first note of Harry's "Unknowns," the beginning of a literary legend.

A researcher and book dealer, Lynn Munroe, produced entertaining, occasionally provocative book catalogs. His bibliography moved the details of

Harry's pile of 200 novels closer to coherence but there were still questions. Munroe wrote: "I have learned that the standard HW bibliographies are incomplete, or rife with errors... I contacted the Whittington family in Florida and they were most helpful.... Our correspondence continued until I sent a letter asking for their help in identifying the 39 "house name" paperbacks HW said he wrote... I hit a stone wall. Either they don't know or don't care to name those books. And so my plan for the first ever COMPLETE HW checklist remains a pipe dream."

Sometimes, before his death in 1989, Whittington seemed to tease about these unidentified novels. They represented nearly one quarter of his bibliography and left him with an odd, hollowed out career, an anomaly for a writer as well-known as Harry. He had already been published with so many pseudonyms, for so many publishers that it took a scholar to follow his career.

As a reader who admired the storyteller I wanted to know: If there were thirty-nine unknown books, were there any that could rival his classic crime stories? Could there be more? Harry was too notable a writer for this black hole and thirty-nine titles to go unnoticed.

Harry took pride in his persistence: his volume, his dedication, the sheer mass of words that he was able to produce. On the other hand, there was his very real discomfort about these "Unknowns." They had been written during a troubled period in his life, a period he was not eager to revisit. Ultimately, he compromised, claiming the number of finished books but none of the titles. He wanted credit for those "Unknowns" even if he was reluctant to name them.

"He could turn out 30 pages of original material a day," his son Howard said. "That was macho. It was his strength, his power. He didn't think many people could do that."

Sometimes Harry would refer to his novels as his hundreds of bastard children. His son Howard believed that this represented all his father's writing, the product of one mind, a father but no mother. The "Unknowns" were the true bastards, however, with not even the thinly veiled "Hallam Whitney," "Whit Harrison" or "Harry White" pseudonyms that Harry had used to designate the parentage of some of the "Knowns".

It was part of Harry's nature that he would divide his life and career into acts. Accordingly it became a three-act play: a rise, fall, and rise again. During the "Cadillac Years" he was literal enough that he actually celebrated his good fortune by purchasing a Cadillac. When he began to write the "Unknowns" he was past the Cadillac years, well into the realization that the old good days were gone. He had manuscripts in the mail but not enough of them were selling.

In 1962 Whittington severed his contentious relationship with his long-term literary agent, Donald McCampbell, and signed with the Scott Meredith Agency, a firm known for taking an aggressive role in generating new markets.

In 1963, after the "Cadillac Years" and writing nurse novels, magazine pieces and westerns, for the lower paying markets, Harry began the regimen of the "Unknowns." This was the last stand. Three years later, at the age of fifty-two, he gave up his career as a writer of fiction.

□   □   □

In 1999 I contacted Howard Whittington and he was kind enough to send me a copy of his father's sales records. The description of the "Unknowns" was tantalizing. So was the description of Whittington's earliest efforts.

Between 1932 and 1942 Whittington wrote five unpublished novels influenced by F. Scott Fitzgerald and John Dos Passos. Between 1944 and 1946 he worked with an editor at Doubleday Books, generating ten rewrites of his novel *The World Before Us*. He abandoned the novel two years later and would never again put so much effort into a single piece of work.

In the accounting of his sales, Whittington wrote: "No record remains of the hundreds of unpublished short stories written, submitted and rejected between 1932 and 1942. Tried every market from *The New Yorker* to *Love Fiction Weekly*. Nothing published. Most rejection slips printed." No copies, only titles remaining: "Slave Girl Down the River," "And Whenever April Comes," and "Hell's Love Song." While he wrote he was a public employee. He worked in the postal service of St. Petersburg, Florida.

Four pages representing the "Unknowns" were missing from this informal bibliography. The title and publisher of one of the remaining books had been scratched out with a pen. This is what was left: "(50,000 wds) Pseud. House name. First of the long 38 months of a 'novel per month.'"

Harry's widow Kathryn was the one who had scratched out the title and the name of the publisher, but even she had left a clue. Beneath the scribbling was "Ember," an unfamiliar imprint.

There was also another clue here: thirty-eight books, one fewer than Harry had claimed in "I Remember It Well," his ironically titled essay. Harry's inexact figure, 38 *or* 39 novels, had given the search yet another level of mystery.

I looked up Ember on the internet and found *Go Down, Aaron* (1967), an "adult paperback," and I began to understand Harry's ambivalence about these novels. The books were written to order, all of them exactly 190 pages long, snubbed-down paperbacks with the look of a Volkswagen bus. Yellow, or pink. Ugly covers with the roughest of charms. Sex books.

It seems that one of the ways Scott Meredith kept his writers working was by serving as a conduit for "Corinth Publications," publisher of "Ember" and other imprints. It was owned by William Hamling, who was also the publisher of *Rogue* magazine, one of the most successful followers of Hugh Hefner's *Playboy* magazine. It was the early sixties, a year or two before the

"Swinging Sixties" really got into gear. The term "Love-in" had not yet been coined. Sex was something that television wasn't selling, at least not to the degree that it could be handled in print. It was the age of sleaze.

I found some of the books from the series. Several featured the work of William Knoles, a clever, facile writer who wrote as "Clyde Allison." Some of the Allison novels were expensive James Bond pastiches, ranging up towards one hundred dollars a book. Well, in that case, I could count them out — they weren't Harry. There were 148 novels, Ember and Ember Library books. If I could eliminate the Allison novels and the others by known authors, it became more realistic to look for the thirty-eight books by Harry Whittington. Rather than trying to pick out the Whittingtons, I could begin by identifying the books that had not been written by Harry. The process of elimination.

□   □   □

I began reading the Ember books and came up with dozens of maybes but not a single book that was clearly written by Whittington. I needed some kind of corroboration, like a panel of experts, someone with a Ph.D. It was the pacing, the cuts, the rhythm of a Whittington I was seeking. Harry's stories hummed without sound. When I read the "Embers" I was not convinced. The closest was a book called *Sin Hellion* (1963) and the connection was not all that close. The hero was Harry Donalds, a combination, I believed, of "Harry Whittington" and his agent "Donald McCampbell," whose apparent lack of interest in Harry's writing had helped lead him to the Corinth contract. *Lost House of Sin* (1964) might be Harry, or *Passion Rap* (1966) or *The Sin Collector* (1966). I put the project aside. It was hard to make a convincing case for any of these books, even to myself.

I'd keep going as long as Harry kept feeding me clues. If he didn't want the books identified, why had he left me so much information about them. He was the one who had brought up the subject. No one knew about them until he began discussing them in his essay and lectures.

At the University of Wyoming's American Heritage Center, where the archives preserved several boxes of Harry's papers, I found another copy of the list of his sales. This one included the missing pages and Harry's titles for the "Unknowns." All the titles on his list of "Unknowns" were identified as "Embers."

□   □   □

I met Earl Kemp, the editor of the Corinth books, at a Southern California paperback show where he'd become a regular. He was cordial and he had opinions, conservative dress, a white goatee. He didn't look retired. He looked like a leftist, a sociology Prof. or a screenwriter about to be blacklisted. Maybe it was the freedom of speech thing.

I asked him how he handled the manuscripts that came in for Ember.

He stopped me. He said it didn't work that way. The books arrived in black boxes, from the Meredith Agency. Then they were shuffled to whatever imprint needed a book. There were no Ember writers. The writers for Corinth were as generic as the novels. Even Kemp didn't know who they were.

Now the process of elimination had suddenly become ten times more difficult. Corinth had published thousands of books from scores of writers. Picking out the work of one voice among this peculiar chorus would be difficult if not impossible.

I asked Kemp something about the novels and he corrected me again.

"Novels?" he said, "These weren't novels! This wasn't literature. These were periodicals, to be read... and thrown away."

Ultimately, a long detective-research effort had left me with nothing. It was a *Heart of Darkness* in paperback. I was done. It cost me nothing to vow that I wouldn't embarrass Kathryn. I was sharing these secrets with no one. I had the name of a publisher but none of the books. If I had just one story I was sure was Harry's I could work from that, and expand the list. So far Harry had been leaving clues and messages. The whole time it seemed like he was pushing the search along. I needed another assist from Harry. If it came.

□   □   □

Kathryn Whittington died August 13, 2005. Three months later I received a Sunday phone call from her son. I had spoken to Kathryn several times while I worked on "The Art and Life of Harry Whittington." We had corresponded. She had read "Tough Luck" and approved.

One morning we had a conference call with Howard. Kathryn had spent half the night watching late night movies (She was a fan of Tarrantino's *Pulp Fiction*). She was the caretaker of the Harry Whittington legacy and had long ago omitted the word "Ember" from her vocabulary. She told me that she had saved all of Harry's papers and books, that his work had been untouched during the years since his death.

I mentioned a fact I wasn't supposed to know. Harry had been visited by the F.B.I.

I had understood, incorrectly, that the F.B.I. wanted to question Harry about his trip to Cuba, when the publisher Pyramid sent Harry and two other writers to the island and asked them to write quick novels to take advantage of the public's interest in the Cuban revolution.

"She's looking daggers at me," Howard had said.

Actually, the F.B.I. had come to discuss Harry's writing, the thirty-eight unknown novels. Despite Cornith's poorly kept, evasive records, the Federal Bureau of Investigation was there because they thought Harry had been sexing up his fiction.

I had already spoken to Howard after Kathryn's death, urging him to watch for any manuscripts, particularly for an English copy of *Mink*, one of the Holy Grails. I also asked him to look for copies of Ember books, and I described the format for the Corinth paperbacks.

Now he had the evidence, dug out of an upstairs closet at Harry's pearl white, bay front home, a new home that looked like it belonged in *Gone With the Wind*. Harry had finally achieved his longtime goal, a house on an island, a dock alongside the Gulf. His closets were filled with books.

"I've found the mother lode," Howard said.

He was reading the titles, and the names of the writers, chuckling as he went deeper into a cardboard box: *Passion Burned, Flesh Curse, Remembered Sin, The Sin Fishers, Saddle Sinners, Baptism in Shame, Blood Lust Orgy, Lust Dupe, Sharing Sharon, Flesh Avenger, Pushover, Wedding Affair, The Sinning Room, Sin Psycho, Shame Union, The Abortionists, The Taste of Desire, Flesh Mother, The Latent Lovers, Flamingo Terrace, Sin Deep, Sinsurance, Hell Bait, Passion Cache, Lust Buyer, Passion Flayed* and *Man Hater*. Perhaps these were author's copies, unloved, but not discarded, either. Somehow, despite Harry and Kathryn's discomfort, these books had been saved. Now they had become part of the story.

Twenty-seven novels! I'd been looking for a starting point, a pseudonym, even a single book that I could identify as one of Harry's novels. Now there were twenty-seven of them. If these were Harry's they were two-thirds of his unknown novels, the best clue yet.

One whole continent away, on the West Coast, it was hard to be sure exactly what these books represented. They could be Harry, or perhaps not. There were sixteen books by John Dexter, four by J. X. Williams, and seven by Curt Colman. I'd been seeking a pseudonym and here were three of them. I'd been seeking Ember books but these were Sundown Reader, Evening Reader, Nightstand, Leisure and Idle Hour. There was not a single Ember book among them.

This, finally, was the new hypothesis, the proposition on which all the facts and clues would be assembled. We'd start with the assumption that all these books were written by Harry. It put us way beyond the process of elimination.

Some of the titles were still the same that Harry had given them: *Pushover* (Leisure Book, 1964), *Saddle Sinners* (Evening Reader, 1964), *The Sinning Room* (Nightstand, 1966), *Hell Bait* (Evening Reader, 1966) and *Sinners After Six* (Leisure Books, 1966). For the remaining novels it was going to be hard to match up Harry's evocative but nonspecific titles like *Love's Lovely Lust, Marry the Devil* and *Private Gallows*, with the Corinth titles.

Later, when I saw the actual books, they didn't look like they had all come from the same source. Some had marks from the newsstand. Some of the covers had been torn off. It looked like Harry had collected this incomplete group from newsstands and used book stores. Random copies from here and there. There had been an intent to assemble these books. They didn't just show up.

□   □   □

The craft of writing long ago made its accommodations to a world of factories and assembly lines. You can add Harry Whittington — with the fastest typewriter in the south —to the scribes who worked the writing factory.

As the market slowed Whittington didn't suddenly begin writing for the New Yorker or literary magazines. He began writing for the true confession and true crime magazines. As far as writing personal journalism, the combination and fact and fiction technique, he was ahead of Mailer and Capote.

Among these efforts, at the end of 1960, was "Prowl, Peep and Prey," sold to Joseph Corona, at Fawcett's *True Police Cases*. "It has all the elements, rape, unnatural violation, violent bludgeoning and a great deal of police work," Harry wrote Corona.

"Finally somebody in Florida solved a murder."

Corona wrote back: "I'm pleased to learn that there is a strong element of sex in the crime, should add up to one hell of a fine story through your skillful handling."

After a dry spell Harry's books were once again being printed by many publishers. The book Harry titled *Hollywood Affair* had been finished in June of 1958 but was not sold to Gold Medal until August of 1962, published as *Don't Speak to Strange Girls*. *Some Like 'Em Cold* was finished June 1959, sold to Belmont Books in July of 1962 and published as *Hot As Fire, Cold As Ice*. That was the year Whittington signed with the literary agent Scott Meredith.

He was considering a six book a year commitment to Beacon Books, a publisher that promoted the sleaze element. Beacon had published Harry's novel *Bier Date*, the follow-up to *Brute in Brass*, as *Any Woman He Wanted* (1961). Since 1960 Harry had recently written five books for Beacon, using two different names, Whit Harrison and Kel Holland. *Naked in Babylon* became *Strip the Town Naked* (1960), *As God Made Her* became *A Woman Possessed* (1961), *The Strange Young Wife* (1964) was originally titled *Feed On My Flesh*, and the first title for *The Tempted* (1964) was *The Glass Scalpel*.

Meredith wrote Harry about a suggestion from the editor at Beacon, a story about "a marriage between a girl of around 18 to 20 and a man in his late fifties. This wouldn't be the typical story of a bad marriage, but rather, the marriage would be a good one on most counts, marred only by the fact that the husband, perhaps because he's subject to heart attacks, isn't able to satisfy the girl completely in a sexual way. A younger third person would come into the picture to provide a sexual outlet for her, and the complications then ensuing would be the basis for the novel."

"This is, of course, similar in some ways to your Nightstand book..."

Whittington had been asked if he'd like to try a "Nightstand" book, the name of the first of the Corinth imprints, a line which began publishing in 1959. Harry wrote one of the books, it was accepted, and he signed a work for hire contract to write one novel a month, $1000 for each manuscript. More than half of these would be crime novels, potent little psychodramas with heroes at risk from multiple menaces, both criminals and the forces of law. Harry found that he could finish one of the books, usually, in a week. That would leave him time for other manuscripts and film jobs and a chance to get ahead financially.

The book that Harry wrote for Beacon was *His Father's Wife* (1964), with a new pseudonym, Clay Stuart. The book for Corinth was *Lust Farm* (1964).

Harry collected gimmicks, odd facts and turnabouts for his books, and he saved his ideas on three by five cards. One read: "No footprints in soft mud, or snow, but man is killed in house. Gimmick is stilts with sharp points."

Another went like this: "Would an absent minded scientist die if he had to compete with a gangster on a desert island?... If there were a woman with them they both wanted?... If a man and a snake fall in a pit, which would survive?"

Howard Whittington recalled another gimmick his father had been pleased with... a beaver will not maintain a dam in polluted or fouled water.

That was where the body went in *Lust Farm*, an Ember Book published in 1964. The body of "Aaron Barr" goes into a beaver pond and the beavers leave. Typically, Harry framed his "fact" by using it in another switch, a frame-up.

This was the sex in *Lust Farm*, Harry's poetry of desire, his conjugation of love: "It was as if he were transported, whirled about the room as if on the gales of high winds. The pale lights of the room were blindingly bright, and they seemed to explode behind his eyeballs, and then there was darkness, and the darkness was sweet and warm and liquid, and he was spinning downward to it." When Harry wrote about sex it was like he was writing about Armageddon.

Lust Farm was the twenty-eighth "Unknown."

This first "Ember" publication may explain why Harry subsequently referred to all thirty-eight of these books as "Ember" novels. Harry's title for the story was *Of Dark Desires*. His manuscript featured another pseudonym, Hal Whitney, that never saw print,

When Whittington joined Corinth he was joining a roster of young New York writers who would later rival the skills of Fawcett's Gold Medal line, a group that would become the best crime writers of their generation, including Donald Westlake, Lawrence Block and Evan "Ed McBain" Hunter. This was their apprenticeship.

There are famous stories about how some of these books would be written at great speed or how they were written collaboratively, around a poker table, a modern version of the surrealist's game of Exquisite Corpse. One book could finance a fine party and if the writing was uneven, well, so was the printing.

Harry had very mixed feelings about these novels. He had always walked a high-tension tightrope of taste: crime, sex, brutality and corruption were all among his themes. The stories he wrote for Corinth weren't far from his oeuvre, but they didn't feel quite right, either.

For Harry, the books were problematic. A lot of people couldn't see past their covers. Harry was from the conservative Florida Outback. He grew up in the hill country during the depression. Some of his relatives felt they had to keep one hand on the Bible, if they read one of Harry's novels.

Like any other paperback, the Corinth books offered promises they wouldn't keep. By the light of 2009, the sex is mild, archaic, politically incorrect. Of course the subject never seems to go completely out of style. The eroticism of fifty years ago has a patina of innocence today.

In 1981 Whittington was interviewed by the pulp culture historian Michael S. Barson for *Paperback Quarterly*. Barson asked: "Did any [paperback] house ever specify that they wanted a more sexy sort of story than what you had submitted?"

"I don't think there was much difference between publishers — and I had many! " Harry said. "Ace never used sex in any overt way. Gold Medal thought they did — but looking back, we know there was no sex in any of those books."

Corinth, at the time, was of a different level of sexuality. If the manuscripts didn't deliver it — the packaging certainly did. The books looked cheap and they were inexpensive.

The publisher was operating out of San Diego, my home town. For a boy of fifteen or sixteen, the books were not an unknown. You could find them in the liquor stores, where you could buy both doughnuts and fiction. When the cover illustrations were on good behavior you might see them in a grocery store. In San Diego, you could find the books when they fell off a truck.

There wasn't always much sex in some of those books. For Harry it wasn't so much a change in style as in presentation, perhaps a change in degree. Sometimes you could read through the whole book and not bend the corners of a page. It was more accurate that there was the potential for sex in the books. The characters consider it as a normal part of human life. Sometimes they spend the whole story thinking about it.

□ □ □

Though most readers became aware of the "Unknowns" in 1987, via the Black Lizard publications, there was an earlier, lesser known reference to the "Unknowns." That was in *Vision*, a literary journal published by the Arts Assembly of Jacksonville, Inc. in 1979. It also identified Harry's Henry Whittier byline, used for the later Corinth novel *Nightmare Alibi* (1972).

According to Professor Gary L. Harmon, chairman of the Literature and English Department in Jacksonville, at the University of North Florida, "...In October, 1963, (Harry) signed a contract to do a novel a month for Ember Books, to be published under house bylines for $1000 each book. He wrote 38 over the next 38 months.

"He didn't like the writing he was doing, though writing was what he had always enjoyed. And writing 55,000 word novels month after month in order to pay off debts, support the family (his son and daughter were college age then) and meet the publishing schedule must have rubbed his

nerve endings raw. By 1968 he was exhausted, sick of the publishing business, truly disgusted with the writing he had to do... The killer pace of the novel each month continued, ending finally in February of 1967."

The interview with Professor Harmon continued: "When I observed to him that his sex scenes are bold and suggestive, but not explicit, his response was instructive. 'When I was young, I read Erskine Caldwell's *God's Little Acre*, and I saw that he was having a great deal of fun writing about the sexual activities of his people. Since then, I've never been inhibited to write about people's sexual behavior.' He observed that "There's the pants-up school of writing, and then there's the pants-down school. I belong to neither. I would rather provide just enough detail so that the reader could participate in creating the scene. Often, readers will tell me how raw and shocking a particular love scene is. But they have filled in the details... and added the "raw" and "shocking" part."

Later Whittington told Barson: "None of the books you mentioned (*The Mexican Connection* (1972) *Nightmare Alibi*) were written as porn, but they may have been spiced up by the editors. I don't know. They told me they wanted books written 'your way,' not 'ours.'"

By the standards of 2009 the earliest of the thirty-eight were relatively chaste. A steamy conversation might end with even more conversation, though by the mid-sixties the scenes usually went further. You might think that this would be the perfect marketplace for some of the noir and hard-boiled novelists, where all the restrictions were off, where sexuality would be a natural part of the characters' lives. Unfortunately these books had their own formulas, and they were written fast and published with mistakes. Few of them are masterpieces.

Harry's daughter Harriet was a stay at home Mom with a young son. She was limited in the other responsibilities she could take on, but Harry had her read these novels and proof them. Harriet said she had to forget he was her father when she read these books. She also confirmed Harry's assertion that the novels had been "sexed up" after they left his hands.

Harry believed the books were adulterated - they were less than 100 % Whittington. That gave him another reason to disown them. It's doubtful that he ever read the printed versions.

He told Barson: "It's like having children, sending them off to compete in school where they excel in every way, and then are failed by the authorities."

Shortly before Whittington's death in 1989, he was interviewed by David Chute, who was enthusiastic enough to credit Harry with "over 300 books." The exchange was published in 1992, in the Australian crime and mystery magazine *Mean Streets*. He was still talking about the "Unknowns," explaining his challenges after *Face of the Phantom*. From beyond the grave, Harry gave his clearest explanation of the "Unknowns":

"I had so much money in that picture that for the next eight years, no matter how much I wrote, I couldn't pay off the interest on my loans. I got a job with a company called Ember Books that paid me $1000 at the first of each month. Within that month I was to send them a 60,000 word suspense novel. They were all published under house names — I don't know what the names were and I never saw any of the books."

Somewhat countering this recollection were the comments of the editor, Earl Kemp. Kemp was unfortunate: he not only spoke to the F.B.I. but he did time for the words and stories. He had gone to prison for the temerity of publishing some of these books.

According to Kemp: "The writers knew what we published and what we wanted. It was simple. If they didn't supply the books we wanted we wouldn't buy them."

Kemp wanted to reintroduce me to Lynn Munroe. "Ask him," he said. "He's the expert."

Finally I confided in Munroe. I gave him the list of the titles found in Whittington's closet: *Sin Psycho* (Sundown Reader, 1964), *Blood Lust Orgy* (Nightstand, 1966), *The Taste of Desire* (Leisure, 1966) and the rest of them. These were Harry's books, 27 of them in a box, twenty-eight including *Lust Farm*. There were ten more novels still waiting to be identified. Could we find the rest?

As Kemp had promised, Munroe knew the publisher and its titles better than anyone. According to Munroe, there were eleven Curt Colman novels. If we assumed the pseudonym was specific to Harry, we could add *Sinners After Six* (Leisure, 1966) *Mask of Lust* (Companion, 1967), *The Grim Peeper* (Pleasure Reader, 1967) and *Balcony of Shame* (Companion, 1967) to our list of Whittingtons. Thirty-two books.

Lynn Munroe could find copies of the additional Colman titles. He could also hunt up "Dexters" and "Williams" books from the period of Whittington's employment. Several of his hunches turned out to be paydirt.

Munroe and I compared notes: "If *The Latent Lovers* (Sundown Reader, 1966) had not been one of the books in the box, we never would have found it in a million years," he wrote. This despite a clarinet-playing hipster named Gil with stacks of LPs around his pad. Be warned, however, that this may have been the only resemblance in this novel to Harry's friend Gil Brewer.

One way Harry was able to write twelve novels every year was by canni-balizing the novels he had not been able to sell during the past ten years. These were the books that had gone back into the files after being rejected by, Fawcett and even the secondary, off-brand publishers. One of the revisions was *Blood Lust Orgy*, originally written as *The Crooked Window* in 1956. Readers who expected, blood, lust, or an orgy were apt to be disappointed. Harry wasn't writing about any of those three nouns. This is one of the stories where you can almost hear Harry counting off the bloody twists of plot on his fingers. Just a few months after it was published as a Nightstand Book, it was published as a 30,000 word novelette in *Shell Scott Mystery Magazine*. According to the magazine's editor, "...Some things no man can take and stay sane."

Two of the novels were adapted from Harry's confession stories. *Passion Burned* (Sundown Reader, 1965) was also published as "I Needed A Man Now" in *Daring Romances* (May 1966), *You're Deader You Think*, a rewrite of a 1954 *True Confessions* novel *The Stranger Within Me*, was published as *The Abortionists* (Nightstand, 1966).

Others were rewrites of Whittington's published novels, different versions of the same story, a process that helped us find several more of the unknown Whittington novels. His second novel, *Her Sin*, published by Phoenix in 1947, was rewritten and sent to Fawcett early in 1963 but rejected. Three years later it became *Baby Face*, (Idle Hour, 1966), the thirty-third "Unknown."

To Find Cora, rejected by Gold Medal and Newstand Library, was published by Novel Books as *Cora Is A Nympho*, an inaccurate and inelegant title, then rewritten and sold to Corinth as *Flesh Snare*, (Sundown Reader, 1966). That was book number thirty-four.

Clearly these rewritten stories had been revised, retouched by a second pair of hands. What could not be certain is whether these were still Harry's hands, years later, or some other retoucher. Many of these revisions were generic, with swoons that suggested not only sexual satisfaction but oblivion.

Flesh Snare illustrated some of the problems with the novels. A violent and sexual scene at the beginning of the book fits the characters but destroys most of the story's suspense. This time Cora really is a "nympho." After that, the version is not so bad, good enough that readers are likely to prefer whichever version of the story it is that they have read first.

One of the stories, *The Crowded Bikini*, was adapted from a screenplay Whittington had written. Another, *Sin Phantom*, was originally written in 1959, after Harry wrote, produced, directed and failed with, *The Face of the Phantom*. It is not clear from Harry's notes whether this novel was accepted by Corinth. None of the books seem to follow the plot of the movie or feature a bikini.

Despite the "mother lode" and the titles we had added to the list we were still no closer to an American edition of *Mink*. There was still no manuscript.

The French edition of *Mink, T'as Des Visons!*, certainly did exist, but the idea of translating Harry to French, and then from that French back to English had all the integrity of a ruined carbon. How exactly would you translate a croissant back into Harry's world.

Harry had, however, submitted a manuscript to Corinth titled *Like Mink, Like Murder*, in July, 1965. None of the 28 books we had identified as Whittingtons featured mink as anything more than a status symbol, a background detail. With Harry's habit of reusing titles, there was no way to be sure if this was the English version of *Mink*.

There were still more pieces of this puzzle to be found. During a trip to Florida, I was allowed to shift through Harry's note cards, his lists of published and unpublished novels. Since *Mink* had never been published in the U.S., Harry felt few compunctions about submitting it to Corinth. He rewrote the novel and submitted it as *Sin Doll*. It was the same manuscript that he later identified as *Like Mink, Like Murder*.

Munroe brought a French-speaking friend into the hunt and matched *T'as Des Visons!* with *Passion Hangover*, (Leisure, 1965), the thirty-fifth of Harry's Corinth novels. Obviously, it was Harry. Later I found a copy of the novel mixed with Harry's books in storage.

When I read *Passion Hangover*, the additions that made it a Corinth title seemed clear. I was reading two stories at once, the revised novel in my hands and the original novel hidden within it, as it must have been when it was submitted to Gold Medal and Ace. The dialogue was identical even when some of the descriptions had been changed.

Harry added scenes and perhaps even dropped a few. There were the sex scenes, which Harry could write convincingly. Harry typed every one of these new pages, so there were changes as he went along, little improvements, because he couldn't help but tinker with the prose.

I was asked if I could restore the novel, to bring it back as close as possible to Harry's original manuscript. It was an intimidating prospect but one I couldn't avoid, the chance to bring to life a "lost classic" and study the writing from the inside. It was a book that should have been published in 1957, when it would have been known as one of Harry's most striking pieces of storytelling.

Unlike some of the hurried, pieced-together efforts for Corinth, this, at its core, features deft plotting and ever-increasing suspense, with a sexual angle on par with Harry's novels for Gold Medal. One female character, a neighbor who makes friends easily, was added to the narrative, and most of "Peggy Austin's" scenes are as subtle as a third eye. Harry could have rewritten these or they could have been added later at the Corinth offices. In this Stark House edition these distracting add-ons were removed. It was a feat of subtraction, bringing *Like Mink, Like Murder* into the main current of Harry's storytelling. Everybody was always "gazing" and "shrugging" in the Corinth novel. You will find less of that here. It was the kind of work Harry might have put in if he'd ever spent a day or two rewriting, a tedious task without a computer and it's keyboard.

This is the fourth version, the fourth retelling of this story. There was Harry's original manuscript... then the French, the Corinth, and finally this book in your hands. It is a quick, lean read. Harry's original manuscript was 50,000 words, *Passion Hangover*, 55,000 words, *Like Mink Like Murder*, 36,000 words. It is the essential working out of a plot by Harry Whittington. The taut bones move.

Three years, one book a month, a lot of production and all the time Whittington was just hating it. He had not been able to generate enough additional work to escape his financial nightmare. He said he felt like he was in a coffin, already dead. He tried everything to keep going. One time he rented a cabin at the beach, so he could get away and finish one of these novels. The forced march quality of the effort wasn't making the quality any better. Kathryn Whittington said: "He'd written his brains out."

One of the last of them, *The Grim Peeper*, is barely a novel at all, more a series of vignettes with one mysterious, continuing character. It was the first time Harry had ever cheated his readers by grabbing the supernatural card:

"'You,' Billy whispered.

"He peered at the wizened, monkey-evil face, the empty eyes, the amoral smile of the old man, and he understood at last why the old man hadn't come forward to save him, but had come now.

"It was such an insane joke that it made the whole world the object of laughter. 'So that's who you are. Death.'

"Billy began to laugh, sick with laughter. 'So that's it. Death is a dirty old man!' He laughed until he couldn't stand. He laughed with his head thrown back, and he laughed doubled over, with the laugh-cramps twisting his belly.

"He laughed all the way to the chair, and beyond."

Harry didn't have many books left in him after that one.

When Harry finished the last of his books for Corinth he was physically, emotionally and economically exhausted. In his essay "I Remember It Well," Harry wrote: "I wanted to go on, pay no attention to setbacks, overlook discouragement or double-cross. With all my heart I wanted to, but I was too tired, too disappointed, too depleted... I threw away every unsold script, put my books in storage. I quit. I had reached the low point where writing lost its delight." That was when he left Florida and went to work for the Rural Electrification Administration, Information Services Division.

Harry wrote that he had thrown out his manuscripts. It was even more likely, according to his daughter, that Harry had gone out and burned his words in a backyard incinerator.

So ended 20 years of freelance writing.

□   □   □

Contrary to what you might be thinking, Whittington didn't receive quite enough punishment during his lifetime. Now I had to punish his words, to put them through a wringer as I read the novels back to back, not to consider them as individual stories but to see how they fared as a group. This is not the appropriate treatment for an author; the act of reading should be more like wine tasting, with a clean palate. This time I wasn't looking for elegance. I had to find the quirks and birthmarks, giveaways that proved to me these were Harry's novels, thirty-eight of them, as many pages as three or four copies of *War and Peace*.

So I read them all, a long sequence of memorable scenes and a style and point of view that was clearly Whittington. I tried to read one of the novels every day. A novel a day. It's the closest I could get to that book-a-week intensity with which Harry had turned them out. Wall to wall Whittington. All the books from the box were written by Whittington. There were many connections that linked these stories to him, the names of characters, the turn of a phrase or a certain mode of seduction. Sometimes it was the way the words looked on a page.

A couple of our own guesses flunked out. They didn't belong among the bastards.

Many of these books are hard to love, scarred by Harry's hurried effort and the twists that also made them a Corinth product. None of them are without flaw. There are also treasures, particularly for those who enjoy the style and pace of Whittington's writing. Sometimes it wasn't that difficult to see Harry's real story behind the garish Corinth facade.

Several of the books were crime novels and were probably rewrites of stories created years earlier. *Flesh Curse* (Sundown Reader, 1964) and *Passion Cache* (Sundown Reader, 1966) were two of them, stylish crime thrillers with unique situations and twists. First the girl — then the money: this was Harry's math. *The Taste of Desire* was a strong — if sentimental — story of class and desire in the south.

There were touches of autobiography in the books. Two of the biggest events in Whittington's life had been trips to San Francisco and Hollywood. During his first trip to California he served in San Francisco before being shipped to Pearl Harbor. His duty would be communications. He'd still be delivering the mail.

Harry wrote about those war years in *Sin Psycho*, referring to: "...a shy young man from some country town. He had worked in the post office in civilian life, and the Navy assigned him to the Fleet Post Office in San Francisco. There were no quarters for the post office personnel, so they were paid living expenses and found rooms where they could in the bay area. She remembered him telling her parents all this in his hesitant, shy voice. He read a lot and didn't go out much, catching a street car and coming home from the fleet post office in the old John Deere Plows Building at the foot of Sixth Street..."

After World War Two Harry returned to San Francisco and was mustered out of military service. Kathryn and a neighbor woman drove to San Francisco to join the husbands for a week before returning to Florida. In California they sold the car and returned home by train. Howard Whittington's first memory of his father was a figure walking out from the smoke of a train.

Harry returned to his job as a postal worker, until 1948, but he was single minded in his devotion to the craft of writing. His hobby was writing — and directing an occasional film, making his own short dramas and comedies with his family and neighbors.

As long as he had written, Harry had dreamed of making movies. The high point of his career was the sale of *Trouble Rides Tall* to Warner Brothers in 1957, $15,000 and a five-week screenwriting contract at $500 a week. This would be his first trip to the West Coast since World War II.

After this Whittington wrote two Hollywood novels, *Don't Speak to Strange Girls* and *Sin Deep* (Leisure, 1966), written by "Curt Colman," that echoed Whittington's own experience in Southern California. In *Sin Deep* he wrote: "Nothing he had ever seen could compare with the burst of color that leaped at him after the long, dark flight across the mountains and the desert," he wrote. "No other city had given him the sense of profligate splendor. It was as if the prisms and colors and gems — rubies — had been spilled carelessly by some giant who didn't even glance back because there were plenty more in this rich, wild, wealthy place, more where that came from."

There is also a portrait of rural Florida within these "Unknowns," a setting that Harry commanded. In *Flesh Snare* Harry moved the action of *To Find Cora* from Oklahoma to his native Florida hill country:

"The landscape was wild with jack oaks and scrub palmettos and lob lolly pines. I got deeper and deeper into the forsaken scrub country. I crossed a river on a narrow, wooden bridge. The water was cypress black and swift. Bay trees and water oaks and magnolias were all strung together with gray streamers of moss.

"...Behind me, the silence of the swamp country thundered like the pressure drop in the sea. The house was silent too, but in a different way, as if tension had stretched the air inside taut, singing quiet, so that even a whisper dropped would smash everything."

What is exceptional is the commonness of these stories. Between the lines Whittington was a Steinbeck made of pulp. These were stories of the American proletariat. Harry was writing about the little guy, the Down-and-Outer and the paycheck to paycheck guy who gets in trouble. They're bank clerks and box boys and an army of hard-case guys who are looking for a job. *Sin Psycho* is about a suburban mother with an out-of-work husband who becomes a prostitute to support her family.

The hero of *Like Mink, Like Murder,* is a college student turned gangster turned milkman. He's been working for two years when his past catches up with him. The story has a good girl and a bad girl. The original was another Whittington charmer that should have been filmed in low light and second-billed somewhere in 1958, a movie starring actors of the second tier. Gold Medal missed this one.

Just as home milk delivery dates *Like Mink Like Murder,* so does the whole basic premise of *Body and Passion.* It very clearly predates the introduction of genetic testing.

If the stories seem sensational, or unlikely, it may be because so many of Harry's stories were based in grade b film noir, with coked-up characters and last minute surprises. High drama from the west coast of Florida. It seemed exaggerated, a violent, unsteady world just outside our experience. Maybe Harry was right, and what these pages contain is truly the reality of life: sex and passion, violence and death. He wrote stories for the wounded and the dispossessed, a class of characters who could not write their own histories.

All these efforts, the long path, had lead us to thirty-five "new" Whittington novels, a display of sex, crime, and social ill with an undercurrent of poverty. These were the same elements, told in the same style you could read in the over-the-counter books but they were cursed by experience.

Thirty-five novels.

Stark House was ready to go to print, the end was near, and Lynn Munroe was still chasing the riddle. It had been a good partnership. I had studied Harry and his writing for ten years and was as close to his plotting and style as anyone was likely to get. Lynn was comfortable enough with some of the Corinth authors to send them plots and ask if they'd written them. He could eliminate the majority of the contenders for the honored thirty-eight, Corinth Books published between 1964 and 1967 written by "John Dexter," "J. X. Williams" and "Curt Colman."

Munroe was urging me to give one of the "possibles" another chance. I was already familiar with *The Shame Hiders* (Sundown, 1964), set on the Gulf Coast of Florida in a mythical town called "Suncrest." There's references to underwater swimming, John Wayne, mink and "golden skin," Munroe's favorite clue. These were all among the clues that would mark a Whittington. *The Shame Hiders* also expressed the sweet but rather persnickety belief that for every man and woman there is somewhere a true, perfect match. It had the "splat-splat" of gunfire, a chase through a swamp and only enough sex to disappoint some of the readers. It was the cannibalism that had thrown me off. Harry had never written about cannibalism before.

Then I read it again, in the heat of thirty-five consecutive Whittington novels. Yes. This was number thirty-six. The clincher was Harry's original, unused title for the story, *Island of Flesh*. This is exactly the title that Harry would have used for this story. After all, who's to say that Harry couldn't write a convincing story about a couple "Old World" cannibals. It was another challenge met.

So it's thirty-six "new" Whittingtons. That leaves us two books short. Harry keeps some of his secrets. His turn on the stage is still not over, his performance unfinished.

"Books do not become classics, or even great art, because of some publisher's logo, binding, or weight of paper. The novel that touches the heart, that comes from the heart, that stirs the emotions, that satisfies and enriches and entertains the reader — this is the truly great work of art no matter where it was published."

HARRY WHITTINGTON, 1983

DOWNIEVILLE, CA,
MARCH 2009

TO FIND CORA

BY HARRY WHITTINGTON

I

I could see her beautiful, nude contours before me. Her skin was like alabaster. On first glance I wanted to fall on my knees and worship her, until I looked into her eyes. Then I wanted her in my bed. Her long, flowing black hair tumbled over her shoulders like molten lava—delicate, bare, white shoulders which begged my teeth to caress them.

That was Cora—my Cora—and those were the images I saw when I looked at that farmer running his disc-harrow in a field across wire fencing from the road. I laughed, feeling the laughter warm and liquid in my throat, feeling better.

I warned myself I was stupid, but I knew I was going to ask him. He was some hick farmer I'd never met before, but he might have seen Cora. It was a chance I couldn't pass up. If he'd seen her, he'd remember her, all right.

I had to find Cora.

It was all that was left for me now. I had to find her soon or I was going to flake up inside.

People tried to talk to me about it. You know how they will—for your own good, Joe, they say. "Why do you want to find Cora, Joe?" people would say. "Looks like you know she don't want you any more, you'd let her go."

They didn't understand. Sure, they said they understood, giving me the sad smile, and the hand on my knee. "Sure, I understand how it is, Joe. But she went away—left you. She don't want you to find her."

Even the police didn't understand.

I went to them—that was back in Hollander, hell only knows how long ago, how many days, how many miles.

I could see the pitying look in those eyes, along with the contempt.

"Hell, Mr. Byars, sure we want to help you find your wife. But you got to help us. You must know something about where she went."

"No. I don't know. We had a fight."

The police detective was thumbing through some papers in a file holder. When I said that, about Cora and me having a fight, he glanced up, square in my eyes and laughed.

I felt choked. I almost hit him. I felt the trembling start, you know the way it does when something sets you off, makes you raging mad all in a flash. I almost lunged across that desk on him and gripped his shirt and hit him in the face.

For that brief space of time, everything in the world stopped and we stared into each other's eyes. I hated him as I never hated anybody, even the newest man that got on his knees with Cora I never hated him the way I hated that police lieutenant.

He saw it all, too, the hate, the way I had to dig in to keep from jumping him, and the office full of cops.

"No use being nervous, Mr. Byars," he said. Nervous. That's all he said. But he knew all right. It was right out there, bare and raw between us.

"I'm upset," I said.

His name was Lieutenant Calvin Thayer. I don't even know why I remembered his name, I wasn't remembering anything very well along then. But that name stuck with me, that fat, flat cretin face with the cigar in it, and the intelligence burning out of those ugly eyes. A man who thought clear and sharp and cold, with that cold detached kind of thinking that considered with a terrible, deliberate calm everything that was going on inside you, too.

"You know the man's name, Byars?" Thayer said.

I shook my head. "No. Not this time. Not this one."

There was a snicker behind me, but when I flinched and jerked my head around, nobody was looking at me, all of them avoiding my face. They had no eyes, just lids fixed on the uncarpeted floor.

"You don't know his name."

"No. I couldn't find out. Not this time. She—"

"She was too smart for you, huh?" Thayer said.

The snickers were louder. But I didn't turn around now. I stood leaning against Thayer's desk, humming to myself.

"Yes," I said. "This time she was too smart for me."

I felt the pain of saying that aloud in the police station of desks, and men without eyes in their heads.

"You got to do something," I said. "You got to find her. We—had this fight, see."

"You were always having big fights, Mr. Byars. Screaming, yelling at each other. We got ten—twenty disturbance calls here on you folks. Looks like she took all she could stand and walked out. Why don't you be smart, Mr. Byars? Why don't you let her go?"

"Listen. I want screwy advice, I'll write to Abby. I want you to find my wife. God damn. You people are cops, a person is missing. You don't hand out advice. You find them. You find my wife."

"Take it easy, Mr. Byars."

"I can't take it easy. I'm sick, man. I'm all torn up inside. I feel like it's coming right out of my eyes. I don't know what to do. I've got to find her. I don't know what else to do. You people got to help me."

"We'll put her description on the wires. If she's around, we'll find her."

That's what he said. They understood, they would take care of it. Only they didn't understand, so they couldn't take care of it.

I kept that phone hot. There had to be some answers to her description. You couldn't lose a girl like Cora, not anywhere. She walked into a room and everybody saw her, everybody looked at her, everybody remembered.

Sure, they gave me the shaft on the deal, the way the police will. First they figure it's classified information, police work, none of your business.

They didn't put me off like that.

They lied to me, they hung up on me, they threatened to put me in a cell if I didn't stay off that god damn horn, but they knew sooner or later they had to tell me.

"All right," Thayer said.

I was back down there, sweated, hadn't shaved, and my eyes were wild.

"We got a couple replies. One in Detroit. Another one out in Kansas City. One in Detroit didn't pan out. She was dead. Fingerprints didn't match."

I held my breath. My chest burned. "And the other one?"

He shrugged. "You think your wife went to Kansas City, Byars?"

"How the hell do I know? What did they say about her?"

"Not much. This woman answers the description. Minor traffic violation. Living with a man named Boston at the Kay Cee Hotel. That's all we got."

"I'll go out there," I said.

"Now wait a minute."

"I got to find her. If I can talk to her."

"Hell, man. A woman who looks like her. Hold on. We got no idea—"

"It might be her. She don't stay mad long. She never did. If I can get there. I can talk to her. She'll listen to me. She'll come back to me."

Only she wasn't in Kansas City. It cost me plenty to find out Jacob Boston had moved on to Hutchinson, Kansas. Topeka. Carthage, Missouri. I caught up with him in Carthage. He was alone. He showed me pictures of his wife, and kids. A fat dumpy woman, and round-faced kids with greedy mouths. No wonder he stayed on the road as much as possible.

"She was a singer. A night club in Kansas City. I met her a couple times in the past few years. Hell, a man alone on the road like this."

"The last couple years?"

"Just a few times, fellow. I don't feel like it's cheating. Not like I had a mistress, you know, waiting. We get together. Hell, you know."

It couldn't be Cora. Two years. Just a few weeks ago I had parked the Chevvy on Main, and run around to the rear at Lerner's, just in time to see her come through that door, moving fast, going somewhere.

"Where is she now?" I said.

"Who?"

"For God's sake. That girl. In Kansas City."

"Cherry?"

"All right. Cherry. Where is she now?"

He stared at me. "What for, mister?"

"I want to see her, that's all. I want to know where she is."

He thought that over, chewing on his fat lips. But I could see him make up his mind. It was easier to tell me where she was, because all he really wanted was to get rid of me.

"Hell, I'm not sure. When I left Kansas City, she was going to Denver."

"Denver."

"That's right. She had a singing job. In a club there. She sings around here—St. Louis west."

"Denver."

"Mister, that was two weeks ago. Hell, she wouldn't be there now. Denver. You know how it is. A few nights in one spot. They move on."

"You don't know where she was going?"

"No. Denver. That's all I know."

How long ago? How many miles? How many days ago? How much black coffee? How many people who just looked at me and shook their heads—their fat, empty heads.

I found Cherry in Omaha, Nebraska. Her real name was Pansy Kluttz. She'd changed it to Cherry. She offered to bed down with me for a steak dinner and a night on the town. I looked at her and my stomach roiled. I couldn't want any other woman, and what really made me sick was the stupid police. They could look at a picture of Cora, even a wire-photo and see this doll. It was a wonder they ever caught anybody, or got home nights, or recognized their own kids.

For a little while I lay alone on a motel bed and watched the lights blink against the drapes. I was low. I was stopped. I came looking for Cora, and I found Cherry. Pansy Kluttz.

Then, slowly, I began to feel better.

One thing was bright and clear, so some of the sickness dissolved in my knot-twisted belly. Somebody would see Cora, and remember. If they thought a dame like Cherry was beautiful, Cora would make them sick and frustrated and ready to clobber their wives in the chops.

If they ever saw Cora.

I was on the phone. I forgot about the time difference between Nebraska and back east in Hollander. Thayer was out, but I stayed after it. I located him, and at first he didn't want to tell me anything. But I knew. It was in the tone of his voice, there had been new answers.

I cursed him, I swore he'd never get a minute's sleep until he told me. Finally, he said there was a woman. She was in this town in back country Oklahoma. "It's a wild goose chase, Byars. Forget it."

The name of the town was Frigate. Frigate, Oklahoma. Somebody with a sense of humor. I got to the police station in Frigate, one room with a single cell out back and a drunk in it, whining and trying to climb the walls.

I told this deputy sheriff why I was there. His face was long and narrow between his ears, and his ears were oversized, and he compensated by making you repeat everything, as though he were hard of hearing.

"Yeah. We got the flyer. Woman named Cora Byars. Right?"

I nodded, staring around the room. Why would Cora be in a town like this?

"A woman was in here at Blackstone's Store. Three. Four days ago. I meant to talk to her. With some man. They had a Buick. Three or four years old."

"What did she say?"

"I didn't get to talk to her. Meant to, like I said. Something came up."

"You know where she went?"

He shook his head. "But she comes in maybe once, twice every few weeks. She don't live in this county. Look, mister. I don't waste nobody's time. If it didn't look reasonable like her, I never would have sent word clear east to Hollander."

"You got no idea where I could find her?"

"Not unless you hang around town. She's been in a few times recent. Maybe she'll come back."

"My God, man. I can't wait. Sit around like that."

"That's up to you, mister."

"When she left town. Did you see which way she went?"

He thought that over, staring at the drunk who had sprawled on his back across a cell cot.

"Yeah, I did notice. She and this tall, blonde fellow. He usually sat out in the car while she went in Blackstone's, or else he had a few beers across the street."

"Which way?"

"I noticed. Each time, now you recall it to my mind. They went west out of town. On County Road Sixteen."

County Road Sixteen was narrow and pitted. I tried to keep down to thirty, and couldn't do it. I kept seeing Cora's face out in front of me, ephemeral, just out of reach, gone beyond me, and I'd find myself hitting eighty on that narrow road, trying to catch up with her.

"Cora. My God, Cora."

I was talking aloud in the car. I was cursing, and I wasn't cursing Cora, or myself, only the people who tried to tell me I was better off without her.

When I was with her, it was like holding my breath, and feeling ready to burst. Sure, I got to admit I was jealous of her. I couldn't help it.

She got with a man, and it was like she couldn't help what she did. It was like this: like she kept telling herself that the next new guy was going to be what she wanted, and she couldn't help trying to find what she wanted.

We talked about it. When I was calm, and she wasn't screaming at me, we talked about it, and I told her maybe she could see a head-doctor, and he might be able to help her.

I thought she was going to have hysterics. "Good grief, Joe." She rolled on the bed, that long black hair wild, laughter spilling all over the floor. "Why don't you tell me to talk it over with my minister?"

"I'm only trying to help, Cora. We got to do something."

She laughed again. "Sure. We got to do something about it, Joe. Try hypnosis. We got to stop this fighting. It's all in your head. You start it, and you make something out of nothing. You go nuts. You make me hate you, Joe. We got to forget it, that's what we've got to do."

...I parked the car on Main. I went running around to the rear entrance at Lerner's. People stared at me, and I knew I looked like something crazy. There she was, coming out that back door, moving fast. Going somewhere.

Different!... Thirty minutes and half a cup of coffee in a roadside diner. Neither one of us wanted the coffee, and she was like something wild before I got on a side road. Only it was different. "I felt different about you, Joe. The first minute I saw you."

I asked all along the street in Frigate, Oklahoma. They all remembered her. Black hair. White complexion, a build like twenty oil wells, all gushers, like dirty pictures so a man felt embarrassed to look if his wife was along. None of them knew her name. Nobody knew where she lived.

I had driven a long time. I was quivering, vibrating with the trembling motion of the car I was so tired.

The country was flat, burned brown, unchanging.

When I saw the fence, and the farmer on the harrow, I stepped on the brake, waving my arm out of the car window. He cut his engine, walked over to the fence, and we got there about the same time.

We were about the same age, just edging thirty, but he was burned and dry the way the earth was, and looked as hard as the rocky ground. His eyes were flat and he stared at me with an infinite patience while I told him about Cora, told him what she looked like, what the man looked like, the car they drove.

"Think I know the people you mean," he said.

"Where are they?"

"I'm not sure it's the same people, but these folks came here a few months ago—"

"A few months ago?"

"That's right. Tall blonde fellow, and this wife that's a looker. They live in the old Petain place. You know where that is?"

"No. You tell me. I'll find it."

He told me and I got back in the car, I wasn't tired any more. I tried to keep it under thirty, but I clattered across that wooden bridge at fifty, slammed on the brakes and took a right turn on a hard-surfaced lane that was too narrow for two cars.

I was sweating. I could smell myself. It was that nervous sweat, like waking up covered with sweat from a nightmare.

Through the trees I could see the house. The sun shone on the black roof, and reflected off the tops of leaves and the upstairs windows, the way light refracts in blind eyes.

A wooden gate stood open and the yard was bare. The house was square and needed painting, and there were corrals and outbuildings beyond it. A Buick stood up in the shade of a cottonwood.

I felt myself drawing tighter.

I cut the engine and rolled near the front porch. I sat a moment trying to calm my nerves, trying to stop sweating, trying to will my hands to stop shaking.

I got out of the car and crossed in the afternoon sun, and went up on the porch, my feet loud on the dry boards.

I knocked on the door. There was the resounding echo as if the sound was coming back out of an empty house. I waited a long time.

At last I could see movement through the screened door. The long hallway ran the length of the house, and someone moved from a rear room and called out, "It's all right, Hall. I'll see who it is."

The voice caught at me, it was her voice, but maybe it was only her voice because I wanted it to be so badly. As she came closer through the shadows and into the light, I felt as if someone had cut me off at the knees. It was Cora coming toward me. It had to be Cora.

2

She came nearer.

It wasn't Cora. I saw this even before she came up all the way out of the nearest shadows of the long corridor.

I went on staring at her. Outside, behind us the silence thundered, flat and dry and hot and silent. The house was silent, too, but in a different way, as if tensions had stretched the air inside the house into a taut, singing silence so even a whisper dropped would smash everything.

"Who is it, Viola?" the man's voice came from upstairs. I let my gaze dart from her for a moment, looking upward past her into the hot gloomy silence of the second floor.

"I don't know, Hall." She laughed in flat exasperation.

"Find out who it is, Vi."

"A salesman, I guess." She flung the words across her shoulder.

She stared hard through that screen door at me, looking from her silence into mine.

I could see her eyes. I could see into them. It was as if there were no dust-rubbed screen between us, and I recognized her, even though she was some girl named Viola whom I'd never seen before in my life. I recognized her, because I'd lived two years with Cora.

There was that desperate, urgent sense of seeking in her eyes. Through the screen I couldn't determine the color of those eyes, but the need and the urgency wasn't in the color....

"Why, hello," she said.

I nodded, not saying anything, because for the moment I could only stare at her, at her body, and her rich black hair, the pale flesh of her face and shoulders, and her eyes....

"Vi!" He was yelling now, petulant and impatient like an invalid.

"For God's sake, Hall," she said, not pulling her head around.

I don't know why I kept standing there. I had my answer. It wasn't Cora; I had known all along it wasn't going to be, and it wasn't. All that was left was to turn around....

From somewhere deep inside me, I knew this was what I ought to do. Get out of there. Run. There was a sense of wrong that emanated from that gloomy house like vapors. It was warning enough for anybody.

I didn't move. For one moment we stared at each other from our prisons.

She leaned against the doorjamb and moved her eyes across me. They were hot with that urgency of discovery that I remembered from Cora.

A secret smiling pulled at her mouth.

The man yelled down the stairs. "What does he want, Vi?"

She did not bother to answer him. She licked the tip of her tongue across the bow of her upper lip sensually.

"To get to this place," she said. "You must have gotten off the road, and lost your way?"

"No." I shook my head. "I was looking for somebody."

It rushed up in me, the way it always did, senseless or not, to pour it out, to tell her about Cora, so young, so whitely fair, with black hair rich and thick and cascading down around her shoulders, so faithless and shallow and gone away somewhere so I couldn't find her.

I didn't say any of this. Always in the past few weeks, I'd find myself telling strangers about her, all about her, every hurting thing. I wouldn't want to, I'd know it was crazy, but I couldn't help it.

But something stopped me now. I didn't tell her about my agony, because I saw she was snarled and twisted into a ball of hurt of her own, and my words wouldn't touch her, wouldn't get through the screen door to her.

She stepped outside of the door.

The man yelled, panic-stricken from the upper hallway. "Vi!"

She seemed like she didn't even hear him.

"You look tired," she said. And it didn't matter what she said. The words didn't matter, they had no meaning, only a soft, throaty sound that was pleasant and soothing, as if I could stay near and under the pleasant sound of her voice and I could rest, for the first time in weeks, I could rest and be restored.

It didn't make sense. I warned myself I had been deranged ever since I'd lost Cora, and I wasn't thinking now, but I had just enough intelligence left to see there was something wrong about this place, and I had to get out of there before it was too late.

"Well, I've been driving," I said. "For a long time."

"Yes, I know."

She didn't touch me. She walked past me to an upright in a yellow shaft of sunlight, but I had the feeling that she brushed against me, the soft, lingering stroking velvety way a cat strokes past you, arching its back.

"Well, I'm sorry to bother you," I said.

I turned to walk past her, but she lifted her hand, her fingers long, pale, shapely. It was as if she laid them on my arm, digging her fingers with gentle insistence on the flesh inside my wrist, only, of course, she didn't. She didn't touch me at all.

"Where are you going?"

"I'm not sure," I said.

"It's getting late. Miles to the nearest town. It's actually a village in the next county."

"Yes."

"Sure is funny, the way you came along like this."

"Why?"

"We don't get many people out here." She laughed at herself, a soft, compelling sound. "Who am I kidding? We don't get anybody."

"It is quiet."

"Quiet? You ought to stay around and try a bottle of it, a week of it. Two days. You talk to yourself, just to hear noises." She shuddered.

For a moment we were silent, standing there, she in the faint warm sunlight, and I as if rooted in the shadows behind her, looking at her, staring at her body in the cheap dress that she wore as if to spite somebody.

"Well, I better get on back," I said.

"You could stay—for supper." She spoke in a low, flat tone, but it was as if she were frantic, pleading with me and her body, unmoving, was writhing inside that cheap dress. It writhed again, whispering, "Stay."

"Thanks. I better not." I inclined my head toward the gloomy stairwell. "He might not like it."

"Him," she said, and it was a violent curse, uttered in a contemptuous whisper.

"It's funny the way you came here," she said, and she laid all the stress in the world on the word you. That's the way it came out, whether it made sense or not, as if she'd been looking for me for a long time.

Ah, Cora.

Ah, Vi.

It was different with you, Joe. I felt different with you. I felt different from the first moment with you, Joe.

I nodded, but I didn't speak. I waited the faintest fraction of a breath, not knowing what I expected her to say, what I wanted her to say, or what there was to say, only that I waited. But she didn't speak, and the moment passed and I knew I had to go back to my search now.

I moved across the yard, the flat empty yard, but I felt as if I were slogging through doughy swampland about my legs.

I glanced back at her. Her eyes were fixed on me, and her face was pallid and rigid, and bleak. "Goodbye," I said.

She did not speak. It was as if when I walked away from her she didn't hope any more, or live any more, or exist at all.

"Just hold it. Right there, mister."

The words struck at me. They were blurted, wild and raging, a man's voice. It came from the corner of the old house.

I turned slowly toward the sound of his voice. It was like something crazy, like something that had no relation to reality, but it was real all right.

It was as real as the German Luger in his trembling fist.

3

I stared at the gun in the palsied hand. I said, "What is this?"

The woman came down the steps. "Hall," she said. "What's the matter with you?"

He ignored her, didn't even glance toward her. His voice shook worse than his hands were shaking. "I heard you, mister. I heard what you said. You were looking for somebody, huh? Who were you looking for, mister? Me? Her? Now you think you'll run get word to the cops, huh?"

"I don't know what you're talking about."

He laughed, and the sound had dry, rasping tears in it. "You don't know what I'm talking about. Oh, that's lovely. That's pretty, all right. You don't know, anything about the money, I guess, nothing about—"

"Shut up, Hall." She moved across the sand toward him, those deeply sultry eyes blazing. "What kind of fool are you?"

"I heard what he told you," Hall yelled at her, keeping his gaze stuck on me. "I heard what he said. I'm no fool."

She stopped walking, stood perfectly still staring at him as if he were insane. Her hands hung at her sides, her shoulders drooped, but her laughter had a hacking edge.

"I don't know why I'm surprised. I don't know why I asked. I know. I know what kind of fool you are, all right. Damn it, I know."

He seemed to wither under her sarcasm. He was the man the deputy at Frigate had described to me, all right, he was tall, and he was blonde.

He had been a big man once, basketball tall and lean with the wide shoulders and thin hips, but something I had no words for had eaten away at him, eroded him. His hair wasn't really blonde anymore, yet it wasn't gray, only dirty and lifeless.

When Vi spoke, his haggard face rutted into lines, and he looked as if he were going to sob aloud. But then the obstinacy set in, the rebelliousness that was the only armor he had left against her.

"Shut up," he said, slashing the words at her from the grinder of his mouth. "What were you going to do? Let him walk out of here, let him go to the police?"

"For God's sake, Hall. Why don't you keep your mouth shut? He just wandered in here.... He got lost. That's all."

"You're lying. You're both lying. Maybe he was somebody you knew— before. Is that it, Vi?"

"Sure," she said. "We slept together. At Vassar. Wasn't it at Vassar we slept together, mister?"

"Funny," Hall said, voice quivering. "Oh, you're funny. You got any idea, Vi, what it would take to blow us to hell out of here?"

Now she did laugh, in a helpless way. "I know I wouldn't care. Even hell would be somewhere else."

"You wouldn't care," he said. "Sure, you wouldn't care. But I would care. You see, that's the difference, Vi...."

His eyes were infested with wraiths. He had grabbed that Luger, run down the back stairs and around the house. Now he had time to think. He began to see maybe he was wrong. The woman was right, he was shooting off his mouth in panic to a stranger, and he was wrong.

He shivered all over. He saw now he was wrong. This didn't make it better. It made it worse. Where he was—with whatever it was driving him—he couldn't afford to be wrong, he had to be right every time. It was more than compulsion, it was the frantic hope of existence with him.

"I got to stop him," he said, staring at me. "You know I got to stop him."

She shrugged. "You going to kill everybody, Hall, everybody that walks in here—by mistake?"

He grinned suddenly, horribly.

"You got lost. Came in here by mistake, huh, pal?"

I glanced at her, she was staring at him.

I said, "That's right."

A cunning look crept into his eyes. "And I didn't even hear what you said, huh, pal?"

I should have seen we weren't going anywhere, we were following the grooves of his thinking, but I didn't look closely enough at him.

"What was that?" I said.

"Oh, come on, pal. What you said. To Vi here. Didn't I hear you say you were looking for somebody?"

The hell with this. "I was looking for my wife," I said.

I heard him catch his breath from half across the yard. Now I'd insulted his intelligence. I saw him tremble again suddenly, going wild, twitching inside.

"Oh, that's good, pal. That's real pretty. Only you got to do better than that."

I was sick of him. "That's the truth."

"That's great, pal. Like you expected to find your wife out here on this farm. Down this road. Three miles from the county road, fifteen miles from the highway. Oh, that's pretty."

"Go to hell," I told him.

"Sure, pal." He laughed now, his face creasing with his melancholy laughing. I stared at him, thinking: you crazy bastard. I wanted to take that gun away from him and whip him across the face with it.

I warned myself to relax, nothing had changed, the world was the same as it always had been. It's not going to end here on this abandoned farm.

"Go have a drink," I told him. "Go have yourself a drink and cool off."

Now the woman laughed. "Sure," she said. "Sure. That's all he needs. One more drink."

Her laughter triggered the wildness in him as nothing I could possibly say or do would inflame him.

He pulled his gaze from me for the first time and stared at her, his gray eyes flat and empty. I saw him trying to forget what they once had had, the things about her that drove him and haunted him, and enslaved him.

I watched him. I had been down that road, too.

Cora had dragged me down all the roads.

"You want a cracked lip, Vi?"

She shrugged. "It'll go with the set."

"Shut up," he said. "Stay out of it. If you can't see what I got to do, I can."

"Look," I said. "It's been fine... I'm going now."

I moved to turn from him and walk to my car.

I heard the sharp whack as a bullet was thrust into the chamber. I stopped where I was, and suddenly my Chevvy was impossibly far away,

"Don't be a fool," I said. "That's a hair-trigger gun. Don't be a fool."

I was watching him again, now, all right. I was standing half-turned from him, the sun across my face.

He had the gun fixed on me. He moved with a fine deliberate movement I had to admire. He knew guns from somewhere; a gun was a part of him, the way a gun can be with a man that truly knows them and understands them. But it was no consolation telling myself that I was going to be shot to death by a gun-expert.

"I got all the medals in the army," he said in a low tone, speaking to nobody in particular. "All the medals. All of them."

Then he tilted the black snout of the Luger away from me, but not very far, not far enough. He pressed the trigger, the sound breaking and reverberating across the silence. The slug cut into the right front tire of my Chevvy, and there was a sharp popping, and then the hiss as the casing pancaked.

The guy stood there and took his time, waiting with the Luger in his fist. He waited until the tire went flat and stopped hissing at all, the Chevvy sitting tilted, then he turned the gun again slightly, pressed the trigger and the other front tire exploded with a sad little plopping noise and a faint sigh.

"You damn fool," I said.

"No," he said. "I'm not a fool. I did what I had to do. I couldn't let you go tell them."

He glanced at the woman, and he seemed pleased with what he had done. But she did not even look at him, and finally he turned to face me again.

His face was gray and he was grinning, the parts not matching, like something hastily pasted on. "One more thing. About that Buick. I got the keys. I keep them put away. Safe. Nobody knows where they are, but me."

I just stared at him, full of rage, helpless with it. But I didn't move. He would put a bullet in me as he had put them into my front tires. Probably quicker.

I could still hear the sharp, perfect firing of that gun in my temples.

"What's your name?" he said.

"Joe Byars." It didn't matter what I said, he didn't really hear me, he was all involved in his own thinking.

"You might have come here by mistake. As Vi said. I've got to try to remember that. " He nodded.

I looked at him as long as I could, then jerked my gaze away and stared at the woman. Her gaze was fixed on me as if she had forgotten him.

4

As the sun set, the wind came up. It wailed, keening and whining around the eaves of the old house.

I sat on the front steps, my thoughts going in crazy circles. Behind me, Hall sat with the gun on his lap, rocking in an old wicker-back rocker, the creaking of the rockers growing fainter as the wind rose.

I watched the wind, like something you could see marching across the flat, empty land, boiling up thick clouds of dust or kicking dust devils ahead of it.

I stared at the flat tires. I kept telling myself even the flat tires didn't really stop me. I could drive on them, on the rims, anything to get out of this. But I knew better. Hall had thought of that. He might even be thinking it at that moment. I could feel the savagery of his grinning fixed on the back of my neck, raising the hackles. His Buick was faster, and even if I let the air out of his tires, it was a long way to the highway, and that Luger made the difference.

It grew black dark.

The front door whined open and slapped shut. Vi said, "Supper is ready."

"Come on to supper, pal," Hall said, getting up from the rocker, floor boards squeaking. "What did you say your name was?"

I didn't bother answering him.

Hall lighted two glass lamps, turning the wicks up, so only three-quarters of the dining room was in darkness.

She had set mismatched plates, cheap utensils on the bare table. Supper was heated hot dogs stirred into a couple of cans of pork and beans. She was no cook, even the beans were charred. Whatever else she was, she was no cook.

She poured black coffee from a metal pot into cups before her plate and mine. I watched the steam rising.

She brought a fifth of whiskey and an empty glass and set them before Hall. He grunted, but did not speak. He sat there, holding the Luger in his lap with his left hand.

I felt faintly hopeful. Maybe she was thinking even when I couldn't. A fifth of whiskey could snarl a man up. Once he was passed out, I could get away. I could reach the highway. I might even get to the nearest farmhouse.

I sat watching him drink, the shadows leaping on the lamplit wall behind him when he raised his arm, moved his head.

"Look," I said. "This is all something that can be straightened out. I know nothing about you. I don't want to know. I came here because somebody told me—in Frigate they told me your wife looked like Cora."

"His wife," she said. She took a long drink of coffee.

He seemed not to hear me, but I went on talking, feeling the outrage, the hopelessness of trying to reach him at all.

"I'm looking for my wife," I said to him. "That's all."

His head came up, elongated shadow leaping on the wall beyond him. His eyes showed an instant of rage, then he shrugged. He said, "Pass the beans, Vi."

We ate in silence for a long time. At last, Vi said across the table to me in that throaty voice, "One thing I'll say, this place looks better by lamplight."

"Don't they have electricity out here?" I said.

"We don't," Hall said. He finished off his third whiskey tumbler, poured another, without ice or water to dilute it.

"Hall doesn't want meter readers coming around once a month," Vi said.

My voice was more bitter than I intended. "Would be bad, having to kill every new man that came to read the meter."

"We don't need lights," Hall said.

"We don't need anything," Vi said, with suppressed savagery. "We've got each other."

The expression on his face did not alter. "That's the way you wanted it," he said. "That's the way you said you wanted it."

She put her head back, laughing. The room shuddered with her laughter in it.

He took a long drink, watching her across the top of his tumbler.

"Wonder what Esther's doing tonight, Hall?" she said, taunting him.

"Stow it," he said.

"Esther is Hall's wife," Vi said across the table to me. "She's a big woman. Breasts like melons."

"I told you. Knock it off."

She didn't even look at him. "Sometimes when I haven't anything else to do, I wonder about Esther. I wonder about what's she doing. Like tonight. Wonder what Esther is doing, wonder if she knows how well off she is?"

He hurled the whiskey into her face, tumbler and all. The glass struck her across the nose, making a sharp, painful sound in the empty house.

I moved fast. I came up out of that chair, kicking it backwards, hoping to jump him while four straight tumblers of alcohol and Vi's needling slowed his reactions.

I got all the way up to my feet, to the edge of the bare table, the mahogany cutting into my thigh as I slid around it toward him.

The gun came up, flicking like a snake, glittering, oiled and cleaned in the lamplight.

He brought it all the way up. He came up with it, moving in a sober, clear-headed way to the balls of his feet so he slapped the mouth of that gun hard on my forehead, between my brows. He kept it pressed there.

I backed up, slowly, sitting down again.

He kept the gun where it was.

Across the table, Vi was wiping the whiskey from her face. There was a red mark across her nose. She ignored it.

"Thanks," she said, to me.

Hall laughed. "He wasn't thinking about you, my love," he said. "He was thinking about himself."

"Thanks anyway," she said.

I tried to match her tone. "It was the least I could do."

He gave the gun one last hard jab between my eyes and then drew it away. He seemed clearheaded now, and pleased with himself.

"It was the least anyone could do," he said, sitting down again. "You had to test me. You had to find out. Now you know, use better sense. I'm not afraid to kill you." He said it casually, and in the same tone, spoke to her. "Vi, get me another tumbler."

I expected her to tell him to get it to hell himself, but she got up wordlessly, went into the kitchen.

"You're a brave man," I said. "To turn your back on her."

Vi brought him another tumbler and sat down. She did not touch her food again, leaving her plate half-filled. Once in a while she would look at the food with revulsion. The mark across her nose was livid, swelling slowly. She seemed completely unaware of it. Physically, he could not hurt her any more.

At last, she said to me, "You have some kind of job, Joe? What work do you do?"

"I was a salesman," I said. "Engineering equipment. But, you see, a few weeks ago I lost my wife. I thought it was better if I went to look for her. I got temporary leave. They were glad to let me go. I was—I was no good to them after my wife left me."

I heard Hall's sharp intake of breath. I jerked my head around. His gaze was fixed on me—his eyes called me a liar.

The wind went on howling. A little while after supper, Hall finished off the fifth of whiskey without asking either Vi or me to join him. He sat in the partly furnished living room with the empty bottle in his fist. He stared at it a long time and then threw it across the room, smashing it in the fireplace.

"Does he always drink in such moderation?" I said to Vi.

She shrugged.

He said, "Once I drank eight fifths between Friday and Sunday. All by myself."

"I believe it," Vi said. "Who'd drink with you?"

"You could drink with me," he said. "You'd be a lot happier if you drank with me."

"I couldn't stand any more happiness," she said. "I couldn't stand it."

He stared at her, his eyes dark and swirling in the lamplight. At last he exhaled heavily. "It was a wonderful feeling, drinking like that. You get a sense of power. You light up. Things are clearer. That's when you can really think. Clear and uncluttered.... That's when I figured everything out."

"You're a genius," Vi said. "Oh, you're a genius. Esther tried to tell me."

He leaped up. "You leave her out of it," he said. "You leave her name out of it."

"Esther," she said up into his face. "Esther. Esther. Esther. Wonderful, lucky, fortunate Esther."

He stood over her, his bony hands bent into claws, his body trembling. Then he shook his head.

He turned his back on her. "You're a slut," he said to her. "That's why you can't stand to think about Esther."

"I can't stand to think about you, either," she said.

He laughed, the sound painful. "She said she was crazy about me. She said there was nobody else. You know the things they say, pal? Sluts. When they are trying to get what they want? That's the way she talked. You should have heard her. You could go real batty just listening to the things she promised."

I didn't say anything.

Vi said. "That was a long time ago. A long time ago. That was before you popped your cork."

"If I'm not sane," he said, "you thank God, Vi. Because God help you if I ever got good sense. God help you."

"I won't worry about it," she said.

She stood up. He heeled around, his narrow face bleak. "Where are you going?"

"I'm going to bed."

He thought that over for a few moments. He nodded. "We'll all go to bed," he said.

He held open a door on the second floor. "You can sleep in here," he said. "There's a mattress on the bed, and a quilt. You won't need a light."

I stared into the room, the lamp sending a wan shaft of light into it. It was even more sparsely furnished than the rest of the house, a chair, a mattress on a four-poster iron bed like I hadn't seen since I was a kid visiting on a farm.

"It looks fine."

"If you think about running away tonight," he said, "go ahead and do it. Please, I want you to. We can get that nailed down quick."

I didn't know exactly what he meant beyond the fact that it was a threat, and I couldn't figure it out.

I went into the room and he closed the door behind me, leaving me in a warm breathless womb of dark.

I felt my way across the room, opened the window, the wind screeching past me, cold and loud in the darkness. The wind chilled the room, and filled it with the terrible sense of the unknown, the unexplained.

I wasn't afraid of anything on the wind. But I decided I'd sleep better, or even think better, with the door locked.

I went slowly back across to the door. There was no key.

I exhaled, not even really surprised. I stumbled awkwardly back across the darkened room and sat down on the bed.

I stared at that unlocked door, wondering at what hour he'd decide I had lived long enough, that it was too dangerous to him to let me go on living.

I sat there and thought about him. I didn't know what he had done, only that there was some terrible wrong in this house that hadn't been in it until Hall and Vi brought it with them. A wife somewhere named Esther, and a crime of some kind, something that he couldn't live with, and couldn't run away from, either.

I got to thinking about Vi. Something kept her with him. She was like a savage tigress caged up with him, but she stayed. Why? Shared guilt? Or was it something else, something she hoped to get away from him?

I was trembling with cold. I got up and closed the window, and it was as if the howling of the wind receded slightly.

I sat on the bed again. If I fell asleep and he came into this room, there was no lock, no way to keep him out. He could put a bullet in my head while I slept.

Then it occurred to me that I was on a two-way street at least. If there were no locks on his doors, and he could get to me in my sleep, I could get to him.

I nodded, pleased with myself, glad that I was able to think. It had been a long time since I had thought rationally. It took something like this to do it.

I felt better. There were a lot of angles to this thing, and yet there was nothing that couldn't be solved. I would have to move carefully. I'd have to find his room. I would have to wait until he slept.

I forgot to be tired. I forgot how long it had been since I had slept more than fitfully, even my sleep tormented.

I waited a long time. Mice skitted between the walls, and the wind was a weeping thing outside those windows, but the house grew still. There was a terrible stillness about it, as if when Hall and his woman slept the evil was suspended in the silence, hanging like a dry mist.

I pushed off my shoes, and got up from the bed, moving with painful slowness so the springs did not squeal.

I went in that same measured way across the room. I opened the door stealthily. I was lucky in one way, the wail of the wind concealed most sounds.

There were many doors along the cavernous upper hallway. It was breathlessly hot and still, with the heat accumulated and left over from the long burning daylight. Sweat filmed my face, dripped along my ribs.

I listened at the doors, each of them unlocked. I found her room, Vi's. I could hear her whimper in her sleep, her troubled breathing. She was alone in there behind that unlocked door. In my mind I could see her rich hair against her pillow. I moved on in the darkness.

Hall's room was beyond hers. Even before I touched the knob to steady myself, I knew. I pressed my ear against the facing. If he were asleep, I could tell by his breathing.

My fingers closed on the knob, and something was wrong. His door was locked. I realized then the way he thought: a man had to have one room where he could lock himself in.

There was a whisper of sound behind me, and too late I realized there had not been any sounds at all beyond that locked door.

I heeled around, throwing up my arms in an involuntary gesture. It wasn't any good. It was too late. Something struck me across the skull, coming down sharply behind my ear. I heard him grunt with the effort of striking me, and then I didn't hear anything else. I toppled against the wall, digging at it with my nails, and sliding down along it slowly, slowly, and never touching the floor at all.

5

"Oh, you're the worst kind of fool. The worst kind. The stupid kind that thinks with his heels."

Her voice raged, striking me like some sonic force where I'd been struck across the skull, shattering my senses all over again.

They were arguing, yelling at each other, standing over me when I came out of it. I opened my eyes and saw them like shapeless reeds wavering over me, and then I had to close my eyes against the shafts of early morning sunlight.

"Suppose he's got a concussion?" she was saying to him. "You going to get a doctor out here to him?"

"He was sneaking around. He was trying to get into my room."

"Where you going to find a doctor? If you find him, what are you going to tell him?"

He said something that got lost in the throbbing inside my head.

I tried to move, tried to roll over on the floor. I could not do it.

I opened my eyes slowly, painfully. A bright chain was linked around my wrist and secured to the wall. I pulled against it. The chain rattled, but I could not move.

"He's coming out of it," I heard Hall say.

"You're getting better than you deserve," she told him. "All you need is murder added to everything else."

"I always got better than I deserved," he said, "I got you."

But there was a tone of relief in his voice.

They went away and I closed my eyes again against the painful thrusts of sunlight. I had been out all night. I had no idea how many hours that was, because I didn't know how long I'd waited last night hoping Hall would sleep with that fifth of whiskey in him.

I was in the bedroom again, only now I was chained, arms spread-eagled on the floor near the bed. I could see the bolls of ancient dust under the bed, the earthenware bedchamber.

When I was alone, I examined the link chain and the metal band that had been pounded vise-tight on my left wrist and the chain looped through it so that to move my wrist at all caused sharp shooting pains that exploded at the base of my brain.

The chain on my right wrist was only linked around my arm, pulled taut, secured with wire. I could have worked it loose easily, only I'd need my left hand free to do it.

Heavy steel hooks had been driven into the baseboards, the chains linked over the prongs and stretched taut.

The house was silent, and it was breathlessly hot up there under the roof. It was as if the sun were beamed directly upon it every hour of the day.

I could hear them talking, moving around downstairs. His voice covered the whole range from pleading to frustrated shouting, but hers had only one tone, bitter, flat, savage hatred. It was in every word.

I watched the shadow shorten at my window. It must have been nearly noon when the door opened and Vi came in carrying a tray.

Hall followed, so tall he stooped to enter the door, his shoulders round, mouth sagging in lined face.

He carried the Luger.

She jerked her head at him. "Untie one arm at least."

Hall nodded. He knelt beside me and loosed the wire, freeing the chain links on my right wrist.

"Too bad you ain't got good sense," he said. "It didn't have to be this way."

I didn't answer. I rubbed my wrist along my trousers trying to soothe it.

I sat up slowly and she placed the tray in my lap. It was an unappetizing bowl of soup and a cup of coffee.

"There's not much in the house," she said. "We haven't been in to Frigate for some time."

Hall went back to the doorway, leaned against it. "He don't need much. He ain't doing anything."

She pushed the tray closer on my lap. She spoke in a low whisper. "He'll sleep. Sometime. I'll come back. We must talk."

I heard her, but I jerked my head up, watching Hall, wondering if he'd heard her too in that strangely silent house.

His face remained blank.

He stood there until I finished the watery soup, the strong coffee. He removed the tray, snagged my wrist.

I fought him. He was big, but he looked as if he'd gone to ashes. He was nothing compared to what he must have once been, but he had quick reflexes, instant responses.

He laid that gun butt across my temple just over my right eye, not with great force, but only enough to cut the flesh, and start the agony crackling behind my ear again.

I lay still until he had me wired up again.

I lay on the floor and stared at him. "You're stacking up quite an account," I told him.

He shrugged.

I didn't know how much sleep he got the night before, but I waited all afternoon and Vi didn't come near me again, and I could hear Hall prowling about the house.

Supper was beans and hot dogs again. Then they went away and I heard them eating downstairs, snarling at each other like caged animals.

I knew he was drinking heavily. Finally I heard the bottle smash inside the fireplace, and he'd finished off his dinner hour fifth.

I heard his steps heavy and sharp coming up the stairway. I saw the lamp-light lunging ahead in shapeless shafts ahead of him and then he entered my room carrying the Luger. He set the lamp on the old bureau near the door, lighting the room wanly.

He stood inside the doorway then, staring at me for a long time with a peculiar look on his face.

The wind had risen again, the way it did every night on those eternal plains, screaming like something tormented under the eaves and across the roofing.

"A few things you ought to know, pal," he said. "What was it you said your name was?"

I watched him and didn't say anything. He shrugged.

He hefted the oiled gun in his hand, looking at it as if it were the last thing on earth he loved or trusted.

He slapped it, whacking a bullet into the cylinder. He lifted it in a slowly casual way, hardly aiming and put a bullet an inch from my left ear.

I lay there frozen, afraid to move. He tilted the gun slightly, and put a second bullet into the floor that same distance from my right ear.

"So you're an expert," I said, holding my breath.

With that same casual movement he put a bullet between my thighs an inch from my crotch, so I felt the floor vibrating, felt my body constrict involuntarily.

"You get the idea?" he said.

I was aware I still hadn't breathed. I said, keeping my voice level, "It's easy shooting at a man chained on a floor."

"No," he said in that melancholy tone. "You don't get the idea at all, do you? That's just practice. A man needs to practice. He needs his exercise every day. I could do that if you were running, or if you jumped me. I was in Korea. Were you in the army?"

I didn't waste my breath answering him. I did breathe though, because my lungs were going to burst if I didn't.

"I'm trying to tell you," he said. "What a fool you were to come looking for me. You found me. What are you going to do?"

I didn't answer that, either.

"You got any idea what those plains are like out there, fellow? How flat and empty they are? You know how far away our nearest neighbor is? You got any idea?"

He was rolling the gun around in his trembling hand. I didn't say anything. I felt sweat burning into my eyes.

"You'd have to run ten miles across open ground to get to the nearest neighbor, pal. That's what I'm trying to tell you.... That's why I bought this place.... I've owned it for years. I came from Oklahoma, and I knew there was some place like this. So I bought it. Years ago. Nobody thought a thing about it. Seven hundred acres and a house."

He nodded, pleased with himself.

After a moment, he said, "This place. It's like Mars."

"Must be like home to you," I said. I licked my mouth.

He didn't hear me. "That's what's so wonderful about this place. If you ran away, where would you go—in that open country out there—where would you hide?"

It was a good question.

He picked up the lamp, shoved the gun under his belt. He stared at me. "Well," he said. "I just wanted to let you know, pal."

They went off to bed. I heard Vi's screaming at him about something in the hallway and then her door slammed, and after that for a long time there was only the crying of the night wind.

I lay flat on my back on the floor. The muscles, tendons and flesh of my hips, shoulders and legs were sore the way festered boils become. My arms felt detached from my body, stiff and wooden out at my sides.

I thought about Cora, and about where she was, and the way I had come to this place looking for her and I jerked hard at my chains, raging. But I only did that once. I felt as though my arms had broken, like brittle sticks.

Once I thought I heard the key turn in Hall's bedroom lock down the hall, but it must have been the wind because I waited for a long time. There was no other sound.

I must have fallen asleep. I was dreaming, running along a ravine and I couldn't see the ground above me, and there was something behind me in the darkness, and I didn't know what it was, only that I was running in terror.

I heard my door pushed slowly open, the dry whine of the hinges bringing me fully awake.

My flesh constricted, all I could think was that Hall had come back to put a bullet in my head. I tried to reason myself out of this. If he had wanted to kill me, why wouldn't he have done it when he was using me for target practice after supper?

"Joe."

I sighed out heavily. It was Vi. She moved like a shadow through the cracked doorway, not touching it at all.

"Joe. We got to talk," she whispered.

Gray light filtered through the window on her. She wore a diaphanous gown she must have bought in some other existence. Her hair was brushed back from her face and in the night her face was gray as ashes.

She took a step toward me away from the door.

Suddenly the door flew open and exploded against the wall.

Hall came through it as if he'd been shot from a cannon. Vi caught her breath and stood as if frozen in the middle of the doorway.

He caught her by the arm, and for a moment there was only the grieving wind, the rattling at the windows, the sound of his breathing. Finally he got himself under control. He managed to laugh.

"You must have gotten in the wrong room, eh, Vi? Took the wrong turn and got in here by mistake. You got lost? I'll have to remember that, Vi.... I'll try hard to remember that."

6

The house grew quieter, and it seemed I could hear Vi sobbing down the hallway, but I couldn't be sure. It was funny as hell.

Vi was nobody's angel. You didn't have to have a file on her to know that. But she was in hell, and for some unfathomable reason she stayed in it. Hall had something on her, something she wanted.

Anyhow, she stayed... and sobbed in the night.

The wind keened, crying around the old house, and I didn't blame it. There was plenty to cry about out here.

I slept....

It was the roar of cannons, the protesting firing of tank engines that woke me. But when I was fully awake, and knew where I was, I recognized the sound. It was Hall's Buick, engine racing down in that front yard.

I heard the engine roar, full, and then the gears were shifted, engine racing and the car screamed, making a turn in the yard, going away from the house.

Before the sound of the engine died along that narrow lane between the fence rows, the door was pushed open and Vi stood there, staring at me, eyes distended and urgent.

For a long time we didn't even speak. We just waited, holding our breath, listening until we couldn't hear that engine any more.

"Get me out of this," I said.

She nodded. She ran across the room and knelt beside me. I could smell her hair, and the faint scent of her lush body, even as sick and scared as I was. Her kind of beauty ate through anything. It had eroded Hall's insides, even after whatever she felt for him had soured into hatred.

Her body brushed me as she worked with the wire and chain on my right wrist.

We didn't speak while she worked with it, her fingers fumbling. Then the chain fell away and I sat up, my arm feeling dead and numb.

"How much time we got?"

She shook her head. "I don't know. We got to talk."

I stared at the metal band on my wrist. "First I got to get out of this."

"I don't know how, Joe," she said. "He hammered it on there."

I stared at her. "You think I'll go away and leave you here?"

"We got to talk, Joe."

I glanced at the band, then her. "We can talk while I'm working on this thing. Get me a hammer, and a screwdriver or a chisel."

"I'll see what I can find, Joe."

She moved toward the door, and there was reluctance in the way she walked. She didn't want me free. Whatever she wanted, she never wanted to be abandoned here on this farm with Hall again.

"You got to listen to me, Joe," she said.

"I told you I would. Don't let him come back here and find me still in this thing."

She paused in the doorway, leaning against it, her body thrusting against the cheap fabric of her dress.

"We got more time than that, Joe."

"I got no time at all unless I get out of this thing."

She shook her head. "Like I said, I got to talk to you, first. You got to listen to me." Her eyes were anguished, pleading. "You might think I'm not worth taking away from here with you, Joe.... But I am.... You got no idea how much I might be worth to you, Joe."

"All right. A hammer. For God's sake. I got to get out of this."

"So have I, Joe. I got to get out of this, too. You got to see that. You got to see how it is with me, Joe.... I can't stay here any more like this, Joe. It's worse than chains, Joe. It's a lot worse."

"Oh, for God's sake. I'm not blind. I see that—"

"No. You can't see it all. You can only see what has happened since you got here."

"It's enough. Too much. Get me a hammer."

She fixed those wild, frightened eyes on me. "You're wasting time, Joe. I got to have help, and you got to help me."

I wailed at her. "Like this, I'm helpless. I can't help anybody. Can't you see that?"

"We got more time than that, Joe. He's gone in to Willoughby, or Wild Horse. One of those places."

I rubbed my wrist along my trousers, sweating. "What are they?"

"They're villages, Joe. One is about sixteen miles away. The other is twenty. I don't know. He wouldn't tell me.... You see, he knew I'd let you free.... He didn't want us to know which way to turn on Road Sixteen."

I could see it as if she had drawn me a map on the dusty floor. Narrow County Road Sixteen. Willoughby in one direction, Wild Horse in the other.

"There's nothing in either village, a train station for loading animals and grain. That's all."

"What did he want?"

She licked her mouth. "That's what I want to talk to you about, Joe. There are telegraph stations at Wild Horse and at Willoughby."

"Yes?"

"Well, that's it. He took your wallet. Your papers. He went through your car. Now he's going to wire east... to the people you worked for, to the police in Hollander, if—if you're who you say you are—and he finds it out for true, he may let you go when he gets back.... He doesn't want to kill you... unless he has to.... He knows he's got trouble enough, without killing anybody."

"You mean I could stay right here, and when he came back, he might let me go?"

"He might. He said he would. When he left here.... He's scared of what he's said to you, but he says if you had a chance to go free, you might be willing to forget anything you heard here."

I looked at those bullet holes in the floor, and remembered the way I had lain there frozen. I was thinking hard.

She saw that in my face. "That s what I got to talk to you about, Joe."

Suddenly I knew there was no sense asking her for a hammer and chisel. She'd bring them when it pleased her.

"That's it, Joe.... If he comes back, and he lets you go, you couldn't take me with you.... He wouldn't let you do that."

Now she took a step forward into the room, more sure of herself and her charms, and the pleading and fear in her eyes dissolved and through some chemical change became something else entirely.

"I want to go away with you, Joe," she said. "It's more than that. I've got to."

"You know better than that. He wouldn't let you go. He'd kill you first. He'd kill me."

"He might," she said. "He might want to. He might try."

She knelt suddenly in front of me on her knees and brought her body close to me, the heat from her stronger than the heat of the sun, different.

"I felt something for you, Joe, the first moment I saw you. When I walked up to that door, and you were there, I knew it could be—different—with us."

She didn't look like Cora, not really, and her voice wasn't like Cora's, either. Not really. Only the words were the same.

"I could be something wonderful for you, Joe."

"I've got a wife, Vi.... I told you."

She moved her face against me, and her hands. She knew everything there was to know.

Her voice lowered. "She went away and left you, Joe. She was a fool. I don't know why she left you, but she was a fool, and I could make you forget her, Joe.... I could make you forget all about her."

"You could get me killed."

"No. You're smarter than he is... we're both smarter than he is... he's all bluff... as long as he's got that gun, he's like God... I've seen him without it, Joe. I've seen him."

"That's when you should have killed him," I said, trying to ignore her face against me, what her hands were doing.

"I couldn't, Joe. Because I didn't have the money then. I didn't know where it was. I got in this mess because of that money, Joe.... I'm not going to give it up now.... I've earned it."

I sat there, watching her, close up, extremely close up, her eyes deep, fixed on mine.

"It's a lot of money, Joe.... It's two hundred thousand dollars.... I didn't know where it was before.... I know now . It's a lot of money, Joe, and it could be ours."

We didn't speak then for a long time. We stayed there on the floor with her body, her hands hot on me, and we thought about the money.

"We could go anywhere," she said. "We could live. We could have fun together.... I'd make you forget... I'd make you forget, everything. It's a lot of money, Joe, and you've got to help me get it."

Her body moved. Her mouth moved. Her hands moved. She whispered, "There's nobody else, Joe. Nobody. You're all I've got. You're the only one who can help me. It'll be different with us, Joe.... I never felt like this for anybody else. It'll be different. You're the only one."

There was the sound of mice downstairs.

She stiffened in my arms, lunged away, and I heard it, too. It wasn't mice at all. It was footsteps. They moved, and they stopped. They went along the rear of the house below my window, and then they eased up on the back stoop.

"He's come back," I moaned. That damned Vi. The chain rattled, the sound like laughter, linking me to that wall.

She pressed her palm across my mouth, shaking her head, warning me to be quiet, listening.

There was a rap on the rear door jamb. There was a brief, breathless silence, then there was another knock.

I stared at Vi. It wasn't Hall at all. There was somebody down there, though, and those raps were signals.

She looked gray. She looked as if she would crumble into hundreds of pieces. She shook her head, pulling away from me, getting up to her knees.

"Stay quiet," she whispered. "Please don't move. I'll come back, as quick as I can. Please, don't make any noise."

She went from the room then, running, and I sat there chained to the wall, feeling my heart slugging raggedly against the cage of my ribs.

I heard Vi racing down the steep stairwell, sliding her hand along the wall, and then she went running through the long corridor.

The rap was repeated, more urgent now, louder.

Then the back door opened, singing, and slammed behind her.

It was a man all right. I could hear his voice from down there in that sun-struck yard. I could hear Vi's voice raised against his, and the urgency in their voices.

I crawled on my knees to the window. I could not quite reach it. My chain was too short. I stretched my arm as far as I could, feeling the metal band ripping my flesh, tearing it. It didn't matter. I had to see them down there. I had to hear what they were saying.

My flesh tore along my wrist and at the heel of my hand. I pressed my face against the window and peered through the glass. I could see their shadows against the sand. They were close together. The man was big, and he held her arms tightly, as if he owned her, as if she had let him believe he owned her.

I felt the laughter and sickness gorging up through my throat. I remembered what she had been saying here in my arms moments ago. Different, Joe. No one else, Joe. In that sick instant, watching them down there, I felt almost as if I had found Cora.

7

For a moment I stood there in the middle of that raging, mad laughter as if the sounds were not even pouring like bile out of me.

I was pulling against that chain with all my strength. It had cut my wrist deeply, and blood covered the metal band and the chain links. I was not aware of the pain at the end of my numbed arm.

I could not think about anything except that ten minutes ago that woman had been in my arms, talking about money, about killing a man for his money, about how it was different with us, from the first moment different. Good God, they're playing our song, only the needle is stuck, and it's not a song any more, it's just plain, ugly insanity.

The sound of that laughter bounced and echoed in that room. Because the funny part, the really funny part was not that Viola had been wheeling and dealing, using all her body and her mouth to close the sale, but that I had listened to her. I had let her get inside me.

Because I had been listening, all right.

In my rage, I jerked at that chain. Nothing happened. It held securely. I didn't even feel any pain. The only way I was aware that I was bleeding was when I saw the strings of blood playing out along the chain link.

Anybody else buying that act from Vi wouldn't have been so hysterical, but me. I would have told you that after Cora, no woman could get at me. Maybe I did tell you that. I had been telling myself that—for weeks.

But one thing helped. My rage made it clear that what Cora had done to me, and what Vi had almost done to me, didn't really matter at the moment. All that mattered was that hook driven into the wall, and this chain. Hall was gone to wire for information on me. He would find out that I was all I said I was, nothing he feared I was, but nobody knew how he would react to this. For some reason he had trusted Vi enough to leave her alone here with me, or he felt sure I could not get away from this vast wasteland until he decided to free me.

Sweat poured along my face. I didn't know how long he would be gone, how long it would take the Hollander police to reply to his wire. All I knew was that I had to get out of here.

I could hear them downstairs now. Their voices had raised. The man had heard me moving around up here, and his voice lifted, accusing, yelling, and slowly, Vi's voice came up higher, protesting.

The hell with them.

I moved across the room to where the hook was driven into the wall. Had no idea that it was a small hook. It was old and rusted, the kind they drive into stables to hang ropes and chains, even saddles and heavy gear. The hook had been hammered into a closed eye with the chain through it.

I sank to my knees beside it, caught the hook in both hands, trying to rip it from the wall.

I had one faint hope. The hook point was so large that the baseboard had been ripped slightly when Hall drove it into the wood.

That hope died quickly. The split was there, but the threaded head was driven beyond it into the studding. I could not hope to rip it free.

I tried to unscrew it. I might have done that, if I'd had anything to use as a lever, but there was nothing.

I hunkered there on my knees, staring helplessly about that room. It looked so bare. The sun was relentless against the roofing, and it had become an oven. My clothing was sweated. I could hear them shouting at each other down there in the yard.

The sounds of their voices got inside me like worms. I couldn't stand the sounds grating on my nerves.

I looped the chain, caught it under the hook and stood up, slowly. I came up terribly slow, using all the muscles in my back and legs.

For a moment I thought I was going to faint. Panic banged around inside my skull, and the room spun. I clung to that chain as if it were the only thing that could keep me from skidding off the globe.

The metal band was tearing along the inside of my hand now. I went on pulling. All I could think was that I was going to faint. But I kept adding one more thought to that: I was going to be free when it happened.

The metal band moved painfully, crunching the bones in my thumb, squeezing my hand into a bloody knot. But the blood helped, too, oozing about the metal band. It made it slide just a little easier.

Suddenly I heard something tear. I didn't know if it were my flesh, or bones crumbling under pressure. I didn't stop to look. My head was back and my eyes were pressed closed, and I went on pulling myself upward.

Abruptly, I broke free and toppled half across the room.

I struck against the iron bars at the foot of the bed.

I stayed there for some moments—I don't know how long before I realized I was free.

I stood up slowly, and gradually the room cleared. I stood there with that chain in my fist. Two things had happened: the split baseboard had splintered and the threads didn't hold in the inside studding; the metal band had slipped across my crumpled thumb and along my fingers.

I didn't waste time thinking about it. I was aware of the blood on my fist, and the way I went on holding that chain.

One thought skittered through my brain, over and over and over—Get out!

I ran, staggering, through the doorway.

Their voices rose from the lower hallway, coming up to strike me in the face.

I ran along the balustrade toward the stairs, staring downward. The man, in overalls and denim shirt was running along the hallway from the rear of the house.

Vi was behind him, snagging at his arm, screaming at him. I didn't care what she was saying. I didn't care about anything she did any more. I was going down those stairs and out of this house.

I reached the newel post at the landing, catching at it as I went around it.

At that precise moment, the man reached the foot of the stairs.

I stared down at him, and he paused, looking back at me, his mouth gaping slightly.

I recognized him. It was the stone-faced farmer who had directed me here.

It was different with him now. His face was not expressionless. Rage had twisted it out of shape, and his eyes were distended.

"You," he said, raging. "I'm going to kill you."

I scarcely heard him. Words like those had suddenly lost their power to affect me at all. And I didn't think he was going to kill me. I didn't believe he was going to stop me from walking out of this house.

I didn't bother saying anything. Nothing was really clear, even yet. The stairwell wavered before my eyes, and I knew I was bleeding, knew I was carrying that chain, knew I had to get out of here.

I moved down the stairs.

He came boiling up them, yelling at me.

"Take her away from me, eh? You going to take her away from me? No. You're not going to take her. She's mine.... She come here.... And she's mine.... You ain't going to take her from me. Nobody is ever going to take her from me."

"Get out of the way," I said.

Viola stood at the foot of the stairs, the girl who could stir up a mess like this, screaming something at us. I didn't even listen.

He was too incensed to hear what I said. Maybe nothing could have stopped him, anyway. Even in that crazy flash of time, I found myself seeing how it was with him, the sad, sick way it was. She had him so snarled up, so frustrated and defeated he had to smash something, or he could not live with himself.

"Clint!" Viola yelled, coming up the stairs behind him. "Clint. Let him alone. Get out of here, Clint, before you ruin everything."

He heard her, even with the sickness bubbling inside him, he heard her. You get so you can never get away from their voices, you hear them, everything they say, no matter what else is going on, no matter what they've done to you, no matter how much you wish you never had to hear them again.

"I'm going to ruin everything. I'm going to kill him. He's not going to take you.... I'll stop you.... I'll go to Hall Weaver—I'll tell Hall all of it—everything before I'll let you go."

"Oh, that's fine," she said in a low voice that was hard with contempt.

We both heard her. He was almost upon me now, and I hoped he'd have sense enough to see what she thought of him. Only he didn't have any sense left at all. For whatever time Vi had been out here on this farm with Hall Weaver, during all that time, she'd somehow gotten at this man, and all he could think was that he had lost her. He had done nothing to hurt her, and he was about to lose her.

He and I were fraternity brothers.

Welcome to hell, Farmer Clint.

He sprang upward at me in that second, his arms out, his hands grasping.

He struck against me, and I went toppling back on the stairs.

I heard Vi screaming. I felt his fists pounding my face, and I heard his sick rage spilling out of him.

I got my knees between us and I kicked outward. I heard his gasping and I felt him going away.

He struck against the stair railing, and it splintered under his weight.

It was like slow motion now. He yelled as the stairs gave, and rolled downward, going away from the place where it was crumbling.

He lost his balance, stumbled and pitched forward down the stairs.

Vi screamed and tried to leap out of the way.

She was too late. Clint's big body toppled against her and broke his fall for only an instant, then they both went tumbling from the stairs into the hallway.

I stayed where I was on the stairs less than a second. I was already up, springing to my feet and running down the stairs again.

Vi was screaming now, fighting to get free of Clint. He seemed for the moment stunned, but I had no time to look at either one of them. I could see the screen door, and through it, the hot silent yard, like some bright lovely place. I ran toward it.

I was still carrying the chain.

"Joe!" Vi screamed at me. "Joe, please. For God's sake, Joe. Listen to me."

I didn't even look at her. I was staring at the sunlight beyond that screen door.

Clint came up on his knees as I ran past. He threw himself against me.

I was still carrying that damned link chain.

I lost my balance, trying to twist away from him, and I fell hard. The house jarred, trembling under me when I fell.

Clint came up off his knees and jumped at me again. I was on my back and I brought that looped chain upward and across his face.

He walked right into it, and I watched it smash his face.

It staggered him. I moved, rolling away, and as we both came up, I hit him in the face with all the rage that had torn this hook out of the wall.

He wavered for a moment on his knees, then he fell forward on his face.

I didn't even bother looking at him. I sprang past him, going toward that doorway and my car, running.

8

I ran across the porch, breathing through my mouth. The air felt hot and stifling and for the moment I was almost blinded by the metallic white of the sunlight.

I paused at the head of the steps. I leaned against the upright and the world seemed to skid away from me.

Suddenly I could feel my head throbbing, and now my arm was bleeding. My stomach burned where the farmer had clouted me. But no matter where the pain originated in my body it clattered against my skull.

I wiped my hand across my eyes, trying to clear them and smeared my face with my own blood.

My legs felt weak, but through an occluding film I could see my Chevvy, tilted forward on its pancaked front tires.

I opened my eyes and went carefully down the steps, still nauseated and afraid I was going to pitch forward on my face.

I hurried when I hit the sand. It was going to be tough trying to steer the car, rough moving through that eternal lane, and along narrow County Road Sixteen.

I brought my head up and stared at the country sprawled endless and tortured with gullies and knolls and ravines as far as I could see it. Impossibly flat, impossibly open....

I felt depleted as I staggered to the car and toppled against the front fender.

"Joe! Please, Joe, wait."

I didn't turn around, but I heard Vi running across the porch. I didn't look at her. I didn't want to see her any more. I knew what she looked like, and worse than that, I knew just what was in her eyes at this moment.

"Joe."

She clutched my arm in both her hands.

"Let me alone," I said.

"Joe, you're bleeding."

I dropped the link chain.

"Listen to me, Joe."

I ignored the frantic quality in her voice. You didn't worry about the Violas of this world; they got along; there was always some man.

"Where's your friend the farmer?"

"Clint?"

I shrugged, moving toward the car door.

She trembled when I moved away from her. I could feel her whole body shaking. She clung to my arm.

"He's gone, Joe.... He won't bother us any more.... He doesn't matter, Joe."

"That's the truth!"

I shrugged free of her hands. She almost fell. I didn't waste the energy I had left looking at her, but opened the Chevvy door and half-fell inside under the wheel.

I fought the keys from my pocket, wondering why Hall had left them with me. I wanted to laugh that I would wonder about that: he was sure I couldn't get very far in this car.

My arm dripped blood as I twisted the key in the ignition. Nothing happened. The engine was dead.

Vi was half inside the car, pressed against me, screaming in my ear.

I cursed when the car wouldn't start. There was no spark of life. I didn't know what Hall had done to it.

I pulled my head up and stared at the barren, open back-country beyond Vi's head. Ten miles to the nearest farmhouse. Wasn't that what Hall had said? And whose farmhouse? Probably Clint's. Good old Clint. He'd welcome me with open shotguns, even if I could make it. Only I knew better. At the moment I was afraid I could not walk as far as this house.

"Listen to me, Joe. I can't stay here any more. You can see that.... I've got to go with you."

I pushed her aside and got out of the car. She ran after me. I pushed up the hood. Hall had jerked all the wires from the distributor cap.

"Joe. You've got to take me with you. He'll kill me if you leave me here."

"There's always Clint." I spoke across my shoulder. I was working with the distributor cap, hands trembling.

"Oh, Joe. Please don't.... I've been out here—almost a year, Joe. Do you hear me? I've been on this place almost a year—with Hall—like he is.... Clint Hales was the only man I ever saw.... I was desperate.... I had to have somebody to help me.... Can't you understand that?"

I went on working with those broken wires. I was thinking with the twisted strings of hope going through me that if this was all Hall had done to the car, he wasn't trying to stop me, only to delay me as long as he could.

"Joe! I helped you. I helped you get free."

I glanced at her. "Why didn't Hall take you with him? Didn't he know you'd do that?"

She laughed, the bitterest sound I ever heard.

"No."

"He's really nuts."

"He really is." Her voice was flat, hopeless. "He knows how bad I want that money, Joe."

I pressed the distributor cap back in place, snapped it shut. "Oh, yes, the money."

She clenched her fists, almost as if she wanted to hit me and keep hitting me. "It's a lot of money, Joe. It'll buy us everything we ever wanted."

"It hasn't bought you much."

"No. It's bought me hell. A whole year of hell. That's why I've got to have it. That's why you've got to help me get it."

I shook my head, letting the hood fall back in place. The sound was like a desecration in the silence.

"Joe, I've been through hell. I've earned that money."

"Then get it."

I moved past her, got back in the car.

She stood there in front of the car, watching me, the sun making her pale and unreal. She did not move until I twisted the key and the engine turned, protesting. The third time it caught.

She ran around the car then, jerked open the door and lunged into the front seat beside me.

"Where are you going?" I said.

"I'm going with you."

"I don't want you. Can't you understand that? I don't want you. I don't want that money."

She shrugged, knotting her hands in her lap. She did not glance toward the house.

I turned the car slowly, painfully in the sand yard, the flat tires twisting and bumping already. It occurred to me the car might move better on the rims, but I knew I was too beat to rip off those casings. It wouldn't be long, the sharp rocks in the land would tear them into strips.

"You're mad now, Joe. Mad about Clint... and what you think he means—meant—to me."

"Oh, hell."

"Maybe I don't blame you, Joe. Maybe I'd be mad, too. Only you got to see what hell I've been in. How terrible it was for me.... Clint came—almost a year ago, to see about selling us milk and eggs.... After that, I met him when I could. I had to have somebody.... I already saw what had happened to Hall.... I had to have somebody."

I stared along the lane. The car wobbled crazily, weaving toward the narrow mouth between the fence rows.

"He—he's married, Joe. Clint is—"

"You have poor luck, don't you?"

"Yes, I have hellish luck... It took a long time. Joe, he's stupid, like a work mule... like an animal... It took all this time.... even with the money. But he came over when Hall left today to tell me he would help me.... Don't you hear me, Joe?"

"All of a sudden you got nothing but helpers."

"I didn't want him any more. But—before you came, he was the only hope I had, Joe.... You got to understand that. He didn't mean anything to me... nothing... less than nothing."

"I believe that."

"Oh, Joe.... Don't hate me like this. You can see I was going insane on this place."

"Sure... but then there's that other question. Why did you come here?"

"Joe. You already know that. We needed to hide—Hall did... He was afraid. He said we would hide out here until—the trouble blew over, and then he promised to take me out of this country. We'd go anywhere... We'd go everywhere. That's what Hall promised. Rio, Paris."

"More bad luck."

"Yes. More bad luck.... He said we would stay out here only until things cooled off.... He had bought this place years ago, through a dummy buyer... He was—he was a certified public accountant, Joe, and brilliant.... He was brilliant.... only he's not any more."

"No. He's not any more."

"He went nuts after we got out here. For a long time he didn't do anything but drink. He stayed drunk all the time. He had hallucinations. They were coming to get him. They were surrounding the house, or sneaking through every shadow. Then, it got so he was having those hallucinations when he was sober. He got so he was scared to leave here. He believed if he went away from here, they would catch him. He was scared to have people on the place—he was afraid of Clint Hales until I convinced him Clint was stupid, and harmless.... Hall would only go into Frigate once every couple of months, even when we'd run out of food, he wouldn't go. He had to build up his courage enough to bluff it out in a little nowhere place like Frigate. He would be full of bravado, going into the beer parlor, talking to people, trying to find out if the law was looking for him yet. By the time we got back here he'd be wild with fear."

I glanced at her. "Why did you come with me, Vi? What do you want?"

"I'm going with you."

"Yeah, I heard that. Only I don't believe it. What do you want?"

She held her breath for a long time. "I thought maybe I could make you listen to me, Joe. You've got to listen. All that money. All the things we could do with it."

"Sure." I laughed at her, only there was no laughter in the sound. "Sure. All that stands in the way is Hall and his gun."

"We can go back. We can get it now, Joe.... I know where it is. He's got it in a safe in that room of his."

"Oh, no."

"Joe!"

"Even if I were fool enough to go back. How could we open that safe? We couldn't open it. And I'm getting out of here. You might live with that character a year. But I couldn't stand it."

"You wouldn't have to, Joe... we'd take the safe. It's small enough we could both push it, down the steps, drive the car right to the porch."

"The hell with it. You hear me? The hell with it!" I pulled my gaze from the road. The car swerved wildly in the snake-like ruts. "You want to get out here?"

"No. There's two hundred thousand dollars back there, Joe. I've earned it. Every penny. It's mine and I'm going to have it."

"Lots of luck."

And then she screamed. The sound was torn out of her throat. I slammed on the brakes involuntarily, staring at her. She was staring past me through the windshield.

Slowly, I turned my head, following the direction of her gaze. I didn't really need to look.

Across the fields, on County Road Sixteen, rousing no dust, but screaming toward the cutoff where we were, was Hall's Buick. I recognized it across that distance because Vi had recognized it.

I didn't move. My hands gripped the steering wheel. I reckoned the distance to the end of the lane, and then thought what difference would it make on these torn tires?

I looked both ways across the rough, stone-pocked fields.

I did not bother to step on the gas again. We were sitting there when Hall whipped his Buick into the lane and careened toward us. He slammed on his brakes and let his bumpers click hard against mine.

I just sat there gripping the wheel. I was too tired and too sick to run, and anyway I could see in Hall's face, that was what he wanted me to do.

9

"So she told you all about it," Hall said. He paced up and down along the sunstruck porch of the silent old house. "So she told you all about me?"

I looked at him. I was sitting on the steps because this was as far as I could make it. I was too exhausted to go any farther, too beat.

I felt my mouth twist. What was the sense in arguing with him?

I shrugged. "What else? You left her alone here with me, didn't you? What do you think we would talk about?"

He stopped walking, standing tall and uncertain on that porch. He moved his narrow head, looking from me to Vi, sagged in a rocking chair. She stared at the bare yard as if she were completely abandoned, as if neither Hall nor I even existed for her any more.

But she existed for him, all right. I felt a twist of shock—shock without any surprise in it—seeing that Hall Weaver still wanted to trust Vi, even with all he knew about her, all she had put him through in this past year.

He stared at her for a long time, face rutted and mouth pulled down. He was trying to see the answer in her face. He wanted to believe that she had not betrayed him to me. But the evidence against her must have been overwhelming, even in his pressure cooker brain: I was free, no longer chained as he'd left me—though my arm was ripped and bleeding. He could see that getting free had not been easy for me. He had met us running away, almost to County Road Sixteen. Still, we had returned quietly enough, Vi crying into her hands. Wherever he was, lost inside that dark labyrinth of his mind, he still wanted to cling to her—or maybe he needed to, because he was a man who had nothing else; he was a man who now could consume a fifth of whiskey as another might drink a cup of tea.

"Vi," he said.

She did not look up.

Going grayer than ever, Hall swung his awkward, scarecrow body around to face me again.

"She told you about me," he said. "Don't lie."

I met his gaze levelly. "I didn't lie to you about who I am."

He flinched slightly, then ignored this. "So I'm on the run. The police are after me... the police may be after me now—"

"Look," I said. "That's all very interesting. But you don't have to tell me. You don't have to do it. All I want is to get out of here. I'll go in my car, without tires, the way it is, or I'll walk.... I don't want to know anything more about you."

He seemed almost sad. "Do you think I can let you go now?"

"You could if you were able to think at all."

He laughed at me. "Maybe you don't know how I can think. How my mind is filled with thoughts all the time.... And not about this mess.... Good things.... Good things I could do for people...."

"There's one thing you can do for me. You can let me out of here."

"No. You know too much about me. I wouldn't be safe."

I shrugged, not answering him.

"Look at me," he said.

I turned my head and looked up at him, waiting.

"I had everything my way," Hall said. "All my life. I was just bigger than the next guy, just better. I had things my way. I got to thinking... that I deserved things that way.... I was better in classrooms, I was better in sports.... It seemed to me that everything ought to fall in place for me when I got out of school, the way it always had."

I went on staring at him.

"Only it didn't."

For a fraction of a second he looked as if he would crumble into all those mismatched pieces. All that was holding him together now was the memory of the wonderful character he had once been.

"Only it didn't," he said. "No. I got this girl in my office pregnant. I had to marry her. I didn't have to. I could have run away. But I didn't want to run away. Not then. I wanted to stay where I was. In a good job, a cushy office. Things my way. I married her.... There wasn't any baby.... Something happened.... We didn't even have the baby.... Only I had Esther.... I still had Esther."

I forced myself to laugh at him. "So then you began to want to run away."

He controlled his anger, hanging onto himself. The gun was too near, making a heavy bulge in his jacket pocket. He was fighting himself. He could use that gun in his pocket, and then, no matter what else he was now, he would then be something else, something to his own mind worse: a murderer.

"All right. I wanted to run away. Look at me, man. What do I look like?"

I glanced at Hall, knowing what he wanted me to say: he looked like a big man, a former athlete, a man who could take what he wanted, mold things to his own desires. Only I didn't have to play the game his way. I saw him for what gallons of whiskey had made him, what fear and frustration and rage had made him.

I said it softly, but straight up into his face.

"You look like an embezzler."

It was as though I had struck him in the mouth. He literally staggered backwards a step, and then he changed, and he pounced on that....

"So she didn't tell you about me!" he shouted.

I kept my voice low. "She didn't have to tell me. What else? You're a CPA. She told me that. Sure, you'd be a CPA. You'd take snap courses in college so you could go out for all the sports. You'd find yourself with nothing left, but a chance for a degree in accounting.... Only it didn't pay the way you wanted it to, the way it ought to, so you rigged up a foolproof plan to embezzle your firm out of—out of a hell of a lot of money.... Now you've run with it, and you're scared in your guts, and you don't know what to do with the money, and you don't know what to do with yourself. Hell, nobody had to tell me that. There's nothing new about it. Jerks pull that stunt every day—jerks like you."

I had rubbed a raw spot. He forgot everything else, wanting to defend himself. "Nobody ever figured it out like I did. It was foolproof. Nobody could prove anything. I covered it everywhere, everyway."

"Then why you hiding out here, scared of your own shadow?" I said.

His voice rose slightly, quavering. "Nobody could prove anything on me. Nobody."

"Nobody except me." Vi spoke for the first time from the depth of her chair. Her face was in shadow, but the flat tone of her voice, the sag of her body showed the despondency engulfing her mind.

He hesitated. I saw his eyes waver. And then he said, voice hard: "I'm going to tell you something, Vi. Something I never told you before. Because I never wanted to. You couldn't have proved anything... you just had a suspicion, that's all. And I could have let you go to the head office with it, and you know what would have happened, they would have audited my books, and they would have fired you. Not me. You.... Only I didn't want that to happen.... I wanted you, almost as badly as I wanted that money.... So I went along with you. I let you think you shared in it." He shook his head.

"And here we are," Vi said, voice empty.

He paced back and forth on the porch. "So you can see, pal, why I can't let you ride out of here, or walk out of here. I wouldn't be safe.... I've gone through too much to lose it now."

"Lose it?" I said, "what the hell. You've lost everything else."

He shook slightly, then straightened his shoulders again. "I've still got that money. All of it... in case Vi didn't tell you. Over two hundred grand. Covered, every way from zero. Mine. I haven't lost anything, and I'm not going to."

I went on staring at him, keeping my voice low, but taunting him. "No. You haven't lost anything. It must be paradise for you, hiding out here, cringing like an animal in a hole, scared of the dark—in a house without electricity—scared of the neighbors, scared of strangers, scared of the woman who lives with you. Oh, you got it made."

"All right. It's a little rough right now. But nobody knows where I am. And it'll blow over—"

"What'll blow over?"

He shook his head, his eyes revealing his insecurity. "I quit my job. They audited me out. Gave me a clean bill of health. Just like I knew they would.

Vi had quit the place months before. I'd bought this place years ago. They had nothing on me. Nobody had anything on me. I was free to go where I wanted to go."

"Paris," Vi said, in contempt. "Rio."

He ignored her. "They didn't have any reason to suspect me."

"So here you are, hiding out," I said.

He breathed raggedly, across his open mouth. "It's because of Esther. I didn't think about that—until after Vi and I were here. What I had done to Esther. I had run away and left her without anything."

"A man with two hundred grand? How thoughtless."

"No. That's where you're wrong. I was thinking all right. I was a guy out of a job. How was it going to look, a guy out of a job, leaving his wife money when he abandoned her?"

"Lucky Esther," Vi said.

He snarled at her, then turned his back on the chair where she sprawled like something forsaken.

"Esther is the one I have to fear."

"You told her about your little embezzling plan, eh?"

"No. Oh, no. I told you I was too smart for anything like that. One reason I wanted that money was so I could get away from Esther. She's a good woman—"

"A good, big woman," Vi said.

"—but she smothered me. She was driving me bugs. I wanted to get away from her, and I never even let her guess what I was doing. But I know how wild she can get when somebody does her dirt—"

"Like walking out on her?"

"Exactly. She's the kind of person that could walk out any time without looking back if it pleased her, but that was no two-way street with her. She must have private detectives looking for me. If she raises a stink enough, they might go over those books again—and again—"

"Until they trap you," I finished for him.

"That's why I've had to stay here all this time. I've got to stay here until Esther gives up on me.... Then when it's quiet, Vi and I can leave here."

"Balls," Vi said.

"Don't talk like that!" Hall raged, swinging around to face her. "I know you're a slut. I've seen you with that farmer.... I saw you trying to get in that room with this guy.... I know by now what a slut you are, but you don't have to talk like one... not in front of me."

Vi laughed at him. "Hall can steal money, desert his wife, threaten to kill you. But he can't stand profanity."

"You slut!" he spat. He was quivering with the rage that made him a wild man, the rage that was steadily harder for him to control, the wildness inside him that he had to fight every minute.

He stood tall, shaking like a sapling in a hurricane, and then he strode past me, going down the steps, crossing the yard.

He leaned against a fence post. From the house we could see his shoulders shaking, sobs racking his body.

I looked away because it stirred something inside me, something I wouldn't let myself think about at all.

Vi didn't even bother to look at him.

Her voice was slow, tense, like something ground against my face. "Still think you're going to walk out of here alive?"

I didn't answer. I was thinking about Cora.

10

"We've got to kill him," Vi said.

I went on staring at the ground. I wanted to cry aloud because suddenly I knew the truth: I was never going to find Cora.

"Even you've got to see that," Vi said. "If we're going to live, we've got to kill Hall."

Her voice grated at me. Her words didn't make sense, all they did was destroy what I was trying to think, to remember. I wasn't going to be able to find Cora. I wanted to think about that, I wanted to go over it in my mind, the way I knew I had to, only I couldn't with Vi's voice hammering at me.

"Joe."

"Shut up. Let me alone."

"He's going to kill you, Joe."

Her voice got to me, and suddenly I was running away from those thoughts about Cora, and I felt gushing relief all through my body. I didn't have to think about it now. I was never going to find Cora.

I stared at that man sobbing his insides out across that sun-bleached yard.

"He's going to kill you, Joe... no matter what he found out in Willoughby... no matter what you were when you came here...."

My gaze was fixed on Hall Weaver, cringing in agony against the fence. He looked like an embezzler, and I wondered crazily if he looked like a murderer.

"You hear me, Joe?"

"Shut up, Vi. Let me alone."

"We got to talk... you been putting me off... you can't put me off now, Joe. You know how long we got? Until he comes back across that yard."

I pulled my head around, away from Hall Weaver and gave her a glance, my mouth twisted. "He's got the gun," I told her.

"But we got everything else, Joe. Everything."

I licked my mouth. "What's the matter with you?"

"I been planning, Joe. Months. Months, I haven't thought of anything else. I knew I'd have to kill Hall if I was going to get away from here, and I know how to do it. Only I need help... it looks like you need me, Joe, if you're going to stay alive... so you better listen to me."

I saw the way her gaze was fixed on Hall down at the fence, the way her tense voice spilled out, racing against time and the moment when Hall Weaver got himself under control.

"It's got to be now," she said. "Tonight."

"He's still got the gun."

"Yes. And the keys to the Buick. They're in his pocket. He hasn't pack-rat-ted them up to that nest of his upstairs. And if we keep him off-balance, he won't do it. Those keys are in his pocket."

"Probably right under his gun."

"Stop wasting time, damn you. Here. Read this."

I turned, frowning to look at her. Still watching Hall Weaver, she pulled a folded sheet of paper from her pocket and thrust it out to me. I took it, read it, and read it again. It was brief enough:

"I'm sorry. Sorry for everything I've done to you. Sorry about the money. The way I hurt you. Please forgive me."

"What is it?" I said.

"It's a note. From Hall. It's his suicide note, only he doesn't know it."

"There's no salutation, no signature."

She laughed, deprecatingly. "Think. Why should there be a signature? It's his handwriting. Even the stupidest police will learn that. And he's started some letters to his wife, even addressed an envelope.... I've got that, too. We leave that on the table alongside the note." Now she was breathing heavily. "Put it in your pocket. That'll prove I trust you. It's my only hope to make it look like Hall's death was suicide. He wrote that note to me one night over a year ago, back home in Cleveland.... We had a fight, and he wrote me that note, begging me to forgive him. Very touching."

"And you kept it?"

She shrugged. "All I know is that you are here.... You came here.... I kept that note and he's going to kill you... and me... unless we kill him first."

"He's still got the gun."

There was triumph in her tone, as if I had agreed to anything she planned. "We can take that away from him."

"We haven't had a lot of luck, so far."

"Luck won't have anything to do with it." She had not moved her gaze from Hall. She waited a moment, then she said, "Tonight, I'll give him a second fifth of whiskey."

"He drinks it like water."

"Doesn't he, though? That's what you've seen.... But it poisons him. It's just like poison. That's why I never give him but one fifth. That's why he's stopped fighting me about it. He knows what more than that does to him."

"So now you're going to make him drink more than one, now when he doesn't even trust you?"

"Joe," she said, "don't you know anything about alcoholics? Don't you see? He wants more. It drives him nuts when he can't get it—all he'll think is how lucky he is tonight to get more—"

"He can't be that dumb."

Her voice was scathing. "He's not dumb. Don't go counting on him being dumb... he is an alcoholic. Sick. He'll believe he's lucky getting that second fifth because that's what he'll want to believe. Don't worry about him. He'll make himself believe it."

Hall came slowly back across the yard.

I sat on the steps with Vi's unsigned note from him in my pocket. My heart beat off-key, as if something had happened to the trigger muscle. I could feel it flutter, and I could feel it slow down so my chest ached.

I had the crazy sensation that if I stood up even, the note Hall Weaver had written would fall out of my pocket to the floor at his feet. And if I spoke, the words would not be what I wanted to say, but a blurting confession. I gripped my mouth shut until my jaws ached, and I sat rigidly on the porch flooring, unmoving.

Vi sat watching him. There was a change in her, and there was nothing subtle about it, she seemed to have gathered new life and new strength. What she looked like was one of those sopranos in an operetta just about to burst into a song.

When Hall reached the place where our cars were parked in the yard, Vi got up and walked across the porch to the front door.

"Vi!"

There was frantic anxiety in the way he yelled her name from the yard.

She didn't even hesitate. The front door whined open and slammed shut behind her.

Hall hesitated out there beside the cars, and then he ran forward, shambling toward me.

I watched the bulge that gun made in his jacket pocket bouncing against him when he ran.

He was breathless when he reached the steps.

"Where's Vi? Where'd she go?" He stared down at me.

"Pull yourself together."

"Where did Vi go?"

"You're going to fly apart."

"Stow it, pal. Don't make the smart chatter for me."

I shrugged.

Hall stood there in the sunlight, his gaze fixed on that door. Neither of us moved.

"You don't know," Hall said, staring at that screen door where Vi had disappeared. "You don't know, how it was... with us.... With Vi and me.... We had something good and wonderful—clean."

"Sure."

"We were in love once.... She was in love with me.... You hear that, pal? She really loved me. She went crazy when I loved her—"

"Moaning. Crying out. Telling you how wonderful you were. The word was different. Wasn't that what she told you? You were different."

"Damn you," he said. His face was rutted and he looked as if he were going to burst into uncontrollable sobs again. "Damn you. What do you know about it?"

I shrugged again. I didn't bother telling him I owned the copyright. I had played all those scenes.

"What do you know about a woman loving you?" he cried out, still not looking at me. "A man like you. A man that his own wife runs away from. What do you know about a woman truly loving you?"

"Not very much," I said.

He laughed, pleased with himself. He had gotten the word on me at Willoughby, all right. Not that it mattered any more.

"What do you know about it, pal," he said with a rage of laughter in his voice, pushing it. "What can a man like you know about a woman loving you?"

"She loves you when it's convenient—for her," I said, knowing he wasn't really listening to me. What he was listening for was the sound of Vi's feet in that hallway coming back toward him. It was pathetic as hell. At least it hit me that way, because it was as if I were seeing myself in a distorted mirror, the kind of distortion that shows you the real truth. "She'll love you when it helps her get what she wants, when there's not somebody that looks better to her."

"Oh, you got it figured, pal." He laughed but didn't look at me. He couldn't pull his eyes away from that door. "You just never had a woman crazy for you. Crazy and wild, and scratching to get closer to you. I'm sorry for you, pal. I'm really sorry."

The front door was pushed open, and it was as if the sun had suddenly brightened, warming Hall Weaver's lean face, relaxing the grooves and ruts in it.

He almost laughed aloud. Vi had gone away from him, and now she had come back.

For almost a whole minute he didn't even see the unopened fifth of whiskey she carried, because he was concentrating on her face.

I looked away from Hall's face. I'd had enough of that distorted mirror for one day; I'd had enough of the truth.

He saw the bottle of whiskey then, and his gratitude made him almost childlike. "Ah, Vi," he said. "Vi."

"You've had a tough time," Vi said, meeting his eyes. "You got to relax. You got to unwind."

He licked his lips and then drew the back of his hand across his mouth. "Yes," he agreed. "I got to relax."

He reached for the fifth of whiskey. His hand was trembling.

I glanced at the brassy sky. By the sun I figured it was between two and three o'clock in the afternoon.

When I pulled my head down, I saw the way Vi was watching him, her smile grim and satisfied. But Hall didn't see anything except the bottle that he usually got to drink along with his supper.

I held onto the edge of the porch because the world tilted even further, and I clung, like I might fall off. I watched him drink, and knew it had started. We were going to kill him. It was like the night wind that rose at sunset out here and howled all night, nothing could stop it. We were going to kill Hall Weaver; it had started like that night wind, and nothing could stop it.

He took a long drink, gripping the bottle greedily in his fist, glancing at me as if he were afraid I was going to ask him for even one drink.

He smiled, nodding as the whiskey burned into him. "Thanks, Vi," he said, eyes glittering with tears. "You're good to me. Maybe I've not been fair, but I'm going to make it up to you, Vi. Everything's going to be fine for us. Everything. It's all going to work out, Vi."

"Yes," she said, smiling at him. "It's all going to work out, Hall."

11

That afternoon died away slowly. Sometimes, from the steps where I was sitting, I'd glance at the sun, and it seemed not to have moved. It was as if it were hung there, burning itself out.

Only one thing hadn't stopped me, and that was my mind. One terrible idea kept rolling through my brain: It had started. We were going to kill Hall. It had started.

Hall was certainly unaware of the fact that he was breathing his last, drinking his last. All his thoughts seemed turned in on his bottle, all right.

He strode up and down that porch in the heat, sweating and nursing from the mouth of that bottle. You could hear him gulping it down, even when you didn't look at him.

And I didn't look at him any more than I had to. He would say something, slurring his words, laughing at nothing, and yell my name when I didn't look up.

"Pal! I said something. Didn't you hear me, pal?"

"I didn't hear you." I still didn't look at him.

"He didn't hear me," he said to Vi. "How about that, Vi? He got something on his mind. That it?"

"Maybe he's got something on his mind, Hall."

I looked at her, all right. I had never seen anyone as calm as Vi looked just then. She sat with her hands folded in her lap, her head back against the chair rest. There were no such thoughts in her mind, murder, money.

A fly buzzed across her face. She didn't bother to brush it away.

Hall staggered back along the shaded porch to where I was sitting. He stood over me, bottle in his fist.

"You poor bastard," he said.

I stared at the ground.

His voice rose. "Didn't you hear what I said, pal?"

"I heard you."

"You poor bastard. I said, you poor bastard. You wander in here, looking for your wife, and get mixed up in something like this. You poor bastard. I'm sorry about you. I want you to know that."

"Don't waste your pity," I said.

I looked up. He was holding that Luger in his fist, looking at it with loathing, but the kind of loathing that was meaningless. He hated it, but he was going to use it. The way he had it figured, he had to use it.

I jerked my gaze past Hall to where Vi sat calmly. Her eyes were dry, and brushed against mine, as if to say, well, that's it, the time you got, Joe, is whatever time Hall decides you've got.

"I don't want to do it, pal." Hall was almost blubbering. "I wish you could see that."

Vi's voice taunted him. "Don't worry, Joe. He won't do it until he builds up his courage. Isn't that right, Hall? You've got to build up courage first, haven't you?"

"Stay out of this, damn you." Hall spoke across his shoulder.

Vi shrugged. "That's the way Hall is. That's the way he is, all right. Hall has to build up his courage even to go into Frigate for groceries. Don't you, Hall?"

He spun around, pivoting. "Lay off me!"

"Oh, go on and drink," she said, speaking defiantly up into his face.

He stood there a moment, staring down at her, and then he laughed in a bitter way. "You think I won't, huh?"

"I'm sure you will."

As if to spite her, Hall turned up the bottle and chug-lugged it. The bubbles burst upward in the emptying bottle.

When he removed it from his mouth it was almost empty. But now he had shoved the gun back in his jacket pocket and for the moment he seemed to have forgotten me.

I looked toward the west. The sun seemed to be stuck there in a flat, cloudless sky.

Hall finished off the bottle. He reeled down the steps and then stood looking around in the yard.

He drew his arm back and hurled the empty bottle toward my Chevvy. The bottle struck the windshield, breaking. The windshield shattered in a thousand wavy lines.

He turned, looking down at me. "I'm sorry about that, pal," he said. "But it don't matter.... Really, it don't matter...."

"No," I said, looking up at him. "You'll bury the car along with me."

He met my gaze for a moment, and involuntarily lifted his arm, forgetting he'd emptied the bottle.

He pulled his gaze away from mine and stared at his empty fist. The bottle of whiskey was gone. He stood there unsteadily looking around, lost without a bottle.

It was still daylight when Vi called us in to supper. Usually it was well after dark before she even went near the kitchen. Tonight she was hurried. We could see in the gloomy dining room without the lamps. But she lit them anyway, setting them in the middle of the table.

"What you want to eat so early for?" Hall wanted to know.

"We got a big dinner," she said, putting the smoked pans before us. "I just couldn't wait."

He leaned forward, stared into the pans and then sat back, looking ill.

"Beans and hot dogs again," he said. "My God. Beans and hot dogs again."

She stared at him flatly. "You were expecting steak?"

"Beans and hot dogs." He shuddered.

"It's your own fault, Hall," she said loudly, standing near him. "I cook what I've got, and that's what I've got left. It's not my fault you won't take me out of here—even to the store in Frigate."

"All right. We'll get into town, as soon as we can."

"When, Hall? I want to get out of here."

"You will." He glanced at me. "Things are going to be better, Vi. I got a few things—I got to take care of—and then things are going to be better for you."

"Sure they are," she said.

I glanced up, found her eyes fixed on me.

Hall cursed, leaned forward, slopping beans and hot dogs into his plate. Vi put coffee cups before my place and hers. I saw Hall glance up, scowl, but he said nothing.

Vi went into the kitchen. When she came back she was carrying an unopened fifth of whiskey. She put it down casually beside Hall's plate without speaking.

Hall's head came up warily. I watched him, holding my breath. He almost spoke, almost protested, and then a faint smile showed around his mouth, a secret, triumphant smiling.

I saw the look of cunning that gleamed for an instant in Hall Weaver's face. He did not say anything. Clearly, he was putting one over on Vi. She had already given him his daily ration of whiskey, but she had forgotten, and he was too smart for her. He was not going to remind her.

Vi sat down across the table from me. She said, and her voice had calm in it. "The coffee isn't ready. I'll bring the coffee in soon, Joe."

She spoke directly at me. I didn't look up. I nodded.

She said it again. "It isn't ready yet."

Hall was ripping the top off the bottle, doing it quickly, expertly, thirstily. Without watching him, I knew he was trembling with anticipation. Maybe even like a child, he was trying to drink as much as he could before Vi took it away from him.

He tilted up the bottle, drinking without even pouring it out into the tumbler. I saw the way he watched Vi as he drank, but she ignored him, letting him think she'd forgotten the first fifth because she had something else on her mind.

She had something else on her mind, all right.

I glanced across the table at her. The lamplight made deep shadows in her cheeks, making her look drawn and haggard, even her flesh ready to crack with the tensions in her. It occurred to me that if she were still beautiful after a year in this mad paradise, she must have been sensational in the good old days before she met Hall Weaver.

Hall's hands trembled on the bottle when he tried to pour whiskey into the tumbler. I began to see how well Vi knew him: she'd been right about his making himself believe she'd allowed him this second fifth of whiskey by accident.

Neither Vi nor I ate anything. Both of us heaped food on our plates, but all we really did was sit and watch Hall drink. It was something to see. His insides had built up a tolerance for the amount of whiskey he usually consumed, but more than that truly poisoned him.

I sat, my heart slugging, watching a man drink himself to death.

First a muscle twitched under his left eye. It was barely noticeable at first, but then it was vibrating like a pulse under his skin and it jerked his lid down in an odd, upsetting way.

He was unaware of it.

Then I saw the muscles in his arms twitch just the way his lower eyelid was pulsating.

Vi must have seen all this, too, but she remained calm. She said, "This damned wind. It's starting earlier tonight, and it's louder than ever."

"Wha' say?" Hall said. "Wha' you say, Vi?"

"Go to hell," she told him.

His eyes brimmed with tears, and when his lower lid jerked, the tears spilled across his cheeks, and he wiped at his eyes with the back of his hand the way a small boy might.

"You don' love me, Vi.... I don't think you ever love me."

"What do you know about it?" She said, to him. "What do you know about it, when you drink like that?"

His face muscles constricted, and his arms trembled with muscle tremors. You could look at him and see he was a sanitarium case at that moment, but Vi went on calmly sitting with her hands in her lap.

And I was jumping almost as badly as Hall, with nothing to drink in me.

"It's your fault, Vi," Hall said, gripping the bottle in his palsied fist. "You ought not to let me drink like this, Vi.... You loved me.... You wouldn't let me drink like this."

Hall was swaying in his chair. The change was taking place in him, just as Vi had vowed it would. Even his head would twitch on his shoulders, and his body would lurch suddenly in his chair.

He removed the Luger from his pocket and laid it in his lap. He did this with elaborate show, as if he wanted to convince me he had everything under control, and knew what he was doing every minute.

"Whiskey don't trouble me, pal," he said. "Because I've learned to handle it."

His head twitched on his shoulders.

I glanced at Vi. From that moment there was a static tension in that lamplighted room that hadn't been there before. There was a visible change in Hall as he sank into the depths.

The change in Vi almost matched his. I could see the way her eyes glittered yellowly, and the way she watched him. How many times in the past year had she watched him just like this, reading him as you might read a gauge?

The sounds were louder inside my head: the wind, the way Hall breathed, and the sudden creaking of a board on the porch.

Both Vi and I reacted.

I sat forward at the sound of that noise. I wanted to cry out, warning her. It struck me hard that Clint Hales had returned. I had beaten him and run him away, but that didn't mean he had to stay away.

Her voice had a dreadful calm in it. "It's only the wind," she said.

Hall hadn't even heard the noise.

"Wha's matter, Vi?" he said. "Wha's matter?"

"Nothing," Vi said, staring into his upraised face. "Eat your beans."

"Hate beans. Get out of this, never eat 'nother bean. Not long as I live."

I strained, listening for the sound the dry boards would make if a foot moved on them. I don't know how many moments went by, the sound was not repeated.

Vi stood up. I trembled at the sudden movement. I glanced at Hall. His head was back against the chair rest and he was humming gently to himself, eyelid twitching.

"I'll get our coffee now," Vi said. "It's ready."

She was staring hard at me. I did not move. For a moment I wondered that Hall would not think it strange that it had taken almost an hour for that coffee to get ready. But then I saw that where he was, it didn't matter, time had lost any meaning. As far as he was concerned, it may have been only moments ago that Vi first mentioned coffee. Anyway, he didn't care; he didn't drink coffee.

We sat there, waiting for Vi to comeback from the kitchen.

12

Vi came through the doorway from the kitchen.

"The coffee is hot now, Joe," she said. "It's good and hot. Isn't that the way you like it?"

I stared past Hall Weaver at her. Vi wasn't even carrying a coffee pot at all. What she was carrying was a steaming kettle, the steam so thick it was like a solid mass rising from the kettle's spout.

Vi's face was as gray as the steam.

I shook my head but Vi didn't even look at me. I wanted to warn Hall what was going to happen, to yell at Vi that we couldn't do it, we had to wait. But I didn't do anything. I just sat there, watching numbly as if I were inside some plastic bubble, seeing it but unable to change anything. And I didn't speak because suddenly I wasn't thinking about Hall and Vi, and this moment. I was thinking about Cora. Sick inside with my thoughts of Cora.

"Our coffee is ready now," Vi said, her voice as calm as Eve's must have been when she handed Adam that apple.

From this detached place where I was, I saw her lean across Hall's chair at the head of the table as if to fill my cup from the steaming kettle.

Hall screamed.

I didn't even see her suddenly pour the water, sloshing it down the front of his shirt and over his thighs.

All of Hall's reactions were delayed. He screamed, but only because he saw that she was pouring something on him. The message of scalding pain was slow getting to his mind and he came upward like a diver in slow motion, swinging his arms and yelling at her.

Vi was screaming, too. She hurled the kettle aside, yelling at me. "Joe. Now, Joe. Now."

I may never have moved at all, but the clatter of the Luger on the floor was loud, loud enough to shake me out of the terrible apathy in which I found myself. The gun. I had to have that gun.

I shoved back in the chair and fell forward on the floor, searching for the Luger.

I saw it on the floor, in the shadows under the table, and I lunged forward on my belly, scrambling for it.

Hall moved, too. That water had been boiling hot, scalding enough to peel the hide off a hog, but when I leaped for that gun, Hall forgot the pain, forgot Vi and what she had done to him.

He stepped forward and as I reached out, he brought up his foot and kicked me in the face.

He must have kicked field goals like that ten years ago on somebody's college gridiron. I thought my head was torn loose from my shoulders.

My head jerked upward, and for a moment my brain was in a red fog. But I was desperate, too. If Hall could keep moving, poisoned with alcohol, scalded with boiling water, he wasn't the only one who wanted to stay alive.

My hand closed on that gun, and when I went toppling over away from his foot, I had the Luger in my hand.

Hall was slobbering, his eyes distended and face rutted. His lower left eyelid twitched wildly. He leaned forward, his arms extended, hands like talons to claw that gun away from me.

He might have made it. His shoe had caught me under the chin, and though I was aware of everything, I was moving slowly.

But when he leaned forward, he lost his last wispy memory of equilibrium. He had had it. His mind and body succumbed to the poison and he crumpled.

Hall would have plunged forward on his face, but Vi moved quickly, catching him around the chest. For a moment she staggered under his awkward height and the dead weight of his body, but then she moved back and let him sag into his chair at the head of the table.

"Joe," she said to me.

I heard her through the boiling pressures inside my temples.

"Now, Joe."

I could hear her, all right.

I came up on my knees, waiting for Hall to spring forward from his chair. But he was out cold, head lolling awkwardly on his shoulders.

I stood staring at him with the Luger in my hand.

I don't know how long I stood there, because suddenly Vi was screaming at me.

She ran around the chair, yelling at me, her voice keening, cutting into me like the wail of the wind.

"What are you waiting for, Joe?"

I only shook my head, standing with the gun poised out in front of me.

I felt Vi's body strike against me, and I wavered slightly under the impact of her weight. Her hand closed over my hand on the gun, and her flesh was chilled, but her pressure was firm. My hands seemed paralyzed, but hers were not. Her hand pressed against my fingers. There was the explosion of the gun, held only inches from Hall's head. He jerked the way a target does when struck by a bullet, and then there was blood over everything and I could not look at him.

"Give me the gun, Joe," Vi said. Her voice had that ice-cold calm in it that was worse than hysterics for me.

I released the Luger, and she took it from my numbed fingers.

I turned away. Hall Weaver was dead and part of his face was blown away and I could not look at him. I stared at the shadowed walls, hearing Vi move at my back.

She placed the gun in Hall's hand, and pushed his body forward so he sprawled face down on the table. I looked only long enough to see that he looked as if he had passed out with his head in his unfinished plate of beans, his arms out on each side of his head.

"Give me the note, Joe," Vi said.

I nodded, without speaking. I took the note Hall had written to her in passion and need a long time ago in Cleveland.

"There was somebody out there, Vi," I said. "I heard them. I know there was somebody out there."

"Don't be a fool," she said. "We've got to hurry."

I nodded. This was the first thing that made any sense to me. Hall Weaver was dead and I could get out of here. She was right. I had to hurry.

She was going through his pockets. He had a heavy key ring and she tossed it to me. I caught it. Her voice crackled with impatience.

"Take the kettle back in the kitchen, Joe. Bring me the coffee pot."

I nodded again, and walked into the kitchen. I set the kettle on the stove. The coffee pot was near it, and hot. I carried it back into the dining room.

Vi had gotten everything from Hall's pockets that she wanted. She brought several envelopes on which Hall had scribbled Esther Weaver's name and her Shaker Heights address in Cleveland. The envelopes were crumpled as though Hall had wadded them up and thrown them away, but she had smoothed them out.

Vi took the coffee pot from me and poured coffee in our cups, then spilled most of the rest of it on Hall where she had scalded him with boiling water. Calmly, she set the pot on its side at his elbow.

"Come on, Vi," I said. "Let's go. Let's get out of here."

Her head jerked up, and she stared at me for a brief moment with that scorn she'd once reserved for Hall Weaver.

She didn't bother to answer me. She put Hall's fountain pen, opened, near his hand as if he had just scrawled that old note.

She replaced our chairs at the table, scraped most of the food from our plates back into the pot which she left near Hall's head.

"That's it," she said at last, looking around. "That's all we can do right now."

"Let's get out of here."

She spun around on her heel.

"What are you talking about, Joe?"

I was calmer now. I was all right as long as I didn't look at that spreading pool of blood on the table.

"We've got to get out of here. We got to run."

Her face told me the brand of idiot she thought me. "You going to run, Joe? Where you going to run?"

I shook my head. I had not thought that far ahead. I did not know.

"We got to run. We got to get out of here."

"Why?" she said, still staring at me, mouth twisted.

"We killed him. We got to get out of here. We can take his car. We can be out of this state by morning."

Suddenly she laughed. It was a rasping, taunting sound without a trace of mirth in it. "We didn't kill him, Joe. Hall killed himself.... And we're not going to run. You might as well make up your mind about that. If we ran, they might think we killed him.... Forget it, Joe, we're not going to run any-where."

13

I forced myself to calm down.

There was something in her voice that made me see hysteria wasn't going to buy either of us anything. She had said that she had planned Hall's death for almost a year, and the way she behaved now convinced me.

At least she had a plan, and I had nothing to fear, and for the moment there was nothing to do but to go along with her.

I watched her checking everything in that dining room, amazed that she could move in that businesslike manner around the man she had run here with as if he were some stranger asleep with his head on that table.

"We've got to be careful, Vi," I said.

She appeared not to hear me. I felt a sudden flare of hatred. For some reason, this murder was something she'd been unable to accomplish alone, but she acted now as if I were no more than the Luger she'd used to shoot away part of his head, and now left clasped in his fist on the table.

"We got to be careful," I said again.

She moved purposefully about the room. She glanced at me, at the table. "Wrap up your hand in something," she said. "An old towel. Anything. You look like you've been in a fight, but that's fine."

"Sure," I said. "Fine."

She threw me a handtowel from a closet across the room. I wrapped my hand in it, watching her.

"It's more than killing him," she said. "It's that money. We've got to have that money. We haven't got a chance without that money."

"All I want is to get out of here."

"You fool. If you ran now, they'd hang you."

"Can't we hurry it up?"

"I'm not going anywhere without that money. Come on. We'll get it now."

She took up a lamp and moved out of the room. I glanced at Hall's body and then followed her.

Vi went along the hall, her shadow lunging crazily against the walls as she moved.

She jerked her head at me, and went up the stairs. I followed. Those steps were longer than I remembered, steeper. They seemed impossibly high, impossibly steep.

I was breathing through my mouth when I came off the stairs to the upstairs hallway.

"The keys," Vi said impatiently, "come on. Where are the keys?"

Using my good hand, I dug Hall's key ring from my pocket. She stood near his locked door with the lamp held high. The lock on his door was a Yale. I fumbled through the keys until I found the right one.

I shoved the door open, and then waited. She entered his room ahead of me.

She had called it a pack rat's nest. That was an understatement.

We stood, looking around.

It even smelled closed, crowded, dusty. It was impossible to see how he slept in this debris at night. It was as if he had become obsessed with collecting things, junk, useless objects, as if in the past year he had become afraid to let anything go, and instead had stored it all away here in this locked room.

Vi went unerringly across the room to where the small metal safe stood.

It was small, weighing about two hundred pounds. I saw it was a combination safe. I stared at it helplessly in the lamplight.

"How do we open it?" I said. "Did he leave you the combination?"

Her laugh was sharp. "Don't be a fool. He never told me anything. He hardly trusted himself."

"If we rob that safe, we'll never make it stick that he killed himself."

"We've got to open it. That's where my money is."

"You do want to get hung, don't you?"

She glanced across her shoulder at me, eyes cold. "We don't have to open it here. We don't have to leave it here. Nobody around here knows he had a safe like this." She laughed. "Who would ever miss it from a roomful of junk like this?"

"We've still got to open it."

"We'll open it. You'll open it. Only we've got to get it out of here first. We'll roll it down the hall, take it down the stairs. We can back the Buick up to the front porch, load it up and take it away. I know a place across the fields where we can get rid of it."

Now I looked at her with that contempt she loved to spread around.

"And leave indent-marks across this floor, out in the hall, down the stairs, across the front porch? Why take it away if you're going to do that?"

Her voice flared up against mine. "You got a better idea?"

I looked around helplessly. "You'll never explain those scratch marks that safe would make. We might carry it downstairs, but I doubt it."

"You got a better idea?" she said again. "I'd carry that safe downstairs for two hundred thousand dollars."

"So would I," I said. "If I thought we could do it. But I don't. We'd drop it somewhere, set it down somewhere. We'd have to." I was still looking around. Something struck my attention, but was lost. I scowled, searching again. "Any marks and we might as well leave it here."

"I'm going to have that money."

But I wasn't listening to her. I was staring at the window, locked and closed, the wind loud beyond it, the dark night empty and black.

Suddenly I laughed. I ran across the room, pushed off the lock and shoved the window up. The night wind clouded past me, filling the room, rolling out through the house.

"Get me that quilt," I told her, jerking my head toward Hall's rumpled bed.

She smiled suddenly, pleased, and grabbed up the quilt in her arms, running with it to me.

I spread the quilt carefully across the window sill and along the sides.

The safe was heavy, but I managed to lift it off the floor. I staggered with it to the window, then paused, holding it. I let it touch the quilt as gently as I could, then I lifted it. It was only partly through the open window when gravity took over for me. It was as if the heavy safe were torn from my grasp.

We held our breaths, standing inside the room. When the safe struck the ground it was as if a tree had fallen. We could feel the vibration inside the house.

I jerked the quilt out of the window, closed and locked it as it had been, while Vi tossed the quilt across the bed, even spreading it neatly as if the bed were made up, waiting for Hall.

Her face was gray, the way wet ashes are gray, but there was a smiling in her face, and she stared at me, nodding.

The Buick bumped along the back roadway through the fields. The night wind was cold and inside the car, neither of us talked.

There was nothing to say. Both of us were trying to think our way out of this maze now. It was as if we had made it, part of the way, but the roughest stretch was still ahead, and we could not afford to make even a small mistake. I wanted to laugh crazily, because I abruptly remembered this fear of being wrong was the way it had started with Hall Weaver. A little fear that kept growing and festering inside his mind....

I ticked off in my mind the way it had gone since we dropped the safe out the window.

We came downstairs together, breathlessly. We left lamps burning in the house. There was only a faint chance anyone would come near, but we wanted them to see the reassuring gleam of light in the house if they did look at the old place from the road.

Vi got an empty suitcase from a downstairs closet and we ran out on the front porch.

My Chevvy sat there, tilted and useless in the front yard. It seemed to me we were going to ride to the gallows on that thing.

"We've got to get rid of it," I told Vi.

"It doesn't matter," she said. "It doesn't matter at all. We're not trying to hide. We're not trying to hide anything, not even your car, or even what Hall did to it."

I let it go for then. We hadn't had time for her to tell me what her plan was, and there was no time for it now.

We ran across the yard to the Buick. I got in under the wheel. Vi put the suitcase in the back seat and sat as far as she could get from me against the door.

I drove the Buick around the house to the place where the safe had dug itself a small crater in the ground.

I unlocked the trunk, lifted the safe again and crouched, crabbing around to the trunk. The car seemed to sag under its weight.

"We'll have to go slow on those back roads," I told her, "or we'll break a spring."

She stood watching me, but didn't speak.

The safe door had sprung slightly when it struck the ground, but this was going to make it no easier to open. I took a flashlight from the car and went into the barn. I came back with a sledge, hammer and a crowbar. I put them in the trunk beside the safe and closed it.

We got into the Buick.

"All right," I said. "Which way?"

She nodded toward the rear fields, away from County Road Sixteen. I turned the Buick, following the vague outlines of a dim trail. We went through a fence, its gate hanging broken, unused, unrepaired.

The car bounced on the rough trail. The car lights seemed weak in the wind-swept night. There were no lights anywhere before us to mark a horizon. Against the deepest black sky, I could see the rise of foothills.

I tried to keep the car at a slow speed, but I couldn't do it.

I glanced at the dash, found the speedometer needle at thirty-five on the pocked, rock-strewn lane.

"Slow it down," she said.

I tried to, but it was impossible. I drove faster, my foot seeming to step harder on the accelerator, no matter what I told myself I wanted to do. What I really wanted was to put miles between me and that body back in that house.

"Slow down, Joe!"

I managed to pull my foot off the gas pedal. I was sweating.

"You wreck us out here, and we're through—finished—in jail," she warned me.

I nodded. I had sense enough left to see that, but in a moment the speedometer was creeping upward again. I couldn't hold it down. It was almost as it had been when I started out driving to find Cora. I'd start out slowly, but before long I'd be hitting eighty, ninety, breaking all the speed laws, looking for Cora ahead of me, trying to find Cora. Now I knew it was too late. I wasn't going to find Cora. Not now.

But still I was driving too fast, only now I wasn't running toward anything, I was running away from that body back there, or from myself.

14

"Stop," Viola said. "Stop the car here."

She was sitting forward on the seat, peering ahead in the darkness.

I stepped on the brakes. The car rolled to a stop and I cut the engine. For the space of one long breath we sat in the silence.

I got out of the car.

I caught my breath.

I almost laughed aloud. It was good that Vi had spoken the instant she did. The car was less than ten feet from the brink of a pit.

I stood looking around, feeling the helpless laughter inside me. It had been so close, it was almost all over. My arm ached, I was tired and beat. I told myself we could not get out of this anyway. Maybe it would have been better if Vi had not spoken at all.

"Good grief," I said. "What sort of place is this?"

Vi stood on the other side of the car. "Hurry, Joe."

I glanced around at the desolate badlands into which we had driven. The land was eroded, broken, chopped, slit with long ravines and arroyos. The trees were stunted pines, the only other life was tough clumps of grass and small cactus.

I opened the trunk, managed to lift the safe one more time.

I needed light, more light than the flash would provide. I wasn't about to carry that safe to the front of the car. The answer was so simple that I laughed at myself, and despite everything, began to feel a little bit better.

Carefully I reversed the car, turned it around, fixed the headlights on the safe.

I studied the way the door was sprung and decided the easiest way to get in was to use the sledge and the crowbar on the slight opening made where the door was sprung.

I put the crowbar against the opening and holding it with my hurt hand, struck it with the sledge hammer. It was slow because I was not naturally left-handed.

Vi ran forward, got on her knees and held the bar in place. Using both hands I drove it into the safe in four different places before the lock suddenly snapped.

Vi sighed, as if she'd been holding her breath. I lifted the door and let it fall open.

It was as if someone struck me full in the face with a mailed fist.

Maybe I hadn't really believed all Vi had said about that money before. I believed it now. It was there, stacks of it, carefully embezzled, carefully hoarded and stashed away for a long time.

Vi was making whimpering noises in her throat.

She crawled nearer on her knees, breathing through her parted mouth, whimpering.

She acted about this money the way Hall Weaver had behaved with his second fifth of whiskey.

I didn't say anything.

I stood staring at the green, beautiful stacks of money. I didn't know how Hall Weaver had gotten away with that much cash, but that wasn't my problem. It had been a beautiful plan, even if it hadn't brought him very much.

Vi was making those odd, moaning noises, swaying and dipping her arms into the money, letting it caress her flesh up above her elbows.

At last, she looked up at me across her shoulder.

Her eyes were almost dreamlike, soft and luminous in the light from the car.

"Joe," she said softly. "Get the suitcase, dear."

Still feeling oddly that this thing was a dream with nightmarish overtones, and not real at all, I nodded.

I returned to the car, opened the door, got the suitcase.

When I came back, Vi was still there on her knees, laving her arms in the stacks of money.

I opened the suitcase and sank to the ground beside her.

"We better hurry, Vi."

She smiled and nodded, but I wasn't sure if she really even heard me.

We stacked the money in the suitcase, and it took a long time because we did it so carefully, touching each stack with tender loving care.

It was placed in the suitcase neatly, and the old safe was empty.

Vi closed the suitcase, locked it, secured the straps and then, holding it in her arms as if it were a baby, she walked to the car.

I stood a moment looking after her, then I rolled the safe slowly across the rough ground to the brink of the pit.

By the time I got there, gasping for breath, unable to think because of the pain in my right arm, Vi had walked dreamily from the car and stood near me, watching.

"Be careful, Joe," she said in that dreamlike voice, "don't hurt yourself, Joe."

I looked up, and laughter burst across my mouth.

"No. I can't hurt myself," I said. "Not now.... We don't want to waste any of that lovely money on a doctor, do we?"

She giggled. "Money. All that lovely money."

Her voice sounded so odd that hackles quivered at the nape of my neck. Yet she looked the same. It was nothing I could explain.

I shoved the broken safe over the side of the pit, and we heard it rolling and bouncing, striking against flint rock, sparking as it plummeted down into the abyss.

"Let them find it," Vi said behind me. "Let them look for it."

I turned around. I was feeling better. I forgot the pain in my arm. I had this sense of triumph that I must have contracted from her, like a contagious fever.

"We're going to make it," I said.

But she hardly heard me. The look was still in her eyes that had come into them at the sight of all that money. She stood, staring at nothing, lost in thoughts all her own, already spending that money in the marketplaces of the world, tossing it wildly with both hands, and she seemed to have forgotten all about me.

I said, "Come on, Vi. We better get out of here."

"What?"

"You heard me. Come on. We can't stay here."

Her laugh was low in her throat. "Why not?"

"Come on, Vi."

"Why can't we stay here?"

"Stop acting like a fool."

"Why can't we stay here?" She looked around her as if we were standing in the courtyard at Monaco. "I might buy it."

"Hell, maybe you already own it," I said. "Maybe Hall left it to you. In his will. Come on. Let's get out of here."

The laugh moved upward in her throat. "That's lovely, Joe. Maybe it's mine. Maybe Hall willed it to me. Maybe he did."

"Vi, for Christ's sake. You're acting nuts. I don't mind that, but you're wasting time. We're rid of the safe, we got the money, let's get out of here."

I tossed the sledge hammer and the crowbar out into the darkened pit.

"I came here with Hall once," she said, standing on the brink of the pit, the wind whipping her black hair from her face, gluing her dress to her body. "We stood here on the ledge of this pit, and we were fighting. I was sick of this place—I was fed up, and I told him I was leaving." She laughed. "He went a little nuts—a little more crazy.... He went wild.... He said if I ever tried to leave him he would kill me, and he'd throw my body in this pit and nobody would ever find me."

The laughter rose inside her, spilling across her mouth.

"For God's sake, Vi. Let's go."

She turned then, her hair riffling across her face. "Where are you going in such a rush, Joe?"

"I don't care. Anywhere. We got the money. Let's go."

Her laughter rose higher. "Are you crazy, Joe? I told you, we can't run.... When we leave here we got to go back to that house."

I stared at her, certain she had moved out upstairs. I couldn't have blamed her if she'd flipped, she'd been through hell.

"Are you in a hurry to go back there, Joe?"

I still didn't speak.

She thought this was funnier than ever, the way I stood speechless looking at her.

The laughter spilled out of her, gushing out now.

"Vi!" I yelled at her.

She didn't even hear me. Her laughter was as untamed and violent as the night wind.

"For God's sake, Vi!"

I ran to her. I grabbed her arms and shook her. This only made her laugh harder.

"What's the matter, Joe?"

"Are you crazy, Vi? Is that why you're laughing?"

This was funnier than anything else. Her knees buckled, she was weak with her laughter.

"Why shouldn't I laugh, Joe?"

"I don't know."

"Sure you don't know.... And sure, I got plenty to laugh about, Joe.... I got more to laugh about than anybody you ever knew."

"Come on, Vi, back to the car."

She stared up at me, tears of laughter standing in her eyes. "Would it be better in the car, Joe?"

"What are you talking about?"

She laughed again. "Oh, that's right. Poor Joe. You don't know, do you? You don't know what I feel right now. How free I am. I'm free. Have you ever known what it's like to be free, Joe? Have you ever been in hell, and then got free? Have you ever, Joe?"

"I don't know."

She managed to stop laughing for a moment, looking up at me with pity showing in the mirth-wet eyes.

"Poor Joe.... I pity you, Joe.... Oh, I pity you. I pity everybody that's never been in hell, and got free."

"Look," I said. "Listen to me. We haven't made it yet."

"Oh, I've made it, Joe. I've made it all the way. No matter what happens, I've made it, Joe.... I'm free."

"Listen to me—"

"No matter what happens to me now, Joe, I've made it. I've got that money, that beautiful green money.... No matter what ever happened to me in my life, no matter what ugly things—the men that pawed me, the lies I had to tell just to exist, the ugly things they did to me—they never even happened, because I've got all that money, and I can buy it all back, and it never happened, none of that ugliness ever happened, because I can buy it back now, and none of it ever happened."

Her laughter subsided slightly.

"I've been miserable, Joe. All my life. I've been unhappy, because I was too lovely to be poor. If you're going to be poor, don't be what people call pretty, Joe, because then you're in trouble. Men do things for you, Joe, because you're pretty, and if you want anything you have to trade on how pretty you are, and what men will do for you because you're pretty... and soon you feel trapped, and dirty, and all you can think about is when you are free, and no matter what you've done before, you'd do more, you'd do anything to be free of what they—what they did to you."

"Come on, Vi. Come on to the car."

She laughed and took my arm. "Sure, Joe."

When we got to the car, she pulled open the rear door.

"Get in, Joe," she said. "Get in and let's sit with our money for a while.... Don't you want to feel rich, Joe?"

I got in the rear seat of the car. I reached across and pushed off the lights. I fell back against the seat beside her.

"We're going to be all right, Joe," she whispered against my face. Her breath was hot, frantic. Her body moved on mine. "All we've got to do, Joe, is stay here and forget it—we've got to forget all about it for a little while."

"You're crazy," I whispered.

"Yes," she said, kissing my throat, I'm crazy.... Don't worry about it, Joe.... Don't think about it.... Just forget all about it."

"I can't forget it," I said. "I know what's ahead—"

"I'll make you forget it, Joe." Her laughter was warm and excited in the car. "The way I promised.... I'll make you forget it, Joe.... I'll make you forget all about it."

The excitement and the madness in her was getting to me. I pulled her closer, feeling her laughter bubbling against my mouth. I saw that she clung to the suitcase handle with one hand. But she was clinging even more tightly with the other, to me.

"Oh, Joe.... Joe—"

I pressed my mouth on hers.

"I'll make you forget," she whispered. "I promised. We'll stay here until I make you forget."

As Vi talked, she began pulling her sweater over her head and fondling the full breasts inside the straining brassiere. "Do you like them, Joe... they're all for you... here... feel how warm they are...." And she took my already trembling hands and placed them on her heaving bra. "Wait a minute... Joe." She said, as she pulled the straps down over her shoulders. The two full globes bounced as the cups fell away.

It seemed like it took ages to get out of my clothes—Vi was stripped in seconds.

She pressed her lush contours against me feverishly—her hands explored my body as our mouths locked.

I tried to roll her onto her back, but she resisted. "Wait... Joe," she moaned, "there's something I want to do just for you...."

And she did.

15

Dawn oozed syrupy and wetly gray across the rough back country. I came awake suddenly, cold and disturbed, the way you will from a bad dream.

Vi was curled against the far side of the seat, asleep.

I couldn't think what was troubling me, only that I had to get out of here. I wasn't going to wait to talk it over with Vi. I would get the car moving on the trail before she woke up.

I got out of the car slowly, carefully so as not to waken her. I remembered what she'd said last night about our having to return to the big old house this morning, but decided she'd been jumpy, saying things she didn't really mean. I shivered in the morning chill, thinking about going back to that house. I couldn't force myself to do that.

I nearly missed seeing Clint Hales standing a few feet away from the car.

For a moment we stood and stared at each other. Beyond him, far down the twisted trail I saw his pickup truck, clay-spattered and dented.

He stood in those overalls and denim shirt, his face battered from my fists and that link chain. But there was a look of cold calm in his eyes.

I turned away, moving toward the front of the car. The hell with him.

He moved after me, walking jerkily on the stone-rough ground.

"What do you want?" I said.

His face twisted into some sort of grin, looking colder and grimmer than ever when he attempted to smile.

"Whatever I want," he said. "I'm pretty sure to get it, huh?"

"Are you?"

"Yes. Oh, yes."

His mouth pulled into that smile again. I shrugged and turned away. "I don't know what you're talking about," I told him. "But good luck."

His face went gray and he grabbed my arm. "Mister," he said. "Just a minute. Where do you think you're going?"

"What is it to you, Hales?"

He clung to my arm. "It's this to me, mister. We got to talk. You and me. We got some things to talk about."

I shrugged free of his hand, and stared at his swollen, bruised face. "We've said everything we had to say to each other. Now get out of here."

I moved toward the door again, but he stepped in front of me with that chilled smile, barring the way.

He said, "I know everything that's happened, mister. I been around the whole time, and I know all about it and you ain't going nowhere, until I tell you okay—you and that evil woman in there."

He jerked his head toward the rear of the car. He was so full of hatred he was practically jumping with it. He wiped his hand across his mouth.

"You two done gone too far," he said. "And you played into my hands. Things are going to be done my way from now on."

"What are you talking about?"

"About you, mister. And that woman. Oh, she tried to get me. She tried every way she knowed to get me. She turned me against my wife—a good woman. She had me all confused and full of evil thoughts. And then she made a mistake. She done all the things with you—all the things that she had talked about she was going to do with me."

The first flares of the sun showed across the bleak sky, burning my eyes, drying me out, stretching me taut.

I had thought Hales was bluffing, but I didn't think so now. I remembered the sounds I had heard at the house early last night, and my stomach tightened in knots, and I stared at his cold face, wondering if he had followed us all night.

There was something in his face that shook me good, it was implacable confidence. The fact that he had almost stood in my shoes didn't matter to him, suddenly he was the righteous, he was the judge and the jury. And more than that, there was the chilled assurance that everything was in his grasp now.

"I seen it all," he said. "I watched you with her. I saw what she was, what she done, what she really is I don't want her no more... but she's told me about that money...." He nodded, sure of himself now. "I don't want her no more.... But I reckon she's going to cost you that money.... all that money."

I hit him. I wasn't thinking anything except that he stood in our way, and we had to get past him somehow, even if we had to throw his body into that pit along with that broken safe. It outraged me to think this dirt farmer stood between us and freedom.

Hales staggered under the impact of the blow. His face turned red, and a bruised place was torn open, leaking blood. He toppled to his knees on the rough ground, and stayed a moment, bracing himself, looking up at me.

"It won't do you no good, mister," he said. "That won't do you no good.... you know you got to pay me... and you got to pay me high."

As he straightened, I moved toward him again.

"Joe!"

Vi came out of the car. She'd hastily pulled on her dress, and it was twisted high on her legs. Hales stared at her with a sick longing in his eyes, a yearning that showed through the hurt and the hatred.

"What's the matter with you, Clint?" she said. "What are you doing here? What do you want?"

"He wants that money," I told her.

"I followed you two out here," Clint Hales said to her. He stood up, dabbing at the blood on his face with the back of his calloused fingers. "I seen everything you done." His voice rose slightly, full of agony. "Everything. You hear me, Viola?"

"You're a low-down animal, sneaking around, following us."

"It won't do you no good, Viola," he said. "I seen it. I seen it all."

I reached for him, but Vi caught my arm. She stepped around me, going nearer to Clint Hales.

She said, "What did you see, Clint? Tell me, what did you see?"

"You know what I seen." His voice was defiant, but he didn't meet her gaze. His face was sick. "'I seen your man lying across that table back there.... And I seen you two come out here, and get together like no-goods out here on this road."

Her voice was very quiet. "I told you, Clint. You are wrong. You're wrong about everything."

"No use lying to me no more.... You lied to me for nigh on to a year, and I believed your lies, but ain't no good in this world you trying to lie to me no more."

"I'm not lying to you, Clint," she said. "I tried to tell you. But you wouldn't listen.... Think... you told Joe how to find our farm, and he didn't know us—any of us—before then. You went wild, accusing me of terrible things when you found him at the house while Hall was gone... I tried to explain, but you wouldn't listen.... You got all stirred up, and you made me hate you—because you doubted me.... You made me hate you, Clint... You... And then Hall got drunk last night, and Joe—Mr. Byars and I—we had to run out here to get away from Hall."

Hales spat on the ground at her feet. "Don't lie to me... woman, don't foul me with your lies no more." His voice rose, shaking.

"I'm not lying at all. Hall got drunk, and went wild. We tried to go out the lane, but he threatened to kill us. We drove this way, hoping we could get away... The road ends out here, Clint, and we stayed here last night, hoping that Hall would come to his senses by morning... that's all you saw...."

"I seen you. You and him, pounding it to death in that there back seat," Hales' voice exploded.

"In the dark night you saw us, Clint?" Her mouth twisted. "You've let your evil mind destroy everything in you that was decent, Clint—"

"No. I never done that. You done that, woman. You. Turned me from my good wife. Turned me from a churchgoing man to—to what I am now."

"You did that, Clint." Her voice remained soft. "I offered you love—because that was what I thought you wanted. You came to me. You came every time Hall left the place. You asked me to signal so you could come when it was safe.... I thought you cared about me. But all the time your mind was full of evil, and doubting and suspicions that crazed you and—made me hate you.
"

Hales shook his head, staring around helplessly, out of his depth with words. "No," the word exploded across his mouth. "It won't do you no good. You ain't mixing me up. Smooth talking me out of what I seen—and what I know. You talked to me about taking Hall Weaver's money and running away. You wanted me to help you kill him, and take his money, and run away."

She stared at him a moment as if he were insane. If I had not seen her, I wouldn't have believed she could have remained so calm, unruffled.

"What are you talking about, Clint? Have you gone mad?"

He spread his hands helplessly. "I don't know. Maybe I have.... But I'm giving you two people just one chance.... You give me the money you took off him... and I call it quits."

"I don't know what you're talking about."

"Damn it. I'm talking about that money. About you taking Weaver's money and running away."

"Running away, Clint? Who has run away? I'm here. I'm right here... and Mr. Byars is here... I don't know anything about any money."

He looked for a moment as if he would leap upon her and choke the life from her. He cried out, in agony. "Stop lying to me, woman."

"You better get out of here, Clint," she said in a cold, quiet tone. "I don't have to take this wild talk from you."

His face got a crafty smile in it. "Would you rather I talked to the sheriff at Torrance?"

She stared at him a moment as if she had never seen him before, and then she calmly nodded. "Yes. Yes, I would, Clint. I don't know what kind of wild accusations you'll make, but that's what I want you to do. If you know anything about Hall being dead, and my having any money, and running away with it—"

"You planned it all with me—" he whispered.

"Or did you, Clint? Was that what you talked about to me? I think you better go back to your wife while you can, Clint...."

He took a backward step, shaking his head. "You ain't going to get away with this, Viola. You ain't... I won't let you."

She looked through him. She spoke to me. "Come on, Mr. Byars. I think we can go back to the house. I'm sure Hall has calmed down by now."

"I don't ever want to go back there," I said, playing along with her, putting pathos in my tone.

Clint Hales caught Vi's arm. "It won't do you no good. I seen it, and you better think on it good. You two are going to pay me, or I'm going to the sheriff at Torrance with what I know. It's going to be one or the other."

She shrugged. "You do what you want to, Clint . If you want your wife to know what you've been doing—if you want the people that know you to see how insane you've become, you do that."

We left him standing there beside the pit, staring after us. I started the car, moved along the trail, pulled around his pickup truck.

We were five miles away along the trail. Vi looked back through the window. His truck was still there.

"Where to?" I said.

"We've got to go back to the house, Joe."

"Are you crazy?"

"No. More than ever, we've got to now. We've got to leave some of this money hidden there, Joe.... Maybe ten or fifteen thousand. It'll make that note stand up—poor Hall. He embezzled fifteen thousand from his employers, ran away with me—and I didn't even know anything about it—and then his conscience drove him insane, and he committed suicide."

I stared at her, the Buick rocking along the back trail. "My God," I said. "You've really got this all figured out, haven't you?"

She nodded. "I really have." She reached over and removed three small stacks of money from the suitcase, then locked it up again. "This will be the best money you and I ever spent."

I felt ill, thinking about returning to that house. "Let's get it over with as quickly as possible, and get out of there."

She laughed. "Why, Joe. You won't even have to go in with me. I'll hide the money where they can find it without any trouble, and you can wait in the car."

"That suits me."

She touched my arm. "Don't worry, Joe. Everything is going to be fine. As soon as we leave Hall his share of this money, we'll go into Torrance and talk to the sheriff."

"I'll let you talk to him," I said. "You know all the answers."

She nodded. "That will be best. You just let me do all the talking, Joe."

I glanced at her. She didn't look like she had been part of the way through hell, with more of it ahead of her. There was a faint twisted smile on her face. I might have believed she was thinking about me, and last night in the back seat of the car, but I knew better. I knew she was thinking about that money, and how badly she wanted it, and all she had done to get it, and all she would do now to keep it....

I came over a knoll behind the bleak old farmhouse. I almost stepped on the brake, almost whipped the car around to run, only there was no place to run.

She saw it, too, as I did. I heard her catch her breath. She stuffed the money into the front of her dress, and didn't say anything.

What was there to say? We weren't going to have to go into Torrance after all to talk to the sheriff. His car, with the emblem gleaming in the early sunlight like the bright eye of hell, was parked near my Chevvy beside the house.

16

The sheriff and his deputy were standing on the front porch awaiting us when we drove into the front yard.

I killed the engine, let the car roll to a stop, and then I sat there, for the moment unable to move.

"Let me talk," Viola whispered.

I nodded.

We crossed the yard in the early morning sunlight. The sheriff came to the steps, watching us. He was a broad man, dour looking, with a ten-gallon Stetson, a striped shirt, khaki trousers in hand-tooled boots.

He said, "I'm Sheriff Tex Crawford, folks. And this here is my deputy Marve Venters. Looks like you folks got yourself a mess of trouble here."

The deputy nodded, as if stressing the sheriff's words. He was in his twenties, but already going to lard on the public payroll and whatever petty graft he'd latched onto.

"Why, what do you mean, Sheriff Crawford?" Vi said, with the precisely correct tone of awe in her voice.

The sheriff frowned and didn't answer this at once. He gazed at her a moment, gave me a quick glance, and looked at her again. His voice lowered. "You Mrs. Weaver?"

I saw Vi bite her lip, then decide to let it go at that for the moment. "Yes."

"I've seen you and Mr. Weaver in Torrance a few times the past year."

Vi smiled. "Yes. We shopped in Torrance as much as we could. It's such a lovely little town, but Hall—Mr. Weaver—always insists that we go into Frigate, over in the next county. Not nearly as nice a shopping town, but it is nearer."

The sheriff's scowl deepened at the casual way Vi spoke of Hall. It was evident he and his deputy had been through the house.

"You folks mind saying where you been this early in the morning?"

"Why no." Now Vi's expression changed, her face became a sad, gray mask. "We had some trouble here for the past day or so, Sheriff Crawford. It's so bad—well, I hate to talk about it. Hall's acting so queerly—almost as if he were losing his mind. Last night he threatened to kill Mr. Byars here, and we went in the car, trying to get away until Hall cooled down."

He stared at her another moment. "And who are you, Mr. Byars?" he said.

Vi tried to talk, but Sheriff Crawford insisted that I answer him. He did nod at Venters, and the deputy took Vi by the arm and led her to a rocker. The sheriff went on looking at me while I told him who I was, where I was from, how I had started out looking for my wife, and had been told in Frigate that a woman answering her description was on this farm.

Vi unobtrusively took over then. "Neither Hall nor I ever saw Mr. Byars before three days ago, Sheriff. But Hall is so strange lately. As if he has something on his mind, some terrible guilt. He accused Mr. Byars of being a detective who had trailed him here, and meant to take him back to Cleveland—that's where Hall and I came from, Sheriff. But if Hall is wanted for some crime in Cleveland, I don't know anything about it."

The sheriff stared at me. "And you ain't looking for Hall?"

"I never heard of him before I got in this place. But he went wild, Sheriff."

"He shot at Mr. Byars." Vi stood up. "Oh, it was terrible. I tried to stop them. Hall shot the tires on Mr. Byars' car there. And then he threatened me because he said I was taking Mr. Byars' side, that I was trying to help him. He was drinking, out of his head. We were frightened. We got in the car and tried to get away, but Hall wouldn't let us go down the lane to County Road Sixteen, so we drove out the back way, hoping to get away, but that—that road doesn't go anywhere."

The sheriff nodded. "No, ma'm. It don't." His eyes narrowed. "And that's where you folks been all this time?"

Vi exhaled and nodded. "Mr. Byars wanted to come back. He thought Hall would calm down. But I knew better. He's gotten worse—fighting with everybody—"

"The reason we came out," the sheriff said, "we got a complaint from Mrs. Effie Mae Hales that her husband Clint had been beat up when he came over here trying to sell some eggs... but we didn't expect—"

"Oh, it's been terrible," Vi said, covering her face with her hands. "Poor Mr. Hales. Hall attacked him without any reason. But he's gotten like that when he drinks.... Then when he sobers up, he's all right again for a while." She removed her hands from her face, looking around. "Where is Hall, Sheriff Crawford? I'm sure he'll be reasonable now."

The sheriff took a deep breath. "Mrs. Weaver," he said. "I'm afraid I've got some bad news for you—"

"Hall," she whispered. "He's—killed somebody."

The sheriff shook his head. "No, ma'm... but it looks like he might of—killed hisself."

Venters was young and reacted quickly. It was good he did, or Vi would have hit the floor when she fainted. He caught her and half carried her to the chair.

We were standing over her when she came out of it.

She looked around, eyes dazed, hardly focusing.

"Hall?" she whispered. I was staring at her, and I believed she had fainted. Her eyes had that clouded, glazed look. The sheriff had to be convinced, because no matter what he might have suspected, he could not know all the things I knew.

"Your husband is dead," he said, again.

"Why?" she said, her face twisting. "Why? Who killed him?"

The sheriff put his hand on her shoulder. "We don't know that yet, Mrs. Weaver... it looks like maybe he killed hisself... Maybe after he run you folks off... maybe he got despondent—"

"He had terrible fits of depression," Vi whispered, "but I'm sure he wouldn't kill himself."

"—maybe he did. Maybe he didn't. Right now, it looks like he killed hisself. Of course we're going to have to do a lot of investigating yet, but he left some notes.... Your name is Esther?"

"Why no," she said, frowning. "My name is Viola."

He got a wise look on his face, glanced at the deputy. "Well, we're going to have to look into this." He spoke to Venters. "Take the information you have on Mr. Byars here, Fred, and go into Willoughby, wire east to Hollander and check on him." He glanced at me. "This here is just routine, you understand, Mr. Byars?"

I nodded.

He turned and looked at Vi again. "Your husband left some notes, looked like addressed to Esther Weaver—maybe his mother."

Vi looked up at him, her eyes brimming with tears. "I've got something I've got to confess to you, Sheriff."

He held his breath, waiting.

"All right, Mrs. Weaver. What is it?"

"Well, that's it," Vi said in a small, helpless tone. "I'm not really Mrs. Hall Weaver.... I mean—I was never legally married to Hall—he has a wife back in Cleveland. We fell in love—and ran away together here."

The sheriff was silent a moment. Then he said, "I'm afraid that changes things a little bit again, ma'm."

"Why? What do you mean?" she said.

I sat down on the top step. I could not go on standing up any more, but they didn't look at me. The sheriff was watching Vi narrowly.

"I mean, you're not his wife. He left this note." He handed Vi the old note that Hall had written to her a long time ago in Cleveland. Vi held it in trembling fingers and read it as if she had never seen it before.

I held my breath, watching her. Her face betrayed nothing, and she took a long time, going over the note again and again, as if it puzzled her.

"I don't know what it means, Sheriff," she said at last.

He took it from her. "I'll just have to have that, ma'm. Evidence." He tucked it in his shirt pocket. "From the way I read it—like knowing all I do now—about you and him—and the—uh... relationship between you—looks like that note wasn't written to you at all, but to his wife."

"Esther," she whispered.

"What?"

She glanced up. Her eyes were full of tears. "Esther," she said. "His wife. Back in Cleveland. I guess he really never—stopped loving her—after all."

The sheriff nodded. "I reckon this is kind of rough on you, ma'm.... But there are some things I'll have to ask you sooner or later.... Maybe we best do it right now."

She swallowed hard, twisting her hands on her lap. "I guess I've something else to tell you, Sheriff."

"Ma'm?"

"Something about that money." Her eyes filled with tears again. Her voice sounded odd. "You may not believe it, but I didn't know about that money. Not until after we got out here."

"What money is that, ma'm?"

"The money that poor Hall—stole from his company."

"He stole money from his company?"

She cried out. "You got to believe me, Sheriff. I didn't know anything about that. I didn't know about that part of it.... I knew Hall was leaving his wife Esther, and wanted me to come out here with him. Everything was—fine— until I found out about the money, and Hall was afraid of everybody, afraid that his company had found out what he had stolen from them and would send somebody looking for him.... He thought Mr. Byars had come from his company looking for him...."

"Well, that explains a lot, all right," the sheriff said. "That and the note he left, saying he was sorry—about the money—and what he had done to her... if he was writing to his wife."

"He never stopped loving her," Vi whispered, crying softly into her hands.

"There's another question I got to ask you, Miss," the sheriff said.

She looked up. "I'll tell you anything I can."

He nodded. "Well, it's about that money. Do you know anything about that money?"

"Yes," she said. "I didn't know. Not until we came out here. I was in love with him, and I came out here with him, and I didn't know anything about the money, but I found out—and I know where he hid it."

The sheriff pounced on that. "You do? You willing to show me that money?"

She nodded. "Yes. It's so terrible. I want to do anything I can to straighten it out.... I feel so rotten... so evil."

"Well, now don't you carry on like that.... We get that money, we might straighten this here whole thing out."

She cried a moment into her hands. Then she looked up, smiling wanly. "Thank you, Sheriff," she said. She sighed. "I'll show you where that money is now."

We followed her up the stairs. I was glad that the sheriff had not made us return to that dining room now. I didn't think I could stomach it. I was twisted in knots. I knew where Vi had hidden that money, and I didn't see how she was going to fool the sheriff any more.

She led us to Hall's bedroom. She hesitated, with just the right amount of reluctance, at the door.

"He ain't in there," the sheriff said. "His body ain't in there, ma'm."

"It's his room," she said, looking up at him in an almost childlike way. "No matter—what he became—how morose and wild—no matter what he did—I did love him."

"Well, now, you just take it easy."

Vi went ahead of us into Hall's bedroom, and walked slowly across to an old unpainted bureau. By some sleight of hand when she opened the top drawer and removed some underclothing, the sheriff whispered in awe. The stacks of money winked up at him.

I stared at Vi. I had watched her every second and her hand had been too fast for me, just as her mind was too fast for the sheriff.

I wiped the back of my hand across my mouth, sighing. Of course I saw what she had done, why she had chosen this room in which to find the money. It was a packrat's nest and she gambled that the sheriff had been so busy downstairs he had not seen this room before.

He had stood looking around, amazed at the accumulated junk, and in that time, he hadn't even realized he was not watching her.

It was more time than she needed.

The sheriff was breathing through his mouth, counting that money.

"My God," he said at last. "Fifteen thousand dollars. Fifteen grand. Why that guy was the worst kind of crook. Why he stole fifteen grand from the folks that trusted him. No wonder his conscience chewed away at him like it done... no wonder he couldn't live with himself no more."

I was aware of Vi's blazingly triumphant eyes fixed covertly on me. But I didn't meet her gaze. I didn't trust myself to look at her or the sheriff. I stood, wondering what he would say if he ever saw what was in that suitcase in the Buick.

Gradually, I became aware of some noise from outside, loud in the morning silence.

"A car," Sheriff Crawford said, looking up. "Venters couldn't have got to Willoughby and back that quick."

I walked woodenly to the window, stared through it across the back yard. I felt as if the flooring were going to sink away beneath me. It was Clint Hales' pickup truck, racing toward the house.

"It's—" I hesitated.

Vi said, "Why, it's Mr. Clint Hales in his truck."

The sheriff managed to pull his gaze from the fifteen thousand in his fist long enough to check through the window.

"Probably come over here to see what I done about his wife's complaint." He shoved the money in his pocket. "Well, folks, we might as well go down there and talk to him. Nothing more we can do up here."

They went ahead of me into the hallway. I tried to follow, but for the moment, I was unable to move. Vi had fixed everything, but here came that damned farmer to blow us to hell.

Clint Hales had parked his pickup truck out beside the Buick and had run to the car, and grabbed the back door.

We came out on the porch.

The sheriff said, "Hales. What are you doing out there? What do you want?"

Clint Hales' mouth fell open. He stared at the sheriff. "Where—did you come from, Tex?"

"Why, damn it, man, I came in answer to your wife's complaint. She said you got into some trouble over here last night."

"Yesterday," Clint said. He walked away from the Buick. "I got to tell you what I know, Sheriff. I can't help what happens. I got to tell."

I stared at him. I could not pull my gaze from that farmer who was going to send Vi and me to the gallows, and ruin his own life because he was so full of hatred.

"I got no time for that now, Clint," the sheriff said. "I got more important things to do. When a man beats you up, you ought to have sense enough to stay off his place."

"I seen them, Sheriff," Clint cried. "Ask her. Ask him. I seen them. Out there. All night on that back road. Ask them what they was doing. Ask them about the money."

"You mean this here money, Clint?" The sheriff held up the packs of greenbacks, and once more Clint Hales looked as if he would fall. He shook his head. The sheriff said, "Miss Vi here has turned all that money over to me, Clint. Told me how Hall Weaver stole it."

Clint shook his head, unable to believe it. "Did she tell you—about us?"

The sheriff frowned. "What about you, Clint?"

"Go on, ask her," Clint yelled.

"Sheriff, I guess I better tell you.... When Hall began to act so strangely, I turned to Mr. Hales here—for friendship. I was frightened. Sometimes when Hall drank I was afraid to stay here alone.... Maybe I did say some things to Mr. Hales that I'm sorry for now.... I told him that Hall had stolen that money—"

"And you told me you wanted me to help you take it away from him, too," Clint shouted.

The sheriff stared down at Vi's bowed head.

"Did you do that, Miss?"

She nodded slowly. "You see, Sheriff. I needed somebody. I thought—maybe if I offered Mr. Hales money—that money that Hall had taken, he might help me get away from Hall. I was so afraid. I needed somebody. I know I was wrong, but I did tell him he could have the money—if he would help me."

"Looks like you've made a plumb passel of mistakes, Miss Vi," the sheriff said.

"And last night—up there on that road. She was with this here man, all night. And I saw Hall in there with his head on that table," Clint said.

"You saw Hall in there, and you saw these folks up on that back road?" the sheriff asked.

"That's right. They took that money, and they went up there."

The sheriff shook his head. "No, Clint, looks like you're full of rage, and not talking right. Here's the money. Miss Vi just give it to me from the drawer upstairs where Hall Weaver kept it hid. All of it. And Hall was alive, refusing to let them leave here through that lane, so if you can swear that they was up there on that back road all night, looks like we can wrap this case up as a suicide."

"A suicide?" Clint stared at the sheriff.

"That's right," the sheriff said. "After Hall Weaver chased these folks off last night, he wrote a suicide note and took a gun and blowed the side of his head away. Looks like everything falls right in place... a man like that, so full of remorse and guilt that he can't stand to go on living with hisself."

17

Hall was buried two days later.

The funeral services were simple in the somber chapel at the funeral parlor in Torrance. Sheriff Crawford handled all the arrangements because he wanted to spare Vi as much as he could. He had a minister from one of the local churches speak a few words over Hall's cheap, sealed casket.

I had thought there would be nobody there except the law officials, the funeral parlor people and Vi and me. I was wrong.

The services took place at two in the afternoon, and there were a dozen people in there, staring at Vi, and whispering.

At the back of the room I saw Clint Hales, watching, face grim and taut, like some albatross around our necks. A stout woman with a childish, round face in black hat and print dress, stood close to Hales, and clung to his arm. I guessed she was his wife. They didn't come near us.

They didn't have to. I could smell Hales in that room, the way you can smell wrong. It was the last thing he wanted, but his testimony to Sheriff Crawford about where he saw us the night Hall died had been in our favor, and made Hall's death seem more like suicide than ever to the sheriff.

Sheriff Crawford couldn't stop telling people about the way Viola had come forward with the money that Hall Weaver had stolen. Fifteen thousand was a fortune to him, and he believed it was the tops any man could possibly embezzle and hope to get away with.

But I saw Clint Hales didn't believe that. Maybe Vi had told him the truth about how much there was, or maybe he was so full of hatred for us now that he couldn't stay away, he had to be near, watching, looking for a chance to spoil everything for Vi and me.

"The fool," Vi whispered under her breath to me. "What does he want here?"

I shook my head. "That money, I guess."

She made a sound under her dark veil like sharp, cutting laughter.

Just the same, I sweated through the service. We drove in a black Cadillac out to the flat, desolate looking cemetery. I glanced over my shoulder while we were standing beside the open grave. Clint Hales and his wife were there.

I clenched my fists, sweating. Was he always going to be there? Could a stupid, dirt farmer mess up a plan that was going the way this one was?

Already, I was beginning to think how I might kill Clint Hales... kill him and get away with it.

My shirt was sweated and the backs of my legs trembled before the services ended and we moved back toward the black funeral limousine.

Sheriff Crawford came to us, his ten gallon hat in his big fists.

"I hate to ask you this, ma'm, but until after the grand jury meets, I hope you folks ain't planning to leave Torrance?"

"Why no," Vi said, looking up at him. "We want to stay, and be all the help we can, don't we, Mr. Byars?"

"Yes," I said.

The sheriff nodded. "Well, that's just fine... it won't be much longer. Few loose ends to straighten out, that's all."

"We want to help all we can," Vi said.

He held her hand a moment, pressing it. I watched them. She had something that got across to a man, all right, even in a cemetery.

"Thanks, Miss Vi. We'll try to make it easy as we can."

She nodded. "I know you will... there's just one thing, Sheriff."

"Yes, Miss Vi?"

"I can't stay out at that house... I don't think I could stand to go back out there anymore."

"I understand, Miss Vi. I don't blame you one bit."

I kept it all bottled inside me until we got out of the Cadillac at the Holiday Stripe Motel on the wide highway just outside Torrance.

We had adjoining rooms. I was afraid this wasn't going to look good when we first came in, following the sheriff's car into town from the old farm.

Vi had laughed at me. "It'll look worse if we try to stay too far apart. Separate rooms is good enough... as long as there's doors between them... just don't worry, Joe."

I was worried now. The door between our rooms was locked. I knocked on the door, and stood impatiently waiting for her to unlock it from her side.

I could hear her moving around in there. It even seemed to me I could hear her humming to herself. But she didn't come near that door.

Impatiently, I put my mouth against the facing, whispering, "Vi. Vi. I want to talk to you."

I could hear her moving around in there as if I didn't even exist.

The sweat broke out on my face and I was ready to tear that door down only I knew better. I couldn't do that. I couldn't do anything that might attract attention. I could not even take a drink for fear I might do something that would focus attention on us.

I stood, staring at that closed door. Just when I felt as if my lungs would burst, it opened and she smiled at me.

"Hello, Joe."

She was wearing a shorty negligee of some transparent material that made her more naked than bare flesh.

"Are you crazy?" I said. "Suppose somebody came in here?"

She smiled again, coming close against me. "Isn't your door locked, Joe? Mine is."

"My God," I said. "We've got to be careful."

"I've been careful. For over a year. For a long time. I've got what I want, Joe, I've got you, and that money, and I'm tired of being careful."

She was waltzing me back in a slow, odd dance step to my bed. I tried to resist, not wanting to resist because every moment we had been alone since the night out by that pit, we'd been at each other as if the only way we could find breath to live was pressed closer and closer in each other's arms.

"I'm not afraid when I'm in your arms, Joe."

"You saw that Hales. You don't think he's let up on us, do you?"

"He's just a jealous, hick farmer, darling. Sure he wants revenge... but what can he do?"

"I don't know."

"I know. Nothing. Stop worrying about him. Even when Hales talks nobody will listen to him."

"Somebody will listen, Vi. Maybe that sheriff will. He's on your side now, but he wants us to hang around here. Why? They've been over it with us twenty times. What else can we tell them?"

"You worry too much."

"We've got to be careful."

We were on the bed by now, and we weren't being careful. Her breath was loud, and hot, against my face.

"I don't want to be careful. Why do I have to be careful? Hall stole money. Hall killed himself. He's dead and buried. That's all I know about him.... I've been in hell, and I'm out of hell now, and I'm free.... Nobody can touch me... nobody can make me do anything I don't want to do, ever again."

I tried to think about the fears that had hounded me all the way in from the cemetery, but I couldn't think of anything except Vi in my arms. I wanted her. I wanted her. I didn't want anything else. As long as we were like this, I didn't have to think about anything, and as long as I didn't think, I was all right.

"You know what I am," she whispered against my throat.

I knew what she was. I knew what we both were. I didn't speak.

"I am in love with you," Vi whispered, tension in her soft voice. "That's what I am... maybe you don't even know what I'm talking about.... I'm in love... I know what they mean by love now... I know.... For the first time.... For the first time in my life, I've really, truly, fallen in love.... I'm crazy about you... I know I am. I want you. Now! Even more than I want that money.... I love you.... But maybe you don't even know what I'm talking about."

I knew what she was talking about, all right.

I didn't sleep that night.

Vi had wanted to stay in my bed, in my room, with me. But I wouldn't let her. "We've got to be careful, Vi."

Reluctantly, she went into the adjoining room, left the door open.

After a long time I could hear her deep breathing in there. She was asleep. I envied her. How I wanted to sleep.

But I was troubled. Thoughts kept piling upward in my mind, and no matter how I tried to push them back, refusing to think at all, they kept thrusting upward until the pressure was like the blood throbbing behind my eyes.

Vi said she loved me. She said she truly loved me. I'd heard that song before, and I tried to be cynical about it, now, and I couldn't.

I believed her. I felt inside that what she said was true. All my life—even with Cora, especially with Cora, I always thought of love and doubt in the same breath. It was something you could believe in, but being a first class idiot helped.

And now I believed Vi. I had heard her lie to Hall, to Clint Hales, to the sheriff, and she admitted she'd known dozens of men, and even thought she had loved some of them. A long time ago she had thought she was in love with Hall Weaver.

"Only I never knew," she said now, "what a simple, overwhelming thing love is."

It had happened to me, too.

I had not thought about Cora, about trying to find Cora in the past three days. I had not thought about anything except Vi when I was with her, when I was loving her, I was all right.

It was when I was alone like this that the nightmare started, when the thoughts piled up in me, and I was afraid to think at all.

I got out of bed. I was sweated. I felt ill. I went through the doors that joined our rooms.

Vi was lying naked across her bed, breathing deeply.

I went to her. "Vi," I whispered. I sounded like a child frightened in the dark. I was.

She wakened just enough to raise her arms to me, and I sank down on the bed with her, getting as close to her as I could, so close I didn't have to think anymore.

The phone rang on the table beside Vi's bed. It rang four times before it roused me, and it didn't get through to Vi at all. She went on sleeping, face down.

I sat up in her bed and before I thought I reached out to lift the receiver.

I stopped as if I had been hit in the face. I had almost answered her telephone, in her room.

The early morning sunlight streamed through the windows. The phone went on wailing.

Breathless, realizing how close I'd come to making one of those little fool mistakes we couldn't afford to make, I shook Vi until she opened her eyes.

"Vi. Your telephone. I can't answer it for you."

She smiled at me, toppled her body across mine and picked up the receiver. I sat with her heated flesh resilient and lush against me, watching her push her dark hair from her ear and place the receiver against it.

"Oh, hello, Sheriff," she said. I felt the crazy slugging of my heart. She said, laughing, "I was asleep. It's the first time I've been able to sleep since this—this terrible thing happened.... Oh, it's all right... I had to get up sometime."

She writhed against me, smiling at me, teasing me while he spoke. At last she said, "All right, Sheriff Crawford."

She replaced the receiver and pushed me backwards on the bed.

She let her hair fall around our heads, making it dark where our faces were pressed close.

"What did he want?" I said.

"Who?" She was giggling.

"My God, Vi. The sheriff. What did he want?"

"Do you love me?"

"I love you, Vi. What did he want?"

"He wants us both to come down to his office as soon as we can. He said he'd been ringing your room, but you weren't in there. He said maybe you had gone out somewhere for breakfast."

I tried to smile with her, but there was a sharp pain across my chest, a terrible sense of wrong.

"What did he want?"

"He didn't say. Just wanted us to come down there."

"We better go, Vi," I said.

"We will," she said. "Oh, we will. But not right now."

18

I parked the car outside the sheriff's office.

I wore sunglasses because while I shaved I had seen the sleeplessness, and the agony eyes. I couldn't believe Sheriff Crawford or anybody else could look at me and not see what I saw, the terrible guilt, the paralyzing fear.

Across the street, half a block away, I saw Clint Hales' pickup truck parked at a curb. I went a little crazy, the fear mixed with rage. I could feel myself shaking, my stomach tying in knots.

Sheriff Crawford looked up and smiled when we went into his office. It was hot in there, even with a fan stirring up a tepid breeze. It was a crowded office, and small.

"Thanks for coming down, folks," he said.

"We want to help you all we can, Sheriff," Vi said.

"You've been real cooperative," he said. "Both of you."

I looked around. Clint Hales wasn't in this office at least.

"Got some good news for you folks," Crawford said, and at first it barely registered on my mind. "Few more days this here thing ought to be all over.... First, we got word from your town, Mr. Byars. From a Detective Lieutenant Calvin Thayer. He says he is looking for your wife Cora, and that you came out here looking for her. That all checks out."

I nodded, not trusting myself to speak.

"Now that company in Cleveland is running a special audit on their books, Miss Viola. They said they still had not found where Hall Weaver could have embezzled as much as fifteen thousand, but that you never had anything to do with auditing, and at any rate they would have no charges to make against you."

"That's wonderful," Vi said. "I can't thank you enough, Sheriff, for all you've done for me."

"Well, like I say. Maybe you was wrong, taking a man from his wife, and coming off here with him, but that's a mistake—not a crime. I want to help you all I can."

"Thank you," she said in a low tone.

"May we go now?" I said.

The sheriff said, "I'd like you folks to stay in town a couple more days. The Grand Jury has decided to bring in a no-true bill against you folks, saying you had no part in the death of Mr. Weaver. You're free to go. I might as well tell you that. But I'd like it if you'd stay just a day or so longer."

"Why?" I said. "What's the matter?"

"Why, nothing is wrong, Mr. Byars. Like I said, you are free to go. I can't keep you. I'm just asking that you stay around until it's all cleared up."

"What else is there to clear up?"

"Nothing. It's just that I'm sure you folks want to go away from here completely freed of any suspicion, and that's what I'm trying to do."

"Of course we'll stay," Vi said. "I'm sure Mr. Byars is worried—because he wants to find his wife... but I'm in no hurry at all."

"I'll stay around," I said. I looked at Vi from behind my dark glasses, knowing I was never even going to try to find Cora.

But I was nervous when we came out to the car. Hales' pickup truck was gone, but this didn't make me feel any better.

"What does he want?" I said when we got in the Buick. "Why do we have to stick around here?"

She laughed. "What do you care? It's a nice motel, isn't it? They've got beds, haven't they?"

I tried to smile, but I couldn't do it. "We got to be careful, Vi. Not for me. For you. We're supposed to be strangers.... Now maybe they're watching us.... Maybe that's it.... Maybe we ought to stay away from each other."

Now she did laugh aloud. "Sure," she said. "That's what we'll do. We'll stay away from each other."

But that was all we couldn't do. We couldn't stay away from each other.

Apart we were lonely, insecure, frightened. Together, there was no world at all beyond that motel door.

The next morning, Vi woke me, kissing my chest. She looked up, smiled. "The sheriff called."

I sat up, wide awake, gray. "What did he want?"

She laughed at me. "What could he want? What are you afraid of, Joe? He just called to say he wasn't asking us to hang around any longer."

"What?" Even when I heard it, I couldn't believe it.

"We can go," she said. "We're free. Whatever it was Sheriff Crawford was having us stay around for, it's settled. Maybe something about Clint Hales. I don't know. Anyhow whatever it is, it's settled. There are no charges against us. We can go anywhere we want."

She pressed herself against me, but I was cold inside, chilled. I said, "You better go. Without me."

She only laughed. "I'm never going anywhere again, without you."

"You might have to, Vi."

"Why?"

"I've been thinking about it. Whether I wanted to, or not... you've got to go without me."

"No," she said. She lay close against me. "I've thought about it, Joe. Because I've seen the way you acted. I know you've got something on your mind. I've waited, but you haven't talked to me about it. But I want to stay with you anyway, Joe."

"You can't."

"All I know is, I was never truly in love before, I'll never truly be in love again."

"You're a rich woman now. You don't need me."

"No, Joe. That's where you're wrong. Maybe I could go on alone, but even with all this money, it would be the same—the ugly way it was before you came along. I would just go from one man to another, looking for something I would never find... looking for you, Joe... the way I have been looking, all my life...."

I held her close, but I felt chilled with loneliness, already knowing I could not keep her. It was as if she were already gone away from me.

"I want you, too, Vi," I said. "Maybe you're the first person I've ever really wanted, too... but it's too late.... For me, it's too late. I've got to leave you. Today."

She didn't say anything. I felt her shiver against me. I tried, but I could not form the words even inside my own mind that would explain to her why I had to get away from her, because my mind still refused to touch the truth.

But there were reasons enough. "You'll be all right," I heard myself saying, and I didn't even believe it. "You got away—with all that—at the farm.... But if I stay with you, I'll ruin it, sooner or later."

"We could run away. Anywhere."

"I know. I've thought about that. It wouldn't matter. Sooner or later, no matter where we went... you've got to believe me, Vi...."

She was silent a long time.

At last she said in a dull whisper. "It's on account of Cora, isn't it?"

I felt the pressures inside my head, the agony.

"Yes."

"You still love her?"

"You know better than that. I don't love her. I know now, I never did love her. I was—all snarled up in her, and she made my life hell, so I couldn't think—"

"I'll make you forget all that, Joe."

"No. I thought I could forget her. But I couldn't. You see, all the time I was looking for Cora, I didn't really want to find her.... I just couldn't force my mind to admit the truth. But then I got on that farm, and I saw Hall, and you, all that was happening, and I had to think about it, whether I wanted to, or not."

She shuddered. "Joe. Something in your voice... in the way you talk—it scares me."

"You don't have to be scared," I said. "Just get out of here, Vi. Take your car, and your suitcases, and get out of here. Right now. Fast."

"Oh, Joe. I can't leave you."

"If you want that money you went through hell for—"

"I don't want the money! I want you."

"I'm sorry, Vi. So help me, I'm sorry."

"Come with me, Joe. You don't have to talk about it. You don't have to tell me anything. Just come with me. We'll go right now. I'll make you forget all about it."

"I'll spoil it all, Vi. Don't you understand? I'll ruin everything for you."

"Maybe not," she said. She sat up, breathless, her breasts moving with her rapid breathing. "Maybe not, if we go now, if we move fast enough, if we run far enough."

I sat for a long time, looking at her, watching her, moving around the room, throwing things into her suitcase.

"Hurry, Joe. Please hurry. Let's go."

At last, I nodded. "All right. Maybe we got one chance. If we go. If we get out of here right now."

She came to me, pressed my face against her. "No matter what happens, Joe, we'll have whatever we do have—together. We've got to try."

I got up. I said, "All right, I'll get my things together. We'll get out of here. Right now."

She kissed me, laughing. But her mouth was wet with tears.

I clung to her for a moment, then I went through the adjoining doorway into my room. As I stepped into it, I heard the rapping on the outside door, knuckles hard and loud.

I closed the door between Vi's room and mine. She tried to hang onto it, but I closed it, anyhow.

I slipped into a pair of pants. The knock was repeated, louder. I opened the door.

I was not even surprised to see Detective Lieutenant Calvin Thayer all these thousands of miles west of Hollander. But I knew now what Sheriff Crawford had delayed us for.

Thayer smiled at me. "Hello, Byars," he said. "I got news for you, after all this time."

"Have you?"

"Yes, Joe," he said. "I've found Cora."

19

I nodded.

He stood there staring at me, his mouth pulled oddly. "That's right, Joe. I've found Cora for you."

Behind me, I heard Vi catch her breath, and then I knew she had let the connecting door close, and there was the faint whisper of sound as the lock snicked into place.

I watched Calvin Thayer's flat, ugly face. But if he heard that sound, he gave no sign. He ignored it, he was watching me, smiling, really enjoying himself.

"Isn't that funny, Byars?" he said. "All the running around you did trying to find Cora—and I found her for you."

Beyond Thayer the sunlight was brilliant on the white concrete driveway of the Holiday Stripe Motel. The reflection was painful against my eyes, and I felt blinded, and my eyes stung. I could hear the cars whistling past on the broad highway out front, and I kept thinking, a motel in an Oklahoma town hundreds of miles west of Hollander, the sun brilliant like on a million other days, the sounds the same, people hurrying, nothing different at all.

"Aren't you going to ask me in, Byars?" Thayer asked in that soft voice that was somehow like the prickling of a needle.

I stepped back. "Come on in," I said. "You will anyway."

"Yes," he said. "I guess so."

He stepped into my room, and closed the door behind him. For a moment he leaned against it, looking around. I saw the disordered room as he saw it, clothing thrown around, my suitcase open, gear spilling from it.

"Didn't sleep last night, eh, Byars?"

"What?"

"You didn't even go to bed."

My gaze jerked to my bed. It was carefully made up, as the maids had left it the day before, not even turned back, and in the disordered room it stood out painfully.

I looked up, met Thayer's gaze. His mouth was pulled into that wry grin. "Living high, eh, Byars?"

I held my breath as long as I could. The room was spinning, only Thayer remaining fixed and unmoving in it.

"What do you want with me, Thayer?"

He sighed heavily and stepped forward into the room. He pulled off his felt hat and sat in the chair near the door. He peered up at me with those cold, penetrating eyes for a long time.

"I think you know, Joe. I think you know now. Maybe you didn't know all along... maybe you really didn't. I'm just a cop, I don't know. The doc says it's likely you didn't truly consciously know."

He stopped talking, staring at me as if I were a specimen he'd never encountered before.

I felt I could hear Vi's bated breathing on the other side of the door that connected our rooms. I was sure she was standing with her ear pressed against the facing, listening.

"That's what the doc keeps insisting—that you didn't really know, Joe."

"What are you talking about? What doctor?"

"Oh, come on now, Joe. This is Thayer. You don't have to put on any act with me."

"What doctor, Thayer?"

"Your wife's doctor, Joe. Don't you even remember Cora's doctor?"

"I don't know what you're talking about."

He frowned. I saw the rage flare up deep in his eyes and the conscious effort he made to control it. And at last he spoke with great patience. "Dr. Leonard Voss. Now. You remember now?"

I shook my head, but I could feel the tensions working in me. I didn't remember, even now, but I had to admit something I never had admitted in all these weeks: I didn't remember because I didn't want to, because the memory was too painful.

"The headshrinker, Joe. Oh, I know plenty about that. It seems you wanted Cora to see a headshrinker, because she was a nympho. Is that right, Joe?"

I licked my dry lips. I remembered the fight Cora and I had had about the men, the new men. I had begged her to see a psychiatrist and she had hysterics laughing at me.

"She was already seeing a doctor, Joe, when you told her. The doc told me that she came to him and said that you thought she ought to see a headshrinker. The reason it was so funny to Cora was that she was seeing a psychiatrist, all right—but after hours, on his free time, and not as a patient."

"Dr. Leonard Voss," I said, but it had no meaning. I merely spoke the name because I was too ill, too full of all the sickness that Thayer was stirring up in me like some poison brew in the cauldron that my mind had become.

"You remember now, Joe?"

I shook my head. "I don't know him."

He scowled, then forced a grin, and retained that cold, patient tone. "Well, I know him, Joe. I had a little trouble finding him. You were no help. You said you didn't know the name of your wife's latest boy friend. You kept saying they had run away together.... And then you took off—looking for Cora. You had to find Cora, eh, Joe?"

I stared at him, not speaking.

After a moment he laughed in that cold way and went on talking. "After you were gone, a couple things troubled me, Joe. Cora was missing, and you kept hounding us about that. But what about her boy friend? If she had run away with some man, why didn't anybody come looking for him? Hollander is not that big. You see how I figured, Joe? If she had this boy friend, and she had run away with him, why didn't anybody say anything about his being gone?"

I swallowed hard. "I don't know."

"I didn't know, either, Joe. And it troubled me. So I decided if I was going to find Cora, I better find her latest boy friend. That make sense, Joe?" I didn't speak, and he didn't wait anyhow. He was really going over because it gave him pleasure to tell me how brilliant he was. "So I asked around. People in Hollander watch things like that, Joe.... If you didn't know Cora was beauty-resting with Dr. Leonard Voss, you should have asked your neighbors, They could have told you... they told me...."

It was silent in that room, and silent in the room next to it, too. I stared at that connecting door.

"So I went to see Dr. Voss. He was very upset. At first he didn't want to talk to me. A man like that. It was funny, Joe. I guess you wouldn't have laughed, but I wanted to. Thirteen, fourteen years he spent studying all about medicine and minds and psychology to get where he was, and he was a chain-smoking, hand-trembling psycho when I found him.

"You know why he was all snarled up, Joe?" Now Thayer did laugh. "Because Cora Byars had run out on him. She was gone, and the good doctor didn't know where she was, and he was climbing the walls. How about that Joe?"

"All right. Get it over with. You found her."

"That's right, Joe. I found her. Right where you left her."

He waited, but I didn't speak. I sank to the side of the bed, the unmade bed. My legs didn't want to go on supporting me, and the things I was being forced to remember, the terrible, heavy things, whether I wanted to or not.

"Temporary insanity, Doc Voss said. That's his diagnosis. You killed Cora in a fit of rage that blanked out your mind, and later on because you'd been living with that fear Cora was going to run away with some man for two eternal years, your mind blocked out what really happened—what you really did to Cora—and you truly believed in your conscious mind that Cora had run away from you.... Is that the way it was, Joe?" His mouth pulled down. "You see, Joe I'm just a police detective. Some of this psychiatry looks like Mumbo Jumbo.... I've been in courtrooms where psychiatrists on opposite sides testified to exactly opposing views on the same matter.... But no matter how you did it, or why, you're going to have to come back to Hollander with me."

I stared at him. "You asked the sheriff out here to keep me around until you could fly out?"

He nodded. "That's right, Joe. I didn't tell him why.... I've found out, you whisper something, and people hear it. So I just asked him to delay you as long as he could; you see there weren't really any charges against you and your friend Viola Massey—or Weaver—or whatever her name is."

I stared past him at that door where Vi was listening. He didn't even glance that way. He went on watching me, the way psychologists watch white mice in a lab.

"Then you'll let her go?" I said.

"Who, Joe?"

"Viola. She had nothing to do with me. You'll let her go?"

He shrugged. "That's not up to me, Joe. I got nothing to do with that. If it was up to me, I'd hold her—but it ain't up to me. The sheriff believes her story—and yours. He's a little sick now he knows you murdered your wife back in Hollander, but that don't touch Viola."

"She had nothing to do with me," I said.

"Sure, she didn't. But there's this farmer. Guy named Clint Hales. Got a real cob up his tail. Keeps insisting there's a lot more money than the fifteen g's Viola so willingly turned in to Sheriff Crawford."

"The guy's a jerk, burned up, jealous—"

"You'd know about that, wouldn't you, Joe? Maybe he is a jerk. But I'd listen to his story. In fact I did listen to it. I got nothing to do with it, like I say. All I want is to take you back to Hollander, but it strikes me odd that she would turn over that fifteen thousand so willingly. Doesn't it hit you that way?"

"No."

He smiled in a tolerant way. "Well, that's because you're not a cop. You don't see people the way I see them. A grasping dame, running away with a guy that's stolen money. Why would she turn it in like that?"

"She had to. He admitted stealing it. She had to."

I was staring at that door, sweating, hoping that Vi was listening. I glanced at Thayer; if he knew she was beyond that door in the next room he didn't seem to care.

"She had to turn it in, Joe? All of it?" He shook his head. "She was too willing... now, the sheriff... to a hick like him fifteen grand is a fortune... he believes that's all Weaver stole... it was enough to satisfy him... and I figure like Hales, that's what it did, and maybe she's got the rest hid out somewhere. You figure that, Joe?"

I sweated. Get out of there, Vi, I was praying inside. Get out of here while you can. Get away from here.

"No."

"Why not? What's she going to live on? That's what I ask myself."

"I don't know." My voice rose. Run, Vi. Run.

"Well, I told them to let her go, and watch her. She'll turn up that money for them, and then they'll have her."

My voice was louder, with panic in it. "For what? They'll have her for what?"

"Hell, Joe. Calm down. It's nothing to you. Nothing to us. They'll have her for murder, for withholding evidence."

"Murder?"

"Oh, come on now, Joe. You think that was suicide? That guy? Killing himself? Setting everything to look like suicide? Oh, hell. Anywhere except in a hick town it would have fallen apart in five minutes... suicides aren't careful, Joe, they're sloppy. They don't fix things up neatly, they mess up everything... no, fella, that was too neat, just the way her turning in that money so meek and mild was too neat... she ain't going to get away, Joe."

I spoke loudly. "She's got to get away. They've freed her. They've got to let her go."

He laughed. "She won't make it, Joe. She won't make it."

My hands twisted, and the sweat poured off my face. "She's got to," I yelled. I wasn't even talking to him any more. I was yelling through that closed door.

"Take it easy, Joe," Thayer said. He stood up, watching me.

I came up on my feet, too, ready to jump him.

This was the moment when that connecting door was thrust open so that it banged against the wall.

Thayer spun around on the balls of his feet, moving fast for such a big man.

Vi stood there. Her face was gray, and she was crying, but all I could really see was that old German Luger in her fist, and I stood thinking crazily that I didn't even know where she got it, maybe the sheriff had returned it to her, but it didn't matter, because she had it and it was fixed on Thayer, and her hand wasn't even trembling.

20

"Come on, Joe," Vi said, voice throaty and filled with her crying. "Come on, I'm going to get you out of this."

"For God's sake, Vi," I said. "Don't be a fool. Get out of here."

"The man's right, lady," Thayer said. "You better get out of here."

"I'm not going to leave you, Joe," Vi said, ignoring Thayer.

"You got to," I told her. "They got nothing on you. You can still get out of here."

"Not without you, Joe. Where would I go? What would I do?" She shivered. "I need you, Joe... oh, I need you."

I stood a moment, looking at Thayer, and then at Vi, thinking about what he had told me, what they were planning to do to her. Maybe they'd stop her in her car, search it, and bring her back to the jail at Torrance, with that dirt farmer Hales to witness against her—Hales and that money.

"Come on, Joe," Vi said. "Please. Come on."

I nodded. I wasn't running from Thayer now, or from the truth that I had never let myself admit about Cora, and Cora's being dead, and what I had done to her. I owed Vi something—I owed her everything—I owed her the chance to get away from this, even running.

I grabbed up a shirt from the bed, and moved across the room to her.

I heard the laughter sigh out of her.

Thayer spoke then. "Don't be a fool, Byars. You got all the trouble you need without this doll and her bad news."

I nodded at Vi, telling her to go through the door into her room.

I took the gun from her, snatching it quickly when Thayer set himself to jump me.

"Get out of here," I said to her.

Vi moved toward the door, then stopped. "Not without you, Joe."

Thayer's voice rose. "Don't go along with a fool thing like this, Byars. You got no chance. None."

I laughed at him. "I got a chance, going back with you?"

"I don't know," he said. "I tell you true. I promise nothing. I don't know. But maybe you have. If the doc's right. She drove you bugs—off your rocker. Temporary insanity. I don't know. You might have."

"I never loved her," I said, backing through the connecting door into Vi's room. I wasn't even talking to him. I was talking to Vi, wanting her to hear me before it was too late, before I could not tell her all I wanted to tell her. "Cora drove me crazy... I hated her."

"Sure you did," Thayer said. "Go back with me... maybe you got a chance... temporary insanity, Byars... that's the only chance you got... you won't have any if you throw it away with this broad now."

By now Vi had her door open, the suitcase in her hand. Her whisper was urgent. "Joe."

I drew in a deep breath. I knew what I had to do. I had to buy her a chance to get away. She had been in hell, and I had been there. I knew what she had suffered, and it seemed to me they'd done enough to her, too much.

I stepped toward Thayer. He saw me coming and threw up his arm. He yelled, "Don't be insane, Byars!"

But he stopped talking when I clubbed him with that Luger. He stared at me a moment as if he were sorry for me and then his eyes reeled upward crazily in their sockets and he crumpled toward me.

I stepped back and he struck the floor.

I set the door catch, locked the door from the inside, closed the connecting door, locked it.

Vi's door stood open. I went through it, closing it.

Vi was already at her car, the suitcase thrown in ahead of her. She slipped in under the wheel, started the engine.

I went across the walk, shirt tails flying.

That was when I saw Deputy Venters lounging in one of the sheriff's cars. I knew why he was there. He had driven Thayer out to the motel to pick me up. Neither of them had anticipated any trouble, but when Venters saw me running across to the car, shirt loose and gun in my hand, he slapped at the door handle, yelling.

I lunged into the Buick beside Vi. "Get out of here," I said.

She already had the car in reverse. Her mouth was compressed into a thin line in her gray face. Her eyes were wild.

The motel was u-shaped and opened out on the highway. Vi roared backwards, headed the car toward the highway, changed gears and stomped on the gas.

Venters was out of the car, yelling at us.

People ran out of the motel rooms, transients, maids.

We were moving fast, too fast, but I saw it all, the people standing, eyes distended, open-mouthed.

Vi screamed.

I jerked my head around.

"Joe," she said.

From the west, a pickup truck was making a fast turn into the mouth of the motel driveway.

I saw the pickup, I saw the man driving it, and Sheriff Crawford beside him, but it wasn't real. It was a nightmare, because in life people don't grin when they drive headlong at you.

Clint Hales was grinning.

Vi jerked the Buick hard to the left. The car struck against the right side of the oncoming pickup. The metal screamed as the headlight was ripped off the truck and hurled out into the highway.

For an instant the Buick was tilted at an angle as the pickup scraped along its side, almost upsetting us.

Vi stepped hard on the gas. Our car scraped past the truck, wobbling across the parkway, and careening out into the six lane highway.

There was a wailing of horns.

"Go east," I yelled at Vi. "Hit out of this town."

She nodded, clinging to the wheel. The car skidded and careened to the far road-shoulders before she got it under control.

She pressed on the accelerator and we moved away from the motel, going east on the highway.

Breathing through my mouth, I looked back through the rear window. The pickup had smashed into the first of the motel rooms, and people were running toward it.

I saw Sheriff Crawford already leaping out of the car, and then we went around a curve and I couldn't see them any more.

I sat, trying to think. I said, "They'll get on the radio to state police. We got to ditch this car."

"Joe." That was all she said.

"If we can get rid of this car," I said, "we'll be all right."

"They're after us back there, Joe."

I glanced across my shoulder. The sheriff's cruiser, siren blasting, was coming around that curve. Venters and Crawford.

I turned back. There was no sense in watching them racing after us.

"We got to get rid of this car," I said again, senselessly.

"We got to get out of this, Joe," she said. "We got to get out of it."

"Sure," I said.

Far ahead of us, like a small black cube on the highway, a car sped toward us, and as it came nearer, I saw it was a highway patrol car. Crawford was busy on that radio.

"Get off this road," I yelled at Vi. "Take the first turn."

She was going eighty. But she clung to the wheel, nodding. We saw a turnoff, far ahead of us. She pulled her foot from the accelerator, trying to brake down just enough to swing off the highway.

I heard her whisper in anguish, "Oh, no."

I didn't know what she meant then. All I was thinking was that she wasn't going to be able to make the turn.

The tires squealed, and smoked along the highway, and at the last moment, Vi pulled the car around and we bounced along the wrong side of the turnoff road.

We were several miles along that road before the two police cars turned into it behind us.

I was twisted on the seat, watching through the rear mirror. The country was flat, treeless, a plain, and I could see the two cars clearly back there on the road.

"We can outrun them, Vi," I said. "We can still outrun them."

"No," she said.

"We can move as fast as they can, we got a start on them. We'll get rid of this car, I'll get you out of it, Vi. Some way."

I frowned, staring at her. "What's the matter, Vi? You sound beat."

"I know this road," she said. "You don't."

I looked around. There was something familiar about this flat country. But it didn't hit me yet. My mind was too full, trying to plan ahead.

"Dead end?"

"Oh, no," she said. "It goes to Willoughby."

It hit me hard in the belly. I began to be sick.

"It goes to Willoughby," she said. "If we can make it."

"County Road Sixteen," I whispered, wanting to scream the way I was screaming inside my mind.

"Yes, Joe."

"It don't matter," I said. "We'll make it. We'll still make it."

I glanced across my shoulder. I was sick, but I saw the police cars had not gained on us. They were still back against that flat open country behind us.

"Joe."

I turned around.

"Joe," Vi said, again.

I looked around. At first I didn't see anything. What was there to see out there on that twisted, open land?

Her gaze was fixed on the highway, that thin line narrowing to a point on the horizon.

I saw it, too. There was a car speeding toward us, its roof-light whirling and blinking, red in the sunlight.

I jerked my head, looking behind us at the two cars. I looked down at the Luger gripped in my fist, the useless gun.

"We got to get off this road," I said.

"Yes," she nodded. This was what she had been thinking all along.

I said, trying to keep my voice calm, "Take the first turn you see, Vi. No matter where it goes. We'll get all three of them behind us."

"All right, Joe."

We raced toward the speeding patrol car. It grew larger. The highway seemed narrower than ever, enclosed by rusted fencing on both sides. And then I saw a turnoff across a bridge. Not even thinking, I yelled at Vi. "There is a cutoff, Vi. Take that cutoff."

Her voice sounded dead. "All right, Joe."

We were already across the dry creek, slowing for the turn, before I saw what Vi had seen all along because she knew the road, knew what the turnoffs were.

"Oh, no," I whispered. "Oh, no."

She whipped the car off the highway, but went on braking it down until we stopped. She was not hurrying anymore.

We sat there in that hot, breathless car. The police cars were speeding toward us from both ways on County Road Sixteen, and ahead of us was the long narrow lane between the fencerows, that one way road and the bleak old farmhouse at the end of it.

THE END

LIKE MINK
LIKE MURDER

BY HARRY WHITTINGTON

REVISED BY DAVID LAURENCE WILSON

1

When I got back to the office from my delivery, I was sweated down, and only partly because it was another hot morning and I had run, trying to stay ahead of my thoughts. It was a losing battle and I didn't feel any better when I saw the note pinned on my time card.

I felt a moment of quick panic. I warned myself my old insecurity was showing again. Still I hesitated before I pulled off the paper clip. I tried to laugh at my tremors. Don't they pin notes to your timecard continually?

I stood reading it. It contained nothing but an address scrawled on a memo sheet: "612 Charles Street, Apt. B." It didn't mean a thing to me then.

I stood beside the time clock, not hearing the noises around me, bottles rattling on the conveyors, men calling to each other, machines starting, stopping, cars and trucks out beyond the loading platform.

The dispatcher leaned out of his wicket. "Hey, College."

"Yeah?" I turned around, trying to remember to smile. He was a good joe. I wanted him to like me.

"You get the note?"

"Yeah." I nodded.

"Some dame," he said. "Wants you to start delivering milk. Says she wants you to drop by this morning and see her first."

I nodded. "Okay."

"On the phone she had a voice that dripped, College. Sounded like a real doll."

I checked in my route books, waited until they told me they balanced, and then I walked out of the office and went down the steps.

"Baynard."

I stopped because I recognized the boss's voice. Here was the owner of the milk company. He'd inherited the business, but the way he'd expanded his inheritance should happen to all businesses. Dexter City had a hundred thousand population, but the Gorten Milk Company was the largest in the state.

"Yes, sir."

I turned halfway down the steps and looked back up at Bonnel Gorten. A big man, he had the kind of energy Diesels have, or IBM machines. He kept a finger on every detail of the organization, even the little cogs, like me. He was forty-nine, but only beginning to be gray.

"Just saw you passing, Sam," he said. "Wanted to say hi. I want you to know, we think you're doing good work, Sam. I'm proud of you. I want you to know I've got my eye on you."

He winked, trying to take some of the pep-talk flavor out of it. I suppose that even after a year, I still wore a chip on my shoulder, the way some men wear a carnation in their lapels, from habit. I couldn't help thinking he sounded like the warden.

"This is a big operation, Sam. A man can go places, to the top, after he proves himself."

I nodded, sucking air between my teeth. I remembered to smile, but I was thinking that what he meant was, when he decided he could trust me, if he ever did.

I drove out to Charles Street and started looking for 612. I forgot about what I had to say to Lois tonight. If I didn't forget it, at least I shoved it a little deeper in my mind.

I kept telling myself that Bonnel Gorten was a big man trying to be nice, but it brought all the evil back, the kind of evil that had sickened me until nothing would help.

Six-twelve was a four-storied white stone apartment building. I parked the truck out front, went in. Apt. B was on the second floor. I decided to walk up.

Everything about this place was double-distilled chic, smart and modern. Rich plants flowered in corridor planters.

I found Apartment B, thinking how cool it was up here, like living in an exclusive, rarified world apart. The sort of place I dreamed of having for Lois and me, but with the salary I took home after taxes we couldn't afford even a wedding ceremony. Anyhow, after I told Lois the truth tonight, it might all be phased out.

I pressed the doorbell and it was opened almost before the clapper stopped pounding. Actually, it was thrown open, as if she'd been standing inside, waiting for me to ring.

The ringing still racketed around inside her apartment. Then it started in my tense brain, full-range, stereo!

With a rush that was inner sickness I remembered the dispatcher had said a real doll.

She was a real doll. She stood stockpiled in that doorway, a symphony of silver-blonde hair and silk-dry blue eyes, clad only in accentuating negligee and provocative smile. I stared at her, sucking thin comfort from the fact that I'd seen all this before. It had been a long time, and time had been more than kind to her, as if dedicated to annealing her in a supersonic concept of loveliness from the ceramic textured skin of her face and throat to those legs that had always looked fourteen miles long and en route to excitement.

She had the kind of body that disarmed a man and made him atavistic. You got hungry looking at her. There was a boldness about her beauty, a sable fullness of her hips, her whole body speaking a language of witchery.

I stared at her blankly.

I would have sworn, burning the sleek hallway with curses of rage, but I couldn't speak at all.

I forced myself to drag my eyes from her wanton mouth, down across her body, away from her. I looked over the top of her head. I looked back across five eternal years, and the topsy-turvy wreckage of everything I'd wanted to be. And here she was.

Her throaty voice hadn't changed, either. "What's the matter, Sammy? Aren't you happy to see me?"

"Elva," I said. "I'm speechless."

She nodded, inviting me in. I hesitated, but I knew I was going inside. I walked like a robot. She closed the door behind me.

I didn't really see the room, the chic gray couch, matching chairs, contrasting walls and bright pillows. I saw nothing but gray, and that gray was inside me. The world was gray.

"Don't be speechless, Sammy. Kiss me for old times, because I've missed you."

She stepped toward me, but I shook my head, my mouth twisting with the bitterness of old memories, all ugly and dark with evil.

"Turn it off, Elva." My voice shook. "You don't want milk. You hate milk. Buy it from another company. Drink water."

"I don't want to drink it, darling. I want to bathe in it. You start delivery tomorrow. Two quarts and coffee cream. Meantime, stop staring and kiss me."

"I don't want to kiss you."

"No. You want to kill me, but you can't do that, Sammy. Besides, that's such a waste. So enjoy."

That wide mouth pulled into a faint and taunting smile that was a painful, hurting memory all in itself.

She moved closer and I could smell the elusive scent of her. I thought a hundred things, none of them good, but what I really thought was the way she smelled, the faint wave of it that got inside me and shook me again.

I reached out and pulled her to me.

I kissed her. My lips were cold and rigid, but hers were warm and swollen, and they parted slowly so I tasted her mouth in hungry, tantalizing sips.

I tried to pull away, but I was held by the touch of her body. I always had been.

She had a way of pressing her thighs upward, yet not quite going all the way. Her breasts flatted against my chest, but they were ready to spring back, as if denying it had ever happened.

After a long while, she spoke, teasing against my mouth. "They call you College down at the milk company. What's the gimmick, Sammy?"

"Somebody heard I went to the university. It makes me a kind of freak down here, a college man delivering milk. It gives them a laugh."

"It gives me a laugh too," Elva said. "A smart guy like you."

I stepped away from her, feeling the chill when her body was removed from contact with mine, the old, remembered cold. I moved back two feet where I couldn't smell her any more.

"Look," I said. "I never got smart until I started delivering milk. They like me down there, Elva. The boss knows about my prison record and my parole. He says when I've proved myself, he'll promote me. Maybe he doesn't mean it, maybe he does. I'll take the chance. Only he means he's got to be sure he can trust me. Go away, Elva. Don't you and Kohzak come around queering me when I'm just getting started. It's been a long time, Elva. Let's leave it that way."

At the mention of Kohzak's name, a chill formed in me and surged slowly upward through my spine and exploded like nitro against the base of my brain.

It was as if he were in this room with us. It brought him back.

I lunged away from Elva. I ran across the smart front room into the bedroom. I threw open doors, searching everywhere. The bedroom was neat except for Elva's vanity dresser. It looked like the wreckage of a well-stocked beauty parlor.

Just searching the place wasn't enough. I jerked open the closet doors and racks of Elva's dresses expanded outward toward me, the scent of her on all of them.

I heeled around, leaving the door open.

I dropped to my knees, looking under her bed. There wasn't even a speck of dust.

She stood in the doorway, watching, amused.

I walked past, shoving her aside. I checked the aqua-tiled bath, the small kitchenette.

She watched, her mouth pulled into a scornful smile. "What are you looking for, Sammy?"

I panted. "You know who I'm looking for. Where is he, Elva?"

She just laughed.

"Collie's not here, Sammy. He's not going to be here."

"I don't believe you."

"It's the truth, Sammy."

She walked across the kitchenette to me, the negligee curling back from her knees.

She peered up at me, the scorn dissolving from her face, a tender look replacing it.

"I don't blame you for doubting me, Sammy."

I laughed emptily. She touched my face gently with the flat of her hand, but I drew away, thinking about us, remembering, and sick with what I recalled. It had been a long time, like something I'd seen in a half-forgotten late-late television movie, and could not believe was real.

I'd been in the university five years ago. I won't pretend I didn't want kicks, big charges. I was in my third year at school, working my way through the hard way, waiting tables, tutoring, writing themes, selling sandwiches in the dorms after ten at night. Anything for a buck because that was the only way I could get through. After three years the bit was beginning to pall. I was sick of it, I'd worked all my life, nobody ever gave me anything, and it looked to me like plenty of other kids were handed everything.

I met Elva Higgens when she came to the college town to sing at a big fraternity party. I was no fraternity man, they'd hired me to keep things moving for the performers and clean up afterward. I brought Elva coffee during a break and we started to talk. She invited me to visit her if I ever got into her town. She thought I never would, she was just being polite, I know now, but Elva was the most extraordinary thing that had ever happened to me.

I couldn't get her out of my mind, even when she was gone. It was like walking along a quiet street, turning a corner and walking into a strange land of neon, B-girls, strip-acts, gambling, and money.

And lovemaking. I had obsessing dreams of the way it would be when I saw her again, but it was different from anything I ever imagined, better and worse at the same time. She let me hold her against me and I throbbed, hurting with the way I wanted her. Somehow she held me away from her, not quite at arm's length, but away from everything I needed, frustratingly, maddeningly.

She introduced me to Collie Kohzak. A slender man, about my height, he was in his thirties, polished, the rough edges of his beginnings all smoothed, the old scars of the tough climb healed. He was an ugly man, dark and thinning dark hair, heavy brows, black eyes sunk deep and too close together on each side of his hawk nose. He could stare at you and you could feel the beginnings of fear, even of panic, because those eyes told you that human life, except his own, meant nothing to him.

I progressed from being afraid of Kohzak, without really having any reason to fear him, to seeing him as a smart cookie, the cleverest I'd ever met. He changed Cadillacs the way I changed suits. He'd started in back alleys and now he had bank accounts all over the country, even Mexico, the Bahamas, and a numbered account in Switzerland.

He had money but he never spread any of it around unless he got a thousand per cent profit. He told me that because I was a friend of Elva's he was willing to help me make some cash.

The first job was a bank in a country town of five thousand. It was like opening a pop-top beer can. I'll never forget that peaceful town with elms growing in the parkways, and two of Collie's boys robbing a bank. I drove the car. I was the lookout.

A teller got heroic and gummed the works. They shot him, and both Collie's experts who were old pros, panicked. I was the only one who stayed cool. I saw the three town cops running toward us, guns drawn. I gunned the motor, getting us out of there, and I remember I wasn't even sweating. I was thinking if I fouled this, Collie Kohzak was going to look at me with contempt from those black eyes. I didn't want that, I wanted to own Cadillacs the way Collie did, and I figured there was risk in anything that paid off well.

"I like you, kid," was all Kohzak said to me when I got those two cats out of that town and eluded a highway dragnet.

For the first time in my life I had some dough to spend. All I'd done was to follow the exact plans laid down by Kohzak. He never left anything to chance, and I followed his orders.

It paid off. Elva and I celebrated. We did the town and ended up back at her apartment. I had four martinis in me and I'd never seen anything like Elva. She let me slide the straps of her evening gown off her shoulders, baring her breasts to my bleeding gaze. I kissed them, burying my face in the resilient fragrance of them, begging her to let me have her. But she pushed me away. I don't know how. I was wild, but Elva was an expert. She knew how to stop me, and yet to keep me dangling.

She was all in my mind, like a fog shrouding everything else. And when I didn't think about her, I thought about the money to be made following in Kohzak's wake.

I quit the university. Why should I go on to school when Kohzak liked me? Sooner or later Elva was going to get half as excited as I was and give in to me. It was all I lived for, that moment when I'd have Elva, the way I did in my wild, agonizing dreams.

She kept carrying me along that way, letting me think that the next time would be our moment. I knew it had to be her way and I was willing to play along because I wanted her so badly and I knew that it was going to be worth it if I ever did have her.

That was when I started living in hell. Unless you've ever wanted a woman so badly that you ache physically in every part of you, you may not know how I felt about Elva.

And Elva made it worse. She had other boy friends, and she made no pretense about it. She warned me that I didn't own her, and she had to be nice to certain men, and I might as well accept it. Only I couldn't because I was too wild for her, and it was an off-and-on thing with her. She'd pull me up close then shove me away. She'd make dates and break them. When I was sick with despair she'd call me back. When I'd think I had her at last, she'd send me out for coffee like some kind of errand boy.

"You can't treat me like this, Elva!" I raged.

"Buy me mink, Sammy," she said. "Nobody ever gets me just by needing, or wanting or asking. You ought to know that, a smart boy like you."

I lived in torment. I was the yo-yo in a push-pull romance. She let me dangle until I almost fell off the string, then she'd yank me back into her palm and I snuggled there, trembling, begging.

I needed more money to please her and I started taking chances. Once Collie called me in and chewed me out.

"Look, kid. I don't spend weeks on these plans to have a punk like you monkey with them. You do what I say, just what I say, and you'll be all right. Just as you were that first time when you followed orders exactly. Stop being a hero, Sammy, or I won't like you."

He looked up at me, smiling, and that was the first time I ever realized how granite-hard a friendly smile could be.

He and I could be friends as long as I wanted it that way — his way. It was up to me.

I wasn't thinking clearly any more. I stood in dark corners spying on Elva when she wouldn't see me. She dated Collie more regularly than any other man. I followed them, spying on her like a cheap private detective. I was the only one hurt by it. I stood in the shadows across the street from her place late at night when she and Collie went inside after an evening on the town. I saw the lights go out and, no matter how long I waited, Collie didn't emerge. I knew she wasn't teasing Collie and then pushing him away. I was sick, bent over in an alley.

Later I yelled at her but she just smiled at me, coldly.

"You don't own me, Sammy. Remember that. You don't own even my little finger."

"I'm in love with you. I'm crazy about you!"

"I don't want you crazy about me. I need nice things, Sammy. You're a sweet kid. But that's what you are — a kid. And I want mink. Don't get in my way, Sammy."

I hit her across the face, raging with the sickness in me. She fell back on her couch and stared up at me, laughing.

Tears streamed down my face. "Then let Collie buy it for you!"

I had to press my fist against my throat to be able to speak at all. I ran out of there.

I told myself I'd clear out, go back to school, get this witch off my mind somehow. Two hours later I was back, pounding on her door, begging her to see me, to let me apologize, let me hold her so I could go on living.

Collie called me in and told me our next job was one of those exclusive jewelers, the sort of establishment that would rather give you their stones than have you rob them because they like the gem-owning public to believe they're as impregnable as a small fort Knox. And pretty nearly they are, with all the latest safety devices and warning systems. Only Collie had picked up a drunk who'd been a v.p. of this firm, and together they figured a gimmick based on time. The jewelry shop was wired so well that police would be swarming over it in minutes after the first alarm.

We studied floor plans, time and getaway until I couldn't concentrate on anything else. Collie and the ex-v.p. had figured the exact take to the precise instant of peril. Then when the moment came, I put aside all the precisely measured movements. I wanted more than Collie ordered us to take. I knew I had to bring back something extra for Elva.

The rest of them got away, but I didn't make it.

I sweated in prison and I told myself I sweated Elva out of my system. Another con told me that Elva was five years older than she looked and she'd been Collie's personal property for the past six years.

She set me up for Collie. I saw that finally, but it didn't matter any more. I was doing five to ten. If I hadn't been so wild for her from the first I'd have known she belonged exclusively to Collie, or to nobody except herself, like a cat that never really gives it's affection except in return for pleasures, comfort. Looking back from the cell, I saw how it had to be, but before I'd been too mixed up to see anything except my ungovernable need for her.

I stared at her now in her kitchenette.

Five years had been like gilding a lily to Elva, she was lovelier, in her sleek, chilled way, than ever. "Four years," I whispered through my taut throat. "I served four years in that pen before I could get you out of my mind, Elva. That was a long time ago. A lot of suckers under the bridge. Go back to Collie and let me alone."

"Collie!" She spat the word. "I'm through with him. I ran away from him. I looked you up. It wasn't easy finding you. I've missed you, Sammy. I was a fool, it was my fault what happened to you."

"You're too modest."

She tilted her head. "I was a fool, Sammy, and we both got hurt. It doesn't have to be like that."

"That's the way I want it. I really got hurt, Elva. You didn't do four years in prison." I gazed about her kitchenette, the white stove, white refrigerator, white sink and a white sun burning through white window curtains. "I'm all right now, or I will be."

"Won't you even let me say I'm sorry?"

"Sure, if you'll say it just before you say good-bye." I got that creepy feeling at the nape of my neck, as though Kohzak were watching over my shoulder. I looked around for him again, feeling hopeless.

"Sammy darling, I'm not going to let you get away again." She put out her arms.

I took a deep breath. "Why kid ourselves, Elva? Where you are, there's trouble. There always has been. I've had the whole bit, up to here. If you ever cared anything about me, Elva, get out of town. Let me alone."

She just smiled. She reached out and smoothed my name tag stitched on the pocket of the Gorten Milk Company's white uniform.

She let her fingers trail urgently along my ribs.

The tantalizing scent of her struck my nostrils again.

"One date, Sammy? Tonight? Then, if you still don't want me around, I'll leave town. I promise."

"I can tell you now," I said. "I've got the word for you. Don't wait for tonight."

"You've got to, Sammy." She smiled again. "Not just for me. For yourself. You'll never know, Sammy, what might have been between us —"

"I'm sure."

"No. You're wondering right now. You'll always wonder, that's why you'll be here because I promise, Sammy, I won't hold you away, not this time."

I felt the sweat all over me. I shook my head. "Don't wait up, not unless you've got a boy scout to burn in the window with you."

I turned and walked to the door.

She was undismayed. Maybe all women are sure of themselves when they make an offer like that, hold out a promise like that.

"Eight o'clock, Sammy. I'll expect you."

At the door, I paused. I turned and stared at her. "Get out your knitting," I told her. I closed the door behind me. I didn't run getting out of there, but I wanted to.

2

I walked out and got into the white truck with Gorten Milk lettered on its side. I sat in under the wheel and glanced across my shoulder at that apartment. Suddenly her very physical presence and the intense memory of what she'd done to me shook me.

I started the truck and drove slowly, thinking about Lois, and telling myself I didn't know where I was going, only that I couldn't work any more today. I'd had it.

I drove the truck through the quiet elm-lined street where Lois lived with her parents.

I stared at the pleasant, middle-priced homes, with cropped lawns, manicured hedges, clean driveways, decorated with Buicks, Olds, and an occasional Caddy.

The Rowells lived in the middle of the block. I parked out front, thinking Lois's old man was going to hate that, but not really caring. Nothing I did pleased Ned Rowell and I'd given up trying.

I rang the doorbell, feeling alien suddenly to this whole world out here. Ever since I met Lois I'd been telling myself this was what I wanted, fooling myself that I could accomplish the vast leap from what I'd been to what I wanted to be.

Standing there, I saw how fouled up I'd become. I should have told Lois the truth about myself a long time ago. I had been building up courage to tell her tonight. If I told Lois the truth, I was going to lose her.

A quiet, two-storied brick house, solid, secure, paid for, an attorney's home, that's what this place was. Rowell had grown up in this town, married his school sweetheart, made his career, had his children. What was I doing out here? Collie Kohzak's ex-punk, in love with Lois Rowell. It was for laughs, only just then I wasn't laughing.

I saw Lois coming along the corridor. Even in a frilly apron she was something special. Her chin was smeared with flour and her hands were pocked with dough. A tiny speck glistened on the tip of her nose.

"Oh, Sam. I'm a mess. I wasn't expecting you until tonight."

"You look good to me," I said. I opened the door and stepped inside. She turned up her lips for a hasty, floury kiss.

Lois was a tiny, golden-skinned girl. Her deep-set eyes were violet-blue, gentle and yet with excitement swirling deep inside them. The excitement was in her, but you had to reach it, you had to be man enough, and she had to want you, because Lois was that kind of girl. I had been the other way. She was what I wanted.

I stared down at her, wanting to grab her close, not because she was worried but because I was. What I really wanted was some assurance I could ever really have her.

"You'll have to come into the kitchen," Lois said. "Mom and I are baking a cake."

We followed the warm cooking smells out to the kitchen. I watched her going ahead of me, loving the trim firmness of her hips, liking the way she walked, the way she was put together. This good and gentle girl with the depths of excitement waiting.

Mrs. Rowell looked up and smiled from beside the electric range. A youthful-looking thirty-eight, Mrs. Rowell was whistle-bait too. The kind that could cook.

"Lois said you'd be over tonight," Mrs. Rowell said.

"Got dark early. Did you win the club selection?"

Mrs. Rowell nodded, pleased. "By two whole votes."

She looked at me, frowning. I suppose she saw the tautness in my face, the way my mouth pulled, or maybe she could read the troubles plaguing my mind.

I should have told Lois about myself a long time ago, but now with Elva back in town, tonight was too late.

I exhaled. It had been too late from the moment I met Lois. But I'd tried to fool myself.

"What's the matter, Sam?" Mrs. Rowell said. "You look worried. Is something wrong?"

I tasted the cake batter, licked my finger.

"No, I'm all right."

Lois smiled and tossed me a kiss from across the table. "It's not that now you've seen me in the kitchen, you've changed your mind? You don't like me?"

"You look elegant." I raked my finger around the side of the icing bowl. She swiped at my wrist with a wooden spoon. I glanced at her mother. "Lois, could I talk to you a moment?"

Lois smiled. "Sure. A nice boy like you. Any time. Just mention my name."

I looked helplessly at her mother again. Usually Mrs. Rowell was astute, diplomatic and always three steps ahead. But today her mind was on her cakes.

I couldn't say anything with her mother there. It was bad enough having to tell Lois, but the things I had to say I couldn't say before her mother. Not the first time anyhow.

Every time her father saw my white truck parked out front he had a mild form of apoplexy. Lois dating the milk man. Her mother wasn't that bad, but I had to be alone to say what had to be said to Lois.

I glanced around the kitchen. I heard the clock of the oven timer, the small radio turned low to dance music, the shouts of kids on the streets outside. I gazed at Lois's dark hair bent over the cake mix. I'd wanted to tell her the truth, but I never had the nerve. Lois was sweet, beautiful, but she'd lived all her life in this little town. I'd spend four years in jail for robbery. Lois wasn't going to be able to understand that. I'd been there, and I hardly understood it myself. But she wouldn't even know what I was talking about when I tried to tell her about people like Elva and Collie.

She glanced up, busy, and I loved her and I knew I was going to lose her. The kids were louder out in the alley. The radio battered away at a love song. The oven timer clicked its heart out.

I'd lose her. Having Lois was everything I wanted to build a decent life for.

She waited, but what I might have said alone to her, I couldn't say in this room now. In my mind I could see Mrs. Rowell telling Ned that Lois's Sam who had seemed so nice — even if Ned hadn't liked his being a milk man — had served four years in prison for robbery. After that I could see the top of the Rowell home going up in a mushrooming cloud.

Finally I said helplessly, "I've got to work tonight, Lois. I won't be able to see you."

Her head jerked up, and I saw the flash of hurt in her eyes. Then she smiled. "All right, darling, if you've got to work. I understand."

That made it worse than ever.

I drove downtown, hardly aware of the cars that passed me. One old man changed lanes, almost took off my truck fender and went on, unaware.

Why had I thrown another curve at Lois? Why had I lied about having to work tonight? Was it because I knew I was going to keep that date with Elva, or because I just had to say something and that was the first thing I could think of?

I stared at the street gliding past my truck. I had said it because I saw Lois was lost to me. It was all over except the confusion. Sometime I'd make my pitch and beg for her understanding, but I knew better, and it made me sick knowing.

I drove the company truck into the company garage. It was a huge and empty hangar full of echoes at that time of day. The chief mechanic looked up from his worksheet. "Anything wrong with the truck?"

"No, I just got through early."

"Man, you've hardly had time to deliver your milk."

"I didn't deliver it. I poured it down a sewer."

He grinned and took my place behind the wheel, moving the truck back into the cavernous parking area.

I walked out into the sunlight. This was a cheap part of town down here, like the neighborhood where I grew up. I began to think about Mom, an ambitious woman who wanted her son to be an engineer, doctor, lawyer — and the best, whatever he chose. As I grew up, I understood her dream, and that comforted her. She stayed tired, trying to keep us clothed and fed. Her dream was to someday say: "Oh yes. Sam Baynard, my son, the cardiologist."

How many quarts of milk today, lady?

At the bus on the corner of Dexter Drive and Tenth Street, I stopped walking and leaned against a light pole to await a bus.

I hadn't been there more than a minute when this black car pulled up out on Tenth. It was jerked in against the curb, the tire walls scraping. A man was alone. He leaned over, swung the door open. "Give you a lift, Baynard?"

I caught my breath. The day was adding up to trouble, all right. First Elva showed up. Now here was Del Lantis. She and Del would make a great pair, I thought miserably. Unbending Lantis, and Elva as unyielding in her own way.

A detective assigned to the lottery detail, Lantis had checked up on me my first day in Dexter City, and he'd stayed close behind me ever since. He started in on me that first moment we met: "Keep your nose clean in Dexter City, Baynard."

"Get off my back. I served my time. I'm clean."

"Don't smart talk me, Baynard. You're here in my town. That doesn't mean we want you."

The first day in town and that was my welcome. I had just stared back at him, unblinking.

"You don't fool me, Baynard," he said. "Coming to a small burg like this, after being caught in the big pond. Maybe you figure you can outsmart small town cops. Do I look like a hick to you, Baynard?"

"Well, now that you mention it—"

"I warned you, boy, don't smart off. This is the word: In my book a crook is a crook, born that way and dying that way. Is that clear enough, or do you want it clearer?"

"I don't know, Lieutenant. What are you trying to prove?"

"Just this." His eyes bored into mine and neither of us gave at all. "You're here. You got a job that's on the level, even if you're not. You stick to it and keep your nose clean. This town is clean, Baynard. You'll stay on the level, or I'll hound you out of it."

That was our tender meeting scene, Lantis and me. I hadn't seen him in months, except maybe to pass him on the street, or read his name in the newspaper.

Now suddenly he was here.

"What you want with me Lantis?" I got into his car, slammed the door.

He pulled away from the curb, driving fast and recklessly, the way cops drive.

"I don't want you," he said. "Just going your way."

"Oh, sure."

"No. That's right. You got any complaints? Everybody treating you all right?"

"I don't ask but one thing of anybody. Just let me alone."

"Still tough, aren't you?"

"That's right."

He laughed, making a mirthless sound of it. "They given up on you down at the milk company yet?"

"You still stealing apples?"

He shrugged. "Still haven't made you a payroll guard, though?"

There were some sheets of drawing paper on the seat between us. He picked them up and tossed them into my lap. I looked over the pen sketches, quick sharp strokes with attention to detail. Meticulous work. The first sketch was of a scowling man, flat nose and cauliflower ears.

"Who is this?" I said. "Your mother?"

"May not be anybody," Lantis said. "A composite. You know, I draw them from eyewitness accounts. I'm hoping that's an accurate picture of a gent who slugged a woman in a supermarket parking lot."

"I don't think so," I said. "Wide open eyes mean a loving nature. This man would never slug an old woman."

He glanced at me as he drove. "Too bad you're a no-good, Baynard. You could be a nice guy. Smart, but it's just a matter of time, huh? How long before you think you've got the people around here lulled into accepting you?"

I thumbed through the pictures, ignored his question. All the pictures were painstakingly done, as if trying for photographic detail.

He said, "You'd be surprised how often those things pay off. We've picked up crooks from them as often as from a photo."

"I don't guess you cops have trouble with pictures. It's the words with spelling in them that must give you boys fits."

"Typical hood thinking, Baynard. Cops are stupid squares, but crooks who break the laws, prey on innocent people, they're the smart gents."

I didn't want to talk about it. I watched the buildings whip past on the reckless wind stirred by his reckless driving. The town had grown to look familiar in the past year, but now it was different, cold and alien.

He took the sketches from me, returned them to the seat between us.

"I use gimmicks like those sketches." He glanced at me. "Used a violin as a gimmick once. Had to watch a known bad boy who frequented a night spot, so I held a violin under my chin and sawed away at ersatz strings until I got the evidence I needed."

"You're a hero," I said, making it sound stupid. "You are a real hero, Lieutenant Lantis, sir."

"Sure. I'm a square. I believe in law and order. I hate crooks. I especially hate smart-mouthed crooks."

"I can get out anywhere along here."

"Never mind, I'll drive you home. Like to know what's in your mind. Wish I had some gimmick to read what's in your head."

I sighed. "There is one, Lieutenant."

"Oh? What is it?"

"My mouth. You want to know anything about me, ask me."

He stared straight ahead. His voice was level. "I'll do that, Baynard. I'll remember your promise, and I'll do that."

"You don't need gimmicks on me, your listening devices, your transom peeks. You just ask me."

"Don't think much of my gadgets?"

"I don't think much of you."

"I don't care what people like you think, as long as I keep hauling in the crooks." His hands tightened on the steering wheel, knuckles showing white. "It's more than my job. Nothing I hate worse than a thief—"

"Why don't you get out of my face?"

"Am I boring you?"

"Frankly, you are."

He scared me, too. Or maybe it was just that Elva was here, and trouble followed Eva. My nerves were getting all twisted in the pit of my belly. I felt empty and taut, riding along beside him.

I glanced at him, thinking he was a cop twenty-five hours a day.

Lantis was a smart cop, too good for a town like Dexter City. An honest cop couldn't hope to draw more than four or five thousand a year. He worked for something besides the money. He had to. His shirt collar was frayed, his tie stained.

He was a tall man with a wide frame, but he was lean and spare, looking like a man who had gone on a quick-starve diet and lost too much weight too quickly.

I hated to think about this hungry character always watching me. The skin crawled across my neck. He was always thinking up new gimmicks for watching through walls, listening to a particular pinpointed conversation clear across a crowded room. He was the guy watching me, figuring out cute ways to trap me.

Like he said, if I didn't like it all I had to do was to clear out of town.

If I was honest, what did I care about Lantis?

That was a good question, only I didn't have a good answer.

Mostly, all these months, I hadn't worried about him and sometimes I forgot him altogether.

Now Elva was here. He'd read about her in my mind, scent her perfume on my jacket, find a blonde hair on my shoulder, ferret her out. When he'd found Elva, he'd find out she was Elva Higgens, and after that he'd never rest until he found who Elva Higgens was, to the second generation.

He'd dig up her past in that same patient way he drew those composite pictures, with attention to all details. When he had Elva pinned down, he'd find me and Collie as part of the details.

He'd feel good about that. Maybe he wouldn't even sleep a couple nights, drooling over it. He'd add Elva to my past. And Collie. He'd have all the links to my trouble in the past, digging the way anthropologists search for a missing link.

"That's my apartment place," I said. "Right up there."

"I know, Sam. I know."

He skidded into the curb, jarring the tires against it.

When I got out, he gave me the look cops reserve for hoodlums temporarily at large. A look that begged me to make just one misstep.

"See ya, Sam."

"Yeah. I know."

He pulled away, gunning the engine, burning a quart of oil and laying down a smoke screen across me.

I shrugged. I didn't have to have trouble with Lantis. All I had to do was give up Lois, stay away from Elva, get out of his town. It was really simple.

I walked into the apartment building where I had my efficiency apartment on the fifth floor.

Walking, I saw Elva's face in my mind. Once I'd really loved her. When I learned the first truth about her, it had left an empty place inside me.

She never visited me in the state penitentiary even once. Kohzak never came either, but he'd sent an elderly, motherly woman who had leaned close to the wire separating us in the visitor's crib and she'd whispered: "Collie says if you don't keep your trap shut, he'll have you killed, in the pen or out of it."

I had stared at her. It was like hearing Whistler's mother telling dirty stories. It impressed me plenty. Kozak was smart. He'd counted on the impact of shock. He was right. When I was released I tried to run to a place where they could never find me. And here was Elva.

I got off the elevator, wondering if I could escape them now by clearing out. Once I'd prayed to have her. Days and nights were interminable, locked in that pen away from her. Unfulfilled longing, that's what Elva was. I'd spent four years in prison, hot with hating her, feverish with wanting her. But when I ran from her, here she was all smelling of violets and smiling.

3

My telephone was wailing when I walked into my apartment. The ringing had a tired, persistent sound as if it had been ringing for a long time.

The walls seemed to crowd in on me. My apartment had never seemed large. The bed was a three-quarter deal. You had to squeeze past it to get into a shallow closet. Two doorways led off the end of the bedroom, one had no door and this led into the kitchenette, the other had a door and beyond it was a midget bathroom. There was no tub, just a standup shower.

I lifted the receiver. "Hello."

"Hello, Sammy."

Elva's voice made my apartment smaller, almost formfitting. This was no longer a place to live because Elva had traced me here and now it was a cage and I was trapped in it.

"Sammy, honey, where have you been?"

"In bed with the doll next door," I said coldly.

She laughed. "Why, Sammy, you're trying to make me jealous."

"I'm trying to make you disappear."

"What a terrible way to talk. I've been calling you all day."

"I work for a living."

"How perfectly bush-wa-zay." Bourgeoisie was a word Elva had picked up singing at fraternity stags; she loved being around college men, it was so educational.

I was the boy who picked up the education.

"I've missed you, Sammy. Once you didn't treat me this way."

"Once I robbed banks, too. Now I deliver milk. If you called to say you changed your mind about taking milk from me, I forgive you, I understand. It's all right."

"I called about tonight."

I didn't say anything. My hand tightened on the receiver.

"You are going to keep our date, aren't you, Sammy?"

"I told you no. You want it in writing?"

There was a slight hesitation. Elva wasn't used to begging for anything. "Please, Sam, keep the date. You'll never be sorry."

I glared helplessly around my forty-dollar-a-month trap. Whether I'd be sorry or not, Elva wasn't going to leave me alone until I made her see I wasn't buying what she was selling.

If there had never been anything between us, and by now I knew there never had been anything except my own longing, it was over.

I replaced the receiver. In the time it took her to dial, the phone rang again. I paced the room, letting the noise beat against me like hailstones.

I cursed, remembering the running I'd done since I got out of prison. I thought about the Gorten Milk Company. Bonnel Gorten wasn't spreading malarkey. I had a chance to go places with them, once they finally started to trust me.

I stared out of the windows at three kids walking along the street, laughing and playfully fighting. I thought about Lois. Together she and I had what Nature meant when love was invented, if nothing fouled it up. My past gave me two strikes against me with Lois. Elva's showing up here was striking out.

If it weren't for Elva's abrupt arrival I could have gone on living here, maybe even proved to Lantis that he was wrong about me, that I'd never been a crook as much as a mixed-up kid, hungry and tired of slaving his heart out, and who would have done any crime for the chance to be held close in Elva's scented arms as a reward.

Whether Lantis liked it or not, this was my crime, and I'd paid for it. That was what I was going to tell Elva tonight.

It was eight o'clock when I rang the doorbell at Elva's apartment on Charles Street.

When the door opened it was as if a lethal jack-in-the-box erupted from it and struck me.

Collie Kohzak stood there.

Was I surprised to see him at Elva's place? Was there any reason to be? Elva belonged to Kohzak, and where Elva went, trouble followed — there never was a tighter-tamped package of trouble than Collie Kohzak.

I could not look at him and know his age. Maybe evil is ageless. It is Lolita, Fagin, the devil himself. It's a guy named Kohzak.

He was paunchier, filled with champagne, thick steaks, pheasant under glass, pizza, and his own success. There was a touch of gray at his temples that I didn't remember.

There was still that hardness in his narrow, dark face, and the promise of death in those black eyes, even when he smiled. There was that old look of hard self-assurance. Collie was a man who'd been places. He knew what he wanted, how to get it. Two hundred dollar suits and white shirts of imported linen, hand-woven ties, and seventy dollar boots from London.

"Here's our boy," Collie said. "Come on in, Sammy."

I walked in, empty and sick. The running and the moving in the night, and the loneliness and the fear, the praying that he'd never catch up with me again. I'd run around the block and here he was, and here I was, back where I'd started.

Collie said, "My boy, Sammy, it's been a long time!"

I stood there and didn't say anything. He closed the door and called to Elva. "Break out the champagne, baby. Here's Sammy. He's come back to us."

He'd twisted that a little, but it didn't seem worth an argument.

"Sit down Sammy, be friendly. I have nothing but the friendliest feelings for you. You got in trouble on your own, you took your rap. You didn't drag anybody down with you. You were a good boy, Sammy. You're a good man. You've grown, filled out." He laughed. "I remember a hungry kid. Now he's a big man, with muscles."

"He delivers milk," Elva said.

"Don't knock it," Collie said laughing. "A lot of big men had little jobs somewhere in their lives."

I stood, feeling like a man drowning in a dry room.

I turned and stared at Elva, my face muscles rigid. My voice shook. "You were through with Collie. That's what you said."

Collie laughed. "Elva was having a little joke."

Elva shrugged. "I must have been drinking some of your milk, Sammy. You know how I get when I drink milk."

Collie couldn't get over the big joke. "Did you really say that, Elva?"

"I thought he was the census man," she said.

I stared at her. "You thought I was still a sucker."

Collie's voice was soft, full of smiles. "Just a joke, boy."

I ignored him and stared at her. "You never did tell me the truth, did you? Why should I have expected you to start now?"

"That's right, boy," Collie chuckled. "Elva never told anybody the truth. She's opposed to it."

"She's a pathological liar." My voice shook. "A tramp. She's got you, Collie, and that's just what she deserves."

"Take it easy," Elva said.

I just went on staring at her. Her gaze fell away under mine.

"The boy's right," Collie said. "He has a right to be sour. We let him rot in jail. We can't expect him to be as glad to see us as we are to see him."

"You can tape that," I said. "And run it back."

His voice persisted. He was smoother than ever. In the past five years the final rough edges had been rubbed away. "Matter of fact, Sammy, Elva didn't lie to you."

"She lies to herself."

"Just a minute, Sammy." Collie was casual, and smiling. "She told you the truth when she said she'd left me. I hate to lay this on myself, but I'll make any sacrifice to get along with you, Sam. I stepped out on Elva. She blew her top and walked out. She ran away, I followed her. I'm here to get her back." He moved nearer and his gaze slid over me like rancid oil. "Might have known she'd follow you, Sammy. Elva was always sweet on you."

I laughed, but it was laugh or cry. What a beautiful setup I'd walked into.

I stared at Kohzak, seeing the wheels churning under that slick exterior, seeing the plans he was making for us behind that smile that was already wearing thin.

I knew what Kohzak was, how he operated. He was a big spender one moment, penny-pinching the next. I knew how he handled people who ran out on him. I'd seen it happen. I saw how hurt they got. Collie liked having an audience when he taught anybody the futility of running.

My voice was taut. "You never followed her out here to get her back, Collie. If she'd split the scene on you, you'd have sent two goons after her and roughed her up so she wouldn't try it again."

The smile died on Kohzak's face.

My voice went on, low, dead. "You didn't come out here to get her. So now we can get it out in the open. You might as well tell me the truth."

Collie held my gaze a moment longer, evil squirming like shadows in his dark eyes, then he laughed and sank into an easy chair.

"All right, Sam. You were always smarter than the gents I'm used to dealing with. I'll level with you."

"Yes, you do that."

An odd smile worked at his thin lips. "I followed Elva, but like you say there is another angle." He leaned forward, his gaze fixed on my face. "We waited patient a whole year for you to get sick and fed up with this honest-job bit. By now you got to know what that buys you. We can offer you a lot better. We are planning a small payroll heist of a couple hundred thousand in the area, and I might be able to cut you in, for old times."

"Thanks, but no thanks. You cut me in on a couple jobs. I did time."

"But this is a lead-pipe cinch."

I shook my head and took a step backward toward the door. Elva had showed up, and trouble followed Elva. Funny, they arrived the day I got fed up with being kicked around, but I wasn't buying any more time in prison. I thought about Lois but it seemed she was receding, drifting away down a long corridor from me. Then I thought of Del Lantis, how pleased his laugh would be if he saw me now.

"Count me out, Kohzak. This is all real cute, but I'm not buying."

He stood up. The smiling was gone, all of it. "Maybe you didn't hear me, boy. I said you were in."

"And I told you to shove it, Collie!"

"No, Sammy. It's easier than that. One other little jewelry job you pulled for me, Sam. That one is still on police books. Open. They'd love to know who worked it. You'll go along with me on this job, or I'll call the fuzz about that old jewelry heist, and there you'll be, Sammy, on your way back to the pen. I'd hate to see that."

I was surprised that the floor remained solid under me.

"Time is important, Sammy. So you ain't got much time for making up your mind. You're going to help me, or you're going back to the big bars. You wouldn't like it, Sam. You're too smart for that."

I looked over at Elva. She was seated in an easy chair, holding a goblet of wine in both hands. She took a long drink. She did not look up.

I walked out but I didn't know what to do or where to go. I was lonely and scared, and all I could think was I could never stand it inside a prison again.

A bus stopped at the corner. Without knowing why, I boarded it. I don't know if it was crowded or empty. It rolled through the night, air brakes hissing when it stopped, motor straining when it moved again. Lights fled by, the dark shadows of houses, the sudden brightness of an illuminated window, a drink stand, the flashing green of traffic signals.

The bus stopped at the corner of Elm and Highlands. Somebody must have pulled the cord. I didn't remember doing it. I walked off the bus and went along Elm Street, moving through the deep shadows, feeling as though someone were at my back with a switchblade.

I rang the doorbell at the Rowells. After a moment Lois answered the door. She never looked lovelier. How lovely something looks when you know it's lost to you. It was like that with Lois.

"Sam darling." She wore a pastel blue house dress. I smelled the faint scent of perfume about her. "Oh I'm so pleased you could come after all."

She took my hand and led me inside the house before I could protest.

Mrs. Rowell looked up from reading a magazine. "Hello, Sam. I hope you're feeling better. I told Lois this morning you were not well."

"I'm fine."

Ned Rowell glanced up from his chair under the reading lamp. The light glowed in the premature gray of his hair and glinted off the dark rims of his reading glasses. He did not smile and his mouth tightened just perceptibly. He said, "Evening, Baynard."

I nodded toward him. I said, "Lois, it's such a nice evening. Couldn't we walk somewhere?"

"Of course."

Mrs. Rowel watched me narrowly. "Are you sure you're getting enough rest, Sam? You don't look well."

"Maybe Sam's been having to wake up the cows," Rowell said.

I remembered to smile at his pleasantry. I wanted him to like me because he was Lois's father and it would be so much better and easier if he liked me. Then I remembered why I was there, and I knew it no longer mattered whether he liked me or not.

Lois and I had this secret place beside Elm Lake. It had always given us a sense of belonging to sit close together in the shadows and watch the distant light glimmer in the water when there was a breeze, or sit in wavy shafts when it was calm. The lake smelled good at night, and the park was lonely. Sometimes the night birds called, no matter how late we were there beside the shore. Tonight the darkness had a chill in it, the call of the birds was a sad sound.

"May I have something?" Lois whispered when we sank down together into the grass. I saw far lights reflected in her eyes.

"What do you mean?"

"I want a kiss. You've made me wait long enough."

I caught my breath. I had not kissed her, barely touched her on the walk from her house. My mind had been swirling with ugliness. It never occurred to me she would want to kiss me, then I realized I had just a few more moments. I hadn't told her the truth about myself yet.

Her eyes closed and her lips parted as she waited. Feeling guilty, I touched her lips lightly.

Lois laughed wanly. "You really don't feel well tonight."

"I've got to talk to you, Lois."

"Not now, darling. I've waited so long to be with you like this. I thought you weren't coming, and then you did, and now you treat me as if I were poison."

"Oh, no!"

"Oh, yes!" She caught my face in her hands and kissed me on the mouth. Her lips parted, sweet and hot.

"That's the kind of kiss I wanted," she whispered.

I tried to pull away, but she would not let me. I didn't say anything.

"Don't you love me, Sam?"

"Oh, yes."

"You don't act like it. Please, darling, act like you love me.!"

I caught her, held her hand tightly in mine. "I've something to tell you, Lois. I should have told you first, it'll change everything."

"How silly," she said in a whisper. "What could change what you and I have together?"

I shivered. "Just the same, I've got to tell you."

She lay back and I could see in the faint dark that she was smiling.

I couldn't put it off any more, so I told her everything. I didn't try to spare myself. I'd been sparing myself too long now.

I brought the whole sordid business right down to this present moment, even to the part about Collie's being able to send me back to prison.

I watched the smile die in her face.

I saw her face go pale and the muscles of her cheeks get rigid. Then she lowered her face into her hands so I couldn't see her any more.

"Lois."

"What, Sam?"

"I love you. That hasn't changed."

"I'm all numb, Sam. I don't know what to think."

I reached out, caught her chin, turned her face up. "Look at me."

"Sam, I just don't know."

I stared at her, knowing that all this time I'd been hoping she'd understand, and tell me it was all right. I wanted her to say she'd stay with me, try to help me, and go on loving me.

She lifted her head, and she was looking at me as if I were a stranger with two heads, both of them green.

"Sam, I thought I loved you. And all this time I didn't even know you."

I stared at her. I'd known she'd have a hard time trying to understand all that I told her, but I hadn't thought she would walk out on me like this.

The heartbreak made my voice savage. "You know me. You've lain on this grass with me. In my arms. You know me, all right."

"No." She pushed away from me, tried to stand up. I caught her arm. I felt her tears splash on my hand.

"Don't leave me."

"Sam, I don't know. You loved that girl. What kind of girl was she?"

"I don't know. That doesn't matter now. I don't love her, I never did. There was never anyone like you, Lois."

She pulled away again, shuddering. "You robbed people. You went to prison."

"Yes. I was arrested, tried and convicted, and I went to prison. I stood in line to eat, to be counted, and they locked me in a cell by number for four years, and no matter what I did, I paid for it."

"I'm sorry for you, Sam."

"Sure. Like you'd be sorry for a skid row bum."

"That isn't true, Sam. But you're in such terrible trouble."

"Maybe I could stand that, Lois. Don't you see? I need you. I need somebody."

She pulled away from me, holding her arms locked across her breasts, shivering in the cold wind off the lake.

"Go to the police, Sam," she whispered.

I shook my head, helplessly. "Didn't you hear what I told you, Lois? They'll frame me back into jail. Kohzak will. The police have nothing on him. If I said he was with me, he'd produce twenty witnesses to prove he wasn't. All he'd have to do to frame me would be to call from a pay phone and the police would arrest me again."

"Oh, Sam!"

"I don't care about that right now. What about us?"

"Oh, Sam! I don't know. What will my parents say?"

"Lois, no matter what I've done, I'm still Sam Baynard, the guy you said you loved."

"It's all different now."

"Not if you love me."

She stared at me, shaking her head. She looked ill. After a moment she tried to smile. "You're joking, Sam? The prison and all that other? A test?

You're trying to find out what I'd do?"

"I wish it were that simple!"

She shook her head, pressing her hand against her mouth. "You've got to be joking."

"No." I got up on my knees, facing her. I caught her arms. "I was a fool kid, Lois. Crazy. I got in trouble." I shook my head. "Looks like I'm never going to quit paying for it."

She shivered, staring across the lake. Her voice was flat, distant. "What do you want me to do, Sam?"

My voice went bitter again. "I don't know. Get up and run, I guess. Yell for the cops."

"Stop, Sam."

"I can't help it. I've loved you. I've tried to be honest with you."

"I know, Sam."

"Maybe you could forgive me."

"There's nothing to forgive. I'm so sorry for you."

"Stop saying that."

"It won't help any to yell, Sam."

"It won't help any to treat me like a bum in a soup-line, either."

"I don't, Sam. I just never was prepared for anything like this. Can you understand me?"

"I need somebody, Lois. I need you."

"I don't know what to do." She shook her head. "What will father say? Why, he didn't like it because you were a milkman. I could laugh at that. But what now, Sam? When I tell him you served time in prison." She shuddered, pressing her fists against her stomach.

"I want to be decent, Lois. I paid in prison. I've been honest since I got out. That ought to count for something."

She only shook her head.

"I've been level with you. Stick by me, Lois, and I'll fight Kohzak, only I need somebody to believe in me."

She shook her head. "I'm so afraid, Sam."

"Of me?"

She didn't answer.

A night bird cried in a thicket and was suddenly still. Across the lake a light flickered out and darkness leaped up from the water like a striking fish. I looked at Lois and I knew this was what I'd expected, what I had known had to be. Yet, I couldn't stand the thought of losing her.

After a long time she whispered again. "I don't know, Sam."

"You don't love me?"

"Give me a little time to think. I've got to think what I'll say to father." She licked at her lips. "I hate to say it, Sam, but what will my friends say? People I've known all my life in this town? What will they think?"

"I don't know. It's you I want. You I care about!"

She touched my hand. Her fingers were icy but they clung to me, as if she were making a final desperate effort to find a way out for us. "Will you talk to father?" she said. "Will you tell him what you told me? Sam, he might know what to do."

4

When Lois and I walked into the Rowell's front room, her parents were where we'd left them. Ned Rowell had laid aside his newspaper and was watching television. Mrs. Rowell still read her magazine.

"You didn't stay long," Mrs. Rowell said.

"No," Lois said.

Mrs. Rowell's head came up. She frowned. "Lois, is something wrong?"

I saw Rowell turn from the television set, watching us.

"There's nothing wrong," Lois told them.

I glanced at Lois. She was no longer looking at me. She stood slightly apart from me, as if she couldn't stand to touch me. I kept reminding myself that nothing had ever prepared Lois for the kind of shock I'd given her. She was hurt, but she seemed to have forgotten about me, as if whatever I thought no longer had any importance.

I drew a deep breath. "Mr. Rowell, I'd like to speak to you alone, sir."

He stared at me, and I was aware of everything being suspended in this room for the moment, even the physical act of breathing.

Rowell peered along his nose at me. I could see myself as he saw me. A nothing who's been in Dexter City less than a year, a man nobody knew anything about, the man who delivered their milk. What right had I to love his daughter after the fortune he'd spent on her in protection, clothing, medicine and schooling? Who was I? What was I doing in his house?

Come on, Mr. Rowell, you ain't heard nothing yet.

His gaze raked across me. The fact that I was healthy, had all my teeth, was sound in body, meant nothing to him. That extra something he defined as background — if he gave it any conscious name — that was what he sought in the man for Lois.

You want background, Mr. Rowell, come listen to me.

He was a handsome man in his early forties. He removed his dark-rimmed reading glasses, shoved them into a case. He pressed the flat of his hand against his graying temples and stood up.

That was when I caught the smirk tugging at his lips. It occurred to me that he was sure I was going to ask him to allow Lois to marry me. I didn't have to be a clever opposition lawyer to follow the uncomplicated direction of his thoughts. He wanted me to ask. The sooner the better.

He couldn't wait to say no.

"Surely, Baynard." He strode ahead of me out of the room, glancing first at Lois with a protecting look, and then at his wife, with a faint smile that said, thank heaven, this will soon be over.

A room across the foyer had been converted into a book-lined, leather-upholstered study. He snapped on a light, closed the door behind us. He gave me a chilled, polite smile. "Sit down, Baynard."

There were two leather covered easy chairs. I sat in one of them and Rowell sank down into the other. Neither of us relaxed. My hands were sweated. I wiped them on my handkerchief.

I saw that smirk on Rowell's mouth again.

"All right, Baynard, what is it?"

I didn't know how to begin. A story such as I had to tell this respected professional man who had protected his family from even casually brushing against the ugly seaminess of the life in which I'd wallowed, needed a lengthy preamble, and a humble supplication that it be understood. Here was a man who'd never even understood the type of college man who never pledged a fraternity. And I had to try and make him know how it was with Collie Kohzak.

"I told Lois about myself tonight, sir. I mean I was in some trouble once and—"

"Trouble, Baynard?" He leaned forward in that chair, the leather squeaking. His face congealed into a rigid mask, faintly marked with contempt. "What kind of trouble?"

"I'll try to tell you, sir. I won't hold anything back. I want you to know all of it. As I said, I told Lois, and well, it was more than she could face alone. She wanted me to talk to you about it."

"I shouldn't wonder."

"I know that Lois has been sheltered—"

"I've tried to protect her from ugliness."

"I know. Still, because I love her, and believed that she loved me, I had to tell her the truth about myself. You can see that?"

"I don't know the degree of your trouble yet, of course. But I'll say this now. If the trouble is as serious as it appears, you should have told her a long time ago, the very first time she invited you into this house."

"But at first, I didn't believe there was anything serious between Lois and me. I didn't see how there could be. Then, when it was serious, I knew I had to tell her, but I kept putting it off. Can you understand that, sir?"

He just stared at me. "No, Baynard, I can't. I make no compromises with right and wrong. I expect at least that much from men who visit my daughter in this house."

I felt helpless. I met his gaze. I said, "I've been honest with her, Mr. Rowell. And honest with you about her."

"I can't agree with that, either. If the whole association was built on a lie from the first, I'm sick with the deceptions that must have been practiced from then on."

"Can't you believe me? Would I be here now, telling the truth, if I'd been lying all along?"

His laugh was chilled. "That would depend, Baynard, on why you are suddenly being truthful. Are you driven to being honest? Is there some reason for your sudden desire to unburden yourself? Are you pushed into a corner where the only escape is predicated upon your telling the truth finally, and begging for clemency?"

I didn't speak for a moment. Finally I said, "I suppose so. At least you'll see it that way. Maybe I would have prolonged it, but only because I love Lois, not because I wanted to deceive or betray any of you."

He waved that aside. "Suppose you tell me what it is you've done, Baynard. I know how Mrs. Rowell feels about you, and I'm not blind to the fact that Lois has not dated any other men since the two of you began to see each other steadily. These factors must weight heavily in your favor. I love my family, and I put their happiness above my own. I can accept many things as long as I feel they will be made happier and will benefit."

"All right," I said. "I was at the university about six years ago. I was in my third year. It was tough, and when I met this girl and she introduced me to a criminal, I had a chance to make money swiftly. I know this is impossible for you to understand: being in a college, continually broke, needing a haircut, shoeshine, sometimes hungry."

"I'm not completely devoid of human understanding, Baynard." Rowell tried to smile, but he was withdrawing from me. "I admit my father gave me most of the things I wanted, but he impressed upon me, too, that not every boy grew up with the same advantages."

"Whatever advantages you had, I had none of them."

"I won't hold anything like this against you, Baynard. I have nothing but respect for the fact that you went three years to the university under such adverse circumstances. Lois has told me about it. I remember I barely had time to do my studying and I had no outside jobs."

"I don't want to deceive you, sir. When I say the man I met was a criminal, I don't hope to minimize that. He was a wanted hoodlum, and had other thugs on his payroll. He robbed banks—and I robbed them with him."

He caught his breath, and I knew I'd gone too far for any understanding from him. I was lost.

The sense of suspended animation permeated the whole house again. Not even the casual everyday sounds from outside penetrated the walls. It was as if Lois and her mother sat without breathing in that room across the foyer, waiting. As if Rowell and I sat in the eye of a hurricane where there was inaction, vacuum, and gales whipped around us in a wide but narrowing circle.

"A thief," he whispered.

He could have hit me across the face and hurt me a lot less. But it was true, and he was going to get all the truth from me.

"Yes. I was a kid. Mixed up."

"A thief." He would not compromise here, either.

"We robbed a jewelry store and I was caught."

"Arrested?"

"Yes."

"You were sentenced?" He looked ill.

The eye of the hurricane was closing. "Four to ten years," I said.

For some moments Rowell did not speak. His gaze held against my face, and the only expression on his cheeks was contempt. The look deepened and called me bum, and worse than that, because I had dared to sully the inside of his home by entering it.

"Please, let me explain."

He lifted his hand. His voice was cold steel thrust against me and twisted.

"I've heard enough, Baynard."

"There's more—"

"It's enough, too much. What do you think I am, to sit and listen to you recite your crimes? I'm interested in one crime. I want to know how you dared to come into my house? How could you dare to lay your hands on my daughter?"

"Mr. Rowell—"

"That's enough. I don't want to hear any more of your alibis, your lying."

"I haven't lied to you."

"I've felt all along that you were low and vicious, and yet I couldn't let myself believe it. More than once, I wanted to have your past investigated, and I couldn't bring myself to do it."

"Mr. Rowell—"

"I don't want to hear your voice any more. I want you to get out of this house." He stood up, his fists clenched at his side, waiting for me to stand up.

I stood up. He whispered through his taut throat, "Get out of my house."

I couldn't even blame him, or hate him. All he was thinking was of Lois and his wife, their security and their place in Dexter City and the way I'd jeopardized all he held worthwhile.

I nodded and turned toward the door. All the old bitterness welled back up through me. Wonderful, the way people helped you when you were in trouble.

"Wait a minute, Baynard."

I had my hand on the doorknob. I turned, hoping he might be relenting just a little because you hope as long as you breathe.

"Just one more thing, if you ever come here again, if I ever hear you've spoken to my daughter again, I'll call the police myself."

I stalked woodenly across the foyer toward the front door. Lois ran out of the living room. Mrs. Rowell stood up, magazine in hand, watching, her face gray.

"Sam."

I stopped at the front door, looking at Lois.

"Sam, what did he say?" Lois nodded her head toward the study.

"It wasn't so much what he said. It was the way he said it."

"Sam, you sound so bitter—"

"Shouldn't I? He told me what I was, as if I didn't already know."

She sighed. "What did you think he would do?"

"Lois, if you love me—"

"Baynard!" The word was like a stone hurled at me from where Rowell stood in his study doorway.

"Lois," I said. "I need you. I need somebody to have a little faith—"

"Maybe you didn't believe what I said," Rowell spoke again, moving into the foyer. "I want you out of my house."

Lois touched my arm. "Please, Sam, you better go."

That was it. Not, please, Sam, go and I'll call you tomorrow. Come back tomorrow. I promise I'll see you. There wasn't even a kind word tossed as you'd chuck a dog a bone. She was worried only about her father. "Please, Sam, you better go."

I stared at Lois, but she would not meet my eyes. I moved my gaze to where Mrs. Rowell had walked to the living room entrance, still holding that magazine at her side.

I exhaled heavily and I walked out, closing the door behind me. Somewhere along the street music spewed from an upstairs room, flooding down around me in the darkness. I moved slowly out to the walk, glanced back at the door. It remained closed and I knew it would. All the hours I'd spent inside that house were gone, and had never belonged to me: they'd belonged to some stranger named Sam Baynard that neither the Rowells nor I really knew.

I walked through the shadows, the only movement on the quiet street. At the corner I stood at the bus stop until I saw the bus coming.

I shivered. I couldn't get on that bus, sit near people, hear them talking about everyday things as if the world were going on, business as usual. I had to be alone. I had to think, to get used to being scum beneath the feet of a well-fed attorney.

I turned my back on it and the slowly moving bus picked up speed. I walked toward town, my hands shoved into my pockets. I remembered the way Lois and I had met, and the first day I knew I loved her, and the way I'd begun to plan because loving her made everything different and gave me something to hope for.

In my mind I saw myself running with milk bottles because walking with them wasn't working hard enough. I saw myself making sales pitches at back doors when I should have been sleeping because extra sales meant bonuses and there were many extras a route man could sell if he worked at it, cottage cheese, cream, yogurt, buttermilk, things people wanted but had to be reminded of.

I stared at cars racing past on Highland Drive. All the work I'd done — for nothing. All these months I could have been crooked, back in jail or well heeled; it was a gamble and they weren't going to let me be honest.

The bitterness and the loneliness were as they'd been in my prison cell, only deeper now, because I had something I wanted and the loss added to the hurt. I walked faster, trying to get away from it because I couldn't take it any more.

At street corners I paused, looking both ways, unable to tell if cars approached or not. Highlands Drive curved away and I started along Jensen Street.

A black police car lunged from the darkness, brakes snarling, aerial lashing. It slammed into a curb and two men jumped out, crossing the parkway toward me. I saw a gun glinting in the hand of the uniformed cop.

The other man was detective Lantis.

The uniformed cop stalked around me warily. When he got behind me, he holstered his gun and frisked me. It was all I needed to set me off, I was ready to explode.

In my mind I saw myself wheeling around and giving him a knee in the groin, a fist in his face, the side of a hand hard enough across the neck to stun him. Then Lantis would shoot me and that would be fine, too. It was the kind of violence I needed right then.

I clenched my fists, standing tall, suffering the indignity of being frisked on a public street when I'd already had all the hurt I could take.

"He's clean, Mr. Lantis." The cop had respect in his voice for the detective. "Nothing on him."

"You were expecting atom bombs?" I said.

Lantis stepped nearer on the walk. "What you doing out here, Baynard?"

"Mugging old women." My voice rattled. "Unsaddle, Lantis. Let me alone."

"Watch your tone," the cop warned me.

Lantis's voice hardened. "You want a ride downtown, Baynard? Want to sweat out a night in the tank? Learn to speak civil."

"You guys never let up, do you?"

"Want me to put cuffs on him, Mr. Lantis?" The cop sounded anxious. He stood behind me but I didn't have to see his face to know he wanted me to make a break. He wanted to club me to show the lieutenant his muscles. He was aching to demonstrate how tough he was.

Lantis looked from the cop's face to mine. He exhaled and his voice softened. "He's clean, ain't he?" he said to the cop.

"Yes sir, there's nothing on him."

Lantis's voice mocked me. "Well, we don't want to make a false arrest, do we, Shuffold?"

"I guess not, sir."

Now Lantis looked me over. His voice was overly polite. "There's been some burglaries in this neighborhood, Baynard, so it don't look good, a gent like you picking this area for your nightly exercise."

My hands trembled. I shoved them in my pockets so he wouldn't see. "I'm on my way home."

"Sure you are." Lantis stepped nearer. "See that bus stop, Baynard? You walk over there. We'll be right here, sitting in this car. You catch that next bus and go on home, or I'll take you in."

I stepped away, moving from between them. I looked from Lantis to Shuffold.

Lantis stood waiting. Shuffold's hand lingered near his holster. I swallowed hard and turned from them crossing the walk toward the bus stop.

Lantis's laugh followed me backing at the nape of my neck. "You can drop this honest routine any time Baynard. Bad boys don't change."

I glanced over my shoulder. "They don't get a chance," I said.

He laughed again. I walked to the corner. They got in the cruiser, sat in the darkness watching me. The bus pulled in close, air brakes hissing. I stepped into the bus and it pulled away.

All the way home, I tried to keep my mind off Lois. I was still alive, I was still working.

I got off the elevator and went along the corridor toward my room. My apartment door was ajar spilling light down the carpeting toward me.

I didn't slow down. I was too tired, too bitter to care about the door or whoever might be in there.

I nudged the door open wider and stepped into my room.

Elva sat on the side of my bed, light glittering off the curves of her taut black dress.

She pulled patiently at her cigarette. She looked lovely, bad and dangerous. "Hello Sammy."

"Get out."

"Sammy, I didn't lie to you. I came over to tell you that."

"Now you've told me."

"I did run away from Collie. When you were gone I missed you. I came all the way out here to find you and you treat me like this."

"Cut. You're Collie's shill, you always were, you always will be."

"You didn't treat me this way before, Sammy."

"I used to have rocks in my head, but now they've been beaten to dust."

She crushed out her cigarette, watching me. Her eyes went sleepy and her lips pouted. She touched at them with the tip of her tongue, raking it slowly across her full underlip. She made her face into a contrite mask.

"I'm sorry, Sammy, for the way I hurt you."

"That makes it feel all better. Now get out."

"I want a chance to make it up to you."

She wriggled her bottom on the mattress, light shimmering in that black dress and its hem riding high above her knee, exposing the golden inside of her thigh.

She wanted me to look at her, but I turned away, slammed the door and walked over to the window.

"I am sorry, Sammy."

I shook my head. "Right. You win the Academy Award. Elva Higgens running the gamut of phony emotions."

"Don't, Sammy."

"You don't. When I think how stupid I must have been, chasing after you when you belonged to Collie. How stupid you and Collie think I am, you coming up here like this."

She undulated slightly on the mattress again, unworried, unhurried. "Why shouldn't I want a man like you, after Collie?"

I stared down into the dark street. "Because no man would mean anything to you after an animal."

She met my gaze levelly. She smiled slowly, eyes melting in a way she might have patented. "Come here, Sammy."

"Get out, Elva. Tell Collie to get himself another pigeon. Tell him it didn't work."

"All right," she said. "I'll tell him, but first I want to prove to you, Sammy, how sorry I am."

She got up from the bed and moved across the room to me. "You really hate me, don't you?" she said.

"For a long time now."

"Very honest, eh?"

"For a long time now."

"Can honesty ever buy you anything like this, Sammy?" She stood very close, her hand resting lightly on my shoulder, and her chin tilted. I could smell her, I could feel the faint eager thrust of her breasts. She slid her hand around my neck, pulled my head down to hers. She kissed strongly, her mouth parted. I fought against it but she felt the tremor that went through me.

She laughed, a soft, satisfied murmur. I could tell she figured she had me hooked again, just that easily.

She turned slightly. "You don't need to be afraid of me."

"I'm not afraid of you."

"Are you afraid of Collie?"

"I'm afraid of nothing."

"Then kiss me. Show me."

I wanted to hit her and throw her out of there. I was filled with rage against her, against Collie, and Lois and Ned Rowell, but mostly against Elva.

It pleased me suddenly to think that she was so sure she could dangle her body like bait before me, tempt me right back into the fold, and then somehow escape before she paid off, the same old Elva script we'd played a hundred times in the past.

My lips covered hers, and I had to keep myself on leash, not because of lust, unless hatred is another name for lust. I felt her mouth part and her tongue dart into my mouth and start probing. Her arms tightened around my shoulders, pulling her to me.

I pulled away from her.

"What's the matter," she whispered, frowning.

"Nothing. I've had it. I'm just not interested in having it any more—"

"Sammy!"

"Get out, Elva. It's all over. Finished. We're quits."

I expected an outburst from her, but it didn't come. Her voice was low. "I did run away from Collie, Sammy."

"You put up no fight when he found you."

"What would you have me do, Sammy? No matter where I went in this country, Collie would find me in twenty-four hours."

I shrugged, admitting this.

"I don't have much chance," she said.

"We're a great pair."

Her breath quickened. "We could be, Sammy."

"I tried to tell you that five years ago."

Her voice got sharp. "Sammy, it's time that you knew that love is for the birds, the bees, and people who can afford it. What did it matter if I loved you? If I'd played around with you, the way you wanted, I'd have gotten a one-way ride to the river."

I shrugged again, knowing she was truthful now, at least.

"Maybe I wanted nice things," she said. "I came from a rotten town, Sammy. I had one chance to escape that place — my looks. I knew the price of what I wanted, and I knew I had to pay it."

I didn't speak. She found another cigarette, lighted it, took several quick, nervous drags. The smoke drifted upward and dissolved in flat gray clouds.

"Collie gave me nice things. No matter what kind of animal he was, or the things I had to do for him. Once I was his, I was caught, you ought to understand that."

"Very touching. But you didn't come up here to cry on my shoulder. What do you really want?"

She pressed against me again, her naked body like the red coals of a once-blazing fire. "We could get our cut out of this job with Collie, this last one, Sammy! We could get out of the country together."

I sat up, the rage cold. "Collie sent you up here with this same old pitch."

"No, Sammy! Not this time."

"I've had Collie up to here."

"You don't even know anything about being sick of Collie. I'm stringing along on this job because if I can get my hands on enough money this time I can get away from Collie forever. If you've ever been smart, Sammy, be smart enough to see it. We could go anywhere, you and I. We could have what we always wanted."

I heard the tom-toms under her insincerity, the pulsing beat of every lie I'd listened to across those lips, but one truth remained: anybody who'd been with Kohzak as long as she had would want to get away, and to escape. But she'd have to be well heeled.

"We could make it, Sammy. You and me."

This was all wrong, like some scene left over from five years ago, and now spliced in at the same place in time so nothing made sense, and it was out of focus. Only one thing kept it glued in tightly. Hate.

Anyhow, what else did I have?

5

It grew quiet outside my closed windows.

Inside my room, Elva stretched and writhed her naked body beside me. Watching her loveliness, I was able to forget everything else for the moment, even the chilled certainty that she was still lying to me.

Her laugh was shaky.

"You could buy me a mink jacket, Sammy. Would you do that?"

I lay beside her. I felt numb, as though this moment belonged, too, five years in the past.

She nuzzled my throat with her parted lips. "Please, Sammy."

I was thinking that when I broke from the side of the law this time, it was forever. It was a long, narrow one-way street, and you gambled that a jackpot was at its end instead of Death beckoning you into the electric chair.

Elva pressed against me, shivering. "That's one thing Collie never gave me, Sammy. He was too cheap."

I barely heard her. I gazed about my room where I'd dreamed so futilely for one long year.

"We'll have money enough this time, Sammy. You can buy me mink. Little Elva Higgens in mink, and her old man used to stagger home blind drunk."

I thought about the way Lois had walked out on me when I needed her, the very first time I needed her. The way her old man listened just far enough to hear about prison. The way Lantis rode me, waiting for me to make one mistake. As far as they cared I had served time in prison, and so I was no good. But I remembered, too, I had served time, and it had been hell, and I remembered that, too.

"You have no idea how smooth I'd look in mink, Sammy."

I moved Elva on the bed, pressing her body in under mine. She was a sickness that had burned like a fever, and burned itself out.

I pressed her down into the mattress, kissing her mouth, getting the same rough kiss in return. We didn't have love, but we had hatred, and it was almost as good.

It was like a battle between us in which we were each driven by the need to destroy the other.

Then we were not talking any more but only living with the terrible emotions that flailed us and then hurtled us downward, exhausted.

We lay there for a long time without speaking at all and then Elva started in again. "You see, Sammy. I could be so nice to the man who bought me mink."

I got up, the backs of my legs quivering. I found a fifth of bourbon and two glasses. She watched me pour and then sat up, drinking, watching me over the glass.

"All we've got to do is get that money," she said.

"And stay alive."

"Yes." She exhaled heavily. "That won't be easy."

I drank deeply, shuddering. "Once I thought Kohzak the smartest guy I ever knew. One thing sure. He's the most dangerous."

"We've got to be careful, Sammy. Careful and smart. One thing sure. If we do cross Collie, we've got to move fast."

I said, "I don't know if we could outrun Collie, even if we had a hundred grand."

Elva stood up, her hands trembling. She drank from the bottle. "It doesn't look good. I never thought it would be easy, somehow I'm going this time, and he's not going to stop me."

I lay back on the bed and watched her dress. Her coat was tossed over a chair. She picked it up, slipped into it. Her mouth twisted. "It ain't mink."

I stared at her, seeing that despite all we'd done, all she drank, she was steady, cool, self-contained. It made you stop and think.

She said, "Come on, Sammy. Take me home."

I was almost off the bed when I remembered Lantis and the curfew he'd set for me. "You go ahead, Elva. You'll be okay."

"Sammy, I'm scared."

I laughed. "Name the man you're scared of."

"Collie Kohzak." She didn't hesitate when she said it. "If he finds out I was here, and stayed this long — I'm scared."

"I'll call you a cab, baby, but I can't take you home."

"You afraid of Collie?" Her eyes were chilled. But I didn't bother arguing it. I called for a taxi and after a few moments we heard a horn bleep down in the street. "Walk down with me."

She was shivering. I guess fear was honest in her. She knew Collie well enough to be afraid of him. We went down in the elevator, out to the street. It seemed tautly silent out there, the cab driver watching us.

Elva paused in the apartment doorway and looked both ways before she went across the walk.

"Real smart," I said. "Standing in the light to check on somebody who might be out in the dark."

"I've never been this jittery." She gazed at me. "You come over early, Sammy. We got to keep Collie thinking we're on his team all the way."

I couldn't help thinking that she was, even now.

I promised and she ran out to the waiting cab, her high heels rattling like a machine gun on the pavement.

Collie sat at breakfast in Elva's apartment when I got there at a quarter of nine the next morning.

All the signs were he'd spent the night. I wondered what lies Elva had been able to make him believe. Things appeared quiet on the surface, at least.

Collie preened in a wine colored silk lounging robe with his monogram on the breast pocket, the sort of item he liked to leave in his mistress's apartment, initialed cufflinks and a white silk scarf at his throat.

He nodded toward me over his breakfast of sunnyside eggs and crisp bacon. He ate delicately, taking small bits and masticating slowly like a health teacher demonstrating how it should be done. He even chewed his milk. The milk was for his ulcer.

"Good to see you, boy," he said. When I told him I'd eaten breakfast about seven hours earlier, he laughed. He jerked his head toward a man lounging in an easy chair under a lamp. "You remember Scotty Pizzari? Say hi to Sammy Baynard, Scotty."

Pizzari looked up, folding his newspaper. "Hi."

I nodded, glancing at Pizzari, or as much of him as I could see around that newspaper. Pizzari had not changed or gained any weight. He looked like a jockey, a crooked one or a disbarred one.

His sleek suits were sharply cut, and I remember the tailor where he bought them and the way that tailor suffered every time Pizzari ordered another suit cut to the same pattern.

Collie had come from the same sordid neighborhoods as Pizzari, but Collie was ambitious, and Pizzari was happy with things as they were. Scotty loved to be left strictly alone. Once I'd wondered what Pizzari did with himself when he wasn't playing shadow to Kohzak. Now I no longer cared.

Collie masticated elaborately, swallowed, dabbed at his lips with a linen napkin.

He stared at me from across the table with that rock hard friendly smile in his dark, narrow face.

"Elva says you've decided to go along."

"You said I had no choice."

He smiled. "I like my people happy, Sammy. You know that. A man cooperates better if he's happy in his work."

"You won't get much out of me then."

He laughed sharply. "If I didn't think so, Sammy, I'd never have dealt you in. It's a big deal. Don't you know you're going to be worth a lot to me?"

"What kind of job is it?"

"A payroll lift, boy. The nice leafy kind. All cash. Heard about this firm that likes to do its employees a favor. Pays them off in cash every second Friday."

"Is a payroll big enough for you?"

"That depends on the gamble, Sammy. You know me. I consider the stakes, the risks, everything. This is a jackpot any way you look at it. No risk, good stakes. Two hundred sixty thousand plus, cut three ways. You had any pie that rich lately?"

"A payroll of that kind of dough means armed guards. Sounds dangerous."

Collie dabbed at his mouth with that napkin. "Now boy, when did I ever let you take chances?" He pushed back from the table, let his knife clatter against his egg-stained plate. "Sure, you served a stretch, but because you got greedy. You didn't follow orders. You got caught."

"Yeah," Pizzari said.

We both glanced at Pizzari, but he was reading his paper again.

"If it's so good," I said, "why do you need me?"

Collie laughed. "You just don't know how good this one is, baby."

Pizzari looked up over his paper and he laughed, too.

I didn't know if Pizzari laughed because it was amusing or because Kohzak was laughing and Pizzari needed to join him.

"I need you, Sammy," Kohzak stopped laughing. "That's why it's so good, because we do need you."

"Yeah," Pizzari said.

I drew a deep breath, feeling the prickling of wrong, a deeper wrong than morals or ethics, an urgent wrong concerned with their actually needing me for anything.

Collie watched me, smiling. "What's the biggest milk company in this state?" he asked and when I went cold, staring at him, he answered himself: "Gorten's."

I touched at my dry lips with my dry tongue.

Collie leaned forward slightly. "Who works for the biggest milk company in the state, with the biggest payroll? Who knows the inside of that plant and office? Answer to all that: Sammy Baynard."

"Our boy Sammy," Pizzari said.

"You must be nuts." I shook my head. "Why, I wouldn't have a chance of getting away with a thing like that. They know me down there. If you're looking for a fall guy, Collie, get yourself another boy. If I'm going back to prison anyway, you got no threat to hold over me."

I turned and walked toward the door. Collie's hard voice stopped me.

"Who said anything about you going to prison?"

"That's what it sounded like to me."

Collie's voice remained calm. "You think I'm bluffing about putting you back in jail if you try to cross me?"

"I think you believe you can send me back to the pen after you use me in a stupid holdup. I'm not buying."

"You're not walking out, either." He said it in a cool, matter-of-fact tone.

"You planning to shoot me to keep me here?"

"I'm not going to shoot anybody. I'm keeping my nose clean until I collect that three hundred grand Gorten Milk Company has for me. But I'll fix you so that you don't get out of this block."

I walked toward the door again.

Collie's voice trailed after me, level, unemotional. Scotty Pizzari sat forward in his chair, dropped the paper. "You got that note I gave you?"

"Yeah, boss."

I had my hand on the doorknob, my back to them.

I held my breath. Heads, I lost, tails I lost on this deal. I hated the idea of Bonnel Gorten knowing I'd crossed him, the first man to trust me. I wanted to walk out, but I knew Collie was calling my bluff. There was an angle and I had to be smart enough to hear it.

"Sit down, Scotty," I said. I turned and leaned against the door. I stayed there watching Collie and the flat smile in his black eyes. "How could I get away robbing a place where they know me?"

Collie shrugged. "Why don't you let me handle the details?"

"It's my life I'm thinking about."

"It's your life I'm thinking about, too. You got to be humble, boy. You got to learn you can't flare up at me, or walk out on me. I'm sorry, Baynard, but any more of this and I'll have to have the boys instruct you."

"Yeah," Pizzari said.

"You haven't told me yet how I'd get away with that robbery. I'm still waiting to see whether I go to jail for that robbery or for walking out on you."

He stared at me for some seconds, no longer smiling. At last he said, "Nobody will recognize you. That silk stocking gag is still the best I ever heard of."

"Pulled down over my face?"

He nodded. "And nobody will know you. You walk in with a limp, maybe, pad your shoulders, wearing the silk stocking."

I did not say anything.

Collie laughed. "Kohzak's still the smart cookie, eh, Sam? That trick will go over like Jayne Mansfield in this town because they never saw anything like it. Sammy, after this caper you go right back to work the next day. You walk right in there cagey. Nobody even suspects you."

"And what about my cut?"

He shrugged, watching Elva come in from the bedroom. She was something to watch in a transparent negligee. She leaned against the doorjamb, buffing her nails.

"You quit your job," Collie said, "your cut is waiting for you, like always, and you're free."

"Free," Elva whispered.

Kohzak laughed. "And rich."

"With mink," Elva said, giving her words a special meaning.

6

So I cut loose from civilization and went back to the jungle where I was wanted, at least temporarily.

"There's one thing," I said.

Collie watched me, waiting. "Yeah?"

"I've done time, Collie. I've been in prison. I've had that bit. I couldn't take it any more. If I keep pulling jobs like this I will go back, maybe I'll be caught this time. But since I have no choice, that's not much gamble."

"So what's the beef?"

"Just what I wanted when I came out here. I want out. You're holding the knife at my back, so I'm in on this job. It's got to be my last one, Collie. There's nothing else except the chance to go back to prison. I'd be finished in a cell again."

"If that's the way you feel, I can understand," Collie said.

I drew a deep breath, hating everything in that room.

"This one last job, Collie, and then we're quits. When I walk out, you don't come looking for me."

I heard Elva's soft intake of breath.

Collie shrugged. "This one job, boy, and then you are out. Then I never knew you. Like that."

"I have your word," I said.

This penetrated deeply enough to bring him to his feet. He got white around the mouth. "Nobody calls me a liar. Collie Kohzak never broke his word with anybody."

"It doesn't matter," I said. "I've got to trust you."

He nodded, relaxing slightly. "Right. You've got to trust me. Best security you ever had, boy. Collie Kohzak's word."

Here I was, back among the wolves. When I finally spoke, my voice sounded cold, even to me. "I need five hundred, Collie. Right now."

Collie stared at me; he was a hard man with a buck of his own money; it came in fast and he liked that one-way operation. He paid off quick and to the dollar, but he hated having anybody into him for anything.

"Five hundred? What's the matter? Ain't you working?"

"You got it? Or is that why you're pulling this tank-town job?"

His face got livid again. "I don't like that kind of talk."

We stood, our eyes meeting, clashing.

He said, "You know I don't operate like that."

"You need me, Collie. You want to keep me happy?"

"You could run on five bills."

"Run?" I stared at him. "Where could I run?"

He shrugged. "What do you want it for?"

"I want to buy something."

I saw Elva straighten over near her bedroom door. She stopped buffing her nails. Elva really wanted the mink, and she couldn't think of anything else I might need five hundred for.

Her soft voice wheedled: "Give him the money, Collie."

His head jerked around. "What kind of thing is this? You know I can't start running a loan company. Once word gets around I'm a touch, every guy gets his hooks sharpened."

This was so unlikely that even Pizzari laughed.

"No word will ever circulate about you like that," Elva said.

Collie started to speak, changed his mind. He gazed at me and I could see the wheels churning. "Five bills."

He'd smelled an angle. It had a bad smell but I'd already considered it. It just didn't matter to me. If I were going crooked, I might as well go in style.

Now Collie began to see how the money might work for him. He had the blackmail telephone call to hold over me, but the five hundred paid to me before witnesses was added insurance.

"Sure, Sammy. Always glad to help my boy."

Sure you are, I thought, watching him count out five crisp new bills. You've figured the angle, haven't you, Kohzak?

He wanted me to take that money now. He figured me smart enough to know nobody ever took five bills from Collie Kohzak then tried to cross him.

Collie liked the lid down tight.

I took a shower, letting the water wash me a long time, as if there were really a chance of washing away all the evil.

I put on the only suit I owned, caught a bus downtown. I suppose all this time I kept hoping something would yank me out of this nightmare and that everything that had happened since Elva turned up would be an evil dream and I'd wake up and hurry down to my milk route.

As hard as I hoped and sweated, nothing was going to wake me from this nightmare. This wasn't the kind you could escape by falling off your bed.

I felt a dull hatred for the solid citizens I passed on the busy street. Busy making a living, voting the straight Republican ticket, contributing to the community chest, doing all the right things and somehow making it impossible for a guy like me ever to get out of a mess.

I walked into Bochmeir's. There were better furriers east of Dexter City, but he was tops locally.

A saleswoman glided toward me across ankle-deep carpeting that crunched like crisp corn flakes under her toes. Her nose turned up, and there was even a chill in her smile. A tall blonde, with hard hip lines and long, nylon sheathed legs. She was polite, but barely.

"May I help you?" she wondered.

"A mink jacket," I said. I could hit at Collie with mink because he'd never bought mink for Elva, the one thing she wanted badly enough to cross him for.

I wanted some added insurance, too.

The blonde motioned me toward an air-conditioned booth and snapped her fingers. A lean-hipped model paraded mink jackets slowly past me.

The jacket I liked best had gray in it, like a dark-haired woman getting touches of silver so you weren't sure if it was there or just a trick of the lights.

Blondy smiled remotely, almost admiring my taste, warming slightly toward me. "A lovely jacket." She snapped her fingers and the model shrugged reluctantly out of it.

Blondy handled that short jacket as if she were afraid to touch it. The gray highlights shimmered in it, disappeared, shimmered again.

I said, "How much?"

Her nose tilted. One didn't ask the price of mink, it was like admitting you couldn't afford it. "This jacket with tax is just twenty-eight ninety-five."

"Two thousand, eight-hundred ninety-five?"

She smiled. "Of course."

"If I bought it," I said. "Would you accept five hundred down?"

"I believe credit terms can be arranged if you're a local resident, employed, with a good credit rating."

"You see, it's a gift. I want to give it now, and I don't care how long it takes to pay for it."

She smiled again. "Somebody knows a very lucky, nice girl."

No, I thought, a very bad one. Nice girls seldom get mink. Look at Lois — no, I didn't want to look at Lois.

Sometimes it doesn't matter what you want. I walked out of the furriers with that mink jacket boxed elegantly and my installment-payment card in my pocket. Lois was the first person I saw.

I looked at her, feeling uncomfortable warmth flood upward through me. She was so lovely. I'd never seen her so beautiful.

There was an aura of goodness about her that contrasted with this mink under my arm, and every reason why I wanted it.

It was as if I'd flipped, planning to rob the milk company, cross Collie, and run. This was insanity, a paranoiac dream. Looking at Lois I felt all that madness lose its contact with reality. It was as if I suddenly regained my senses and became sane right there on that street.

Lois was what I wanted. All right, she'd walked out on me. But I'd been in trouble before and I didn't give up, I fought back. If I wanted Lois, I'd have to fight now.

I watched Lois walking toward me.

I opened my mouth to speak her name.

She stared at me a moment and for that brief instant, there was nobody near. We were alone on that crowded thoroughfare. I saw tears glint in her eyes, and I saw what I meant to her, or maybe I saw the way I felt about her, my longing and need, reflected in her eyes.

She wanted to speak to me, this was clear. The tense way she paused there showed this. She let her gaze rove over my face, and move downward to the box with the mink jacket in it.

She didn't speak. She shook her head abruptly and turned, pretending to stare at something in the furrier's window.

She kept her face averted, kept walking past me. I felt my heart slugging and an awful ache of emptiness spreading beneath it.

I stared after Lois. I stood in the middle of the busy walk with a boxed mink worth three grand, staring after a girl who was too good to give me the time of day because I'd once been in trouble. I was no good.

I walked along the street, passing people who were no longer like me. I was a person apart, a thief. I had walked back into evil that made everything in the past seem mild.

I caught a bus, rode back to my apartment. My stomach was tied in knots, and I was shaking. Suddenly I saw that I was slated for prison again, as surely as I breathed, as surely as I lived long enough to be arrested. My mind sweated back across those cold gray days in the pen. Tin plates, inhumanity of bored guards, endless nights behind bars.

I couldn't gamble on that again, no matter what high stakes Collie held out. But what else was I going to do? If I didn't play along with Collie, I was on my way back to stir anyhow.

Run? Where? I'd disappeared once, and I had worked hard to make that disappearance stick. I'd sweated out my parole, left no forwarding address. But when I went to work at the Gorten Milk Company, word had gone back to the prison, and routinely they kept a record of my new address. This was the only way I could figure Collie's finding me.

I got off the bus, walked along the street, hurrying to nowhere, trying to outrun my thoughts and knowing I wasn't going to make it.

I couldn't stand the thought of being alone in my room. I stepped from the elevator and the corridor was empty, quiet. It was as if the whole world moved around me, past me, without touching me anymore.

As I turned toward my door, the elevator opened behind me but I did not glance that way. I was too filled with my own woes to care what went on around me.

"Baynard."

Del Lantis's voice lashed along the hallway and flicked at me. I paused and watched him walk toward me. The illness spread in me; now that I'd gotten involved with Kohzak again, Lantis was always around.

Had he learned to smell evil?

"Hi, Baynard."

I exhaled heavily. "What do you want?"

He grinned flatly at me. "Heard you bought a mink jacket today."

"Down payment," I said.

Staring at Lantis, I got a crazy idea that if I told him about Kohzak and the threat, he could help me. I didn't know how I could convince him I was on the level, maybe I couldn't, but I could try. If I got him on my side I had a slim chance of getting out of this alive, and free. No other one guy could help me as he could. Not only was he a smart cop, he could figure angles the way Kohzak could.

I held my breath, thinking that in Lantis maybe I'd found the one way to escape Collie and live.

I bit my lip, remembering the threat of that phone call. No matter what Lantis did to Kohzak, there was no way he could stop Kohzak's having me put away for the old jewelry heist. I couldn't stand prison, as long as there was a gamble that I could stay out.

I stopped thinking about telling Lantis anything.

"Something on your mind, Baynard?"

I jerked my head up, startled. He gave me the creepy feeling that he'd read my mind.

"No."

No matter how much Lantis might help me, he wasn't going to help me serve the stretch in prison Collie would see I got for crossing him.

Lantis stared at the chic box under my arm. "A down payment on a mink coat," he said. His eyes narrowed. "Must have taken a sizable wad even for a down payment."

"Five hundred dollars," I said. "As though you didn't already know."

Lantis nodded, admitting he had been in contact with Bochmeir's. "What I don't know is where'd you get five bills?"

"Isn't that my business?"

"You got no checking account that size."

"I saved it. Pennies in a milk bottle."

"You been robbing the milk company, punk?"

I wanted to hit him. My fist closing was an involuntary reflex. My muscles tightened. I knew he could probably take me in a fight, but just then I didn't care. I wanted the satisfaction of hitting him, no matter what it cost. My gaze chose the spot on the side on his jaw, point of violent contact.

He stared at me, his twisted smile daring me.

I managed to control my rage. "I robbed nobody. You got nothing else to say, get out of here."

"What kind of girl is it, Baynard, that would expect a mink coat from a milk man?"

"It's your wife. Now get out of here."

"The dame can't care much about you, putting you in hock like this. She must want to see you back of bars again. Is that what she wants, Baynard?"

"I don't know." My voice shook. "Get off my back."

"I'm not on your back, Baynard, she is." Lantis moved as though stepping aside. "Don't let me stand in your way. Run. Give it to her. Don't waste any time. Hurry into trouble. She says she wants mink but what she really wants is to see you back in stir, whoever she is."

"I'll give it to her when I get ready."

"Tonight, Baynard? Going to trade a down-payment mink for a quick tussel in bed? Man, you got a real bargain there. One night with some broad and back in the pen."

I met his gaze. "You've said it. Now get out of here."

He laughed. "Don't wait until tomorrow to give it to her, Baynard. You might think it over tonight. You might come to your senses by tomorrow. Oh, no. You run on over there with it now."

"You sound like a broken record—"

"I want you to hurry up. Get it over with."

"You got nothing else to say, I'm going to my room. Alone. Unless you came with a warrant, of course."

"Now, why would I come to see you with a warrant? When I come to get you, we won't need one."

I inserted my key in the lock. My hand shook. "Is that all?"

He shrugged.

7

I walked into my room and slammed the door shut behind me. To my ears it had the sound of metal bars clanging together in a cage. I prowled the room, bumping things. There was not even enough room to walk, no space to think.

And I was too full of rage to think. Lantis and his talk about mink — the terrible part of it was, he was right.

I'd bought that fur in a flash of rage and a desire for revenge. Before I gave it to Elva I had to be sure of a lot of things. Right now I was sure of nothing.

I opened the closet door. I pushed the Bochmeir's boxed mink up on the top shelf and stood looking at it. Smart cop, Lantis. So sure I'd give it to Elva today. Well, I'd wait. I'd choose my own moment.

I sprawled across the bed on my back and stared at the ceiling. In the late afternoon, a shaft of sunlight lay wedged between the bed and the bathroom door. Outside, the street was silent and then as people returned home from work, cars hurrying, the sounds increased and there was a steady throbbing of noise. Then the traffic quieted, kids yelled on the walks, skating and riding bicycles before dinner. Then the kids were quiet and there was only an occasional car and the sunlight dissolved and the window spilled gray all over the floor and it flooded the room, staining everything with darkness. And all that time I did not move.

My brain was like the balances on a pair of scales. Mink or milk route. Robbery or jail. Run or die. My thinking did not change, it just tilted first one way and then the other.

When it was dark in my room, I sat up, thinking it was time for my date with Elva. I had wasted all these hours and had gotten nowhere in my thinking because there was nowhere to go.

All the time I knew the cards were stacked and I had no choice.

I undressed, showered, shaved and dressed again. I knew I should eat something but I was not hungry, the thought of food made me nauseous.

I had a quick drink from a bourbon bottle, smoked a couple of cigarettes.

I stood before the mirror, knotting my tie. My face looked like a stranger's, a frightened stranger's.

I remembered the way I would have hurried to keep a date with Elva, the excitement I'd felt. All I felt now was trapped.

I started toward the door, turned and walked back around the bed, slid along it to the closet. Why should I let Lantis dictate when I gave Elva this mink? I was lonely, I wanted somebody on my side, even Elva.

I opened the closet door, stared up at the swank box with the mink jacket in it, just what Elva always wanted, something she wanted badly enough to cross Collie for.

I shook my head. I couldn't give it to Elva yet. Not tonight anyhow. I was too mixed up. I closed the door and walked out of the apartment.

Elva let me into her apartment. She held the door open and I looked around for her playmates, Collie and Pizzari, but she was alone. A dark evening dress glimmered along the elegant lines of her body. My heartbeat increased, no matter what I knew about her. I felt the charge of excitement in the room around us.

I managed to keep my arms at my sides.

"I've been cooped up too long, Sammy. I want to go out. I want to have fun. Let's pretend we're just a couple of guys with nothing to worry us."

"Where would that take us?"

She smiled. "Dinner somewhere with music, a nightspot later with a comic, where we could dance."

"I'm a milk man. That's not included in my salary or expense account. You better call Kohzak."

Her smile faded. "You've got five hundred bills."

"Yeah? I spent it already."

I saw the secret lights flare in Elva's eyes. She was really hungry for that mink. She wasn't trying for an academy award this time, this was a girl from the worst slums in town finally certain her greediest dream was coming true.

She came slowly forward and slipped her arms up around my neck, locking them. She pulled my head down to her parted lips.

The kiss and her probing tongue were hot, but I didn't ignite. I'd never realized what an artist she was at this love racket, how smooth and practiced those kisses were. I'd known she was no convent girl, but she never gave love, she sold it or traded it, and she had refined teasing to an art.

"You did buy the mink," she whispered. "Didn't you, Sammy?"

"Maybe."

"Stop teasing me!"

I laughed. "Can't you take teasing?"

Something flashed in her eyes, was instantly gone. She pulled on a smiling, wheedling mask. "You did buy it. You're a doll, Sammy. I can be nice to the man who buys me mink. Let me show you, Sammy."

"We better go out if we're going—"

"Later, Sammy."

"What if Collie comes up here—"

"Look at me, Sammy."

I felt numb, but I stood watching her unzip her dress and step out of it, letting me see what I had bought for my money. Collie and everything else in this world was forgotten except for that mink, and the way she wanted to make me hand it over right now.

"I hope this is worth dying for," I said.

Elva watched me and smiled confidently. I suppose she was already seeing herself in the luxuriant softness of that mink jacket.

For the first time I saw some of the power she held over men. Love and sex as such meant nothing to Elva, so she could withhold her favors forever, giving her body only for something in return. I even saw how she kept Collie dangling when he had to be smart enough to know she was faithless.

But I could not pull my gaze away from her. I was as entranced as if all this were not really just the exchange of one kind of merchandise for another.

She put out her bare arms to me, her body silken and shimmering, a glowing invitation to heaven and to hell.

"Come here, Sammy," she whispered.

I went to her as if drawn by some irresistible magnet.

"Do you like to look at me?" she whispered, and there was something almost human in her question, she needed to be reassured that her beauty was as fabled as it was available.

My hands moved on her, as if her body controlled them rather than my mind.

"Do you want me, Sammy," she whispered. "Tell me what you want, Sammy, and I'll do it for you."

I didn't know how we moved together to her bed. Lust was like a delicious poisoning in my brain.

She was crying out, "More, Sammy, I want more!"

We fought at each other in furious savagery, as if we needed to destroy. She was kissing me and crying out fiery words to burn away my last reluctance, my last will to resist her. She let her voice rise to a screaming wail, and I almost forgot why she had undressed and given herself to me. If this wild lust was not real, it was shaking me like some cataclysm. But then in the more feverish moment she wailed, "Oh, Sammy, won't I look beautiful in mink?"

After a long time, Elva stared up at me. "What's wrong?"

"Nothing. What would be wrong?"

"You're mad because I said that, about the mink—"

"What difference does it make? Why should I think you might want me now? You never did before."

She wiggled closer to me, her heated body naked, clinging to mine. "Oh, Sammy, I never had a mink before. You are going to give it to me now, aren't you?"

I didn't say anything.

She pouted. "Why are you putting me off, Sammy?"

"No reason. You'll get it."

"You think I'm not crazy about you. I told you, I'd do anything for the man who bought me mink."

Going home that night I felt as if I'd consumed champagne for hours. My head floated like a gas balloon on a kid's string, and my legs were rubbery.

When I walked along the corridor I saw that my apartment door hung open like a bird's broken wing. But for the moment I was still too filled with all the excitement that trailed me home from Elva's apartment to care very much.

I leaned against the doorjamb staring into my efficiency apartment. People walking in uninvited. This is what I got for belonging in neither the world of the good nor the world of the bad. I was suspended between them and nobody trusted me and nobody cared whether I'd object to their breaking and entering my room.

I was a guy without rights, without defense.

The rage ate through the warmth and I felt the anger building.

The lights were out. I snapped them on, flooding the small crowded room.

Suddenly I remembered the mink coat.

I lunged against the door, throwing it all the way open so that it banged against the wall. I ran across the room and jerked open the closet door. All I could think was that the mink was gone. Sweat stood on my face, dampened my shirt.

The box was up there with Bochmeir's lettered across it. Frantically, I reached up and pulled the box off the shelf. It was heavy with that same substantial, luxurious heaviness.

I tossed the box on my bed, told myself to simmer down and take it easy. I sank down on the mattress, untied the flossy ribbons and turned back the lid. My hands trembled so badly that I had to fight the knots.

The mink didn't look like it had been disturbed. I ran my hand across its softness.

I finally started breathing normally again. I folded the jacket, carefully returned it to its wrappings and replaced the box on the shelf.

I felt physically depleted. I shook out a cigarette, lit it, took one pull and ground it out in the tray on the night table. I went to the kitchenette, poured bourbon over the rocks.

I sat down on the edge of the bed. Fatigue rode the blood through my veins.

Sitting there, I could see my room had been thoroughly searched. They had not been careful, nor attempted to hide the fact they'd been here. Drawers gaped open, doors were ajar. It was a fast job but one done by somebody who knew exactly what he sought.

I finished off the drink, checked everything I owned. It didn't take long, and as far as I could see, nothing was missing.

I sat in my one easy chair and stared at the darkened window. I wondered if Collie had been here, knowing I was with Elva? What would Collie be seeking? Did Collie need to know I was not planning a double-cross? Collie was a man who had to be sure of a thing like that. Once he lost faith in one of his hired hands, things were never quite the same again.

If Collie no longer trusted me, that meant he was going to have me watched every minute until the robbery was staged. And if he didn't trust me, I knew better than to trust him: he'd throw me to the wolves in a second.

I thought about Elva, wondering if this once she was on the level. Would the mink jacket tip the scales in my favor? Was her lying too deeply ingrained to ever be changed? Or did she want freedom badly enough to gamble on crossing Kohzak to get it?

I shivered. Maybe Collie no longer trusted either Elva or me. If Collie was worried about what I'd done with that five hundred dollars he might have come up here, or sent Pizzari, to find out. Collie would worry about a deal like this until he had the answer.

I glanced toward the closet. Well, now he knew.

All I could feel was helpless.

Elva screamed like a kid on a roller-coaster when she gandered that furrier's box under my arm.

I got there early the next night. If Collie knew I had the fur, no sense holding off giving it to Elva. No reason standing there in the middle of the Rubicon, catching hell from both sides. I went all the way across.

Collie was there when I arrived. He sat at the little secretary desk figuring something on sheets of paper. He glanced over his shoulder and growled some sort of greeting when I walked in.

Pizzari sprawled in an easy chair reading a racing form. The three of them appeared comfortable, relaxed. Pizzari didn't even glance up when Elva yelped in pleasure.

"Sammy. Sammy."

She ran across the room, a sophisticated doll in a blue-white cocktail dress, acting like a child over that box.

She threw herself against me. She crushed her dress, mussed her hair, and none of it mattered.

She locked an arm about my neck. But she had only one arm for me. Her other hand clutched at the box, snatching it from my grasp.

I didn't say anything, I just watched her.

She gave me a single, hard kiss. Maybe it was as nearly an honest kiss as she'd ever given anybody, and it didn't last long.

She pulled away from me, still hugging that box. She forgot me, Collie, everything. She ripped away the cords, making little squealing sounds, and she wiggled with pleasure. Watching her, I thought one might like to think a woman found such pleasure in her lovemaking, but she never did.

Kohzak forgot the papers he was working on. He turned slightly in the straight chair and then did not move again.

He held a cigar between his fingers. He did not lift it to his mouth. It was only in his black eyes where things happened, shadows lunged and crazy wraiths appeared, dancing and weaving. His eyes got blacker, seeming to sink into their sockets.

I glanced at Collie, felt my gaze pulled back to him. I'd never seen anything bug Collie quite like this. No matter what he thought, he never showed it outwardly.

Now he stared at Elva. She oozed into the gray mink jacket and floated about the room, hugging it against her face.

Collie's fingers tightened on the cigar and it crumpled in his fist, a mass of dried tobacco leaf and filler, expensive nothing.

His voice lashed at her, a hard cruel sound. "If you can stand still, tramp, I'll tell you people something important. I've made up my mind when we'll lift that payroll."

8

Elva stopped dancing around the room but she did not remove the jacket. "Look at me, Collie," she said.

"Knock it off," he told her.

She stared at him a moment, her eyes chilled, but then she flopped into a chair, hugging the mink, smoothing it, the way she might stroke a cat.

"Anybody else got anything real important to say?" Collie snarled, glaring around the room. He did not meet my gaze. "If nobody has, maybe you can pay attention to me. Maybe we ought to do something that will bring in some money."

He waited and nobody said anything. I rubbed my hands across my face, just to be sure I was really there, that I'd sunk back into this evil again, that I was with Collie, hearing the date set for another robbery.

Pizzari tossed the racing form aside, staring at Collie, concentrating. He had to listen closely to Collie's plans; sometimes they were difficult for Scotty to follow, even when he concentrated.

Elva pulled the mink collar forward. "Stiff seams down the front," she murmured, speaking to nobody in particular.

"It's just new," Collie snarled at her. "Shut up, will you?"

"All right, Collie."

Collie squatted forward on the edge of his chair. He riffled through his notes. His collar was open, his face sweated.

"Day after tomorrow night. The payroll is delivered to Gorten's tomorrow. The guard relaxes the day after, then it gets a little tighter on payday." He shrugged. "We go in there on their relaxed time. Couldn't look better."

"Sounds all right to me, Boss," Pizzari said.

"How about you, Sammy?"

Collie stared at me.

I shrugged my shoulders. "What difference does it make what I think?"

Collie laughed and Pizzari said, "Yeah."

Elva fumbled with the single large button on the jacket lining. She didn't bother to look up.

Collie's voice snapped at her. "You got that, doll? Day after tomorrow night we take the cream from the milk company."

"Odd buttons," Elva mused. "One on each lining."

Collie sprang from his chair. He ran over to her. Her head jerked up, face bloodless, and she stared up at him. It was as if she hadn't known he existed.

She opened her mouth to scream in protest, but no sound was made.

Collie struck her across the face with the back of his hand, bringing his arm upward. It made a hollow, whacking sound of knuckles against flesh in the silent room.

Pizzari sat forward on the edge of his chair, his eyes glistening. His face twisted, as if he were watching the bloody climax of a cock fight. His head tilted slightly to one side and he breathed through his parted lips.

I did not move. I didn't take my gaze off them. It was not the first time I'd witnessed a scene like this, but Collie had never gotten so quickly aroused to rage before. I knew he was hitting her because of the mink jacket, not because she had ignored him.

"Will you listen, tramp?" His voice was hoarse and he crouched above her, his arms extended at his sides, his shoulders slouched round. His gaze dug into her, waiting to see what she would do. "Will you just shut up and listen?"

He breathed in short, hard rasps.

Elva sprawled with her head against the chair arm where his blow had sent her. She stayed there, staring up at him. If anyone had looked at me with such seething hatred it would have scared me.

Collie was unmoved. They knew each other and all their moods, dangers and weaknesses. He knew her fears and he worked on them. He knew her strengths and avoided them.

He waited while the flaring hatred burned itself out in her eyes.

His breathing quieted and he straightened, running his hands through his hair.

He turned away then and paced the room. He talked about the planned robbery. "Elva will watch. She'll let us out, drive away, and the three of us will go in the plant. It will take the three of us. Pizzari will take the money. So, Scotty, that means you'll carry the suitcase in and out. Sammy and I will handle the clerks and the guards. I figure with bookkeepers and stenos, even the night crew will be plenty for me and Sammy to handle. I've figured the exact number of minutes you'll be allowed for taking the money, Scotty, and if you go overtime, we won't get out of there."

"When did I ever foul up, boss?"

"Just see that you don't!" Collie spoke urgently now, explaining to them the entrances and exits of the milk plant. He had it better than a blueprint. I'd spent a year at Gorten's and I didn't know the place as well as he did.

In my mind I saw us getting in there and moving along the corridor. I could see how it was going to be in every detail.

I could smell the gun smoke.

"Through this door," Collie was saying to Scotty for the tenth time. "We go through this door, Scotty. Now there are several doors along here. None are marked, all have the same colored glass in them. Now, pick it out, Scotty. Which door?"

It had been going on for a long time. Collie left nothing out. He planned every move to the minutest detail. I knew this had always worked before, but I no longer had faith.

Scotty studied the floor plan. "It's this door, boss," he said. He sounded proud. "We come in here, and we go up these steps."

"How many steps, Scotty?"

"Uh, eighteen."

"Right, eighteen steps. That's going to be important when we start out of there, Scotty. Then what?"

"We go up them eighteen steps. We come out into this corridor where all them doors are. It's six doors on the right, and it's double doors. Glassed."

Their voices droned on. They went over it all again, and again. Pizzari's face was pasty and his eyes bulged with weariness. Kohzak's blue-white shirt was soaked with perspiration.

Gradually the livid marks of Collie's hand faded from Elva's cheek. During the interminable planning she had remained sitting crookedly in that chair the way she had sprawled when Collie struck her.

At last she sat up and moved her hands along the mink. She appeared to put everything from her mind except that jacket. Her hands stroked it lovingly.

I lay on the couch half across the gray room from her. The place smelled of cigar smokes, and swirls of it drifted across the ceiling. An empty bourbon bottle had rolled against a chair leg. The ashtrays overflowed and papers littered the carpeting.

I let my gaze move from Elva to Collie to Pizzari. I was exhausted with going over it, and hating what I was doing and hating myself because I didn't know any way out of this death trap.

They were no longer real to me. Being in this room with them was like waking up with people from your nightmares and finding them still with you.

Collie had forgotten everything else except the everlasting details of that robbery. Pizzari was scared in his guts that he might miss something, forget something. Elva was unable to concentrate on what they said because of that fur jacket, and yet unable to enjoy the sensual luxury of it because of their voices and the urgency of their planning.

I hadn't realized how much I'd forgotten in the five years away from them. I watched them snarling like jackals over carrion, and I knew I'd better like it because this was the only world I was allowed to belong to. The world where Lois lived was reserved for people who never made mistakes, or weren't caught at them. They wouldn't let me in.

When they had talked until their voices were hoarse and raspy, Collie called it a night.

He and Scotty left. Neither of them said good night to Elva and she didn't look up when they went out.

I watched them shrug into their coats and go out the door. The tension went out of the apartment with them.

Elva hugged the jacket to her, got up and stood before a full-length mirror. She pirouetted, pleased and fascinated with her reflection.

She went around the room wearing that jacket, emptying ashtrays, closing up for the night.

"Messy," she said. "Collie's always been messy like this."

"He doesn't like you having that coat," I said.

"Collie?" She laughed, hugging herself. She named the place where Collie could go.

I watched her carry the empty whisky bottle out, straighten pillows, collect papers.

I exhaled. I knew then as I had never known in five years away from her how free I was of her. She was no longer what I wanted. In the same thought, I knew what I did want, and I scowled, knowing I'd never have that, either.

"Here I am," I said aloud.

Elva didn't hear me. She finished straightening the room, returned to the mirror to admire herself.

"Looks like I'm where I belong." It didn't matter if she heard me or not, because really I was talking to myself.

"Sure, Sammy," she said distantly. She turned, getting her light at a new angle.

"No matter how hard I fought, I couldn't get away from you people."

"Why would you want to, Sammy?" She stood on her toes, watching her reflection. "Isn't it fabulous?"

She didn't even bother to hear if I answered her or not.

I didn't say anything.

I felt lonely and beaten. I could see Collie, Scotty and me going into that plant, but I could not force my mind to show me how it would be coming out. I couldn't see that at all.

She stared at herself in the mirror. Elva had her mink. Collie had his robbery plans. Lois had her security and her social status.

I poured myself a stiff shot of bourbon over rocks.

Elva's voice touched at me, bemused. "You're just tired, that's all. It's late. You'll feel better in the morning, Sammy."

Sure, I thought. Put it out of my mind. Think about something else. Think about Elva.

I sat on her couch, watching her. No matter what she'd been through living with Kohzak, that mink still set her off beautifully. She glittered like some hard, perfect gem set in a rich background.

I wanted to put the robbery out of my mind, and there was only one way I knew.

"Elva. Come here."

She turned, glanced at me over her shoulder, still thinking about her mink jacket. "What?"

I took another deep drink. "I need you to be nice, Elva. You said you could be. That's what I want. Show me how nice you can be."

"Oh, Sammy, how can you think about something like that now?"

Anger surged up through me. "You mean there's something else?"

I stared around this chic gray room, this world I was doomed to exist in, and tried to find something else, any other meaning for existence.

"We got so much on our minds, Sammy."

I stood up, gazing at that lovely body, the firm breasts, the slender hips, the long legs — a body made for love, wasted on a mind concerned only with avarice.

"So much on your mind." I took a step toward her, feeling the urgent charges of lust and rage flooding through me on bared wires of hatred. Hatred was stronger than desire. Desire could be turned off by contempt, a brush-off, by a lack of returned emotion. But hatred? That was something else again. What could stop hatred?

Elva stared up into my eyes. She tried to laugh. "Don't you ever think of anything else, Sammy?"

"I wanted you for years when I never got to touch you at all."

"Sammy, don't."

It was a warning sound but I didn't bother heeding it. I walked toward her. She glanced about wildly, but did not move. Her gaze returned to my face. Her cheeks paled and her eyes widened.

"Sammy." She shook her head again.

But now it was just a word without meaning. We both knew it. "You're giving me the brush again, Elva? So soon?"

"No, Sammy, but you better think about Collie."

"What about him?"

"You said it. He was sore about this jacket. He might come back up here."

"To hell with him. You're not giving me the brush, Elva. Not again. That's all I ever got from you before."

"Collie didn't catch us last night, *before* you collected your mink."

She took a backward step, or only a half-step because she saw it wasn't going to do any good to run.

"Sammy, you'll crush my jacket."

I caught the mink by its collar and peeled it off. I threw it across the room. It struck a chair then settled to the floor. For a horrified moment Elva stared after it, her face drawn.

Then I caught her arms and shook her, forcing her to look at me and think about me. I was alone and I couldn't stand loneliness just now. I couldn't stand to think. I was afraid to.

Her head jerked around and she stared up at me. I was somebody she'd never seen before. I ripped away the cocktail dress. She started to protest, but she was a smart girl. She got the message from my eyes and suddenly she saw the dress didn't matter.

I lifted her in my arms and laid her down on her bed. She struggled against me, then lay still, neither aiding nor resisting me. Her eyes remained half closed, her lips in a catlike smile.

Something had finally driven the thought of that mink jacket from her greedy little mind.

In that smart gray room I lost all track of time. At first Elva remained limp, like sackcloth spread beneath me on the bed. But hatred did something that my desire had never done. Slowly, but then more urgently, she ignited, growing hotter and wilder.

She cried aloud and clawed, slashing at my throat with sharp white teeth.

The telephone rang. It rang twenty times, a hundred times, it kept ringing as though it was never going to stop. It was a symphony to what we were doing, it was cadence and rhythm and tempo. It was the wild kind of background music the whole frantic affair called for.

Collie was screaming at her, that telephone bell was his clawing at her cage, but I had her and he couldn't get to her and she didn't hear his screaming or his rage, or the way his talons raked her cage. For maybe the first time in her life, Elva forgot herself.

She was mine for this moment and she knew it.

For me she was the narcotic I needed, dissipating the last fear of what lay ahead of me, of what I had to face, or of what was behind me. She was an anesthetic, bringing physical satiety and insensibility to allay all the unendurable pains accumulated inside me.

Finally I toppled away from her and she lay across the bed on her back, exhausted, her panting the loudest sound in the room. Both of us were covered with sweat.

I sank off the bed and leaned against it, sitting on the floor with my head back on the mattress.

I got up at last and prowled the room. She lay unmoving with her eyes wide, watching me.

I saw nothing in that room but Elva's gray, bloodless face. It was like a mask of evil. She'd been an evil goddess for me since the first time I saw her. At a word from her, I sat up and barked; but no more.

When I stared at her too long, she smiled at me, faintly, placatingly, but she didn't change her position on that bed. She lay exactly as I'd left her, except that her whole naked body sagged with her sweated weariness.

"You never meant to leave him, did you, Elva?"

"What?"

"You belong to Collie. No matter what I do to you. Always have. Always will."

Her hand trailed off the side of the rumpled bed, her fingers touching at the carpeting. She did not speak.

After a moment I turned away and walked to the window. I stared out at the silent darkness, wondering if Collie and I had changed places, if he were out here, staring up at this lighted window, waiting.

I'd stood outside once, watching the light in her window until Collie doused it and took her to bed.

I'd stood helpless, raging inside myself. But Collie would be able to vent his rage on me. A knife. A gun from the window of a moving car.

I shrugged, unable to see how he could hurt me enough now to make me care. What difference did it make if I died out there tonight, or in some stupid robbery on some other night?

I no longer feared Kohzak's standing out there waiting. They'd dragged me to the last place I ever thought I'd be: where nothing they could do could hurt me any more.

My mouth twisted into a cold smile. I felt I knew a better reason why Kohzak would not avenge his sweet little tramp tonight. He wanted no trouble in the next two days to upset those precise plans of his; it was too near time for the robbery.

Elva was so silent I thought she had fallen asleep. I turned, gazing at her. She lay with her eyes open, watching me. She had not moved.

I laughed. "Going to sleep in that mink tonight, Elva?"

I waited, but she did not answer. I walked away from the window, looking down at her. That meaningless smile tugged at her mouth.

I dressed, went to the door, opened it. She spoke then. "Don't go, Sammy. Please stay."

He stood down among those shadows all right, like a jealous school boy. His light topcoat was turned up about his neck. He stared up at the light in her window. I was almost past the bush where he stood before he saw me.

"Baynard."

The word was a curse. I stopped, crossed the walk to him.

I laughed at him. I couldn't help it, because I remembered the way I'd stood helpless with rage as he was now.

He seemed to shrivel inside that top coat. He kept his hands thrust deep in the pockets.

"You're not very smart," I said, "standing out here this time of the morning. If the police picked you up now it would foul all your exact planning, wouldn't it?"

He stared at me as if he had never seen me before, would never forget my face.

"You're not very smart either." His voice shook.

I shrugged.

"You act real dumb."

"But you're clever, standing out here like cop bait?"

"I called her. A hundred times. If she was up there, why didn't she answer?"

"I don't know. Why don't you go up and ask her?"

He sounded choked. "You were up there all this time?"

"You knew I didn't leave when you did."

"I didn't think nothing about that. She says she wouldn't let you touch her."

I shrugged again.

"Why didn't she answer the phone?" he said again.

Funny how soft the brain of even the sharpest man gets when he's thinking with his hips about some faithless doll that he's known is faithless but that he can't stay away from. It's like a disease. I should know. Collie was infected, but I'd suffered from it, too.

"Why didn't she answer?" he growled.

He didn't expect an answer, but I said, "I don't know." He trembled with suppressed rage. I had the knife in, and I twisted it. "Maybe she was asleep. Or lying down, or something."

I turned then and walked away, expecting to get a shiv in the back. Collie was an avaricious man, and a cautious one, but he was out of his mind at the moment.

"Baynard."

I stopped again.

"You think you got me where you want me," he said. "You think because of my plans I'll take this."

I shrugged. "Do what you want to do."

His eyes leaped up, struck against me. He saw that I no longer cared whether I lived or died. He almost believed it. His voice quavered. "We got this other job first, Baynard. But there'll be time after that. And don't you forget it."

I shrugged and walked away, leaving him standing there staring at the window. The light was out now.

9

The alarm was ringing when I walked into my apartment. It had the tired sound that meant it was about to run down. It was time to deliver the cow juice. Hard to believe that I'd ever had a life that involved nothing except working and being honest. I'd learned just one truth. You make a mistake, you never stop paying.

I undressed and stepped under a warm shower and let the spray sting life into me. Gradually I cut down the warm water until the shower struck me like icy prongs. I felt weariness washing out of me.

When I stepped out of the shower I heard the telephone ringing.

I hesitated, scowling. It was almost four a.m. I didn't know how long the phone had been ringing, but I didn't want to answer it.

Who'd be calling me at this hour?

I stood there rubbing myself with the towel.

A feeling of emptiness spread through me. Had Collie come up with an angle for hitting back at me?

I knotted the towel around my waist, walked over to the telephone. "Hello?"

It was Lois.

"Sam," she said. "I haven't slept all night."

No wonder, I thought, if there's any empathy between us at all, you must have felt something unusual in the way I spent the night.

Her voice went on, tears in it. "I haven't slept since I acted so terribly when you needed me."

Have you ever heard angels sing? Her voice was like that. It was all the goodness and gentleness in the world. It was the promise of the good that I'd missed on that bed in that gray room with Elva.

It was good to hear Lois's voice, even when I knew it wasn't going to get us anywhere. It was too late for that now.

"I've been lying awake all night, Sam."

I stood there, listening, hearing the charged hum of the wires in the night and then her voice like soft kisses spun across those wires to me.

"I knew you'd be waking up to go to work, Sam. I needed to talk to you. I had to tell you I'm sorry the way I acted, the way father acted."

I pressed the receiver against my ear to hear her better, because her soft voice faltered and had tears in it, and need.

I felt exultant for a moment, thinking that Lois did need me. Then all the rest of it washed across my mind, and Lois's needing me didn't matter much.

If she'd thought I was evil before, she hadn't seen anything. Wait until I pulled this job, robbed the milk company where they'd gambled on me and given me a break, where they actually wanted to trust me, and went around with fingers crossed hoping I'd make good.

I'm going to rob them, Lois, those good people. I'm going to pull a silk stocking over my head so I'll look like a creature from space. Thief. No-good. That's the guy you stay awake all night feeling sorry for, and needing.

I breathed in deeply and it hurt.

"Sorry, baby," I said. "You must have the wrong number. Why don't you try the lonely hearts editor at the newspaper?"

"Sam—"

"Spare me. It's too early in the morning. I haven't had my coffee."

"I love you, Sam."

"Oh, come on now!"

"Sam, you must know I love you."

"Not on an empty stomach, doll."

The line went dead. There was a protracted silence, as if she were sitting there across town in that brick home on Elm Street, and was holding her breath, waiting for me to tell her I loved her.

The silence stretched taut and then I heard the click as she replaced the receiver.

She was gone. This time for sure.

I pressed the phone hard against my ear. I listened to the hum of the wires. I thought, that lonely sound is going to be the only sound left on earth when life ends here.

When? It had ended when Lois hung up.

Finally I dropped the receiver back into its cradle. I beat my fists against the wall, clenched them until there was blood in my palms.

I dialed the milk plant.

"Gorten Milk. Delivery department. Kramer speaking."

"Kramer, this is Baynard."

"College, what you calling at this hour for? You trying to wake me up? You're supposed to be down here loading."

"Not today, Kramer. I'm sick."

"A big boy like you?"

"That's the way it goes."

"No kidding. College, I'm sorry. Is there anything I can do?"

"Will you assign a relief driver?"

"Sure. First time you ever called in sick. Glad to do it. But that's not what I meant. Anything I can do to help?"

"No. I'll probably be all right tomorrow."

"Hope so. Anything you need today, let us know."

I replaced the receiver. I thought about Kramer, about all the people at the milk company. They were good folks. Decent human beings. People — like Lois Rowell — living in the kind of world I wanted to live in, but never could.

I stalked that room, pacing it the way a puma paces his cage at the zoo, not getting anywhere, not expecting to get anywhere, but feeling the cage closing in on all sides.

Lois loved me and because she did, I couldn't go on with this robbery, even if I had broken off with her. That was something I couldn't do.

I knew I was going back to prison, but one other thing might happen that would make it worthwhile. Maybe I could stop Kohzak.

Anyway, that telephone call from Lois at 3 a.m. showed me one thing: what was right. As old man Rowell had said, there was no compromise between right and wrong.

I had tried to believe there was, thinking I could pull this last robbery and then it would end. But I knew. It would never end; only a bullet would do that.

I went over all the angles. I wanted to stop Kohzak, but all the time I tried to figure an angle so I could do it and stay alive, and out of prison.

It looked as if this was asking too much. All the odds were stacked against me. I had nothing to gain by choosing to go honest. But I could play along with Collie and, if I lived and was paid off, I might get away and start a new life somewhere. That's what I could do if I kept my mouth shut and went through with it.

I couldn't have Lois anyway, whether I went through with the robbery or not, and if I didn't go through with it, I was throwing my life away.

Right then, that didn't look like much.

I dressed, refusing to think about anything anymore. There were angels, but not for me — for me there was only the straight and narrow, and that led back to a prison cell.

I walked down to the corner, caught a downtown bus. There were half a dozen people riding drowsily to early jobs. They dozed, but I did not. I sat tense in my seat, watching the town slide past.

I paused outside the police station. It looked bedraggled and grimy, glistening with oily dew before daybreak. Lights glowed yellow in the upstairs cell blocks.

I went in to the duty sergeant and asked for Lieutenant Lantis.

The desk sergeant stared at me as if he were going to give me a drunkometer test.

"Lieutenant Lantis? This time of the morning? Are you kidding?"

"I've got to see him."

"Suppose you come back later today."

"What time does he come in?"

"Around eight."

"I'll wait."

The duty sergeant stared at me. He shook his head. "Okay. Sit over there."

Waiting was bad. It was like sweating out an operation that might save your life but promises pain and long hours of surgery.

As I sat there, vice cops herded in a covey of teen-age dames. Most of them were hastily dressed in stretch pants and shirts or sweaters and shorts. They looked as if they should have been in high school but their eyes were old with evil, and they were charged with prostitution.

They were booked, fingerprinted and herded away along the corridors. They screamed and yelled back over their shoulders. Vagrants and drunks were brought in, but they were not as loud as the young girls.

At eight, the duty sergeant glanced over at me and told me to go up to the second floor. I think he was surprised to find me still there.

It wasn't much better up there, or any cleaner, but it was quieter.

I saw Lantis stride into the long, desk-crowded office. He looked underfed, hungrier than usual, and his shirt was already sweated at this hour. I stood up, and when he saw me his face twisted into an odd smile.

"Come to give yourself up, Baynard?"

Freshly shaved, his shirt loose about his turkey neck, Lantis didn't look much better than he did at the end of a day. His suit was rumpled and his eyes were red-veined.

He jerked his head toward his desk. He kicked a chair around the side of it for me.

While I sat down, Lantis lit a cigarette and took a long, hungry drag.

He sat down behind his desk, watching me through the haze of smoke. "Give me the statement, Baynard. We'll type it up and you can sign it."

I did not care that he rode me — in fact, he seemed less sardonic than usual, but that didn't matter, either. I felt I was exactly what he had called me all along.

Maybe it was the four long hours I'd spent watching cops haul in the drunk and the derelict. They were tired, but they were doing their job. And that's what Lantis was doing. He was a better cop, and smarter, but still doing part of that job.

I glanced at him. A good man, giving all his intelligence and all his energy to apprehending people like Kohzak and me. Some of the criminals, like Collie, were smart and made few or no mistakes, making Lantis's job tougher.

Lantis was on the side of the law where I wanted to be. I couldn't make that, but I wasn't going to be like Kohzak, either. Not any more.

Beyond that, I did not know and did not try to see. It all loomed ahead like a dead-end street. Prison, if Collie acted quickly enough. Death, if Collie could get the word to his goons. It didn't take a lot of figuring.

I drew a deep breath and stared at my hands. I said, "I came here because I didn't know what else to do. What I'm going to tell you, you won't believe but part of, anyway. If I can get you to believe the part that matters, that's all I care."

"Why not try me and see?"

I frowned. "Are you ill, or is this Be Good to a Fink Week?"

He smiled and shrugged. "I'm just waiting to see what kind of gimmick you're trying to work on me now."

"When I came here to Dexter city, I tried to go straight, be honest."

He thrust his tongue around over his teeth and nodded without taking his eyes off me. "Found it too tough, eh?"

I just met his gaze, kept my voice level. "Gorten trusted me. He was the first man who had in six years. I don't care what you think, part of the reason I wanted to be honest was because he had faith in me, when I couldn't even get a job digging ditches."

He shrugged. "I'm filled in on you right up to this morning. What surprised me was seeing you inside a police station of your own free will."

"Okay. So you won't buy it that I wanted to be honest. What matters is that a guy named Collie Kohzak is in this town and he's trying to force me to go along with him in robbing the Gorten Milk Company tomorrow night."

Lantis didn't say a word. He drew hard to his cigarette again and leaned back in his swivel chair, studying me.

Silence thickened between us. Lantis's mouth twitched, he scratched at his eyelid. From the tank a drunk's singing was the loudest thing in the station. Outside on the streets, Dexter City was waking up and cars gunned, roaring when traffic signals changed.

"Kohzak came to this town for no other reason," I said at last.

"There must be more. Where did you know Kohzak?"

I drew a deep breath, then shrugged. "I used to work with him, before I went to prison."

His gaze hardened and he crushed out the cigarette viciously in an ash tray. "He just came here, cased the town, and then followed you?"

"Yes."

"Or did he send you ahead to case the town, and set up a deal like the milk company?" He drew some lines on a scratch pad. "And you're going to help him?"

"He says I am."

"And what do you say?"

My fists clenched on the corner of his desk. "I'm here, trying to tell you about it."

"That's what interests me. What's the angle, Baynard? What's your gimmick? Before you go on with this confession, let me tell you two things. I don't make deals. The D.A. might. The courts might. But I don't. Don't expect anything from me, no matter what you tell me."

"I don't."

"And the other thing you better understand is this: if this turns out to be a gimmick, I'll lean on you, boy, and you never had trouble until that happens."

He gazed at me as if I were a fat rat swimming in a sewer. It made me sick the way he looked at me because I finally realized no matter what I told him, or what I did, nothing could make him trust me.

I drew a deep breath, and talking slowly, I outlined Kohzak's plan, exactly as he had run through it a dozen times in Elva's apartment last night.

At first Lantis kept looking for the gimmick, but finally it got through to him: there was a robbery being planned.

When I finally stopped talking, Lantis sat there for a long time. Only his mind was working, and his face showed nothing.

At last he said, "You want me to buy this, Baynard?"

I shook my head. "That's up to you. You wouldn't listen before. I'll tell you why I'm in it after working for a year at Gorten's under your eagle eye."

He waited.

"I worked on a heist at Kleizac's Jewelers. Most of the stones never showed up, or they hadn't when I was arrested, and that was the last I heard of it. That case is still open. Kohzak says it is, and he never lies when he's using something as a threat. He will turn me over to the police on the old Kleizac matter if I don't go through with this for him."

Lantis's expression did not alter. "You just turned yourself over to the police."

"I told you. I don't care. I'm not going through with it."

He stood up, walked around his desk and sat on the edge of it. "I'm supposed to believe that Kohzak is blackmailing you into pulling this job at the plant where you've worked just long enough to have the layout and floor plans down perfectly?"

I peered at the window. "I don't care what you believe."

"And if I arrest you now, it would stop the robbery, eh?"

"Probably. Kohzak is cautious. He's been operating a long time, and as far as I know he's never served one day in prison."

"And if I don't let the robbery take place, I have nothing on Kohzak."

"I don't know. I'd say you didn't."

"I'd say I didn't, too. I told you I never make deals, but it looks like you think you've crowded me into making one with you. You're a pretty cool type coming up here like this. I'm supposed to thank you and let you go."

I shifted in the chair, sweating. "I don't care what you do. There's going to be a robbery tomorrow night. You know where Kohzak and Pizzari are. You can pick them up, you can stop the robbery. You're the cop. I'm not trying to tell you what to do."

He stared at me. "I know where you are too, Baynard. I could lock you up."

I shrugged.

"Maybe I could sweat you down until you tell me what's your angle."

"I don't have any angle. Why don't you check on that Kleizac's robbery in Detroit? You'd know then if I were lying."

"I'd know then if you were lying about Kleizac's." His voice was sharp. His red-rimmed eyes blinked as if he were dead for sleep, a cop who had nothing to live for except being a cop.

Lantis sat down at his desk again, fiddled with the junk on top if it, scribbled on some papers, looked me over a few times.

At last he said, "For now, Baynard, you carry on, just as you are. You deliver your milk, you string along with Kohzak."

I nodded and stood up.

His voice gouged at me. "And keep me in mind, bad boy, because I'll be watching you."

I walked out of his office, feeling his gaze hard on my back.

10

I walked out of the police station and paused on the steps, troubled without knowing why.

It was a gloomy day without the promise of any sun. Cars raced along the street when the traffic signals turned green, exhaust fumes billowing thick and dingy gray.

I shrugged my jacket up on my shoulders and went down the steps and along the walk to the corner. The light changed to red before I got there. Brakes squealed and cars lined up six deep.

Cars were parked in all the spaces before the police station. I don't know why my attention was drawn to them, maybe it was that unexplained sense of wrong.

I looked over the parked cars and stopped. For a second I stood as though paralyzed on the curb. Finally I forced myself to calm down and to recheck that black car parked second from the corner.

The car's engine was running at idle, its driver ready to pull out into the stream of traffic.

I recognized Scotty Pizzari behind the wheel.

Panic swirled in my gut. Pizzari the trigger man, the killer. Five years ago, I'd seen Kohzak send Pizzari out to lean on some enemy or ex-friend, and I never saw the guy again. And Pizzari never changed. Killings didn't touch him, any more than losing at the races.

I went cold all over. I saw that from the viewpoint of mobsters, I'd finked by running to Lantis, the deadliest sin in their code.

Pizzari's eyes nailed me, unblinking. It was like looking into the eyes of a rattlesnake. The sound of his engine at idle sounded thunderous in my ears.

I glanced over my shoulder toward the open door of the police station. I could turn and go back, but what would that buy me?

I could run back to Lantis, but finally I'd have to come out of that place alone. Pizzari was as patient as he was deadly. He could wait.

I shrugged my jacket up on my shoulders. No sense going to the police. I needed protection, but there is no law that says a man can't warm up his engine in a parking place. Pizzari was playing it so honest that he'd even fed the parking meter.

I wouldn't get any protection from Lantis. He wanted Kohzak to proceed with his plan. There was nothing that was going to save me from what Kohzak had planned.

The traffic signal changed. Cars from the cross street moved across in the pedestrian lane. For the moment I was too stunned to move.

I heard Pizzari gun his motor slightly. I stared toward him, but he appeared completely unaware of me. Only I knew better.

I stepped across the gutter, walking toward the far side of the street. A car made a left turn in front of me and I had to stand there waiting for it. I felt chilled in the middle of my back, as if I was wearing a target between my shoulders.

Pizzari pulled his car out of its parking place. He signaled for a left turn, moving into the stream of traffic beside me.

I moved faster, reaching the far curb. Suddenly I saw I had no place to go. I couldn't go to the milk company. I'd told them I was sick. If I went to the apartment I would be like sitting in a barrel, waiting.

I glanced over my shoulder, sweating.

I stepped up on the walk, sick, wondering where to turn. Ahead of me on the next main street was a large department store advertising a gigantic white sale. I headed that way.

I heard brakes squeal out on the street as Pizzari got too near the middle. He didn't care about the snarling drivers of other cars. He wanted to keep me in sight.

He drove along at less than ten miles an hour, staying behind me. I could feel those merciless eyes fixed unblinkingly on me.

The light was with me but also it was with Pizzari. If I crossed to the big department store, Pizzari could move across the street, too, turn left and block me, or do whatever Kohzak had ordered. Even if hell froze, Pizzari would follow Kohzak's plan to the letter.

I turned left at the corner and walked rapidly away to the near side of the street. I heard the squealing protest of brakes as Pizzari made a sharp left turn in the path of a dozen cars.

I walked as fast as I could, almost running. I heard, above all the other traffic sounds, the way Pizzari gunned his engine. When I was sure it was lunging forward, I stopped dead in my tracks, whirled around and walked swiftly back the way I had come.

More screaming brakes told me that Pizzari had stopped the black car but there was nothing he could do except keep moving with the stream of traffic until he could turn. Horns blared at him.

I stepped between two cars, strode across the street, jaywalking in the middle of the block. I didn't know if Pizzari saw me in his rearview mirror. It didn't bother me now.

I stepped between parked cars to the crowded walk outside the department store, banners strung in the windows. I managed to worm my way through the overflow crowd. I pushed between the grumbling women toward the door and when I reached it, I stopped, breathless.

There was a sale, but the reason why the walks were blocked was that the store did not open for another hour.

I checked across the heads of the people around me. I did not see Pizzari's car.

I worked through the crowd and went along the walk again, hurrying. At a men's haberdashery, I went inside and spent twenty minutes discussing suits and slacks with a salesman.

The shop had only one street entrance, so I was forced to return through it to Broad Street. When I stepped out of the store, I saw Pizzari at once. He leaned against the wall at the store exit.

He walked close to me and I felt the snout of a gun against my spine. I knew it was concealed in his pocket. He was ready to use it. He followed orders.

"Why don't you come quiet?" he said. "You can run all day, but it ain't going to do you any good."

He had logic on his side, as well as the concealed gun. I shrugged.

"Now you're being smart, Sammy. Just keep walking straight ahead. I'll tell you when to stop. And don't try to get cute. You got to know that the easiest way to kill is to shoot in a crowd and just walk away."

We went through the crowds outside the department store. I thought of a dozen things I might do, but discarded them.

We crossed the street to the place where Scotty had parked in a loading zone. A red police summons hung on his steering wheel. Even before he opened the door for me, he reached in, jerked the ticket off and tore it up. He threw the pieces into the gutter.

"Get in, Sammy," he said.

"Where are we going?"

He kept his voice low and flat and deadly. "You want to get in quiet, punk? Or do you want to get a slug in your spine right here in the street?"

I turned slightly, glancing at him. It was as if the contempt and hatred were frozen in his features so that his expression could not alter. No matter what Pizzari had thought of me before, and I never had known, even from the first, I was too low to spit on now. I was a fink who ratted to the cops.

He held the door open. I got in. He closed it after he slid in under the wheel.

"Milk man," he said, putting contempt in the words. "Get up early. You don't get up early enough to outsmart the boss."

Again he had that deadly logic on his side.

"I seen finks like you. They used to come along all the time. Ain't seen one in years now, though. Not since people woke up to the fact that the boss is smart enough to stay out of stir. You stay rich and you stay out of the pokey in the boss's racket, you got to be smart, punk. You ought to know that."

I didn't say anything.

We wheeled through the street.

"Looks like you'd know," Pizzari persisted. "First time you tried to think for yourself, what happened? You drew yourself five to ten in the state pen. What makes you think you're so much smarter now than you used to be?"

"Why don't you just drive?" I said.

He laughed as if this were a joke. "What's the matter, chump? You in a hurry?"

Pizzari drove the car with one hand. He kept the gun on his lap, safety off, trigger fingered.

I sweated. The gun could be fired if we hit a bump, or if someone suddenly stopped ahead of us and Pizzari bumped them.

The set look on his dark face, the smug smile seemed to say he knew all this.

He was a good driver and there was something else: he had no sense of responsibility toward other drivers. He was not worried about taking paint or fenders off, if they got in his way. Other drivers seemed to sense this and gave him room. He wove through the traffic, hurrying.

"Milk man," he taunted. "Ought to know you can't ever outsmart the boss."

He laughed like crazy over this, one of the few times I ever heard Pizzari laugh without Kohzak there to cue him.

Pizzari drove fast, concentrating on the road, and he did not talk anymore. He held the steering wheel with one hand, the gun with the other, toying with the safety just to be sure I kept a strong case of jitters.

He wheeled the car into Charles Street, and long before I was ready, we skidded to a stop outside of Elva's apartment.

He watched me carefully. If I were going to attempt a break, the final moment for it was here. What Pizzari didn't know was that by going to the cops, I'd played my ace, and also all the cards up my sleeve.

I thought about Lois, decided that no matter what happened, I was glad it was like this. Even though Lois never knew it, and it did me no good with her, because of her call I had not gone through with the robbery.

"Walk slow," Pizzari ordered. "Take your time. Ain't nobody but you in a hurry."

We moved along the walk. The building super was at work in front. He spoke to us and Pizzari grunted in his direction. Skinny women walked their lap dogs. Nurses gossiped at their carriages. A day like all days along Charles Street.

Kohzak opened the door of Elva's apartment for us. He slammed it hard when we stepped inside.

Collie paced the floor, chewing on an unlighted cigar. His shirt spread open at the collar and his tie hung awry. His armpits were discolored with sweat, his face looked haggard. He seemed not to have slept in days.

I checked the place, but saw no sign of Elva. I wondered if Collie had come up here last night after I left, and found her the way she was when I walked out, her garments strewn across the floor.

There was an air of sickness about the room. It was as though the people living in here had been under unendurable tensions and did not yet know whether they would recover, or die, or just go on in this tense agony of wait-ing for nothing.

Kohzak studied me, and his narrow face was the gray of the walls.

Kohzak finally pulled his gaze from me and glanced at Pizzari, his thick brow quirked questioningly.

Pizzari nodded, "You were right, boss. Just what you figured the fink would do." There was no excitement in Pizzari's tone, no hint of astonishment.

Kohzak looked at me again, but spoke to Pizzari. "Where'd you find him?"

"Coming out of the police station."

"Spilling his guts?"

"Looks like it, boss."

Kohzak stared at me, his gaze slapping hard against mine. "You know what happens to stoolies, Baynard?"

I didn't say anything.

Kohzak laughed, without mirth. "Thought he could outsmart me and run to the cops."

Kohzak paced back and forth in front of me, as if trying to understand what he saw in my face.

Suddenly he lashed out with the back of his hand, swinging upward. This was the last thing I expected. I'd never seen Kohzak lay hands on his under-lings; this was what he hired goons for. But I saw the rage and hatred was deep and personal with him.

He had to have his own vengeance or it was nothing.

He packed all his hatred in that blow and I sprawled back. I landed against a chair and it toppled on its side and skidded from under me on the highly polished floor.

I fell, but I pushed myself up and sprang at him, full of my own hatred and ready to kill him.

Pizzari moved faster than either of us. The gun in his hand chopped down, clipping me behind the ear. I staggered forward two more steps and then toppled face-down on the floor. I rolled over on my back, staring up at them. I could not move.

"Tie him up," Kohzak said. His face was gray, rutted.

Pizzari nodded. He dropped the gun in his pocket, ripped a lamp cord from socket and wall. He rolled me over with the toe of his shoe. He jerked my arms up between my shoulder blades, securing them. Then he shoved me against a wall as if I were a sack of slime.

I stared at them through an occluding haze of red.

I saw that Kohzak had brought Elva in from the bedroom. She wore only a transparent negligee, and the mink coat on over it.

She stared down at me and her face was pale. I saw that Kohzak had been slapping her around. She seemed afraid to raise her eyes high enough to meet any of our gazes.

Kohzak shoved her so she fell on the gray couch. She stayed there, not really looking at any of us.

When I sat forward, Kohzak lunged around suddenly and kicked me in the side. I retched, toppling forward.

"Look at him," Collie panted toward Elva. "There's your big college man, wallowing on the floor."

She did not lift her face to his. She trembled visibly when he spoke to her, like an animal that had had the spirit beaten from it.

I rolled over on my side, trying to sit up. The toe of Kohzak's shoe caught me in the ribs before I could fall out of his reach.

Kohzak and Pizzari laughed. Kohzak said, "Pretty soon you'll learn to stay until I tell you to move, Sammy. I'm going to show you two what happens to people who cross me, people that I trust." He stared at Elva's lowered head and then at me. "The fink and the tramp," he said.

Collie moved closer, standing over me. He looked forty feet tall, his head in a red-hazed fog.

His voice reached me feebly from some incredible distance.

"Knew I couldn't trust you no more. Saw you sniffing around my woman again. Respectable slob, sneaking around my woman at night."

His voice quavered. His insane jealousy was what had set him off, more even than my going to the police. I had gone to bed with Elva last night, and she couldn't lie her way out of it as she always had before.

"So you and Elva think you can play around behind my back, huh? You think she don't belong to me! You think she ain't Collie Kohzak's woman. Well, that's where you both got something to learn. This dame does what Collie tells her. You hear me, slob?"

He was sweated down now. The stains under his arms had spread and his shirt had wilted like a week-old carnation.

My gaze struck against Elva on the couch. She had pulled her mink to her and she caressed it in a sensual movement of her hands, giving it more adoration than she had ever expended on any man.

Kohzak turned and walked over to her. He grabbed her by the hair and yanked her up from the couch.

He held her against him and tightened his arms around her. I saw the fear in her face: not of Collie, because she wasn't afraid of any man, but of what was happening to her mink jacket.

I watched them, thinking that when they forgot me I'd clear out. Somehow I'd get outside the apartment.

"Take it easy, Collie," she whimpered.

He snagged the jacket and threw it away from them.

Elva stayed pressed against him, her face stricken and pale.

I straightened, pulling myself around, trying to idle toward the door, but when I moved, so did Kohzak. He stood over me, the sweat standing like marbles on his grayed-out cheeks.

"Don't try anything, fellow. You've had it. Where you think you're going?"

His foot came up and he kicked me in the face. I fell over on my back, landing hard on the carpeting. I did not try to move again.

I lay there watching him. Finally I could speak around the blood in my mouth. "Whatever it is, Kohzak, get it over."

His laughter was crazed, wild with rage. "Don't tell Collie Kohzak what to do, slob. You just found out that I run things."

His voice rose to a keening wail, and he trembled.

When I did not speak, he laughed again, shakily. "I got the word for you, punk. You're not out of anything. We're going right on with that robbery. Hear me, punk? My plans have changed concerning you, but they still include taking that plant for three hundred grand."

He began to laugh again, sounding inhuman with the hatred that bubbled up in his mouth so that he could barely talk at all.

"It ain't going to be quite the same, fink. It ain't going off quite like you stooled it to the cops."

He bent forward over me. "You hear me, punk? You thought you were smart enough to get away with crossing Collie Kohzak. Kohzak never made a plan in his life that he couldn't change, and fast, and nobody in this hick town is smart enough to cut off my operation."

He reached down, clutched my shirt and yanked me to a sitting position.

"So you can get up off your dead bottom and listen to me. We're going to knock over your milk company. But not tomorrow night like you ran and told your friends the cops." He laughed again and sweat dripped from his face. "They'll be looking for us then, Sammy, but they're going to be one night too late."

11

I rolled over on my side with Kohzak's words bubbling around in the quicksand softness of my brain.

The words crawled agonizingly through the convolutions of my cranium, making their own terrible kind of logic.

I stared at the gray wall and saw how lost I was and how clever Kohzak was, and how completely I'd alienated myself from both worlds now, the evil and the straight.

Kohzak kicked me in the side. It no longer mattered. My body was a mass of pain and my nerve centers had stopped accepting messages of physical hurt.

"Turn over and look at me when I speak to you, punk," Kohzak ordered.

I rolled over on my back, gasping for breath. Blood filled my mouth and nostrils. I had to keep shaking my head in order to breathe at all.

I pulled my gaze back to Kohzak.

"That's better, smart boy." He laughed, and the sound reverberated in my head. "What do you think your cop pals are going to believe about you when the job is pulled tonight instead of tomorrow?"

"They're going to think he crossed them," Pizzari giggled.

Kohzak nudged me sharply with the toe of his boot. He seemed aware now that physical pain had lost its meaning in my body.

"You better know that's what they'll think, ain't it, smart boy?" His voice gloated. "They'll think you crossed them, and they'll think I ordered it that way. Collie Kohzak making a new move that will throw off the fuzz."

He was right, and I saw it, painfully. They'd talk a long time about the way Collie Kohzak sent his stooge in and let him con the cops.

And Del Lantis? After his long record of successes, he was going to look like a hick, a boob. His hatred was something real, even as full of agony as I was. It would avail me nothing to escape Kohzak, even if that were possible. All the rest of his life, Lantis would be looking for me.

Once a crook, always a crook.

"Them stinking small-town cops, trying to outsmart Kohzak!" Collie's voice shook with righteous indignation. "And you, a jailbird punk that got caught for being stupid, you trying to help them. That's what burns me. That's why I'm going to enjoy this job more than any I ever pulled, because it's so perfect and it's going to pay off the people I hate in a way I like."

He stood, trembling, seeing the way it had to be.

"Them stinking cops will really be looking for you now, Baynard, and not to pin medals on you," he said. "Thought you'd end up a real hero. Ratting to the cops and they'd take care of you and stop me before I could fix your water. Changed your mind about that yet? Because it ain't going to matter about you after tonight, but just to put the lid on tight, and just to show you that Kohzak makes allowances for any kind of errors, we're going to fix you so the cops can have that Kleizac jewelry heist to add to your crossing them. Scotty is going to call the police just before we pull this payroll take. He laughed. "Maybe Scotty and me will get a medal!"

He stuck his boot in my face and turned my head with it, as if I were some animal he'd shot casually.

"You hear me, Sammy? Looks like your stoolie caper didn't buy you much."

I rolled my head away, trying to stop the pain and the blood. My bleeding was messing up the carpeting but they didn't care; by tomorrow they'd be six hundred miles away, drinking champagne with their alibis and their character witnesses.

Where would I be? The guy who finked on his mobster pals, and on the police?

They lost interest in me then. Pizzari sat as if in a trance, watching every move Elva made. His eyes were hungry.

"Get Scotty and me something to drink, Elva," Collie said. He sank into an easy chair, mopping sweat from his forehead and watching me in chilled satisfaction.

Elva brought them drinks.

He got a dish of cracked ice and a wet cloth. She knelt beside me.

Kohzak straightened up in his chair, his face livid. His voice lashed at her. "Get away from him."

Her voice was as hard as his, cutting against it.

"I'll stop the bleeding," she said.

"Patch the slob up? For what?"

Pizzari made that giggling sound again.

The ice felt good, and her hands were gentle. Kindness seemed it's own kind of mockery in this place. Elva pushed two pieces of cracked ice between my teeth and soon I was tasting water instead of blood.

The icy cloth soothed my screaming nerve ends; the banging behind my eyes decreased and I saw there weren't really red streaks in the gray wall after all. Finally I could breathe again through my nostrils.

Elva stood up then and went away. I sagged against the wall, watching Kohzak and Pizzari hopelessly.

Kohzak took a long drink of bourbon. "Think smart boy has learned anything yet, Scotty?"

"Maybe he's learned, boss," Pizzari said, pulling his gaze back from Elva.

"Yeah. Too bad he had to learn too late, huh?"

Pizzari shrugged.

Kohzak peered at me, his mouth twisted. He lighted a cigar, inhaling deeply on the smoke.

"All you did, Baynard, was cost yourself a healthy cut of swag." He laughed, thinking about that. "No sense cutting you in now. If you go anywhere, it'll be back to prison. You can't spend money in jail. Only you ain't going nowhere. Too bad. Way I see it, kid, you probably won't even live to get out of that office." He glanced at Pizzari. "Ain't that right, Scotty?"

"Yeah, boss," Pizzari spoke absently.

And that's how we waited out the day. It was like sitting without a chaplain during your last hours in a death house.

Time plays tricks: careening towards unforeseen tragedy, but creeping when you're forced to think ahead of it.

At three p.m. Elva made toasted cheese sandwiches and they ate them with cold beer.

For thirty minutes Collie sat with Elva on the couch and they talked seriously in monotones. I didn't have to hear them, I knew he was giving her the last-minute briefings on the changes in the robbery plan, her part in it. He was thinking about money again.

She grew steadily cooler. This was her habit of all her years with Collie. She'd been down every road with him, through every alley, and on all capers. She had grown cagey and cool. She followed Collie's instructions exactly. Like Collie, she had never been in prison. It was hard to imagine Elva in a drab uniform in a woman's prison, yet I knew the jails were full of dolls like her.

It was time to go.

They untied my arms, but Collie warned me Scotty would be behind me with a gun fixed on my spine every minute.

Collie said, "We got a new wrinkle. You're going to drive us over to the plant, Sammy."

I stared at him.

"That's right. You're driving, and Scotty sits behind you, that bullet ready with your name on it. He has my orders. If you pull anything cute, you get it. You might foul our plans, but you better think what will happen to your face, Baynard. They won't even be able to identify you."

"What difference does it make?" I said. "Whether I get it before we get to the plant or later?"

Kohzak's smile was cold. "No difference. But I'm not worried. As much as you want to stop me, you want to stay alive more. You'll play it cagey because the longer you stay alive, the more chance you figure you'll have of getting out with your skin. It's fool thinking, but that's the way you'll think."

My heart sank. He was right. It was the way I would think, the way anybody would. Nobody wanted to think about his face blown away with a dumdum.

"So if you got that clear," Kohzak said, "we're ready to go. You drive careful, obey traffic laws. I want no trouble with some hick cop."

With frantic hopes, I thought about the parking ticket Pizzari had torn up. Would the cops be looking for that car license? I knew better. Police never even thought about a traffic offense for forty-eight hours; one always had that much time on a parking summons.

Pizzari and I went down to the car first. Collie hated crowds. He liked everything to look casual.

Pizzari and I looked real casual. He walked close behind me with his hand jammed in his jacket pocket. We looked like the condemned man and guard on the way to the death chamber.

There was no one on the dark street.

When I got in under the wheel, Pizzari slid into the back seat and leaned forward, breathing against my neck. We sat and waited.

We looked real casual.

After a moment Elva came out of the apartment entrance. She stood looking around as if wondering about rain. Then she happened to see us waiting and casually strode over. She got into the front seat beside me.

We three casual people waited some more.

Collie Kohzak's role was the hurried businessman with brief case, cigar, and urgent business downtown.

He came out of the apartment house and started along the walk. He paused as if surprised to find us casual people sitting there. He got in as though accepting a ride in a car pool.

"Okay, smart boy," Pizzari said to the back of my head. "Get the show on the road."

I drove carefully. We passed three police cruisers before we crossed Broad Street. They did not glance our way.

Beside me, Elva stared straight ahead. Once she said, "The mink jacket, Sammy. It's lovely."

"You look fine in it," I said.

"It's the only nice thing I ever got."

"You look fine."

"Keep your mind on your driving," Kohzak said from the rear seat.

We did not talk any more. Elva's hand inched across the seat between us and she pressed my leg.

I don't know why it felt comforting, maybe like the priest at the death house, the final small kindness.

"Stop right here," Collie said. "Under that street lamp. Leave your parking lights burning. We don't need any snooping cops."

I pulled into the curb. Collie handed out to each of us the silk stockings he'd bought. We pulled them down over our faces.

Pizzari peered at Kohzak and giggled once. None of the rest of us smiled.

I got the car moving again.

"A gun," I said. My voice was distorted. "Am I going to have a gun when we go in there?"

Kohzak burst out laughing.

"A gun on you would be dangerous, Sammy. A respectable slob like you. I don't think you ought to have a gun. That face will scare people enough. They won't know if you've got a gun or not."

Elva's hand tightened on my leg slightly. I was too numbed to feel it.

Kohzak leaned forward. "Wouldn't look nice for a respectable fink to be carrying a gun when he was killed. Would it?"

There was no answer for that. At least I couldn't think of any.

The lights of the Gorten Milk Company illuminated the dark street ahead of us. It was quiet in that neighborhood at this hour.

"Slow down," Kohzak ordered. His voice sounded old. My heart slugged and my hands sweated. I was afraid to move my hands from the wheel because Pizzari was getting nervous and might misinterpret my movement.

I turned the car into the gate, slowed down. I saw the watchman step out of his little house and hobble toward us on tired feet.

There was probably nobody else on the parking area. The cyclone fence stretched half a block in the darkness. At our right was the unbroken wall of the building. Ahead and around a corner was the side entrance of the offices, and this was where we were headed.

They waited until the old man walked almost to the car.

Pizzari stepped out of the back door, stepped close to the old man. The guard gasped, staring at Pizzari's stocking-covered face. That was as far as Pizzari let him get. I winced at the sound of the sap against the old man's skull.

I felt sickness gorge up in my stomach. Pizzari hit him again as he crumpled, this time for his own pleasure. The guard sank to the pavement and lay still.

Pizzari caught the guard by his jacket collar and dragged him into the shadows. He left the old man propped against a dark wall so he looked like a derelict sleeping off a drunk.

Pizzari walked casually back and got into the car.

"Hick town," Pizzari said.

"Get rolling," Kohzak said to me.

I stepped on the gas, and the big black car lunged forward, moving toward the office doors.

12

I drove slowly to the side entrance. I parked just outside the ring of light around the door.

Elva moved over under the wheel, shrugging her mink jacket up on her shoulders.

"So long, Sammy," she said when I got out.

I stared at her a moment. I knew how bad she was. I nodded at her.

She whispered, "You were the only good one, Sammy. The first I ever knew."

I didn't say anything.

I heard Kohzak laugh. He and Pizzari got out beside me. We took one quick check around the deserted plant yard and then strode across the cement toward the entrance. I was slightly in the lead, with Scotty close at my back.

We pushed open the thick glass door and walked in. This was when we got our first glimpse of the armed guards.

There were two of them with shotguns, but they had gotten careless. Kohzak moved fast and Pizzari was at his heels. The guards didn't have time to jerk up the guns.

Kohzak held a gun fixed on them and Pizzari used the sap from behind, quickly and efficiently.

It was so much quieter that way.

Kohzak jerked his head and we went up the steps. They stayed close behind me, crowding me.

We came out of the stairwell into the wide silent corridor. It was lined with doors that all looked alike.

Pizzari ran ahead, choosing the door that he had been drilled to choose on the floor plan. He moved as if he'd spent his life hurrying into this office with the big suitcase at his side.

The clerks, accountants, bookkeepers looked up, gaping.

They were like frightened sheep.

"Nobody tries to be heroic and nobody gets hurt," Collie told them.

They stood up on his order and he lined them against the wall, their noses thrust against it, their hands held high.

Carrying his gun and the suitcase, Pizzari strode to the open vault.

I stared at them, seeing how easy it was, seeing how Kohzak had it planned down to the minute, down to the number of steps Pizzari would take, the number of times he would toss those tight-packed green stacks of bills into the suitcase.

A girl whimpered. One of the men in the line sidestepped toward a window.

Kohzak's gun jerked upward, leveling on the man's back. For the moment I thought he was going to kill him.

"You," Kohzak said. "Get away from that window."

The man hesitated. Kohzak stepped toward him. I glanced toward Pizzari, seeing he was intent upon filling that suitcase.

I drew a quick breath and lunged toward Kohzak, reaching out as far as I could.

It was not quite a clean tackle. I snagged at him, but I missed, and he whirled around on his heel as if he'd read my mind.

He brought up the gun, its snout fixed on me.

"This is fine," Collie said. "Kind of fool play I hoped you'd make. Can't wait for it, eh, smart boy? Want it now?"

I leaped at him again. He was caught by surprise, but he pressed that trigger at the moment I clipped down across his gun hand.

I deflected the bullet, but not enough. I felt the sharp sickening burn as it gouged into my side. The impact of the bullet sent me reeling away from Kohzak.

Women screamed and men cried out. All of them wheeled around from the wall, staring.

As I crumpled, still going back off my heels and falling against a desk, I heard the sharp singing warning of Kohzak's car horn. Elva was really leaning on it, and I knew something had gone wrong with Collie's plan.

The horn blaring was the loudest sound in the world.

For a second there was darkness, waves of it enveloping me and dragging me down. The pain was intense and I was still conscious enough to feel all of it.

Suddenly every light in the plant flashed on as if somebody had thrown a master switch, or as if I had awakened in a blindly white heaven.

The place was wailing with burglar alarms. It sounded like the end of the world.

I pulled around on my knees, digging my left hand into the fire at my side.

I wanted to hurl myself at Kohzak, but it was no good any more. It didn't matter. I heard the women chattering in hysterical relief, the men shouting.

I saw the cops burst in like a flying wedge through those double glass doors.

The lead cop, thrusting back the doors and striding in, gun drawn, was Del Lantis.

Lantis knew where Collie stood in that robbery setup as though he'd been reading Collie's plans, and he snapped a shot at Kohzak before Collie could heel around to face him.

I passed out when I saw what happened.

I woke up with lights spinning around me, painful in my eyes. For some time I did not even know where I was. I looked for Collie, for Lantis, Pizzari... Lois.

I moved my hands and felt the crisp white sheets. I felt my side. The pain was there, but milder, as if somehow removed by sedation.

Faces passed above me like shadows, and I heard low, disembodied whispers. I was in a hospital bed.

I opened my eyes wider. It was daylight, but something new troubled me. What day?

I lay unmoving on my back for a long time. Shadows swirled between me, and I moved my head, looking around for the bars on the windows.

There were none, and I thought this odd, because there were always bars in a prison hospital.

The door opened after a long silent time and a nurse came in, crisply white and persistently cheerful.

"So you finally woke up," she said, smiling.

"What day is it?"

"Sunday," she said. "You had a nice long sleep."

I did not like to think about how long I had been asleep. I didn't say anything.

She smiled and smoothed the covers. "You've got company," she said. "Do you feel like seeing him?"

I shrugged. It did not matter. A prisoner has no rights. They visited you and questioned you, whether you wanted them or not.

"Relax," the nurse said. "He won't stay long."

She went out and closed the door behind her. I waited, feeling the dull thudding of my heart.

The door opened again and Del Lantis came in.

"Well," he said in that old taunting tone, "looks like you're going to live."

"Am I? If you'd ever been in stir, Lantis, you'd know death isn't the worst thing that can happen to you."

He shrugged. "I've never been in jail, but you're not going back, not this time around, anyhow. We made quite a haul. Big enough to suit me. You ought to see the places Kohzak is wanted. And Pizzari — there are murder warrants out for him. The girl will serve time, but she'll get the lightest sentence of the three."

I waited, not daring to hope. He'd said I wasn't slated for prison. I lay there watching him. "What about the Kleizac robbery?"

He shook his head. "We checked that job out. By taking in Kohzak we recovered all the jewelry. There were no deaths. The insurance company wants to close its files. The jeweler might have prosecuted you, but he decided Kohzak was the big wheel, and anyhow, he doesn't like the publicity that comes from reopening a robbery case that big. They think the rest of the charges can be handled out of court."

I felt the sting of tears.

He grinned at me. "The witnesses all say you jumped Kohzak. That helps."

I swallowed hard.

"You did a good job, boy," he said. "The best you could."

I stared at him. "But I told you it was to be Thursday night."

"That's right, you did." He tried to look modest but he couldn't make it. He was proud of himself. "But actually, you didn't have to tell me anything, Baynard. It's just a good thing for you that you did. That morning you were in my office, I'd come straight from listening to Kohzak make plans, and all the rest that happened in that apartment. You had quite a time with Elva. I think she really was pleased with you."

He laughed when the color flushed up into my cheeks. Then he returned to business. "I already had all the information you gave me. But everything you said checked. You had to be on the level. I knew everything you told me about Kohzak's plans, just as I knew when he changed to Wednesday night."

"How?" It was like the start of delirium, listening to him.

"I heard everything, Baynard, and got it down on tape. The tape recording swayed a lot of law officials to your side, Baynard."

"How?" I said again.

He grinned. "Man, I'm called the gadget cop, even you called me that. I couldn't wire Elva's room because one of them was always there, and they were smart enough to check for wiring." He sighed, pleased with himself. "Remember the night your room was searched? That was me. I figured you'd give that mink to Elva and that she'd wear it a lot, even indoors — dames don't get mink jackets every day. So I needled you, hoping you'd leave it one night in your room, and you did. Then you gave it to Elva right on schedule, and she couldn't have done better: she wore it all the time."

"What's the mink got to do with it?"

"Everything. Remember Elva complained the seams were stiff? That was because I'd wired the jacket for transmitting, with transistors and wireless sending mechanisms. The sound couldn't carry far, but it didn't have to. We were in the next room with ear phones and tape recorders."

I smiled, seeing the way Elva had preened in the jacket.

"Elva knew nothing about mink jackets," Lantis said, "so I gambled she wouldn't be able to tell those buttons were supersensitive sound pickups, the kind they put on hearing aids, with the volume turned up full to catch everything from all angles. The seams were the test. If she didn't fall for the wiring, we were in." He laughed. "The whole time, Kohzak's doll was a walking broadcasting station." He shook his head. "Some of the things she broadcast wouldn't pass the censors."

He stood up then. "Well, Sam, there's just one more thing. They're going to take you back at the milk company as soon as you're well enough to work. So it looks like you didn't come out of it too bad, playing it straight."

He was gone. I don't know how long it was when the door was opened again and the nurse said, "One more visitor, Mr. Baynard. That's your quota for the day. You feel well enough?"

It was Lois. She came in slowly, smiling hesitantly. She stood beside my bed. She touched my hand.

"I've missed you, Sam."

I stared at her, feeling hungry and empty, knowing I had no life without her.

"I love you, Sam."

"Sure."

"Can't you forgive me?"

"What's to forgive? I was a bad guy, and you're too good for a bad boy."

"You're not bad. You're Sam Baynard. You're all I want."

I sighed. "Your father would love to hear you say that."

"He's heard it a lot lately. But that doesn't matter any more. I know what I want, where happiness is. Besides," she smiled. "Father has almost changed his mind about you since you are a hero."

"Me?"

"He tells everybody that you're our milkman and that you dated his daughter."

"I must be dreaming."

"Wait until you read the newspapers. Lantis really gave you a buildup."

I was silent for some moments. "I'm still a guy with a prison record, Lois."

"But that doesn't matter. Mistakes don't rule you out forever. It's what you are, fight to make yourself, that counts."

"Will you go on believing that?"

"Darling, try to see it my way: nothing had ever prepared me for loving a man who'd been in prison. I was sick when you told me. I couldn't think."

"I'm not blaming you. I'm not trying to hold you."

She smiled. "But that's it, you've got to hold me."

"Don't talk like that. I'm in the hospital. That's cruelty to patients."

"What do you think it does to me, darling, having to wait?"

THE END

BODY AND
PASSION

BY HARRY WHITTINGTON

1

Jeff Taylor parked his Buick Riviera in front of his fishing cottage.

His hideaway had always suited him, and for what he planned tonight it was exactly right. Eaton Lake was desolate back country and his two-room cabin was on an isolated rim of the water.

He killed the engine, cut off the lights. The silence and the darkness of the chilly April night settled down thick around them as if to shield them from all sound.

He nudged Ben Young with his elbow. "All right, this is it," he said. "Get out."

Young slapped down on the door handle, slid out of the car and stood, shrugging his coat up on his shoulders.

Taylor reached over the seat and lifted out a five-gallon gasoline can. He slid out of the car and stood beside Young in the darkness. For a moment the whole world was a maw of black. Then he could see the sliver of moon reflected on the face of the lake, the tufted cypress like a picket fence around it.

He brushed past Young and, choosing a key on his keyring by touch, shoved it into the door. He unlocked the door, pushed it open and set the gasoline can inside against the wall.

He straightened up. "All right. You've been wanting to talk all the way out here. Come inside."

"I don't get the point of this," Young said. Anger clipped his words short and sharp.

"You will." Taylor waited until Young stepped past him into the cottage. He closed the door, locked it and dropped the keyring into the pocket of his coat. "If you'll stand right where you are, Counselor, you won't get a banged shin. I'll light a lamp."

He moved slowly across the room, bumped the table because he reached it before he'd expected to. He removed the glass chimney, turned up the wick, fired it with the flame from his expensive cigarette lighter. He replaced the chimney, lowered the wick. Light glowed in the roughly furnished room.

Taylor took his time turning. He leaned against the table and seemed almost as astonished to see the automatic in his own right fist as Ben Young was.

The young lawyer caught his breath sharply. "So it's like that," he said.

Taylor nodded. "That's the way it is." He jerked his head toward a chair. "Sit down. We'll be cozy about it. And quick."

He watched the lawyer sit down. Young sat straight on the chair, his shoulders back, his head up, face cold and hard. His hazel eyes revealed nothing but contempt.

Taylor turned a chair from the table and sat down facing Young. He hated the man before him but he knew his hatred didn't match Young's. The Assistant District Attorney hated his guts. He was willing to see Taylor go to the chair for a crime even Young must know Taylor hadn't committed. Taylor had thought it over from every angle. It didn't add up. He couldn't figure it. All right, he was on one side of the law. Young represented the other side. Okay. But did that explain the assistant prosecutor getting a murder indictment against him on framed-up evidence?

Taylor's hand tightened on the automatic. It didn't make sense. But his whole life had become a nightmare lately. All he wanted was to be free of the whole dirty mess. He was willing to pay anything for that freedom. But not his life. Not for a crime he hadn't committed.

He tilted the nose of the automatic. Yellow flecks moved in the green irises of his eyes. Deep lines pulled down from his distended nostrils. He tried to speak casually but he was too sick and angry inside, too full of hatred.

"You've driven me as far as I can take, Young. So here we are. Only one of us is going to leave here alive. Since I got the gun that kind of ups the odds on me, doesn't it?"

The assistant prosecutor had been trained to conceal his emotions. "I don't pretend to think you won't use that gun. That's been your answer for everything, hasn't it? A hood with a gun. And now you think you can stay out of Raiford by killing me."

"I know it."

"Killing Rick Vashney wasn't enough, was it?"

Taylor frowned, puzzled. There was conviction in Young's voice. Had he pretended to believe in that frame so long that he had actually convinced himself?

Rick Vashney had been killed in his apartment. There were witnesses who swore they had seen Taylor running out of Vashney's front door after the shots were fired. But Rick's apartment was secluded, and there were too many witnesses. All of them were lying; they must have been. Taylor's gun was found in Vashney's apartment. The gun had disappeared out of Taylor's desk.

Taylor had been in his office during the hour fixed as the time of Vashney's death. Halftime Smith had been with him. But Halftime had a bad record. And everybody in town knew he'd give the flesh off his body, shred by shred, for Taylor. It was the word of Halftime Smith against a half-dozen witnesses the D.A.'s office had rounded up.

Taylor stared at Ben Young. Ben was a good-looking young guy. He had everything in the world a man could want. A good family and plenty of money. Good education and a nice future. What in hell was behind this frame when both knew it was a frame?

Taylor's voice expressed his hopelessness. "I never killed Vashney," he said.

Young's mouth twisted. "I think you did. I've witnesses who saw you running out of Vashney's apartment. You're going to the chair, Taylor, whether you kill me or not."

Taylor shook his head. There was nothing in Young's voice that showed he even believed Taylor would kill him.

"When I step through that door in Raiford, Young, and they let me have the juice, I want to know I'm guilty—that I'm not dying because I've been framed."

Ben Young leaned forward. "How do you think you're going to get away with killing me? Your cottage on your lake. Your hideaway. Your car brought us here. You'll shoot me with your gun. What kind of fool are you?"

"What kind are you, Young? You think I got where I am by being so dumb I'd let you get away with a stinking frame like the Vashney thing?" His eyes searched the lawyer's face, looking for the tiniest trace of fear, the least sign that the guy was human enough to be afraid. "There's just one way you can leave here alive, Young—"

"Yes?"

"Admit you framed me. Admit Rick Vashney was in your way. You had to get rid of Vashney and at the same time you wanted to get me. Why, Young? Why? Because of the splash you'd make? 'Jeff Taylor convicted of murdering rival racketeer.' 'Assistant D.A. Benjamin J. Young leads city clean-up.' Oh, brother, it would make juicy headlines, all right. Is that why you're doing it?"

Young relaxed a little in his chair. "I'm not admitting anything, Taylor. But I'll say this. You brought this on yourself. The first time I called you downtown for a talk, you let me know where you stood."

"And that's where I still stand. That's why you know damned well I didn't kill Rick Vashney. I wanted out. I still do. I was trying to sell out to Rick. Why would I want to kill him?"

"Don't worry, you'll hear that in the courtroom, too. What better way to get the money you need? Sell out to Vashney and then inherit the whole vice mess when Vashney is killed—"

Taylor's hand tightened on the gun. His voice was hoarse. "Whatever else I've done, Young—and I'm almost as rotten as you are—I don't lie. I told you when you tried to make a deal with me, I was selling out to Rick Vashney. I was clearing out, quitting. I was sick and fed up with it."

"That's sucker talk."

"Then all right, I'm a sucker. I've got my reasons for wanting out. They're good enough for me. It just so happens I don't want to go to the electric chair so you can become the youngest and crookedest Governor this state ever had. So that's why you're here—"

"You are a fool. You might get away with the Vashney killing—"

"I didn't kill him—"

"—but you'd never get away with killing me. I'll tell you one thing that'll make that gun in your hand completely worthless to you. Vance Roberts of the *News* knows I've got you over a barrel. He knows that I've witnesses, everything lined up, that you're going to fry for killing Rick Vashney. Vance Roberts has almost as complete a file on it as I do. If you did kill me, he'd know why—"

Jeff Taylor's laugh was ragged. Vance was a college educated tramp. He had managed to drink himself into a breakdown, even though he was only twenty-eight. Somehow he managed to hang on to a job as political reporter for the Rainier *News*. But he was more crooked than the crooks he exposed, more dishonest than any dishonesty he ever revealed. Vance was not only bad, he was weak. Add to that the fact he never stopped drinking once he started, until he had run a cycle of stupor, moroseness and trembling and shaking. When he came out of one of his cycles, he walked around ashen and sweated for a week.

"That drunk," Taylor said. "Who do you think keeps him in Scotch? I do. Who you think bought him his last car? I did, sucker. Vance Roberts works for me just like he punched a clock in my office—"

Ben Young's smile was tight. "I don't think you've talked to Vance lately."

Taylor shrugged. But his pale face was rigid. "All right, so Roberts has sold me out. That listens. If you got to him and showed him I was a dead pigeon, he might bail out early. But now, Counselor, I got a surprise for you."

"Have you?"

"Yes. Stand up." Young stared at him. "I mean it. On your feet."

Young stood up.

"Strip down."

"What?"

"You heard me. Take your clothes off. Throw 'em over here. Nice and easy. Right at my feet."

Young stared at Taylor. Taylor's eyes met his. Taylor watched him, wearing cold hatred like a bitter mask.

Young's gaze wavered first. He dragged his tongue across his mouth.

He removed his coat and tossed it to the floor at Taylor's feet. Taylor looked down at it. "London tailored, eh?"

Young was removing his shirt. "Not this one. I bought it here in town."

"Sure. Election coming up. You got to be a man of the people."

The shirt landed on top of the coat, then a tie and undershirt. Young stopped then, his mouth hard. He glared at Taylor, started to speak, didn't. He craned his neck slightly.

"The bottom of the lake, Taylor? Bodies—" he shuddered, "have a way of never staying where you put them."

"Your pants, Counselor."

Young jerked the narrow belt loose, unzipped his trousers and stepped out of them. He drew back as if to throw them.

Taylor shook his head, "Easy, Counselor. Easy does it."

The trousers landed on the pile of clothes.

"Shoes, socks, wrist watch and if you're wearing a ring, I want it."

Young removed his underpants, shoes, socks and class ring. He looked at the watch and ring for a moment, closing his fist over them. He inhaled sharply and tossed them to the bundle at Taylor's feet. He stood there, naked, his shoulders back, his face set and pale.

"All right, get it over with."

Taylor laughed. He reached down, picked up the clothes under his arm and moved back to the table.

"Beginning to believe me now, Counselor? Are you willing now to write out on paper that you framed me? I don't know if it's got through to you or not. You're not going anywhere, Young. Your wife and her warm bed. The Governor's mansion next year. A court where you want to convict me on lies. This is it, Mister. If you've ever used your brains, now's the time to use 'em.

"You made just one mistake when you framed me. That's what tripped you up. That's what got you here. That's why you're going to die out here tonight instead of running for Governor. Contempt. That's what you've had for me. A tramp, a bum. A hungry guy running. Never knew one after-dinner drink from another. But look at us. Look where we are. Laugh now, damn you!"

He jerked his head toward the far side of the room. "Suppose you stand over there, Counselor. Face the wall. Nose against it."

He watched the Assistant District Attorney obey.

"What was it you said, Counselor? My car brought us up here? Okay, it's parked out there. Why shouldn't I be up here? It's my place. Maybe I committed suicide when that fearless Assistant D.A. got too hot on my tail. Sure. That's the way even Vance Roberts will see it. He'll have to. He knows you framed me. And he knows I was trying to quit the rackets. I wanted out. Your boy Vance was like you. He thought I was crazy to try to quit. So he'll believe I was sucker enough to commit suicide. And who'll be around to tell him different? You won't, Counselor, because you're going to disappear. I've been wanting to get out of this town and I'm going. When I go, I'll be wearing the most expensively tailored suit in town. Now, if you think there are any holes in that plan, brother, let's hear 'em fast, because I've been waiting for this chance for a long time and I'm not going to fool around and let anything spoil it."

Taylor waited. Young didn't speak. But Taylor could hear his sharp intake of breath all the way across the room.

2

Taylor jerked his tie loose. He slid out of his coat and began unbuttoning his shirt so fast his trembling fingers almost tore off the buttons. He removed his keyring from the pocket and tossed coat, tie and shirt across the room so they struck against Young's bare heels.

Young turned, staring across his shoulder.

"What are you doing?"

"I'm giving you a chance to see what the common man really wears. In fact, you're going to wear them."

Taylor laid the gun on the edge of the table under his hand and removed his trousers and underclothes. He tossed them across the room. He pulled off his shoes and socks, throwing them on the pile. His wrist watch and an initialed ring he carried over and placed in the chair Young had been sitting in. He returned to the table and began to dress in Young's expensive clothes.

When he was dressed, he sat down in the chair, strapping Young's watch on his wrist. For a brief moment he admired Young's college ring. He picked up the gun, leaned back.

"All right, Young. Turn around. Get dressed."

Young turned around and picked up the clothes still warm from Taylor's body. His face showed the distaste he felt. Taylor could see all the way across the room that the lawyer was blue with cold. The guy had courage. Taylor gave him that. Hell, until Young started yelling for a murder indictment against Taylor, Jeff had always considered him a brilliant and honest young attorney. But that was a long time ago. Now it was something else again. Either Young died or Taylor went to the electric chair. Taylor's mouth twisted. He didn't have to think twice on a choice like that.

It was taking Young a long time to dress.

"You're gonna get it sooner or later, Counselor. Stalling won't buy you much out here."

Young shrugged into Taylor's coat. It was a good fit. They were almost the same size, the same weight. And that was funny as hell when you considered that Young had had everything and Taylor grew up in the gutters downtown.

Young stalked back to his chair, slid his hand through the strap of Taylor's wrist watch and pushed the ring down on his finger.

"You're up against experts," he said. His voice faltered a little. "You're not going to get away with this. Murder is a sucker's racket and you ought to have sense enough to know it."

"Killing you is murder," Taylor said. "Sure. But sending me to the electric chair, Young, what's that?" His laugh turned into snarl. "Sure, that's different. I'm a bum, a guy the world will never miss. Well, they're going to be weeping and wailing about you, Counselor."

He let the legs of his chair strike the pine flooring hard. He stood up, and watching Young, strode across the room. He picked up the five-gallon can of gasoline. It was less than half full. He slapped the top off of it and began to slosh the pink-tinted fuel against the walls and over the floor, the cheap grass rug.

For a minute, paralyzed, Young sat and watched the dry wood drink up the fluid, leaving a wide stain to show where it had been absorbed.

Taylor, looking at him, laughed. "Whole place," he said, "like matchwood."

Young jumped up and ran across the room. He struck hard against the door, grabbing the knob in both his shaking hands.

Taylor's laughter mocked him. "Locked, Counselor," he said. "Hell, you've got nothing to be afraid of. I don't have to set fire to this place. You can always write out that paper I want and sign it."

He sloshed the can around in his arms. It was empty. He tossed it into the corner. He looked up. Young was backed against the door, staring at him.

"You're crazy," Young whispered. "My God, you're insane!"

Taylor stood across the room, gun held loosely at his side.

"Crazy, Counselor? Why not? How much can a man stand? How much hounding? How much lying and oppression? A man can't take what I been through and go on being sane. It just don't add up that way. And, Mister, I'm gettin' crazier by the minute. If you want out of here, start talking, and talk fast."

Young inched away from the door. He moved out into the center of the room. His arms were rigid out from his sides, his mouth was parted and he was breathing through it. He was scared now. It was eating at his guts. He no longer doubted that Taylor was going to kill him and leave him here. And Taylor meant to burn the cottage with his body in it. Young's sagging mouth quivered.

Taylor said, "I don't like to see you like this, Young. I get no pleasure out of it. I don't want to kill you. I don't want to kill anybody. But I don't want to die, either. So that's the way it's got to be."

He jerked the snout of the gun up.

Young screamed. It poured out of him from the deepest part of his belly. He stood transfixed, his eyes never leaving the ugly black mouth of the gun.

"We're a long way from anybody, Young," Taylor said. The scream had shaken him. He could still feel the waves of it jarring around in his stomach. "Nobody is going to get here in time to save you. It's up to you. You framed me, didn't you?"

The fear in Young's distended eyes was stark and ugly. He was shaking now. He lifted his gaze from the gun but it was an effort. It was as though he believed by watching that gun he could somehow delay the moment of its firing.

He nodded, and once he started moving his head, he couldn't seem to stop it.

Taylor lowered the gun.

Reaction set in and Young went limp. The sweat on his face stood in separate cold globules. He staggered over to the table and leaned on it, resting his weight on the heels of his palsied hands. No matter what happened to him now, he knew what it was to come to the brink of violent death.

Taylor took Young's own fountain pen from the breast pocket of Young's coat. He slid it on the table in front of Young. The lawyer just stood there, staring at it.

"There's some paper in that table drawer," Taylor said. "Get it."

Young nodded. But for the moment he seemed unable to force his arms to obey the action impulses from his brain. At last he pulled open the drawer, his eyes searching it. There was sudden cunning and hunger in his face. Taylor saw it and laughed at him. There were only three sheets of ruled writing paper in there.

Young took the paper out and dropped it on the table. He slammed the drawer. The chimney shivered on the lamp and it smoked suddenly.

"All right. Sit down. Write it."

Young hooked his foot around the chair Taylor had been using and pulled it around against the backs of his legs. For a moment he stood there, unscrewing the fountain pen top. "What do you want me to say?"

Taylor moved a step nearer. "All of it. That you framed me. How you framed me—"

Young kicked over the chair and lunged against Taylor. He hit hard, his shoulder driving into Taylor's chest. He swung the back of his hand around as he moved, sending it across Taylor's face.

Taylor went out backward, cursing. The chair went over on its back. With his left hand, Taylor caught Young's coat, dragging him after him. They went crashing back against the wall.

Taylor caught his balance first and chopped at Young's head, using the side of the automatic as a club. He saw it rake down the side of Young's face, tearing a jagged path.

Young's knees buckled and he crumpled under the paralyzing blow to the side of his head. His hands gripped Taylor. They fell to the floor. For a moment Young lay there, stunned, and Taylor scrambled to his feet, snarling.

He wheeled around, his legs wide apart, and brought the gun around in an arc. Young yelled again and threw himself with all his strength against Taylor.

The gun exploded. The roar and the stink of it filled the room. As they went back, they crashed against the table. The table tottered for half a second and went over. The smoking lamp went crashing into the wall. For half an instant, there was darkness. Then there was an explosion. It was like the simultaneous snap of lightning and the burst of thunder. It was deafening.

The fire was everywhere at once. There may have been the rapid streak of fire along the lines of the stains on walls and floor, but the fumes had caught that flame and the burning was instantaneous.

For a moment—for too long—both men lay in the middle of the raging flames, too stunned to move. In that second they made the short, quick trip to hell.

3

Taylor pulled himself to his feet. He turned all the way around in the room. There were no windows, no doors, no walls. There was nothing but a sheet of flames. He covered his face with his arms and staggered through the fire. It was no worse one place than another.

He struck hard against the wall. The heat was so intense he could hardly open his eyes. He found the doorknob. He grabbed it, pulled. The door was locked.

He thrust his hand in his pocket. He found the ring, fumbled for the key. He found it, reached for the door.

He heard Young screaming behind him. He turned. The rim of the can crashed across his skull and he staggered back, dropping the keys.

Taylor could see Young's clothes were afire. Young seemed not to care any more. He was intent on only one thing. He was going to kill Taylor. Ignoring the flames and his burning clothes, Young swung the can again.

Taylor couldn't dodge it. He threw up his arm and felt it strike. He chopped at Young's bleeding head with the gun. Young staggered, still swinging the can. This time Taylor was moving forward. The heavy bottom of the can connected against his skull. The fire outside his head was nothing to the inferno that exploded inside it.

Taylor took one more step. His weight sent both of them sprawling backward. Young's head struck the floor. The sound was like a pumpkin against cement. Only Taylor didn't even hear it. Both of them lay on the floor. This time they didn't move again.

Old sayings have it that you can't hide fires in the night. The flaming Taylor cottage brought farmers, campers, guides, fishermen and travelers from the highway on the other side of Eaton Lake.

By the time they got there, there wasn't anything they could do. Somebody telephoned to Eatonville for the ambulance and it came screaming along the twisting sand road with its red blinker winking and its siren at full blast.

A lot of the farmers had brought small kegs and buckets. They made a fire line from the edge of the lake to the cottage, passing water along, sloshing it until never more than half a pail ever reached the men at the rim of the fire.

Still, they were doing all they could. All they proved was that human beings never give up. Not even when the odds are fire in pine wood with a twenty-minute start.

One young farmer had brought two firefighter suits that he'd used in the Navy. He and a friend donned them and then waded out into the lake to wet them down so they could get inside the burning house.

The weight of the firefighter suits, water-logged, pulled them down and they almost drowned. A dozen men had to stop passing water to pull them up. They started up the slight incline then, dripping wet, toward the wall of fire.

"They's somebody in there all right. This here is Jeff Taylor's Buick. I ought to know. I seed it pass my place a passel of times gettin' here."

"Even if he be in there, ain't no sense in the world tryin' to get him out. Why, any livin' soul would be cooked and dead. And I ain't heard a sound out'n that cottage."

"That's right. Nor me. I ain't heard nary a one."

"Maybe he ain't in there."

"Yeah. He's in there. Most probably got likkered up and dropped a cigarette. Them pine floor are dry as ary any kindlin.'"

Somebody yelled. A woman screamed. The men passing the buckets stopped working, holding their pails as though they'd been suddenly paralyzed and turned to stone.

The figure of a man walked around the far side of the flaming house. There was only one reason to say that it was a man. It was walking. He was completely black. The hair had been burned from his head. There was still flesh on his legs and face and arms but it was completely blistered.

He had been holding the burned remnants of a cheap grass rug about him. He staggered, the remains of the rug fell to the ground. He was naked except for a strip of underpants. The middle of his body had not been burned. Obviously he must have wrapped himself in the rug and fought his way through the fire out a window or a back door of the cottage.

They dropped their buckets then, the people who were staring at him. As one stunned being, they moved toward the burned man. The ambulance attendants came running with a stretcher.

The people nearest him realized that the man was screaming. The only sound he was making was a croak, but the screams were at the top of his vocal chords. He was completely insane with agony.

When they tried to get near him, he ran. It didn't take long for them to realize, though, that he wasn't running from them.

He didn't even know they were there. He was running because the agony was so terrible he couldn't stand still. That was all that kept him moving any more. All that was left was the instinct to get away from the terrible fires that were burning inside him now. Fires that nobody in that crowd had any idea he would ever escape....

The ambulance attendants finally caught him. He was not really breathing. He was gulping in just enough air to scream with. He was sending it back through his throat in that terrible scream that was with all the power in him, almost unheard.

The attendants caught him about the hips because there he was least

seared. With his head back and screams pouring out of his mouth, he
allowed them to lead him to the ambulance.

"Better drive him right through to the city!" somebody yelled at the driver. "Eatonville's hospital wouldn't be able to do anything for him!"

"Nobody in God's world can now, Mister!"

"The city hospital is best. They got specialists—"

"That poor devil will never live to get to Rainier—"

"Whatever he's done on this earth, he's paid for it in fire—"

"He ain't through, Mister. He's just started."

"No. He's through all right. He won't live to get to the city."

The attendants helped him into the ambulance and forced him to sit on
the side of the bed. One of them sat beside the burned man. The other leaped
out of the car and slammed the rear door.

"We'll get him to the city," the driver told the crowd. "We'll take him there,
whether he lives or not."

"Anybody know his family better get in touch with them."

"Where are the two guys in the fire gear?"

"The flames were too much, they couldn't get through them." The man
who'd brought the fire gear and his buddy stood at the edge of the crowd.
Their faces were singed slightly. They looked sheepish.

"Warn't no use goin' in there," one of them said. "Anyone in that place now
is cooked up. Nothin' we could do."

The ambulance moved across the narrow yard to the sand road and started
along it, with siren screaming. The narrow lane was almost choked by now
with the cars of late arrivals. Two fishermen had to run along ahead of the
ambulance making the drivers pull off the lane so the big car could get through.

But none of the crowd thought it was worth while, all the hurry to get that
man to a hospital in the city. He wasn't going to live to make it.

But there it was, being proved again. People don't give up. Fire is the odds,
but they fight it, even hopelessly. The burned man had lived long enough, at
least, to get through that sheet of fire. Just because he couldn't give up even
when the odds were hopeless. And now the winking light of the ambulance
moved with agonizing slowness along the crowded lane. They were rushing
to save the life of a man who would be better off dead. They didn't expect
him to live, not really. But they couldn't stop fighting, not as long as there
was one chance. Odds? A million to one. Hell, there's still that one chance.

And even stranger was the fact that, though none felt the burned man
would ever live to get to the city, not one would have suggested that the
attempt to get him there was futile and impossible. Every one of them would
have said try. And every one of them prayed in his own secret way that he
would make it.

"Jeff Taylor!" somebody said. "What a hell of a life he lived, but what a hell
of a way to die."

"How do you know it's Jeff Taylor?"

"Why, it's gotta be. That there's his car parked there, ain't it?"

"Might a been somebody with him."

"Not a man," somebody said. "That ain't why old Jeff Taylor kept this here place—"

"If'n there's a woman in there, she's charred now."

"If'n she's in there now, and that's Jeff Taylor in that ambulance yonder—why, I think I'd ruther be her."

"Lawd, yes. At least, with her, it's over."

They looked back at the cottage. It was almost consumed now. The ambulance had reached the highway at last and they could hear the siren only faintly. There was nothing more they could do for that house now. They stood there and watched it burn.

4

A man on the rewrite desk at the Rainier *News* looked up. He whistled. Ordinarily Zoe would have looked at him and smiled. This morning she seemed not to hear him. She went directly across the open room to the desk of the City Editor. The rewrite man stared after her, frowning.

Zoe Gardner was the loveliest girl most of the men in the *News* office had ever seen. Newspaper offices get some pretty women, a lot of smart ones, a smattering of intelligent ones, but few beauties.

Zoe would have attracted a lot of attention and comment anywhere. She hadn't been twenty long enough for that ripe age to leave the faintest trace on her smooth complexion. She wasn't tall but her slender body was beautifully proportioned, with ample hips and full breasts. Her hair and her eyes were black. She was something to whistle about. But now her lovely face was pale and sick with worry.

Merle Cooper, the City Editor, was talking on the telephone when Zoe reached his desk. She stood there waiting. She could tell by his voice that he was talking to someone at the St. John's Hospital. Two days now, the burned man had clung to his painful life. They hadn't allowed any visitors. Zoe knew. She had been there. She had tried to get in.

Merle hung up the telephone and looked at her, grinning. He was about thirty, frail and blonde. A ball of fire.

"Hi, baby," he said, "what's new?"

"That's why I came to see you."

He leaned back in his chair and looked at her.

"What can I do for you?"

"I'm looking for Vance."

"Roberts?" The editor scowled, the lines twisting his pale face. "My God, honey, I thought you'd washed that romance all up. What do you want with Vance Roberts?"

"I've got to find him. I've got to know what happened to him." Her voice was tense.

Cooper shook his head. "Well, I'll be damned," he said. "I don't know what it is about those lushes that gets the dolls. A beautiful babe like you. A model. A corn-fed Miss America. Something the movies are poorer without. And what do you do, come around here with your face all twisted up because a rum-dum, a no-good, is missing."

"Do you know where he is?"

He shook his head. "And I'll go two steps further than that, honey. I don't care. Don't you know yet what that guy Vance Roberts is? He's no-good, honey. He's alcoholic as a bottle of bay rum. Half the time he doesn't know where he is, the other half he's recuperating from the first half."

"I didn't come up here for a lecture, Merle. I've got to find Vance. Has he been in?"

"Not for two days."

"Hasn't he even called?"

"Yeah. Sure. Two days ago. I think he was at a bar then. He said he wasn't but he says that every time. He said he was working on something hot—"

"Jeff Taylor—"

"All right. If you know all my secrets, that's what he said. He said the Assistant D.A. was ready to throw the book at Jeff Taylor—"

"And that's the last time you heard from him?"

"That's all. Maybe he made Taylor mad, and Taylor had him shot—"

"Jeff doesn't kill people."

"He don't? How do you know?"

"He told me so."

"He told you? My God, now you've started hobnobbing with the really bad boys—"

"Oh, for Heaven's sake. Stop worrying about me, Merle. I met Jeff Taylor at one of those night spots he owns. I was there with Vance. Vance seemed to know him very well."

"Oh, he does that."

"And Vance was just starting on another one of his rumdings. I didn't know it when we started out or I would never have gone."

"And Jeff Taylor saw you home?"

She looked at him. "As a matter of fact, he did. He was a perfect gentleman... That night."

She waited for the effect of that to hit him. When he stared at her, shocked, she laughed at him.

"Look, honey," he said. "You're a child. Take my word for it. Those guys you've chosen to know are no good. How do you think Vance keeps his job here? Hell, a cousin of his owns that whole damned joint. They're just close enough so that we can't fire Vance Roberts. Or we would have, a long time ago. I don't know where he is—another bar, I guess. In fact, I'd bet on it. And if that's Jeff Taylor in the St. John's Hospital, baby, I am glad something happened to him before something happened to you—"

Her mouth tightened. "There's only one thing wrong with you, Merle. You've got the wrong job. You shouldn't be City Editor. You ought to be writing the editorials for the *News*."

He shrugged. "All right, Zoe. I say Vance is on another drunk. If not, there's no doubt in my mind that he got too hot on Jeff Taylor's tail, and Jeff Taylor had him taken care of."

She caught her breath, shaking her head.

He watched her. "Whether you want to believe it or not, Jeff Taylor is a tough cookie. He had to be, baby. He got to the top in a rotten racket. You don't get there living by the golden rule."

"He wouldn't have Vance killed—"

"It would be no loss if he did."

"Stop talking like that!"

"But if he did, would that show you what Taylor is—or was?"

She looked ill. She leaned against the edge of his desk.

"You've got to find him," she said. "You've got to find Vance."

"Don't worry, baby, he's probably on his semi-weekly drunk. He'll turn up."

"He's got to!"

Merle Cooper shook his head. "Not as far as I'm concerned he doesn't," he said. "I got too much else on my mind. Will the burned man live? And if he does live, who is he? Honey, we're selling papers like we've never sold them before."

5

Captain Lipsey Beckart was a six-foot-plus gangling man. He wore cheap clothes and they were always an ill fit. He was forty-five and almost bald, but his suits exposed his ankles and wrists, giving him the look of a growing boy. He was a good police officer, as honest as any man in the department. Sometimes when he was sitting around home, drinking beer after work, he would tell anyone who'd listen that the police of every town are always as honest as its citizens. He believed that most police wanted to do an honest job. But there is a lot of politics mixed up in their poor-paying jobs. There are a lot of ways to hamstring the cops. And most people have learned those methods.

He sat in the resident doctor's office in the St. John's Hospital. The man behind the desk was a psychiatrist. His name was Vincent Ricey.

Ricey was between fifty-five and sixty. His hair was gray. But the hair around the sides of his head was darker than on top. Looking at the medico, Beckart wondered if he wore a toupee. There was nothing wrong with that, except that to the balding Beckart a toupee seemed an affectation, and a doctor who treated mental disorders should at least be free of driving personal vanity.

Ricey was undoubtedly an expert doctor. Beckart had seen him work and he knew him to be intelligent. Ricey was tired. You could see that in his eyes. He worked long hours, longer than most psychiatrists. He attempted to reach more people. Beckart smiled to himself. All right, Ricey was a good man. It was just that Beckart always found himself wondering if he *did* wear a toupee.

Beckart sighed. It was that simple little matter that stood between him and complete faith in the famous Dr. Vincent Ricey. On the other hand, maybe it was a good thing. That nagging little doubt made Beckart surer of himself. He didn't always accept everything Ricey did as infallible. He was able to argue with him.

"I'm convinced, Doctor," Beckart was saying. "The man is Jeff Taylor all right."

"We've told you, you're saying that simply because he walked out of Jeff Taylor's burning cottage. Simply because Jeff Taylor is wanted by the D.A.'s office for murder, and you want a murderer. You want that poor boiled devil in there to be Jeff Taylor and that's why you insist that it is."

"That's not the only reason. There are more. One more thing. Wasn't that Jeff Taylor's Buick parked in front of Jeff Taylor's cottage? Not many people in this city don't know Jeff Taylor's Buick. And there it was. He was always running up to that place. He used it for a hideout—"

"A hideout! Did he ever try to conceal the fact that he owned it, and most of the land on that side of Eaton Lake?"

"No. He never did."

"All right, then. Let's be coldly analytical about this thing. Let's give the devil his due. It's the only way we're going to reach a substantial conclusion. Jeff Taylor owned a fishing camp up there. He never made a secret of it. And he was generous, as I understand it. Many people used it in his absence, just as he often loaned his new car. Why, I've heard that even the young Negro porter in his night spot used that car on dates."

"All right. But the heat was on. Nobody was using his car that night—"

"I still don't think that Jeff Taylor would go up to that place alone. He wasn't the kind to seek solitude—not alone."

"Well, he might have taken that brokendown jerk he keeps around as a bodyguard, Halftime Smith—"

"Halftime?"

"Yeah. Halftime Smith. He used to be a wrestler. He spent half the time on the mat and the other half groaning, even when there wasn't anything to groan about. He's gone to jelly upstairs."

"But he isn't missing?"

"Oh, no. He wanders up and down the corridor outside that room up there until the nurses send him away. They won't let him in that room, but he swears that man is Taylor. And for once I agree with Halftime Smith."

"You're letting your wishful thinking get the better of you. Not that it matters. The specialists in attendance in there aren't trying to do anything for the poor devil except relieve his pain as much as they can. He'll never live long enough for you to get him to the chair, no matter who he is."

"I'm telling you, Doc. That man is Jeff Taylor. Look at it this way. So I'll admit you're right. Maybe I was being kind of FBI when I called Taylor's place a hideout. No, he didn't try to hide. But it was a hideaway. He took dames up there. He was always taking dames up there. And that's what he was doing up there this time—"

"No, Lipsey. I'm sorry. But the residue of that body found inside the cabin shows that it was not a woman—"

"How?"

Ricey smiled. "The simplest answer in the world. The pelvic bones were among those remaining. And even you must know the difference, Lipsey, between male and female—"

"All right, all right. Have your joke. No, Doc, I haven't six different degrees from schools in two continents. But since you've proof there were two men in that cottage, I'll have to get scientific proof that the man in there is Taylor. I'll get it!"

Ricey said, "It might be Taylor. But I don't want you thinking that if by some miracle the burned man lives, that you can point at him and say, 'Murderer, Jeff Taylor.' It won't be like that. Fingerprints? You won't get any—not for a long, long time, anyway. Teeth imprints might have been made at some time for one or both of the two men involved. There may be other methods of determining who the man is, but a lot of them won't be acceptable before a court of law. And I know that's what you're interested in. That's why I'm telling you these things."

"I'll use every method—"

"I want you to. But I'm only telling you what you are up against." Ricey pressed a button on his desk. The inter-office communicator on his desk sputtered. Ricey spoke into it. "Will you ask Mrs. Young to come in now?"

Beckart stared at the doctor. The door across the office opened. A nurse stood there. Benjamin Young's wife walked past her. The nurse closed the door.

Beckart now looked wide-eyed at the woman in the tan suit. Her clothes were expensive, they had that look. She wore an expensive hat that sat snug on her blonde head and had a half-veil that concealed her blue eyes. Beckart supposed the woman had been crying. It was difficult to say. But her face was pale, taut, drawn. She was full-breasted, round-hipped and long-legged. She looked society page. That was the way Beckart pegged her. Country Club, horsey set—society page.

Ricey was standing behind the desk. Belatedly, the gangling Beckart got to his feet.

"Come in, Mrs. Young," Ricey said. "Sit there, won't you?"

She sat down across the desk from him.

"This is Police Captain Beckart, Mrs. Young. He is interested in this case. Until today, believing that Jeff Taylor was alone in his fishing camp, Mr. Beckart has been certain that the burned man was Jeff Taylor. I wonder if you'd mind telling him what you have told me."

Mrs. Young sat with her hands in her lap. She looked at Beckart steadily for half a minute. Beckart found himself wishing be could see better through that half-veil.

"It was to have been confidential what Ben—my husband—told me, Mr. Beckart. But he was with Jeff Taylor in that cabin."

"Your husband? The young Assistant D.A.? With Jeff Taylor?" Beckart's voice told how shocked he was.

"I can tell you it was no friendly matter." Mrs. Young's voice caught.

Beckart nodded. "I'm sure it wasn't, Mrs. Young." His tone was kind.

She looked at him. "Still he was there. *I know.* You see, my husband got a telephone call that night. Just before he left the house he told me he was meeting Jeff Taylor on a very important matter. Taylor had insisted that he tell no one. But Ben didn't trust him, naturally. So he told me that he was to be with Jeff Taylor, in case anything happened. He told me not to mention it, and of course if he had come home and been all right, I—I—never would have said anything."

Beckart looked at her. His first impulse was to say something that would comfort her. What would that be in a strange case like this? Should he say that he hoped the agonized devil in that room was her husband? Would she rather he be in a living hell or dead and out of it? He didn't know what to say. He breathed deeply, saying nothing.

The young doctor looked at the laboratory experts that Beckart had brought into the room. Two weeks had passed since the fire. The man on the bed was still alive. At least, you had to qualify that. He breathed, and his heart pumped. For the rest of it, he was kept drugged all the time.

"Measurements, Captain? Certainly, let them make them. Naturally they'll have to be as careful as possible, but they won't *hurt* him. He won't know anything about it."

Beckart leaned on the radiator at the wide windows. He had a chart and pencil in his hands. On each side of the chart were the physical measurements of Young and Taylor. They had been supplied by doctors in the case of Young and from police files in the case of Taylor.

The lab men began to read off the measurements of the man on the bed. Of course, in no instance were they those shown on Beckart's chart. The fire had made a great chemical change in the flesh on the man's body.

"Head. Twenty-two and one half inches."

Beckart wrote and said nothing. With hair instead of the bandages, that head could belong to either man.

So it went, in the distance from the middle of the man's back to the point of his shoulder, the length of his arms, the length of legs. A dentist had supplied a chart of Young's teeth. Despite the fact that he was thirty-two, he had no fillings, no cavities and had lost only two molars, upper and lower back. There was no dental record available for Taylor. Anyhow, the dentist's chart and teeth examination proved nothing. The man on the bed had the same number of perfect teeth as were shown on the dentist's chart for Young.

They called in Ricey then, and he was able to get the unconscious man to open his eyes. They were wide, dry, pale.

"Both these men had hazel eyes," Beckart said.

"This man's eyes may be hazel—when he's well," Ricey replied.

He no longer said "if." It had been two weeks now. The burned man had walked out of that fire. He was hard to kill. Around the hospital they were betting that he was going to live.

In the fourth week the hospital officials agreed, under pressure from friends of Benjamin J. Young, Sr., to allow the senior Youngs to visit the drugged man in Room 318.

Mrs. Young was a heavy woman who had spent most of her waking hours since the night of the fire at Jeff Taylor's fishing camp in tears. She looked at the man swathed in gauze on the bed and found no reason to cease her crying.

She sank into a chair beside the bed and covered her face with her trembling hands.

"My son," she whispered. "My poor, poor boy."

Beckart was leaning against the window across the room. He dragged in a deep breath and pressed his mouth tightly together.

Benjamin Young, Sr., was almost as tall as Beckart, but he was stout, and a lifetime of wealth had given him poise that not even this tragedy could completely destroy.

He touched his wife's shoulder. "Now, Mother," he said. You could hardly hear him across the room. "Now, Mother."

Dr. Ricey was not as affected as Beckart was by Mrs. Young's collapse.

"You must remember, Mrs. Young," he said, "there is always the chance that the man on that bed is not your son."

She looked up. "It must be," she said. Her mouth was set. "If there is a God at all that is my son on that bed!"

"If he weren't drugged, Mrs. Young, the pain would be excruciating. He might be better off—"

Her head went up.

"Don't say that!" she ordered. "Don't ever say that. This is my son. God wouldn't take my son and leave a rotten common thief in the world! That is my son, Dr. Ricey—and he will get well."

The doctor just looked at her. He started to speak, changed his mind, drew in a deep breath and shrugged.

A week later, two nurses met outside Room 318.

"Gracie, you hear the latest about our human toast in there?"

"No, Mamie. I just came on duty."

"Well, it looks like our Mr. X is going to do a lot of suffering. The narcotic wore off last night. When they finally realized it, he'd almost killed himself rolling on the bed—"

"Oh, God!"

"But that's not the worst! You know what else? They said he'd used most of his energy screaming. Screaming, mind you. Screaming in pain at the top of his voice, and not even making enough noise so that the nurse across the room could hear him!"

6

It was like being born.

You came alive in a sea of agony. You were in pain if you moved. It was so terrible you couldn't stand it to lie still. You tried to open your eyes and found a thin strip of gauze covered them. Through the painful slits, you saw that the venetian blinds were drawn, the room was gray. You had no idea what time, what day, it was. You only knew that you were in pain and that time didn't matter....

He could see a nurse sitting in a chair a few feet from his bed.

He turned his head toward her. Maybe she wasn't even real. Maybe she was only a blur. He tried to speak to her. He made his mouth form the word, "Nurse." He spoke it, but she didn't even look up.

At first, he decided that she was asleep. But he stared at her until his eyes ached. She was holding a book in her hands. She wasn't asleep. Her head was too erect.

"Nurse!"

He screamed it at her. He was in agony. He needed help. He realized that he had not even heard himself speak. There was nothing, just a sharp gasping sound.

No wonder she didn't look up. Probably you made that same sound in your sleep.

He began to roll on the bed. He could no longer lie still. She jumped up then, dropping her book to the floor.

He felt her hands on his hips, pressing him down, holding him still.

"Now, Mr. X," she said. She kept her voice low, soothing. "Take it easy now. Take it easy. You're going to be all right. Lie still. Still. That's right."

With her right hand, she pressed the buzzer that lighted the red signal above the door outside the room. Another nurse came in immediately.

"He's at it again, Mamie," the nurse said from the bed.

"Now, Mr. X, you got to be a good boy. How are we ever going to get you well if you act up like this and kill yourself—after we've worked so hard?"

"You better get Dr. Halligan. This looks like another bad one." She was right, it was a bad one. Mamie scurried from the room to summon Dr. Halligan—whoever the hell he was. The pain was so intense—there was no place on his body that did not burn—that he couldn't tolerate it. He passed out. He was unconscious again before the doctor got there.

"Where am I?" He could whisper now.

The nurse bent over him. It was a hell of a thing, but the truth. Whenever anyone whispered at you, your tendency was to whisper in answer.

"Don't you know?" she said.

"Where am I?" His body tensed.

She smiled at him. "All right. All right. I never met a man whose nerves were so terrible. Believe me, they burned the ends off yours, didn't they?"

"Where am I?"

"This is the St. John's Hospital. The city of Rainier."

His head rolled on the pillow.

"Now what's the matter? Please don't act up again. You get yourself in such a mess when you do. Now, take it easy. I've told you where you are."

His unwinking eyes stared up at her, boring into her. Of course she had. She had answered his question. St. John's Hospital. Rainier. That's what he had wanted to hear. It left him deflated. Miserably disappointed. The names were words. Just words. They had no meaning for him at all. They were just letters of the alphabet strung out one after the other to make sounds.

He felt an awful emptiness in his belly. It was horrible hearing that nurse speak the names of a hospital and a city in a tone that assured him they should mean something to him. But they didn't. But not even that was the worst.

He stared at her, his eyes straining to see her clearly. The question that he wanted to ask, had to ask, the one that had him sick, paled the other two into insignificance.

Who, in the name of God, am I?

He took the two orange-colored capsules she offered him, swallowed the water, felt her stab him with a hypo needle in his buttocks. He went off to sleep. Wasn't that the way it was? When a situation was unbearable, you got tired and sleepy. You wanted to sleep until the trouble cleared up.

But his last waking thought was, *At that rate, I'll have to sleep forever.*

Stabbing pain brought him awake the next time. The room was still gray. The blinds were drawn at the window. He had no way of knowing the hour, or even the season of the year.

He could feel the bandages on his body and on his arms. He jumped up in bed, tearing at them. A nurse grabbed him. She shoved him back in bed and began calling for Dr. Halligan.

Halligan must have been just outside the door. Almost at once he was there helping the nurse push the patient back on the bed. Another nurse was making with the hypo needle.

Halligan's voice was smooth and professional. "Now, take it easy. You're almost well. You're going to be all right—that's why you're in such agony now. The healing is almost as bad as the fire."

"Fire?" X lay on the bed, staring up at him.

"Yes, of course. When you were burned."

"Burned?" X knew he was screaming at the top of his voice. But the sound was nothing but a croaking whisper.

"Well, I'll be damned," Halligan said. He was a stocky young resident doctor with a lock of brown hair over his sweated forehead. There was nothing professional about his voice now. "This is really one for Ricey."

The room was getting hazy before X now. But he wanted to hold on just a little longer. It was so important. Halligan knew why he was here—a fire. Maybe Halligan knew the answer to the question that haunted him every waking moment, *who was he?*

"That's right," Halligan was saying. "Rest now. That's right. Easy. Take it easy. No reason for you to tear the place apart every time you wake up."

"Have—I—done—this—before?"

"Have you? Only every time you wake up!"

The next time he woke up, he remembered what the doctor had said about the fire. The feeling persisted that it all belonged in some horrible nightmare. His body was covered with soothing oil and there wasn't this tearing need to rip his way out of the chafing gauze.

Halligan had said fire. He tried to go back in his mind to the moment of fire. But there was nothing. He couldn't do it, and the terror that hounded him was worse than any memory of a fire.

He was nameless. He had no past. Nothing. He was born there on a bed in the St. John's Hospital, Rainier.

"Nurse! Doctor! Nurse!" He was screaming again, and the sound was only a whisper.

"Oh, oh, here we go again," the nurse said. "Now take it easy, X, my love. Take it easy!"

His head rolled on the pillow. "Nurse, for the love of God, who am I?"

"Who are you?" There was shock in her voice, but she was well trained. She kept her tones even. She was pressing the signal buzzer again under his pillow. When a nurse came through the door at a trot, she said, "X is awake and talking again. Ricey said let him know the minute it happened."

"Ricey?" X whispered. "Who is Ricey?"

"He's a doctor. The kind that you'll have to contend with now that we've got you almost whole again. He's going to help you remember things. He's going to help you find out—who you are."

He couldn't see Dr. Ricey very well through the strand of gauze across his eyes. He could tell that Ricey was an elderly man, gray hair and tired face, heavy shoulders, that was all. *God,* he thought, *what was it they said about dogs? Everything is gray to dogs, isn't it?*

That was the kind of vision he had.

"Well, my boy, we've witnessed a miracle here," Ricey was saying. "Physically, you're out of danger. In time I'm sure your vocal chords will heal and your voice will return. Of course, you won't be able to sing in the church choir any more, but—"

"Who am I?"

"That's why I'm here, my boy. Stop fretting. Stop upsetting yourself about it. You've been through a traumatic experience that wounded you mentally as well as physically. But if your body had the stamina, the will to recover, it's fair to believe that your mind has, too."

"But who am I?"

"That should be easy. But through a strange set of circumstances, right now it is an enigma. We don't know. We don't promise to cure you, even physically, so you'll be what you were before the fire. We cannot promise to help you find out who you are. That's going to be up to you. But we are going to give you every assistance. You and I are going to spend a lot of time jawing with each other. We're going to let the nurses read to you all the newspaper accounts of the fire and of the men who were in it together—"

"Now?"

"Soon. We want you to have all the facts on it. Sometimes in cases like these names, odors, associations, or familiar surroundings will be enough to start your memory working. You see, we've used the so-called truth drugs on you several times in the past weeks, and there is a definite mental block— you don't go back of it. Your conscious and your unconscious seem to have been born the night of that fire."

"Oh, my God."

"Don't let it defeat you. As I said, we're going to do everything we can, place you in every situation we can that might hasten your recovery. It is not at all impossible."

The nurse named Gracie began reading from the Rainier *News* the accounts of the fire at Jeff Taylor's fishing cottage. It was all there. In separate columns, the lives of the two men were outlined.

X lay on the bed, sweating, listening.

The schools that Benjamin J. Young had attended. The degrees he'd earned. The year he'd played football in high school. The year he made third string on the university track team. The girl, Myra English, he had married the year he graduated and entered his father's law firm. His record as Assistant District Attorney. And the account ended with the hint that Benjamin J. Young was working on a giant clean-up campaign at the time of death. Rainier's great loss.

Gracie stopped reading.

"Does that sound like you, X?"

"Would my death be a great loss?"

"You seemed to think so, honey. You wouldn't die."

"Go on reading."

The other life story was written in scorn. The article implied rather plainly that money and birth were the sole evidence of human quality. Jeff Taylor had been born in squalor. From that squalor, Taylor had become the racket boss of Rainier. He operated night spots that existed because of the gambling and the other vices they catered to. He lived by appealing to the basest elements of human nature. His death was no loss. It was, in fact, a great civic improvement.

"I hope you're not him," Gracie said.

"It doesn't sound like me. But why?"

"Because all the work we've done here will go to waste if you are Jeff Taylor."

"Yes?"

Gracie looked at him. "I may as well tell you. It'll come out in the next newspaper I read to you. If you're Jeff Taylor they're going to electrocute you—and after all our work, too."

"For what?"

"For murdering a guy named Rick Vashney. Just be patient, though, you haven't heard anything at all yet."

She unfolded another edition of the *News.* He lay there listening to the rustling of the pages. He began to sweat. It fretted him. It brought back a painful memory. And then he knew what it was, the crackling of flames.

A nurse entered before Gracie could read.

"Hold it, Gracie." The nurse came to the side of the bed. "We've got some visitors for our boy. Your wife and mother and father are here to see you. Dr. Ricey said they were to be admitted the moment they arrived."

"My wife? Mother? Father?"

Gracie's voice was flat. "Mamie means it's your wife, mother and father, *if...* if you happen to turn out to be a man named Benjamin J. Young."

7

They filed in. The stout woman whose face was pale and taut; she looked as if she were going to burst into tears at any minute. Behind her, the august-looking man that X supposed was Benjamin J. Young, Senior. Dad. Pop. Father. Pater. He tried the words inside his head. None of them seemed to fit the man who stood at the side of the bed, looking at him.

She came in last. Alone.

He looked at her and something stirred inside him. He twisted on the bed, staring at her. What was it? His heart began to slug. He tried to speak. There was only that whisper.

"It's I, darling," she said. "It's Myra. It's all right, darling. It's Myra."

Myra. A word. That name meant nothing. Whatever it was that had been stirring in his mind, it was gone. It had eluded him.

Now she was just another person in the room, like the stout woman who had begun to cry, the nurse over by the window, Benjamin Young, Sr., clearing his throat.

It was good to look at her. She was something special, all right. Ben Young's career against crime wasn't the only thing he had to be proud of. He had married one of the loveliest blondes X had ever seen. How did he know? What sort of memory did he have? None at all. All right then, Myra looked like an angel. Except for one thing. Her blue eyes were hard, cold. Even when she was bending toward him, her perfume assailing his nostrils, her eyes remained watchful.

She was really something, all right!

"Don't you know me, Ben?" she said. "Try, darling. Think. It's Myra. We want to take you home with us. We want you to get well. Look at me."

"My poor boy," Mrs. Young sobbed. "He doesn't even know us. He doesn't know us at all."

"He's been through a pretty terrible experience," the nurse said. "You've just got to give him a little time."

Young, Sr. cleared his throat again.

"Of course we will. All the time, all the money it takes to make him well. We won't spare anything."

Something about Young's voice displeased X. Young was saying that money was the answer to everything. Since they had all the money, they had all the answers. He wasn't saying, he'll get well. He was saying, we'll pay some money, and then he'll be well.

Still, if X and the nurse were not impressed, Mrs. Young seemed to gather strength from the statement that her husband's money was going to make X well. X rolled his head on the pillow impatiently. No matter who he was before the fire, since that night, he was a man with the shortest temper in the history of temperament.

"There, there," Myra's voice was soothing. "Please, B.J., don't talk like that, as though money were all that mattered. You know Ben doesn't like it. He never has. He seems to think it's some kind of reflection on his ability every time you mention how much money you have. Poor silly darling."

She bent over him closer now, smiling, showing him she was on his side, even though she didn't agree with him.

"Sorry, my boy," B.J. said. "We'll get you doctors. You'll get well."

Myra covered his gauze-tied hand, and then jerked her fingers away when she remembered the pain she must cause him.

"You'll get well. Because I want you to," she said.

The nurse spoke from the window. "The doctor suggested that maybe you could talk about something that was happening just before the fire. It might help. Anyway, it will give him something to work on and think about when he's alone."

B.J. cleared his throat. "Well, my boy, I was sorry you couldn't join us at the Country Club. You remember, surely, we had made up a foursome with Senator Magressen and Judge Ernest Fuller. Ernest was upset when you couldn't make it. We had to pick up a man at the club. It cost Ernest ten dollars, and he'd been set on winning."

"I'm sorry," X said. "I'm sorry I wasn't there."

B.J. had to lean over the bed to hear him at all. "It's all right, my boy. There'll be plenty of time for golf matches. It was just that I was so anxious for you to have that time out on the course with the Senator and Ernest. It wouldn't have hurt you any—in the, uh, campaign, you know—"

"Governor?" X said.

"Name of God, it's working!" B.J. cried.

"I'm afraid not," the nurse said. "It won't be that easy. You see, we've been reading to him from the newspaper accounts. He knows that your son—he knows that he was planning to run for Governor."

Now Myra leaned over him again. The nearness of her moved him, something about her stirred him. He didn't like to believe it was merely the low cut of her dress, the deep cleavage between her scented breasts.

"Norma was ill when we didn't make it to her party the night of the fire, Ben," Myra whispered. There was depth to her voice, a sexy quality that could have made something intimate of a grocery list. "Of course, I didn't go. I was worried about you. You see, I knew you were with Jeff Taylor. I hope you don't mind, I told the police and Dr. Ricey that you were with Taylor. I know I promised. But after the fire and all—"

"It's all right," X said. "Why shouldn't you?"

She looked at him, her chilly eyes widening. "You *are* forgetful, doll," she said.

The nurse looked at her watch. "I don't think it's a good plan to tire him too much right at first," she suggested. "X is—I mean, your son—is pretty highstrung anyway. It won't help his disposition any to be tired out."

Mrs. Young stood up. "We're going," she said. She leaned over the bed, closing her hands on his arms. He tried to scream. But there was no sound. He only reared up in bed. The nurse streaked across the room, grabbed Mrs. Young away.

"I can't help it," she sobbed. "I've got to help him." She looked over the nurse's shoulder at him. "You've got to get well. You've got to. This is too much for me. I can't stand it."

X was breathing through his parted mouth.

He didn't answer. He watched the nurse leading Mrs. Young through the door into the corridor. B.J. followed without a backward glance.

And X turned his head, finding Myra was still near him.

"Hurry, darling," she said. "Hurry and get well. I miss you."

The face had the look that matched the sound of those whispered words. But the eyes remained aloof, watchful. She remained there, just above him, for a long time, and then she was gone.

X shivered.

What had that meant, the swirling memory trying to fight its way into his consciousness at the sight of Myra Young? Was it really only the reaction any man would feel toward a woman built as smoothly and trimmed as expensively as Myra? He doubted that. The thought that she stirred in him had bubbled up until he almost had it in his hand, and then had burst and was gone.

When they were gone, he lay there for a long time mulling over all he had learned until this moment. The name of the hospital. The name of the city. A weeping mother, a saddened father, a beautiful wife.

What more could a guy ask?

But X knew the answer to that, too. Living like this was existing in a vacuum. Nobody, belonging nowhere. It was illness that was a bottomless void and he had the feverish sensation of drifting through it, without anchor or security or hope. He had to know who he was. He had to see Myra again. Maybe if he saw her often enough, that fleeting memory would boil up into his consciousness and he'd have something tangible to cling to in this awful emptiness.

Dr. Ricey came in with Halligan.

Ricey said, "How do you feel, my boy? Was that the answer? Did the sight of them stir you? What do you think?"

"The girl," X whispered. "Only she did anything at all. I almost felt that I had seen her somewhere before. But I wasn't sure. I couldn't be sure—"

"Encouraging," Ricey said. "Definitely encouraging. We'll ask the young lady to visit you here as often as possible. Will you like that?"

X closed his eyes. He was seeing the full swell of her breasts, the creamy shadow between them. The smell of her. He was thinking about the eyes that remained watchful. The man who mastered that woman would be a man indeed. He wanted to see her again, all right. For a lot of reasons. Her aiding him to remember was just one of them.

He nodded.

The next time X woke up, he was resigned to the fact that he didn't remember anything of his past. Just being able to relax a little made him feel better. He opened his eyes and found the film of gauze across them had been removed.

"Well, darling! Isn't it about time you woke up!"

Startled, he turned his head on the pillow. The room was dark but she stood out like a buoy light in the night. Her hair was auburn-red and there was a lot of it. She parted it above her left eye and it curled down about her shoulders. She wasn't tall and she was heavy. But it was the lush kind of heaviness that makes some women delectable. Her lips were full and her cheeks were, too. Hers wasn't the cuddly type, either. Her brown eyes were aware and knowing. Here was a girl who knew her way around.

And he was her darling. At least, he was one of them!

She kind of flowed over the side of the bed, the warmth and the scent of her.

"Darling, we've tried every day, every way, to get in here. But they wouldn't let us. They said you wouldn't know us and we'd only upset you."

He pushed his gaze beyond her face to the two men. One was short, stocky and dark. His hair was slick with grease. His mouth smiled but his eyes didn't. Somehow, looking at the dark man, X thought of the blonde Myra Young. If only those two people realized how much their eyes revealed about them!

The other was taller but he was built like a keg and was topped with unruly sand-colored hair. His nose was broken and flat across its twisted bridge. But there was a man with eyes. X warmed toward the poor, simple devil the first time he saw him. There was a man whose eyes didn't warn you that his mouth was lying.

X smiled, nodding, stalling. This was a visit that nobody had prepared him for. Who were these people? Was the woman maybe Jessie Taylor? The thought flashed through his mind. That's who it was—the one the *News* had reported, scathingly, as being unable to be found for comment the night of the fire.

Jessie Taylor had been out building flames of her own the night her husband died in a cabin fire.

Now here she was calling him darling, and leaning as close to him as she could get. The world knew the truth about her. Hell, it had been on the front page of the *News*. "At a late hour this morning, the racketeer's redhaired wife could not be reached for comment. A source close to the family revealed that she had not been at home when the news of her husband's tragic death came." Now it was "darling." He knew he didn't like this broad, even though she was some girl.

The dark man spoke. "Been up here every minute I could spare, Jeff. I want you to know that."

X nodded. "Thanks."

The tow-headed keg grinned. "Hi, boss." His face beamed with his smiles. "Hi. Hiya, boss."

X tried to let the big man know that he was trying to smile under the gauze.

"Shut up, Halftime," the woman said. "I tried to make him stay in the car. I didn't want him worrying you."

"He doesn't worry me," X said. He remembered more from the newspapers. Halftime Smith was Jeff Taylor's only alibi the night Rick Vashney had been slain. X smiled to himself. It was easy to see Halftime was loyal to his boss.

"No, he never worries you!" the woman snapped. "No matter how busy you get, you've always got time to clown around with that big stupe. A lot of times you're too busy for me—"

The nurse spoke from the window then. "Please don't raise your voice, Mrs. Taylor. There's no use in exciting him unduly."

Jessie Taylor's head jerked up. "All right, all right. I'm glad you're going to be okay, darling."

"Am I going to be okay?"

"Sure you are. The doc said so. He told us, didn't he, Mike?"

The dark-skinned man nodded. "Sure. A little while more in here, then you can come back. To find things just like you left them. Mike Reglen has taken care of everything for you, Jeff, just the way you would have wanted it."

"Mike's been wonderful," Jessie said. "I'm sure I don't know how I'd have got along without him."

X's gaze wandered over to Halftime Smith. The big man's face showed his worry. Something was wrong. The other two could hide it, but it was all there for anyone to read in Halftime's troubled expression.

"I'm glad," X said. But it didn't matter to him. The troubles of that pair, the deadly dark man and the redheaded woman, left him unmoved.

When they said they were going, X tried to keep the relief from showing in his eyes. Jessie came near to him and formed a wet kiss just above his face, and then she went away, moving back from him, taking the heavy scent of her with her.

Mike Reglen said, "So long, and hurry and get out of there, boss."

X said, "Sure" in a whisper and turned his face to the wall.

For a moment, he thought he was alone. Then he heard someone at the edge of the bed. He turned over. Halftime Smith was there. His blue eyes were wet. He was twisting his cap in his hands.

"It is you, ain't it, boss?" His voice broke. "You didn't get burned in that fire, did ya? Gosh, boss, I never knew I'd miss nobody like I been missing you all these weeks. I ain't had no chance to talk with nobody. They let me buy 'em a drink, but they won't talk. They won't listen."

"It's going to be all right," X said through his gauze.

"Like them doctors say, boss, they say it might not be you. You're just foolin' 'em, huh, boss? It's you, all right. You wouldn't get caught in no fire so you couldn't get out, huh, boss? You're just pullin' one on 'em, ain't you, huh? You can tell me. You can trust me. I won't breathe it out to nobody. They couldn't beat it out of me. You're just pullin' a fast one, huh?"

X didn't know what to say. He put out his hand, touched the big man's arm. "You're all right, Halftime. You're an all right guy."

"Sure. Say, boss, remember the night I fought Bashful Barney? You remember, huh? You told me not to pull off his mask, it might be me mudder I was wrestlin'? Ah, you was kiddin', boss. I peeked. I looked under it. It was a guy—some jerk—some ugly character. No wonder he didn't want anybody to see his puss. Gosh, we laughed about that, huh, didn't we boss? Huh?"

The nurse had Halftime's arm and was trying to lead him from the darkened room. Halftime said, "I'll come back, boss. Plenty. Gosh, it was swell to see you, boss."

"Sure. Come back," X whispered. "Any time."

When the big man was gone, X lay rigid on the bed. There wasn't a hell of a lot for him to come back to, it seemed to him. What sort of life had Benjamin J. Young lived? Playing golf with the politically expedient, the men who could do him some good. Going home to a wife who was worried about what a hostess said when he died rather than attend one of her parties. A father who could never stop impressing people with the fact of his great wealth and influence and famous intimates. A mother who wanted him to get well because she had stood all the grief that she could take.

Or Jeff Taylor. Accused of murdering a man named Rick Vashney. A gun found in his apartment. Witnesses. An alibi named Halftime Smith. A smart cookie of a wife who couldn't be trusted to the end of her leash. A partner who looked sleek and deadly, a man who was the perfect complement to the redheaded woman. They were taking care of things for Jeff Taylor. He was going to find things just the way he left them. Yeah. In a pig's eye. Things would be, he thought, evenly divided between the two of them.

Of all the people he had seen, only one had seemed worth the effort. Halftime Smith. The fight racket had used him for a chopping block until he was no good any more. Then he'd made his living taking falls and groaning so younger and ambitious wrestlers would look good in that farce on sports. Only Halftime really wanted him to get well.

He shook his head, closing his eyes.

Dr. Ricey was there with Detective Captain Lipsey Beckart when he opened his eyes.

Dr. Ricey said, "I think both you gentlemen will be interested in hearing the results of certain psychiatric tests which have been made during the past few weeks. We find that the patient is without tendencies toward violence. His coordination and reflexes are good for a man of his age. We assume him to be between thirty and thirty-three. Socially, he might be classified as recovered, and can now exist without attention, supervision or medical care. His mental block is classed as traumatic amnesia. This may be a temporary condition, it may clear up of its own accord, or it may take long and careful attention."

Beckart said, "But you still won't say who he is."

"That's something he will have to tell you. As I told you there are certain tests, but none would be admitted in a court of law, and they would therefore be useless to you."

"Something has got to be done."

"Why? This man is alive only by a miracle. Are you being pressed to identify a man who missed death only by seconds?"

"I certainly am. We're being bombarded. If he is Benjamin Young, the town wants to celebrate. If he is Jeff Taylor, he is wanted for murder. He's got to be one or the other. If he's Young, fine. If he's not, he's a murderer—and I want him."

8

His office nurse announced that Mr. and Mrs. Young, Sr., were outside. Dr. Ricey sighed and told her to send them in.

They came into the office and the nurse closed the door behind them. Dr. Ricey smiled. Without fail he had found that the richer his patient or caller, the poorer his manners. Neither Mrs. Young nor her husband even glanced at the door. They definitely wanted it closed. They never discussed anything except in strict privacy. But both felt that someone else would close the door, push a chair under them, light their cigarette. That's what other people were for.

Mrs. and Mr. Benjamin J. Young, Sr., had arrived.

Mrs. Young's face was still pale, but she seemed now to have her crying controlled. Indeed, the good doctor, glancing at her, was sure he detected even belligerence in the stubborn set of her jaw.

Dr. Ricey sighed again. Obviously these people wanted something. The distressing aspect of the matter was that they seemed to want something from *him*. They seemed to feel that he was going to oppose them. He shook his head. He had dealt with the arrogantly wealthy before. He hadn't the slightest intention of opposing them, whatever they wanted.

Young, Sr., cleared his throat.

"Doctor," he said, "we want to take the boy home."

Dr. Ricey's mouth sagged open. He stared.

"Take him home?" He was shocked.

"It's been six weeks now," Mrs. Young said. She was a determined woman. Her voice rang clear in the small hospital office.

"But surely you understand that almost a third of his body suffered deep second-degree and acute third-degree burns. Only a miracle kept him alive. The ambulance attendant shot him full of morphine on the drive to Rainier. He was given more morphine, intravenous injections of whole blood and salt solutions to combat shock. We applied layers of gauze under pressure. He's been kept alive with morphine, penicillin and injections of blood. Surely you understand that just a few years ago he would have died even though he was alive, either drugged or in great agony, when he arrived here at the hospital."

"But my son didn't die—" Mrs. Young began.

"He may not be your son," the doctor interrupted. "It is almost time to begin skin-grafting operations on his face. It would be criminal to remove him from the hospital, where he can get every care, where every precaution will be taken to insure against joint paralysis or disfigurement—"

Neither of the Youngs seemed to have heard him.

"How soon could he be released to us?" Mr. Young inquired.

Ricey stared. He took a deep breath. "In about five months!" he snapped.

The Youngs looked at each other. Mrs. Young smiled faintly and shook her head at her husband. Ricey decided it was some private code between them.

Mrs. Young's tone was that of an adult with a recalcitrant child. Reasonable, yet firm. Ricey longed to punch her right in the nose.

"Now, my dear doctor, you must admit that my son's body has healed amazingly—"

"Yes, amazingly, if he is your son. And thanks to 300,000 units of penicillin at a time—"

"He is my son, doctor. Do you think a mother can be fooled?"

"Frankly, yes. Most mothers delude themselves. For many reasons."

"Well! I'm certainly not going to argue that with you. But I'd always felt, doctor, that you medical men would be the last to speak snidely of American motherhood—"

"Motherhood is universal. Highly overrated. It depends entirely on the mother. As in every matter concerning a human being, everything is personal. Each individual is different...."

"We are getting away from the subject of my son," Mrs. Young said. "I felt that we could make you understand. You are a doctor who specializes in mental diseases—we were sure you would understand. My son is not suffering physically any more, but mentally—"

"He certainly is. He was subjected to shock so violent, Mrs. Young, that it has—temporarily, at least—caused a complete lapse of memory."

"He'll recover much more quickly at home, among familiar surroundings, where he'll be cared for with love and kindness—"

"Or he may be driven completely over the brink. Doesn't it ever occur to you that this might not be your son? What then? What would your overweening attentions do for him then? Suppose he is Jeff Taylor?"

"Doctor—his eyes—"

"The shape of his eyes has been completely altered by the loss of facial tissue."

"The color, doctor!"

"I should not need to remind you, both men in that house had gray or hazel eyes. No, Mrs. Young, it is not yet time for the patient to leave the hospital. Believe me, when it is time, I'll let you know."

Mrs. Young took a deep breath, ready, Ricey was sure, to continue. But she happened to glance at her husband, and Ricey again saw that private signal, the sly smile, the almost imperceptible shake of the head. Funny, how you could get to hate people. Such an offensive pair!

Mr. Young took his wife's arm and they got up. Young's florid face was decorated with a sudden false smile. "Thanks for your time, doctor. I hope you'll forgive our intruding like this."

Mrs. Young's false smile almost matched her husband's. And then they were gone. They went through the door, leaving it open.

Dr. Ricey watched them go. He felt a faint chill along the nape of his neck. The whisper of disaster.

Dr. Vernon Corbin was Chief of Staff of St. John's Hospital, Rainier. Dr. Ricey was a specialist and knew Corbin only casually. When he got a call to Corbin's office the next morning there was no mystery about the matter in Ricey's mind at all.

The Benjamin J. Youngs had called on the Chief of Staff, of course. Ricey smiled as he went along the corridor toward Corbin's office. Now he was to be called in for a report on the burned man's condition. He supposed it would be best to couch all facts in medical jargon. The man's condition was serious, but it wouldn't hurt to clutter it with confusion. Probably that was all Corbin would want anyhow. Just something to soothe the Youngs with.

Corbin's private secretary looked up and smiled. "Do go right in, doctor. They're waiting or you."

They! They? Ricey felt that chill across the back of his neck again. That whisper of trouble!

Captain of Detectives Lipsey Beckart was at one end of the colorful rainbow that ringed Dr. Corbin's furbished desk. Beside him were the other doctors who had been working over the burned patient since the night he'd been brought in from Eaton Lake: the skin-grafting expert, the authority on post-surgical infections and all the others.

Ricey had been called in as specialist in surgical shock. Now he felt that he was suffering from shock.

At the other end of the rainbow was the pot of gold, Benjamin J. Young. And wife.

Doctor Corbin gave Ricey a brief smile. Ricey slumped into a chair behind Lipsey Beckart.

Dr. Corbin said, "I'm sure you gentlemen all know Mr. and Mrs. Benjamin J. Young. Mr. Young is one of the directors of St. John's Hospital." Corbin's eyes met Ricey's, faltered, and moved on. "He is also one of the most generous contributors to the hospital. As he says, he feels well repaid for the million he has given St. John's over the years. This hospital was able to save the life of his son—"

"If it is his son," Ricey said.

Beckart grinned over his shoulder.

Corbin stopped smiling at all. "We have reached a conclusion, and I've brought you all here to hear it, for I am sure you will applaud it. We are going to allow Mr. and Mrs. Young to remove their son from this hospital to their private home—"

"But, Doctor—" Ricey spluttered.

Corbin held up his hand. "Please, hear it all. He will have the best of trained nurses, twenty-four hours a day. Now, as you know, while once such severe burn cases would have required six months in the hospital and a minimum of two years of reconstructive surgery, the quick healing of the burned areas makes it possible for this patient to leave this hospital in only six weeks. Very little plastic surgery is going to be required and it can be done easily within a few months—"

"He is suffering from shock!" Ricey said. "We have cured the burns and now we must cure the man."

"I'm glad you brought that up, Doctor." Corbin was suave about this. "I feel that under the normal influences of his home, the patient's recovery will be speeded, not retarded—"

Ricey was deflated. Whisper of disaster? This was thunder. He had thought he would be asked his opinion. He wasn't being asked anything. He was being told. He shrugged.

"Mr. Beckart, as representative of the police, how do you feel about this?" Corbin said.

"If there's some proof that the patient is Mr. Young's son, why, I have no jurisdiction in the matter at all. But it may be that the man is Jeff Taylor— wanted for the murder of Rick Vashney. In that case, I'm sure the law would rather have him remain here."

Ricey glanced around the semi-circle at the Youngs. He could see Mrs. Young swelling, the color of her face change. Then Papa Young smiled at her. That secretive, superior little smile. He shook his head at her. Patted her hand.

Mr. Young got up, went to the desk of Dr. Corbin and shoved a letter across it.

Ricey looked at Beckart with real pity. Poor devil. Beckart didn't know the building was about to fall in on him.

Corbin was smiling at Beckart now. "This is a letter from the Police Commissioner, Mr. Beckart. As you know, Mr. Young is on the police board. The Commissioner says that the police department is anxious to cooperate in every way in seeing that Mr. Young's son's recovery is speeded."

Beckart looked stunned. Ricey knew how he felt. But Beckart managed to smile and nod.

"Why then, sure," he said. "I don't see how the police department can object. Whatever you want to do."

"Fine. Fine," Corbin said. "Then we're all agreed, gentlemen? It would be beneficial to the patient to recuperate in familiar surroundings—"

"No!"

Ricey s voice thundered so loudly in the room that he hardly recognized it. He stood up. "I'll call in the FBI," he said. "I'll take it to the American Medical Association. That man stays in the hospital."

Corbin jumped up. "Dr. Ricey, please. It has been settled! I tell you, it has been settled!"

"Certainly! For what? Another million dollar gift? All right. I bow to progress. What can I do? But you have said that the patient will recuperate in familiar surroundings. It might well be that the surroundings of the Young villa or estate or mansion or whatever it is might not be familiar. The patient must be in this hospital two weeks from today for a skin graft operation. I offer an alternate suggestion. The patient will spend a week with the Youngs. But he must then spend a week in the apartment of Jeff Taylor. Taylor was rich enough to afford equally good medical care and nursing. If he's going to be cured by outlandish therapy—then let's cure him!"

Ricey's hands were still shaking as he returned to the office he was occupying in the hospital. It had been a long and bitter fight. Mrs. Young had fainted twice. She and her husband had exchanged forty seven of those little secret smiles and head shakes. But in the end he had won. Corbin had to keep it scientific—at least with the scent of science. And at last the Youngs had agreed. Probably planning, Ricey supposed, to handle the matter of the second week when they came to it.

The office girl said, "There's a Mr. Smith in your office, doctor. A Mr. Half-time Smith."

The ex-wrestler was sitting in a chair by the window. He jumped up when Ricey entered the office. He was twisting his cap in his hands.

"Hey," he said. "Hey. They tell me that my boss is going out of here." Excitement made him stutter. "They tell me them rich swells is taking him home with 'em. Them Youngs."

Ricey smiled. "That's right. The Youngs are convinced that the patient is their son Ben."

Halftime shook his head. "Well, he ain't. Well, he couldn't be. That's my boss. Look, they say there ain't no definite proof. But I got definite proof, I betcha."

Ricey felt his heart hammering. "What is it, Mr. Smith?"

"A tattoo. My boss had a heart tattooed on his left arm, just below his elbow, on the inside. We got drunk together one night. I was gettin' my girl Mabel's name put on my chest. I talked the boss into gettin' a tattoo. But he would just take one about as big as your little fingernail. But it's there—"

"You've visited him?"

"Yes, sir. I have."

"And you saw the tattoo?"

"Well, that's it, Doc. I looked. First thing, I looked. But it was covered up. A cast or something."

Ricey was smiling. "Yes. He broke his left arm getting out of that house. We're removing the cast, Mr. Smith, within the week. We'll know then whether he's Taylor or Young!"

9

Myra came into his bedroom about ten the next morning. The nurses had kept him to his hospital routine so he had been awake and bathed since six o'clock. He had had breakfast at eight.

Since eight he had been sitting in the wheelchair staring out of the window. Looking at landscaped grounds as unfamiliar to him as the middle of his own back. There was no thought that he had ever seen any of it before.

In the mirror across the room, he could see himself. That was an unfamiliar sight, too! Practically all white bandage—a man-shape swathed in white, with only a slit for his eyes, a hole for his mouth. He wiggled the scarred fingers of his right hand watching the reflection. They were the only other part unbandaged, they moved, and they weren't stiff. He'd been afraid of stiffness in the joints. He'd heard talk about that and about disfigurement since his first conscious moments in St. John's Hospital.

First he decided he was lucky to be alive. Then he asked himself cynically what was lucky about being a zombie. Because that was what he was, wasn't it? A walking being without past or memory of the past. Where were the good things a man could look back on? Where were the great deeds a man loved to look forward to in his secret dreams?

And even more urgent, who was he? Who in God's name was he? Would he *ever* know?

Sure, he was lucky. He was alive. He was breathing. He could wiggle the fingers of his right hand. They didn't look like fingers, of course. They looked like overdone frankfurters. But they were supposed to be fingers, and when the skin grafting was done they'd be fingers again.

Meanwhile, wasn't he lucky?

He turned his head when Myra came into the room. Then he decided that maybe he wasn't too unlucky after all.

She was wearing a peach-colored wrap-around of some transparent material. Beneath it was the sheer nightgown. She did something for those clothes. Rounded hips, the round smooth heap of her stomach and, above, the lush ripe breasts.

He sighed heavily, feeling the need for a woman in his arms. Feeling the desire for this woman.

She stirred him, didn't she? Something about her scratched at the buried surface of his memory. Tantalizing him. And now it was more than that. Now, he wanted to feel her in his arms. Feel her mouth under his.

The house might be a monstrosity built by a modern Midas. The estate, manicured by gardeners in relays, might be the topography of some foreign country. But this woman— He had seen her somewhere before. He had known her somewhere. He clenched his right fist, willing himself to remember.

His gaze moved up to her face, the full lips, pouting, desiring, self-centered. And then the hard cold blue eyes. The body was sensuous, but the eyes revealed her mind. And you saw what she was really like: a selfish, scheming woman. Ambitious for herself. She had all the money in the world. But that wasn't enough. She wanted something else. Everything else. He sighed again. This time without the ache of desire, wondering what it was that Myra wanted so badly that she would do anything to get.

"Are you comfortable, darling?"

Her voice had turned-down spreads, fluffed-up pillows, and lowered lights in it, all right. Maybe even pink-tinted ceiling mirrors thrown in as an added fillip. That voice left nothing to be desired, or left you desiring. It came from deep inside her, down underneath the scheming and the coveting. Down where she was what God intended when he made a man and a woman and gave them the elemental needs.

"Yes. Wonderful," he whispered. She could hear him now. His voice was improving. He sounded like a frog croaking when he spoke now. A sick frog, of course. But it was an improvement.

She came across the room to him, bringing the faintest fragrance with her. Elusive. The kind you hated to lose. So you'd miss her when she was away from you. You'd feel lost without her, incomplete until she made you whole again.

She kissed him on the forehead. The place just above his eyes where there was no gauze. His head was still swathed in it. It looked like a helmet. Layers of the stuff had been applied under mild pressure and, except for being changed, would not be removed until he was ready for plastic surgery.

"Not much of me there, is there?" he said.

"I don't care," said the bedroom voice. "Just so you are back with me."

"It makes it nice, all right. In a way it makes it nice. In a way it's torture."

She smiled at that. A smile as faint and elusive as the fragrance she wore. She pulled a chair around with its back to the wide windows and sat facing him. She pulled close to him. She wasn't touching him, and yet he could feel her nearness as though she was in his arms. His heart increased its tempo.

She lifted her head, and the sun behind her gave her blonde hair a sudden halo. If you could forget those hard blue eyes, what a lovely thing she was! If you could forget—

He had no memory at all. He had just begun to live again. And already here was something he wanted to forget.

Myra said to the nurse, "Would you leave us alone for a while, please? I'll call you."

Now, his heart did pick up speed, like a hot-rod thrown into second gear. Myra was sending the nurse out of the room. Maybe she didn't want to torture him any more. Loving her might be a painful business, but there was a fever eating at him that wasn't going to be cooled by hypos or medication.

If she was going to be that good to him, he could forget the watchful blue eyes, the coldness. He would forget! He would submerge himself in that blonde hair and her kisses instead.

She leaned forward, close to his chair, when the nurse had closed the door behind her.

"Ben," she said. "I want to have a talk with you."

His breathing was quickened. "I don't know if we can, but I'd love to try it—"

She stared at him, frowning. "What on earth are you talking about? You'd love to try what?"

His eyes widened, his heart slowed, his breathing subsided. His gaze met hers. And he realized that she did want to talk with him—just talk.

Talk! The way he felt?

With the fever burning hotter than any thermometer could ever register? He shook his head.

"Nothing," he said. "Nothing at all. What did you want to talk to me about, Myra?"

As far as he was concerned the room was suddenly cold, as chilly as the blue of her eyes.

"Have I ever done anything, Ben, to cause you to mistrust me?"

He smiled. Answered truthfully. "Not as far as I know."

"Well, I do know. Ben, I've been faithful to you. Oh, I don't want you to think there haven't been times when I could have cheated. There have been men who have wanted me—"

"I'll bet there have."

"And men that would surprise you. Men you thought were your best friends—"

"Oh, no. I wouldn't be surprised. To find out that a man is a human being has long since ceased to astonish me."

"Ben! That doesn't sound like you. I thought you had a certain code, an honorable way of life that would put you above an affair with the wife of one of your friends."

"Maybe I just never met the wife of any friend who could cause me to turn human long enough to suspend my code. Maybe that's why I never tried it."

"Ben. Please. You're joking. And I'm serious. Deadly serious. I've been ill, Ben, ever since this business started. I'm afraid you don't trust me any more—"

"Myra! What are you talking about?"

"Only this." She straightened up in her chair. "There was a time when you never did anything without taking me into your confidence. Oh, of course, you know that. You always said that though there may not be much sex in our marriage—"

"*I said that?*"

The way he had just been feeling he knew he couldn't have.

"Stop, Ben. I know you've been sick. I know what you've been through. But this is serious."

"Go on, Myra. What did I say? About our marriage? I'm not too sure I remember."

"If you must make me say it, it was that we were great plotters. We worked together. There was nothing we couldn't have, because we were alike in what we wanted—"

"Oh." It was an inadequate little word. But it was the only one he could think of at the moment.

"That's why I've been hurt, and worse than that, worried. Is this a trick, Ben?"

"A trick?"

"Stop it!" There was no trace of the bedroom in that voice now. It sounded like the courtroom, or the gutter. "I mean allowing people to doubt. Even your own folks. Letting the doctors believe that you might be that hoodlum Taylor. What have you to gain, Ben? What is there to gain?"

"Nothing."

She was watching him, closely. Her eyes were odd, doubting. But he shivered. She wasn't doubting his identity. She was doubting his sincerity. She still thought he was trying to conceal something from her.

She leaned forward again. "Or is it a plan? Is that it, Ben? Have you decided that maybe you can get better evidence if you are accepted for a week as Jeff Taylor, live right in his apartment? I've thought of that, of course. It might work. It might get you even better evidence than the murder of Rick Vashney—"

He felt something tighten in his chest. Vashney. That was the name in all the newspapers that Gracie, the nurse, had read to him in the hospital. The *News* stories by Vance Roberts. The exposés. The revelations. The evidence that was going to enable Assistant D.A. Benjamin J. Young to wipe out vice in the city of Rainier. And also give him a boost up the political ladder.

"Better evidence?" he said. "How could I get better evidence living in Taylor's house?"

For a moment she stared at him. She bit her lip. Then she smiled, knowingly. "Stop it, Ben. If this was ever amusing, it has ceased to be. You're wasting time. You've got to run for Governor. We've made promises! Commitments! We can't let the people who are backing you down."

"Why are you talking to me like this, Myra? There is some doubt, you know, that I am Ben Young."

She shook her head. "There may be some doubt elsewhere, Ben. But not with me. I know. There hasn't been any doubt in my mind. Who should know better than I? Haven't I been your wife for five years? How could I be fooled? But, Ben, stop it. We've got to work. And while you are confined here, I could be working for you. If you'd just take me into the plan—if you'd let me know what you're trying to accomplish!"

He regarded her, shaking his head. What he was trying to accomplish? What would any zombie be trying to accomplish in the world of the living?

He was trying to find himself. The key to his own lost past. The way behind the curtain of fire at Eaton Lake.

The stories that the nurse at St. John's Hospital had read to him hadn't wakened any memories. Nothing had touched him at all except the sight of Myra.

Maybe she was his wife. Maybe he was Ben Young.

But if he was, he was a million light-years removed from recovery. Plans. Evidence about Vashney. Campaign for Governor. Promises. Commitments. Words.

It was useless to try to tell Myra that. She was convinced. He could look at her and see that she *knew* he was Ben Young. She was equally certain that this was some new scheme, some plan hatched to cinch the election of Benjamin J. Young as Governor. She was already trying on the gowns she'd wear to the inaugural ball at Tallahassee.

He felt like laughing—or crying. What a choice he had. The Governor's mansion at Tallahassee—or the electric chair at Raiford.

10

A troop of callers arrived the next afternoon. Mrs. Young came in and waved the nurse from the room. She was followed by Mr. Young and a gray-haired man in an expensively tailored suit with a pince-nez over his suspicious and tormented brown eyes. Myra came in last, and her secretive smile told him that she was playing along with him, no matter what he decided to do.

Good Lord, how could he convince her he hadn't the least notion what plans she meant? That all he knew was what had been read to him from Vance Roberts' columns in the *News?*

"Ben, darling," Mrs. Young gushed. "We've brought you an old friend—"

He looked up at the old friend, hoping Mrs. Young would give him a name. Except for looking like a UN delegate on some TV screen, this old friend was a complete blank to him.

"You know, darling," Mrs. Young gushed on. "Why, it's your *boss!*" And her tone really kicked the stuffing out of that word boss. It made it less than meaningless. Of course, he knew what she implied: Her son was going to be the next Governor. The District Attorney had reached the top—for him. "Philip, speak to Ben, tell him how miserable we've all been without him."

Philip Dickson cleared his throat. His eyes remained mistrustful. There might be no doubt in the minds of Myra and Mr. and Mrs. Young, Sr. But Philip Dickson was a small-minded man who had been born doubting. He wouldn't have trusted his own mother.

"Well, my boy," Dickson said, "we are looking forward to your return to the wars, of course. The office hasn't been the same without you."

"The office!" Mrs. Young's voice cracked across Dickson's. "Of course, why didn't we think of that? Myra, wouldn't that be simply lovely? Tomorrow, we'll have one of the chauffeurs drive Ben down to his office. Old scenes. Old scenes, indeed. Ben, that's just what you need. To get down there to your office. The work you were so proud of. The place where you have accomplished so many wonderful things—with Mr. Dickson's help, of course!"

"Thank you, my dear," Philip Dickson said. "It was a great pleasure having young Ben working with me. I'll tell you I'll be proud—mighty proud, to have him sitting up there in that Governor's chair! We'll look for you at the office tomorrow, Ben!"

Philip Dickson didn't stay much longer. He seemed glad to escape. He didn't trust people even when he could look right into their bare faces. But the man in the wheelchair was wearing a helmet of gauze, and most of his face was concealed under it.

There was some chatter about the people who had been calling to see Ben, the plans for campaign offices that were to be set up over the state. There was a great deal for Ben to do when he felt well enough to face it.

X sat there. The unknown quantity. He still didn't know. Philip Dickson meant nothing to him. Less than nothing. A pompous old man.

When they were gone, Myra remained behind. She pulled her chair close to his.

X no longer felt the stirring of desire, the prickling rush of blood through his veins. Now he felt more like a backward child in school. He was about to receive another lesson in life. Myra was his instructor.

"While you're at the office tomorrow," Myra said. "Look through your papers. I've insisted that your secretary keep everything up to date, and destroy nothing that may pertain to the clean-up campaign. Ben, you've got to get back to work. You know that you can be Governor if the vice clean-up works. Otherwise, you're not politically strong enough. You aren't well-known enough to carry the state. The political bosses have told you that. I know you're not well. But surely you're well enough to dig into the Jeff Taylor matter. Clean up Rainier's vice rackets and you can coast in. Your appearance will be in your favor. You'll make an heroic figure, up on the speaker's platform, swathed in bandages—the man who cleaned up Rainier single-handed. Please, Ben, get back to work! You can do it! You must do it, Ben. It's so important!"

The chauffeur pushed the wheelchair along the wide, polished tile corridors of the County Building. He paused at the gold-lettered frosted-glass door. "Assistant Prosecutor, Rainier County, Benjamin J. Young, Jr."

Swank, X thought. Very swank.

His private secretary was a studious, sensible young woman who looked as though she'd been chosen by Myra. She lent the place dignity. And there wasn't the touch of foolishness about her.

She welcomed Mr. Young back to his office and turned immediately to her typewriter. X told the chauffeur to push him into his private office. Even in there he could hear the busy clatter of the secretary's typewriter. He wondered, without any real interest, what her name was.

He smiled under the gauze. Maybe she didn't have a name. Maybe she was a machine. A number. She'd make the perfect female automaton if the machines took over.

He told the chauffeur to wait in the outer office. He wheeled himself over to the desk. It was stacked high with letters. The stacks were neat, but sorting through them would be a big job.

He shook his head. He wasn't well enough to tackle a job like that, even if he was likely to know what most of them were about, which he wasn't.

There was a smaller pile of call messages. He picked them up and thumbed through them. There were dozens of slips with the single message: Vance

Roberts called. He must have called two dozen times. Suddenly that message ceased. Vance Roberts had stopped calling.

X smiled again. Roberts. There was a man who apparently took a long time getting a fact into his mind, but once he got it, he clung to it.

Still, there was something about it he didn't like. The calls from Roberts. Roberts. The name hacked at the wall of forgetfulness almost as strongly as the sight of Myra had done.

Maybe it was because he had heard read so many of the stories written by the political reporter for the *News*.

He wheeled himself over to the filing cabinets. He looked through three files before he found the folder on Jeff Taylor.

He shook his head. Here he was, following Myra's instructions. Was that habit, working its way up through the crust that had formed over his subconscious mind?

Wasn't Myra the unseen motive power behind Benjamin J. Young's campaign for Governor?

He pulled the folder out of the cabinet and wheeled himself over to the wide window. He turned the venetian blind and opened the file.

It was thick. X supposed it must be a case that was almost ready to be carried to court. It listed the names and addresses of all the witnesses who had seen Jeff Taylor running out of Rick Vashney's apartment the night Rick had been murdered.

There was another list of the holdings of Jeff Taylor. X read these with interest. Gambling clubs, numbers rackets, horse betting—there wasn't any kind of gambling place, it seemed, that Jeff Taylor didn't own at least a part of. The file was vague there, too. Maybe purposely. The co-owners were not listed.

X could understand that. When Benjamin Young went to court he would want the court and the jury to believe that Jeff Taylor owned the rackets along with representatives of the huge international crime syndicate. That Jeff Taylor was a big man in Rainier rackets, but only a small cog in a giant evil, an evil that Benjamin J. Young meant to stamp out so far as Rainier was concerned. A fearless attack on the syndicate that would shove Benjamin J. Young right into the Governor's mansion.

He was still reading the file when his secretary glided into the room on rubber-soled shoes. Startled, he looked up.

"I'm glad to see you looking over the file on Jeff Taylor," she said. "Should we proceed as you had planned? Your assistants turn to me as though I should know. And naturally, Mr. Young, I certainly haven't had any secret line to your bedside all these weeks, have I?"

X smiled. "Now, let's not be hysterical. It's been a big load on you, Miss—uh, my dear. But you just let my assistants go right ahead as we—uh, planned. Tell them that is what I want."

She had to lean almost to his face to hear his whispers. He saw the color creeping through her cheeks. Her eyes were getting moist and her breath had quickened. X looked at her again. For the first time, he became seriously certain that he was not Benjamin J. Young.

Obviously, Ben Young had been playing footsie with this perfect secretary. There was a deep layer over X's memory, but he couldn't believe that he would ever have been attracted to a woman like this.

He reminded himself to ask Myra the name of his secretary. And reminded himself further that if he had the ill fortune to turn out to be Ben Young, to have this young lady transferred to another department of the District Attorney's offices.

She kept her face inches from his for a moment and then, realizing that he was not going to say anything more, she stepped back. Her small, narrow mouth tightened. Her eyes chilled over.

"There's a young woman reporter to see you, *Mister* Young. A Zoe Gardner, I believe. She works with Vance Roberts on the *News*. Political reporting. Will you see her?"

X glanced around the office. The very sight of the dismal place depressed him. He wanted to get out of there. And it wasn't that he was certain he had never been there before. In fact, he seemed to feel that he had.

It was just that he didn't like the place.

Zoe Gardner? Reporter for the *News?* The name meant nothing to him. Probably some thick-ankled, breastless dame with inch-thick lenses over lack-luster eyes. And she worked with Vance Roberts. He hated "intelligent" women, and for some reason the name Vance Roberts caused him to feel upset and nervous. The very appearance of that message on the cluttered desk, "Vance Roberts called", made him sweat under the gauze on his forehead.

"No," he said. "I don't want to see her. Get rid of her, will you, like a nice little—doll."

She'd started from the room. Now she turned and smiled at him. That was what she had been waiting to hear. Her slender hips were grinding as she left the room.

11

He felt relief at getting back to St. John's Hospital.

He understood that it was to be temporary. Now he had to face the ordeal of a week in the apartment of Jeff Taylor, with Taylor's lush, redheaded wife and Taylor's cold-eyed partner, Mike Reglen. He looked forward to it with dread.

Still, he wondered if even that would be worse than the tensions that had accumulated within him during the week at the Young mansion.

The gushing mother. The stalwart father with his chin up and his nose up, too. Myra. Looking like an angel and sounding like a female Iago. If the things she intimated were true, she and Ben Young planned to take all the old-time political bosses in the state for a ride, and the state itself was going to know it had been had before the Youngs were through with it.

Myra sweated him down. There was no desire left, either.

It had been a wonderful and enlightening visit. But X told himself he was relieved that it was over.

Still, they lingered in the hospital room. The private room that was his first home as far as he could remember. He had emerged from the fiery womb of nothingness into this room. Here they'd tended him and brought him this far along the road to recovery. Gracie and the other nurses had read to him all about the pasts of the two men he might be, written by a third man—a political reporter who was all tangled up in the lives of both the gambler and the politician.

None of the Youngs seemed to want to leave him. X knew that Benjamin, Sr., had exhausted every avenue before he resigned himself to returning X to St. John's for one more week.

Myra stood beside the chair. She was nervous. He knew what was the matter with her. She was afraid that he was delaying the urgent business that was going to make her the first lady of the state. The Governor's wife. That was Myra Young's immediate goal. This delay was maddening. Right now she should be having fittings for the evening gowns she would need in the state capital.

Mrs. Young had begun to cry again. Her eyes were tear-stained. The thought that her son was being subjected to the life of a hoodlum tore her apart. Even though she had been assured that Jeff Taylor's plush apartment had all modern conveniences and was one of the largest and most luxurious living places in Rainier, it made her ill to think of her son living there, even temporarily.

Benjamin, Sr., was being the stout fellow. Chin up. He didn't like the business, any more than Clarinda did. But if it meant speeding his son's recovery, he was resigned to it. He had at last faced a problem that he could not solve by paying a little money. Or a lot of money.

The door opened and Dr. Ricey came in.

He smiled at the Youngs. It was a sincere enough smile, but the doctor was unable to keep a touch of smugness out of it. He had won. The patient was back in the hospital.

"Well, how goes it?" Ricey said. His voice was hearty.

"Doctor, let me appeal to you again," Clarinda Young said. "My son. You're sending him to live among hoodlums and gangsters. Do you realize what that will do to him?"

"Eh?" Ricey looked at X. "How do you feel about it, my boy? Did you recognize the scenes of your childhood? Are you cured as they promised you would be? Or are you more confused and tautly drawn inside than ever?"

"You're upsetting him!" Clarinda Young cried.

"On the other hand, his nerves are in such a state of tension that it is a miracle that shock has not set in again. As you must know, loss of tissue and blood and the agony of burned flesh were only part of the story with this patient. He suffered the horrors of untold shock. We've treated his body, and now all of you have stepped in to *help* us treat his mind."

"I cannot understand why you have taken this attitude, Doctor," Benjamin J. Young, Sr., declared. "You talk as though we opposed you, as though our son's welfare wasn't our first concern."

"I must remind you again this may not be your son," Ricey's voice was cold. "The two men in that cabin were very similar, in build and in many bodily characteristics. The differences have been—if you will see it that way—dissolved by the fire. We have no definite proof that this is your son—"

"My heart tells me," Mrs. Young said sharply.

"Then your heart may very well be mistaken," Ricey replied. "I must tell you that within a day or two we may be able to make what will be a conclusive examination. Dr. Webster is going to remove the cast from the patient's left arm. Then we may be able to determine our patient's identity more certainly."

They were all staring at him, except X. He was watching Myra's face. He saw the tightness of her painted mouth, the way her eyes narrowed slightly.

"How will you know?" Myra said.

Ricey turned to face her. "I have learned that the gambler Jeff Taylor had a small, half-inch heart tattooed on the inside of his lower left arm. When we remove the cast, we may find that mark—"

X went on watching Myra. He saw her face drained of color, saw the muscles become rigid in her cheeks. What was she thinking? That she may have been wrong? That she had revealed too much to X if it should turn out there was a tattoo mark under that cast?

It was almost as though he were reading her thoughts. He saw her go through doubt, apprehension and then back to that old cold self-assurance. "Have the cast taken off," she said.

"I'm sorry. But that can't be done," Ricey said. "Not even for you. I have talked to Dr. Webster, the surgeon. He expects the cast can be removed by the day after tomorrow at the earliest."

"But he'll be with—with those people—those hoodlums then," Mrs. Young cried. Her voice rose. "I don't see how I can allow it."

Dr. Ricey smiled. "The health of my patient is my only concern, madam. I'm afraid you'll have to allow it." But Ricey was a kindly man. He didn't like to crow when he was victorious. He said in a softer tone, "I promise you, Mrs. Young, he'll be brought back here to the hospital when the cast is to be removed. You'll be the first to be told what we find out."

"I'm not at all worried," she said. But she was. For the first time she was thinking that she might be forced to admit that her son had perished in the fire at Eaton Lake. She was worried, all right.

Jessie Taylor and Mike Reglen came into the hospital room about an hour after the Youngs left. Jessie looked as lush as ever and she was giving little bounces that were supposed to express her happiness. She kept smiling at X and patting his hand.

His gaze moved on to the frozen eyes of Reglen. *If you've ever seen a fish staring out at you from the iced display of a fish market,* X thought, *you've seen eyes like Mike Reglen's.* They remained frozen even though he, too, kept smiling at X and telling him how glad they were going to be to get him home.

X looked beyond them for the huge chested ex-wrestler, Halftime Smith, but he wasn't with them. X felt a twinge of disappointment without knowing why, but he didn't ask the smiling couple about Halftime. He didn't want anything to spoil their happiness at his homecoming.

Dr. Ricey came into the room with them.

"We're not going to send the patient to your home in his wheelchair, Mrs. Taylor. We feel that it is time that he began getting mild exercise. He'll walk from here to the elevator—if each of you will be so kind as to take his arm— and from the elevator to the car."

"Why, we'll be glad to help the boss," Reglen said. He got on one side of X, and Jessie insinuated herself against his other arm.

"I'm just so glad to have him back," Jessie said, "I'm willing to do anything."

Dr. Ricey looked at her. "Just don't overdo anything." He smiled. "Remember, only the mildest forms of exercise for a while. No more walking than necessary. Plenty of sleep and rest—but, of course, he'll have the same nurses with him that he had at the Young home."

"Of course," Jessie said.

"Nothing too fine for the boss," Reglen said. The words were correct and they rang right. That was why X couldn't understand why he felt that the two people were closing in on each side of him—like executioners.

He shivered, wishing that Dr. Ricey would stop impressing upon Reglen how weak he was, how helpless.

If Reglen had ever wanted to take over from Jeff Taylor, what better opportunity could he have than this moment?

"And remember," Ricey said, as they started for the door. "The patient must be back in here tomorrow afternoon to have the cast removed from his arm. As you know, moisture is bad for burns, and we'd never have put the cast on his arm except that it was necessary."

A dark blue Packard with chauffeur awaited them at the emergency exit of the hospital. Again X looked around for the wrestler, Halftime Smith. But he still didn't ask Jessie or Mike about him.

Jessie got into the rear of the car first. She put out her hand to him and he saw her shiver as she touched the overdone frankfurters the doctors called his fingers. He heard her catch her breath, but she went on smiling.

Reglen got in and plopped down in the seat, with X in the middle.

He could not say why the seat seemed too crowded. But he knew he was sweating. And he knew why. They were crowding him, these two.

"Some of the fellows are anxious to see you again," Mike said. "So tonight—"

"No. I'm too tired."

"But, boss—"

He saw Mike and Jessie exchange glances across his shoulders in the back seat. Jessie went on smiling, but her voice was hard. "You've got to see them, Jeff. Just a small party. Drinks and music. Buffet supper. They want to welcome you back."

"Yeah, boss. It might hurt you to call it off. It really might. You see, things are pretty rough right now, and it might not be a good idea to let the boys think you're weak."

X twisted his head, looking at Reglen. That smile never wavered, but the eyes remained cold and deadly.

X shrugged. As far as he could see, it didn't matter who else knew how helpless he was. The most dangerous pair knew it already: the two people crowding against him in the back of the car.

They helped him across the sidewalk and into the elevator. X was breathing as though he had run a mile. But he found himself wishing they would stand away from him just a little. Crowding. They were crowding him. They allowed him too little room to breathe in the small elevator.

Mike unlocked the apartment with a key from his own key ring. Neither Mike nor Jessie seemed to think there was anything remarkable about that.

So X said nothing about the fact that Jeff Taylor's lieutenant had his own key to the boss's apartment.

He shook his head. It must have made it nice during the time Taylor was away. But there was no other feeling inside him. He didn't care. Even if he turned out to be Jeff Taylor, he couldn't imagine himself caring what the red-headed little tramp at his side did.

He followed Jessie into the apartment, thinking that there were plenty of things he would not do if he were either of the men he was supposed to be. Ben Young didn't care what he did to make himself Governor. Ben Young played footsie with a very undesirable secretary. Now here was Jeff Taylor's life: a wife he couldn't imagine himself ever loving, a partner that no intelligent human being would trust.

And he had to be somebody, didn't he?

When Jessie suggested they have a drink, X agreed at once.

He was puzzled at the way both of them looked at him—and then looked at each other.

"You gone off the wagon, boss?" Reglen said.

So Taylor didn't drink. No wonder. He wouldn't dare trust himself around this deadly pair unless his mind was clicking and alert.

"Just to celebrate," he said. It sounded lame. "I'm home. I been away a long time."

"That's right, honey," Jessie said. She put her arm around his waist, pressed her head against his chest. "We'll have a big one to toast my daddy coming home."

Jessie went across the ultra-smart white and black living room to a chrome-trimmed bar set before floor-to-ceiling mirrors. She got out glasses, ice and chaser.

"What'll it be?" she said.

"Bourbon," X answered when they seemed to be waiting for him. And again they looked at each other.

Again he knew that he had failed a test. How the hell should he know Jeff Taylor's preference in whiskey? The doctors had explained to these people— as well as to the Youngs—that X's mind was a blank behind the moment when he came wandering out of the fire. And yet it was obvious that neither this pair nor any of the Youngs completely believed the doctors.

They remembered. It was impossible that he could forget himself.

"Well, you have changed," Jessie said. She poured in a jigger of bourbon.

"You better make that two jiggers," X said. "It's been a long day."

She showed her astonishment, but prepared the drinks and brought them across the white rug. She sat beside Jeff on the divan.

A silence that grew, stretching taut, developed when they faced each other with whiskey in their hands.

"Well, happy nights," X said.

"Welcome home, boss."

"Welcome home, angel." And they drank.

X looked at his empty glass. "Wonder if there is any more in that bourbon bottle," he said.

"Angel, hadn't you better take it easy?"

"Yeah, boss. It's going to be a big night."

"Look, two drinks won't make me looped," X said. "I can take it."

He knew he could, and yet he found himself wondering how he knew.

Jessie got up with the empty glasses in her hand. A door to the rear corridor opened. The smile faded from Jessie's face. Her voice went shrill.

"Halftime! I thought I told you to get out of here! I thought I told you to stay out!"

Halftime nodded, miserably. "Yeah, Miz Taylor. But gee, I hadda see the boss. I hadda see him. Hi ya, boss? Hi ya."

X looked at the battered features of the wrestler. He nodded and whispered as loudly as he could. "Good to see you, Halftime. I thought you'd be at the hospital."

"I had to run him out," Jessie said. "He hangs around all the time. He makes me nervous—"

"Gosh, boss, I ain't done nothing."

Jessie's laugh was sharp. "Oh. I know. Jeff will take up for you. He'll tell you you can stay around. All right, you can. But just get out of my sight. Go out in the kitchen and wash the dishes."

"I already done 'em, Miz Taylor. While I was waiting for the boss to come on home."

X smiled at the exasperation that flew across Jessie's painted face. It felt good to smile. It was the first smile he'd had since he awoke in the hospital. This was a pretty dark part of the world he was supposed to have come from.

The party was a quiet one. X was tired by ten o'clock that night when the guests began arriving. His nurse had helped him into one of Jeff Taylor's dress suits. Except that he had lost too much weight since the fire, the suit might have been made for him. It fit his frame, at least.

As he went to slip into his jacket, he noticed that Jessie had laid out harness, shoulder holster and an automatic. He and the nurse looked at each other, eyebrows raised.

He strapped the shoulder holster on and shoved the gun into it.

He went out into the living room. A buffet dinner had been prepared by a caterer who stood at one side, admiring his handiwork.

The guests began to arrive. Jessie introduced them to Jeff, reminding each of them that Jeff had been through a bad time. "The shock was simply terrible, remember," Jessie told each of them. "Sometimes his memory ain't what it ought to be."

The men looked like businessmen. Hard-eyed businessmen. They wore dinner jackets and their women wore expensive evening gowns.

The wrong note came when he would feel the holster under his arm, and know that the other men were feeling guns under their arms as well. They got their peace of mind and sense of security from knowing that gun was there.

It affected X differently. He felt tense, keyed-up, awaiting trouble. Somehow he was reassured when Halftime Smith lounged in the room and sat in a corner, watching.

Jessie would call out their names to Jeff and he would welcome them. Marty. Snell. Carl. Strossy. Either they had no last names, or X was supposed to recall them upon hearing their given names and seeing their taut-drawn faces.

Mike Reglen arrived last. By the time Mike got there, the girls had had enough to drink to set them laughing and chattering in groups around the room. But the men, if they drank anything, were unaffected by it. Their faces remained cold and set, their eyes watchful and hard.

"Maybe we better have a little talk-talk," Mike said after he'd been in the room about five minutes.

He looked at X. But X was at a loss to know what was expected of him. He saw Reglen's mouth tighten, and the man heeled around, leading the way to another room which, when X followed the others into it, turned out to be the library.

A table was set up in the middle of the room. There were drinks and smokes before each chair. The men went around to their chairs as though they knew where they belonged. Only X waited.

There was only the chair at the head of the table left after Reglen sat down in the one to the right of it. Reglen jerked his head toward the remaining chair. X sat down.

Nobody spoke. He could feel eight pairs of eyes fixed on him. Cold eyes.

He said, "Suppose you run things, Mike. I have to whisper, and I doubt if the boys can hear me."

That pleased Mike. He began to get reports from the boys the table.

Each man got up. And each man had trouble to report. Something was out of line in every situation. Competition. Tough police. Or suspected doublecross.

As each man reported his trouble in a cold flat voice, he would watch X at the head of the table, waiting to see what he would say.

And X noticed that after each report Reglen's smile widened a little.

When every man had made his report, Mike turned to X and said, "So, what do you think, boss?"

X made his whisper as loud as he could. "I think you've let things go to hell since I've been ill, Mike."

It was exactly the last thing Mike had expected to hear. It was a showdown, and Mike had apparently been sure that Jeff Taylor was going to back down.

For a second, Mike's olive black eyes were murderous. Then they went flat again, and he grinned around his mouth.

"Well, boss, you know you been away a while. And, you know, boss—" now Mike's voice was as dead and frozen as his fish-market eyes "—even before you went away, you were letting things go to pot some."

There was a mumble of agreement around the table. X glanced around at the men, one by one. Each held his gaze defiantly for a moment, and then let his eyes drop away.

X felt a cold knife up his spine. There was trouble here. Bad trouble. It was bubbling like a cauldron, almost ready to spill over.

He stood up. His croaking voice ended the meeting. "Well, I'm back now. I'm glad you boys have saved your troubles for me. Now I know 'em, you don't have to worry any more, huh? Let's go back to the ladies."

This wasn't what they had expected. The table was heavily loaded with drinks and smokes. They'd planned to be here for hours. Some kind of showdown had been arranged. X waited. Mike stood up at last and, as though that was a signal, the others got up, too. The showdown wasn't coming off. Not tonight.

They went out of the room in pairs. They were whispering together as they went. X was left standing at the table in the heated yet cold room.

He stayed there a long time. He could hear them laughing and talking in the huge black and white front room. The whiskey was getting to them now. The polish was being washed off.

He didn't see how this was helping his recovery at all. He looked down at his overdone right hand. Those swollen fingers were trembling. Ricey ought to see an x-ray of my nerve centers right now, he thought.

He wanted less than anything to go back into that black and white room where those cold eyes would all be picking a place in his back for a bullet, to be delivered when they got the nerve to use a gun.

The laughter reached a crescendo. He poured himself a stiff drink and drank it down straight. It burned all the way through his chest, but there was no effect, no lift.

He got up from the table. There were French doors at the end of the library. They opened on a darkened terrace. He could see that much. He went to the doors. They were locked. He twisted the key and stepped out on the lowered terrace. There were potted palms, and boxed evergreens out here. The air was fresh and cold and good.

He stepped nearer the wall, and that was when he saw them. They had been talking together so tensely they hadn't even heard him step through the doorway.

When they heard him, they leaped apart and turned facing him. Jessie and Mike. All the guilt in the world was on their faces. And Mike's mouth wasn't smiling now. It was hanging open.

X bowed. "Sorry," he said. "So clumsy of me." He stepped back through the French doors. Closed them again.

And locked them.

12

He went back across the library. As he came out into the living room, somebody's blonde caught his arm. She dragged him over to the couch. At first, she was very cuddly.

He wondered who she belonged to. Mildly, he wondered why her keeper didn't object to her friendliness.

But he soon found out. She wanted something. She wasn't as drunk as she pretended. Probably she wasn't drunk at all. There was a man asleep in a club chair across the room. X supposed the blonde belonged to him.

If so, his name was Marty. Marty was in a lot of trouble with the other boys, the blonde said. Marty wanted to stay loyal to the boss—*That's me,* X told himself—and there was a lot of talk about getting rid of Marty. And then he found out what the blonde wanted. Some kind of assurance from Jeff Taylor that Marty was going to be safe—and saved from the wolves.

He didn't have to answer her. Before he got a chance to say anything, the blonde suddenly began to laugh and sing at the top of her voice. The man across the room opened his eyes and jerked his head erect, sat up in the club chair. X saw why. Mike Reglen and Jessie had come in from the terrace.

"Well, now, ain't you the scream?" the blonde wailed at X. And under her false laughter, he could feel the tension. The tension and the fear.

Marty got up from the club chair across the room and staggered over to the blonde and X on the couch.

"Come on, Ellie," he said, his words slurring. "Stop pestering the boss."

"Yeah, kids," Mike said then. "It's been a big night. The boss ain't been out of the hospital long. Maybe we better all call it a night."

And with that, the laughter and the music and the loud talk in the room ceased. Everybody had been drunk, and everybody had been having a good time. Abruptly they were all sober, and were getting ready to leave.

Mike managed to be so busy saying goodnight that he didn't have to face X, or to shake hands with him. He seemed to get pushed out of the door in a mob. But X smiled to himself. Mike had maneuvered that exit very adroitly.

Finally, they were all gone. They were alone together. Jessie and the man she believed was Jeff Taylor. And the residue of a party—overflowing cigarette trays, overturned glasses, somebody's forgotten wrap.

Jessie closed the front door, locked it and then leaned against it. Her carefully brushed hair was mussed a little over her right eye. And her lipstick had smeared at the corner of her pouting mouth. She seemed to be overflowing her lime-green gown the way the cigarettes overflowed the ashtrays.

"Well, all right," she said. "Say it."

He had started across the room toward the corridor. He stopped and turning on his heel, faced her.

"Say what, Jessie?"

"All right. So you sneaked around and caught me out on the terrace with Mike. Sure, I was out there with him. And sure, Mike likes me—"

"That's wonderful."

"All right, smart guy. That sounds like you. You always thought that you were too good for me, didn't you? Well, we'll see if you are or not. Maybe you won't he so high and mighty when you try to take over again—and find out—"

"Find out what?"

"Find out that maybe you can't do it!" She walked toward him, her hands on her hips. "Oh, Mike told me. You cut quite a figure in there at the meeting tonight. He said you almost fooled some of them into thinking you were the old Jeff Taylor. But he knows better. He knows about the money—"

"What money?"

"You think you're pretty clever, closing out all your checking accounts here in town. You really were getting ready to run, weren't you, before the fire?" She laughed, her voice strident in the silent room. "Well, maybe Mike will let you run—when you turn over that money."

X felt his heart slow. So that was why Mike and Jessie had been so anxious to get him back to the apartment. All that "boss" and "angel" talk. There was money involved. Jeff Taylor had secretly moved his checking accounts out of town. These two meant to get that money.

How much money? And where was it? What would they do to him in order to find out where that money was? And which of them would ever believe that he had no notion where the new accounts had been opened?

So that was the point of the meeting in the library tonight. Mike had rehearsed the boys carefully. He was showing Jeff Taylor that he could not take over again—ever.

And when X had called his hand? Why hadn't Mike forced the showdown then and there?

The next thing the redheaded Jessie said answered that.

"Mike let you get away with the big talk in there... tonight. He said to tell you. He'll see you again tomorrow night. Things will be different then."

X frowned, and then he remembered. Tomorrow the cast would be removed from his arm. Mike was willing to wait and see if there was a heart tattooed on X's lower arm before he started working him over.

X looked down at his left arm. He could feel the skin burning and itching under that cast.

Mike turned up at eleven the next morning to assist Jessie in seeing that "good old Jeff" got back to the hospital safely.

X was playing double solitaire with Halftime Smith on the polished table in the library.

When Jessie came to the door she was dressed in a gray tailored suit with a fox fur. She looked cheap. She made the clothes look trashy and brassy.

"Come on, Jeff," she said. "It's time to go to the hospital."

Her honeyed tone, X knew, was for the benefit of the nurse who sat near the French doors.

"You needn't go, honey," X said. His voice was a nice croak this morning. One that any self-respecting frog would be proud to go a-courting with, "I'll have Halftime drive me over."

"Sure, boss. Sure," Halftime said.

"But, angel, I insist." Jessie was keeping her tone sweet, but the steel was showing through. She was afraid that if he got out of that house without her and Mike he might never come back. Might? He never would.

Mike came through the door. "Why, boss, you know your little woman wants to be with you at an important time like this."

"To remove a cast? Nothing to it. I don't need you."

Jessie came into the room. "Now, sweetheart!" she began. But then Mike shook his head at her. She shrugged and tried to laugh it off. "Oh, all right then. If you want to be mean to me."

"Don't you worry, Mrs. Taylor," Mike said. "He can't keep us from being there at the hospital. I know how worried you'll be. I'll drive you over to the hospital."

"Yeah. Do come," X croaked. "If I'd known how important a thing like this was, I'd have had cards engraved." He pushed back from the table and stood up. "Halftime, have we a spare car we could use for the drive?"

"Sure, boss. Sure. You come with me."

They went out the rear of the apartment and down to the basement garage in the service elevator. Halftime led him to a gray Plymouth. They drove almost a block in silence.

Finally, Halftime said, "Boss. I'm worried. Things sure look plenty bad. And that Mike. He might tell you he's looking out for you—but he's a bum. He's looking out for Mike."

"Maybe there won't be a tattoo on my arm."

"Boss, don't say that! Don't you see what that means? You ain't got no tattoo, you ain't the boss. Ah, gosh, boss, I couldn't stand that. You'll have that tattoo. And when we get that settled, you can get back to work. You'll take care of that Mike!"

X wished he could share Halftime's confidence in his ability to make everything all right. He wasn't so sure. It would be a hell of a thing to have a tattoo on his arm right now when he had no memory of moving checking accounts to out-of-town banks. A man with a heart tattooed on his left arm was going to have to account to Reglen for a lot of money.

He could feel an ache at the nape of his neck as though somebody were staring at him. He twisted around in the seat and looked through the rear window.

It was back there. The black Packard. His executioners. They were still crowding him. They were following back there, keeping their deadly eyes on the gray Plymouth.

Mike was mighty interested in seeing that cast removed.

He was waiting to be sure there was a tattoo before he lowered the boom.

The Youngs were waiting outside Dr. Webster's office in St. John's Hospital when X and Halftime arrived.

Myra got up and came across to X. She gave him a cool, impersonal peck on the lips.

Clarinda was weeping again. "Are you all right, darling boy?" she cried. "Did they hurt you? Did you sleep all right? Are you sure you had enough to eat?"

Benjamin, Sr., cleared his throat. He patted X on the shoulder. "Chin up," he said. "It will soon be over... son."

Halftime said, "You folks lay off the boss. He's got enough to worry him wit'out you making him noiviss."

Clarinda turned slowly and looked down her nose. "And what is that?" she said.

Halftime only stared back at her.

Dr. Ricey came in then, followed by the lanky police captain, Lipsey Beckart.

"Well, at least," Dr. Ricey said, "this will settle one matter for good and all. We'll know which of the two men we are treating. We'll know how to proceed."

"Won't we, though?" Beckart said.

X thought the police captain's eyes looked hungry. He was hoping for a tattoo. He was looking for a murderer.

Mike and Jessie came in then, hurrying.

"Well," Mike said. "Anyway, we ain't too late." His eyes were dead, but they were fixed on X.

X shrugged his coat up on his shoulders. He said to Ricey, "I think, Doctor, that I won't go back to the Taylor apartment."

"Why not?" Jessie cried.

"An excellent idea," Benjamin Young said.

"Have you decided you're not Jeff Taylor?" Ricey asked. He took a step forward, watching his face.

X looked at Mike Reglen. He bit his lip. Mike's face was flushed. But his eyes were still cold.

X said slowly, "I'm sure I'm not."

Halftime Smith made a sound. It was as though someone had struck him unexpectedly in the solar plexus. All the air gushed across his lips in a dry sob.

Clarinda Young cried aloud, "I could have told you all the time!"

"Why," said Mike, his voice as dead as his eyes, "don't we just wait until they take off the cast? Then we can see."

Dr. Webster asked X into his office then. He allowed only Ricey and Beckart into the room along with two nurses.

They gave X a shot of narcotic and then removed the cast. He stared down at the arm.

It was a burned wreck. That was the best he could say for it. Where the rest of his body, left open and treated with penicillin to keep down infection, or covered with gauze under mild pressure, had healed quickly, the arm under the cast looked as bad as it had when it was put in the cast to set the broken bones.

Webster ordered penicillin and a bandage.

Ricey inspected X's lower arm and then stepped back. There was a smile on his face. Something pleased him very much.

The nurses went to work giving X injections and applying the gauze to his arm.

Beckart began to shift his weight from one foot to the other. He stared at Ricey, but the doctor continued smiling, said nothing. Beckart's tension began to build.

When the bandage was secured, Ricey and Beckart walked beside X out to the waiting room. They were all sitting down out there, but they were sitting on the edge of their chairs.

Ricey said, "I know you're all interested and I won't keep you waiting any longer. First, there *isn't* any tattoo."

Halftime Smith sagged. The breath sighed out of him.

Clarinda Young sniffed and looked around the room. Her look said, "I could have told you. I knew it all the time."

Benjamin Young straightened his wide shoulders. The long battle was almost over.

Mike Reglen's eyes were cold and dead.

Jessie Taylor looked baffled. Plainly, she was thinking about money.

Money that Jeff Taylor had moved out-of-town. Money she was never going to get her hands on now.

Myra's smile was enigmatic. Her eyes remained cold, but there were dreams in them again. Greedy dreams.

Beckart just shrugged.

Ricey said, "I had promised that this would be conclusive. I now must qualify that statement. In the first place, most tattooing is deeply done, through two or three layers of the epidermis at least." He went across to Halftime Smith. "Could I see the word that you had inscribed on your chest at the time the heart was drawn on Mr. Taylor's left arm?"

Halftime unbuttoned his shirt, baring his massive, pale chest. The word "Mabel" was visible there, in faded blue ink.

Ricey took a look at the tattoo on Halftime's chest. He called in Dr. Webster. Both men examined the work, probing, pinching and studying, while Halftime grinned, wriggled and blushed alternately.

Ricey said, "Dr. Webster agrees with me. Mr. Halftime Smith was sold a very inferior grade of tattooing. Not more than one or two layers deep. There seems no reason to doubt that the heart inscribed on Mr. Taylor's arm was equally superficially done.

"The man who escaped from the fire in the fishing cabin at Eaton Lake wrapped a grass rug around him. That's why the trunk of his body escaped anything but minor burns while parts of his legs, arms and head received acute third-degree burns. His left arm must have been on the outside of the rug. That would explain its being fractured in his fall, and would also explain the severe second-degree and third-degree burns it suffered—burns that destroyed so much tissue that it is now impossible to say whether he was ever tattooed or not."

13

X walked slowly along the corridor. Halftime shuffled along beside him without speaking. X was thinking, *there's still trouble, still confusion and I'm still in the middle of it.*

Mike's lips had smiled when Ricey had explained that there *might* have been a tattoo on that arm. Mike had nodded at Jessie. Jessie's face was white under the rouge. They sat silently while the Youngs filed out, still protesting against returning X to the Taylor apartment for the balance of the week.

As far as that went, X himself was protesting that. He had no intention of returning there.

"Just a minute!"

A woman stepped around the corner of the corridor as X and Halftime passed it. They stopped, looking at her.

"Why, Miss Gardner!" Halftime said. He put out his great paw. Here was someone the ex-wrestler was really glad to see, X thought.

There was no wonder. She was lovely. She would have made any man's dreams a pleasure. The soft smooth texture of her skin, the full young breasts, high and firm. The eyes with the youthful innocence still in them. He sighed. To be a man and not a zombie. To have a girl like that in love with you. To have a past—a decent present—and a future.

"Gosh, boss, you know Miss Zoe Gardner. I'll say you know her!" Halftime guffawed at that, so that a nurse passing on crepe soles frowned and shook her head at him.

Zoe Gardner. For the third time, he felt that stirring in him. Here was another one that he remembered from somewhere. And then he decided he knew. Deflated, he recalled that the secretary in the D.A.'s office had told him last week that Zoe Gardner wanted to see him. A woman reporter. From the *News.*

He kept his voice cold to conceal the disappointment he felt.

"Do I?" he said. "I'm sorry. You see, the doc says I've suffered some kind of shock and—"

"Yes. I know." She was looking at him. Trying to see inside those layers of gauze that he wore like an old-time knight's helmet.

"Do you?"

"I've tried to see you. I came every day. They wouldn't let me in. I even tried the Young estate."

"You're a newspaperwoman, aren't you?"

She winced a little. "Why, yes. I am. I was. I—I—well, I quit my job recently."

"And still trying to interview me?" he said. "I must be important to a lot of people."

Her voice was cold. "You're very important. I suppose you must have sold thousands of extra copies of newspapers. Who are you? Will you live? Are you the next Governor? Or will you die in the electric chair? Oh, yes! You're very important."

Her voice cracked a little. Almost as though she were going to flood the hospital with tears.

"I'm sorry," he said, baffled. "I didn't mean to upset you. You said you had tried to see me here every day. I remember at the office in the County Building my secretary said a newspaperwoman named Zoe Gardner—"

"It was the only way I knew to see you. I didn't tell her I was from the *News*. But when she asked me, I simply passed it off, as though that was why I wanted to see you."

"And that wasn't really the reason?" He frowned. "Why then? Why did you want to see me?"

"Don't you know?"

Odd, he thought, it was almost as if her voice begged him to know.

"The boss has been sick, Miss Zoe. Real sick." Halftime was apologizing for him.

He shook his head. The removal of the cast, the tension in that waiting room, all of it had tired him. And now there was this young girl who wasn't a newspaperwoman, but had been one until she quit her job recently, who had been trying to see him every day, for some reason that was supposed to be clear to him.

"Let's get out of here," he suggested. "Maybe we can go in the car. Halftime can drive us around. We can talk as we ride. I want to get away from here."

"Sure, boss."

The girl smiled wanly and nodded. To ride with them was a little thing, but somehow she accepted it as a triumph. At least it seemed to be what she wanted. She took one of his arms, Halftime took the other and they hurried him out to the gray Plymouth.

He was baffled. He was sure he knew her from somewhere, and then equally certain that it was nothing but wishful thinking. What had he to offer a lovely young girl like Zoe Gardner?

The best thing to do was find out what she wanted and send her on her way. The sooner he got away from her, the less it would take to get her image out of his mind.

She sat on the outside in the car, linking her arm through his. Halftime drove at thirty along the parkway that wound out of town.

She seemed indisposed to talk, content to ride with her arm linked in his as the buildings of the town slid past.

"What was it you wanted to see me about?"

She took her arm away.

"You really don't know?" Her voice was cold and hurt all at once as if she could not believe him.

He shook his head. "I honestly don't."

"Boss!" Halftime said.

"It's all right," Zoe said. "If you've lost your memory, all right. We'll let it go at that. If this is a convenient way of telling me that you don't want to know me, all right. There's just one thing I want to ask you."

Her words were calm enough, but they had to push their way through her choked throat. Her voice had the nasal timbre that accompanies a summer cold.

"Ask me," he said.

"What happened to Vance Roberts?"

He felt the ice water flow through his veins. He had anticipated all kinds of questions. But not this one.

She turned a little, so she could watch his eyes.

"I've been looking for him," she said. "He disappeared—the night of the fire. He hasn't been seen since."

"Look. Take it easy on me. I've been ill."

"All right. I'm trying to believe that. I hope so. With all my heart I hope so. They even say that you're not Jeff Taylor at all. They say that you're Ben Young. You can't be! You just can't be! That awful Ben Young to go on living—and Jeff Taylor dead! No! Not if there's justice in the world!"

He shook his head. "That's the damndest thing. Clarinda Young said those same words—only the other way around. For her I've got to be Ben Young—or there's no justice."

She buried her face in her hands. Her shoulders slumped round. "Oh, I've been so ill," she said. "I've been through this a thousand times in the past six weeks. I haven't been able to sleep. I've looked everywhere for Vance. I haven't been able to find him. Then I would try to see you. They wouldn't let me in. Nobody would let me near you. I've been crazy, telling myself I had to know. Are you Ben Young or are you Jeff Taylor? I've got to know!"

"God help me," he said. "I don't know. I don't feel like Ben Young trying to be Governor. I don't feel like Jeff Taylor who killed Rick Vashney—"

"You never killed Rick, boss!" Halftime declared. "I was in your office the whole time. I was right with you."

Now the girl uncovered her face. Her cheeks were tear-stained.

"No. Jeff Taylor never killed Rick Vashney."

"The police think so."

"Sure," she said. "Why not? Ben Young framed Jeff for that murder. To run him out of town wasn't good enough for that high-class society lawyer who wanted to be Governor. He had to get him for murder. If you're Ben Young—I've nothing to say to you."

"And if I'm Jeff Taylor?"

She faced him squarely. "If you are Jeff Taylor there's one thing I've got to know before I can say anything else, *where is Vance Roberts?"*

"Right there," X said. "Stop right there. That's where I came in. What have I got to do with this newspaper reporter who disappeared the night of the fire?"

"I'll tell you." She took a deep breath. He watched her breasts heave. Watched hungrily. "I'm going to talk to you as though you're Jeff Taylor. I can't help that. I can't stand the thought if you're not—" she stopped shortly.

"Okay with me. Only I don't know what this is all about and you've got to explain it to me."

"I will. Just because I want you to be Jeff Taylor—and I want to believe that you're ill. First, Ben Young wanted to be Governor, so he framed Jeff Taylor for murder. Okay?"

"Go ahead."

"Jeff had an alibi. But nobody will accept it."

Halftime broke in. "They said I'd lie to save you. They said I'd do anything to save you. And—damn 'em—they was right, boss. I would. You know that."

Zoe's smile was gentle. "Only this time Halftime wasn't lying. Jeff Taylor was innocent. I was working with Vance Roberts just before that on some newspaper exposés on crime in the city of Rainier. Vance had a file on Jeff Taylor. Gambling. Running rackets. Yes. But no murder."

"That's right," Halftime said. "The boss and me, we was on the up and up."

"Yes," Zoe said. "But Vance learned something. I had quit my job about then so I didn't know what it was. Only that it was about Jeff Taylor. Vance said he was working on something that was going to be the hottest story in years." She stared at him. "You must remember that?"

He was sweating. Something was fighting to be recognized in his mind. Something. Something. Something. What? The whole secret. The whole mess. The answer. It did no good. He couldn't reach down far enough.

He shook his head.

"All right. So you—so Jeff Taylor told me he was going to take Ben Young up to his fishing camp where he could talk to him. He promised me that he wouldn't use force—only threats. He thought Ben Young might break under threats if he saw that Jeff was serious. If he could get Ben Young to admit that the Rick Vashney murder was a frame, it would break the whole case against Jeff."

"So what happened?"

"So I know that Vance Roberts found out that the Assistant D.A. and Jeff were having a meeting. He was drinking. He came to see me. Wanted to know if I knew where he could find Jeff. I wouldn't tell him, but he must have guessed. He ran out of the house. I saw him get in his car and drive off. It could have been toward Eaton Lake. That's the last time I ever saw him!"

"And his car?"

Her voice was starting to crack now.

"The police were told that his car was found near an Eaton Lake bar about three weeks ago—in the woods, abandoned. Close enough to Jeff Taylor's cottage that Vance could have left it there, gotten some camper or farmer to drive him the rest of the way to your—to Jeff's fishing camp. But he has never come back. There's never been any word."

"Could he have sneaked in the house, got caught in the fire?" Halftime said.

She shook her head. "Only one body was found."

"Then he wasn't in there," Halftime said.

"And why would I—if I were Jeff Taylor—why would I know what had happened to Vance Roberts?"

"Because of what you—what Jeff said the night of the fire at my house. I told you—told Jeff that Vance was snooping around. Jeff said if that whiskey tenor didn't stay away from him, he'd kill him. I didn't pay any attention to it then. I didn't think you—didn't think Jeff would kill anyone."

"And now you're not so sure?"

She was crying now. "I know Jeff didn't kill Rick Vashney. There isn't anything I wouldn't do to help prove that. But now Vance Roberts is missing. He's been missing for six weeks—"

"You think I—Jeff Taylor—may have killed Vance Roberts because of what he might know?"

"I don't know. I don't know what to think. I only know that everything is lost for you—for Jeff—unless we can find Vance Roberts."

14

He stared at Zoe.

Everything was lost for him unless he found the missing reporter, Vance Roberts?

He wanted to laugh aloud. Bitter and cynical laughter. He had wondered how things could get any worse. Jeff Taylor was wanted for murder. Ben Young had been framing a man for murder. Jeff Taylor's wife and partner were planning to doublecross him, maybe even kill him for money that Jeff Taylor had hidden. Ben Young's wife was a cold piece of baggage with her eye on the state capital. And now here was another girl. And she was telling him that everything was lost unless he found a drunken newspaper reporter named Vance Roberts.

"I was on your side before," Zoe was saying. "I believed in you—in Jeff and in Jeff's innocence. But if Vance Roberts has been killed, that changes everything. Only Jeff would gain by Vance's death. At least, that's all I can see."

"Hey," Halftime Smith said. "Hey, the boss ain't killed nobody. Looks like you'd know that better'n anybody, Miss Zoe."

She looked past X at Halftime, who had taken his foot off the accelerator, letting the car slow down on the highway.

"I hope you're right," she whispered. "I hope so, Halftime. Only we've got to find Vance."

"All right!" X croaked, his voice angry. "Stop worrying. I'll find your precious Vance Roberts for you."

He couldn't say why it angered him so that she should be so anxious to find another man. But it did anger him. It made him tremble. He wanted to smash something.

He looked up just in time to see the big car cut directly in front of them. He yelled.

Halftime jerked hard on the wheel, whipping the gray car to the dirt shoulder of the road. He slammed on the brakes and they stopped, inches from the embankment.

The other car pulled in just ahead of them and also stopped on the embankment. This was a lonely stretch of the road. There was nothing to be seen on both sides except palmettoes and slash pine growing in fields of saw grass and wild wheat.

X leaped out of the car, pulling the automatic out of his shoulder holster. It occurred to him that whoever he was, he was not afraid of a gun.

But he didn't have time to give any thought to a matter like that.

The two thugs wriggling out of the big car had guns drawn. But he stood there, his gun leveled across the radiator of the Plymouth.

"Don't even try to lift 'em," X croaked. The voice belonged to a bullfrog now. A hoarse bullfrog. "Drop those guns as you come around the car."

Halftime got out of the car on the other side of it.

"Okay, you guys, you hear the boss. Drop 'em."

The two men looked at each other. For a second they hesitated. The stout one edged the snout of his automatic upward.

The gun in X's fist spoke. Smoke sprang in a spiral up from it. Sand jumped between the stout man's legs. He yelled. And then he dropped the gun.

The smaller man didn't hesitate after that. He held his automatic far away from his body and dropped it.

"Gosh, Mr. Taylor," the fat man said. "We didn't mean to harm you."

"The hell with that," X said. "If Halftime hadn't been driving slow, you'd have run us off this road. Would you have apologized to us then?"

"It ain't us, Mr. Taylor," the small one whined. "We're just following orders. We're just doing what we're told."

X took a step forward. "All right. What were your orders? Run us off the road? Kill us?"

"No, sir! I swear it. We was just to be sure that you came back—"

"Came back? Where? To the apartment?"

"That's right, Mr. Taylor. That's all. That's right."

The black Packard parked behind the Plymouth now. Jessie was at the wheel. Mike Reglen was at her side, a gun resting through the window.

"Suppose you drop it, Taylor," Reglen said. "I'd hate to shoot you on the side of the road like this. But I will."

"I don't think you'll shoot," X said. "You started the attack. And there's always the chance I may not be Jeff Taylor."

"I can blast that gun out of your hand," Reglen said. "No matter who you are. Now, why don't you be smart and drop that gun?"

"Why don't you come and get it?"

Halftime chortled. "Them doctors can talk all they want to. This is my boss, all right."

Reglen's mouth formed itself into a smile. He jerked his head at Jessie. She got out of the car. X saw she was carrying an automatic. He couldn't turn, for the two thugs were waiting to leap for their fallen guns. Now that Reglen was here, some of their courage had returned.

Jessie walked over to the car. She spoke to Zoe. Her voice was a snarl. "Get out, sugar. We can shoot *you* all right. We know who *you* are."

Zoe looked at X for a moment. Her face was white. She started to slide out of the car.

"Stay where you are," X ordered.

"Don't be a fool," Reglen said. "A bullet would mess her up. You know that. That pretty face all smeared with blood. You better get out, Zoe. Do what Jessie tells you."

"All right," X said. "Go with them. They won't hurt you. God help them if they do."

Zoe slid out of the car.

"He's right," Reglen told her. "It isn't you we want, sweetie. It's the man with the gun there. So maybe you better tell him. You don't want your toe-nails torn out, do you? One by one? Tell him. That's what's going to happen to you, baby, unless he decides to come back to that apartment like a nice lit-tle rat, and behave himself."

"You touch her," X snarled. He turned a little and both the thugs jumped for their guns. He wheeled back around, firing.

Reglen fired, too. The bullet struck the automatic in his hand, an inch from his fist. The gun was jerked from X's hand.

Reglen laughed. "That's nice shooting, if I do say so myself. Now I can put a bullet anywhere I want to. So let's quit stalling now and get back to town. I may decide any minute to move one closer in."

The two thugs had retrieved their guns now. They moved in on X. The stout one jabbed him in the ribs. "Do what Mr. Reglen says."

X turned and walked to the Packard. Jessie had the back door open. Mike twisted around so his automatic rested on the back of the seat.

"Get in," Jessie said.

X looked at her. "You used to call me darling," he said.

Her mouth twisted. "Get in, darling."

He got in the rear of the car, sat with his hands in his lap. He faced for-ward. But all he could see was the cold eye of Mike's gun. It was as though Reglen had three eyes now. Three deadly eyes fixed on him.

Jessie slammed the door. She spoke to Zoe. "You can go back to Halftime now," she said. "We don't want you any more, baby."

Mike spoke. "You, Phil and Jersey. Follow those two into town. Maybe you better impress on them what will happen to them if they try to ring the police in on this little game."

"I'm going to the police," Zoe said.

Before anyone could move, Jessie had slammed the gun across Zoe's face. The girl staggered back. She would have fallen, but Halftime caught her as she stumbled and just before she struck on her knees. She straightened slowly.

Blood eased from the red welt along the side of her face.

"Get in, Jessie," Mike snarled at her. "Let's get out of here."

X leaned forward. But Mike only shook his head, lifting the gun. Mike's mouth smiled. "Just relax, brother," he said.

Jessie got into the black Packard behind the wheel. She pulled it around on the wide highway. X was watching through the back glass. He saw Zoe and Halftime get in the Plymouth. One of the thugs got into the other car and turned it around while the second stood on the shoulder, watching Zoe and Halftime.

He heard Mike's cold laugh. "Just forget 'em. They'll be all right. As long as they're smart."

X's bullfrog voice croaked at him. "They'd better be all right."

"I tell you. They will be. Just like you'll be all right. As long as you're smart."

They didn't speak again on the swift run into Rainier. Jessie whipped the Packard through the side streets without even slowing down at intersections. She pulled into the down ramp and entered the garage under their apartment building.

They got out at the entrance and let an attendant park the car.

"Now, just take it easy," Reglen advised. "You may think I won't shoot you here in this apartment house. Okay. I don't want to shoot you yet. But the side of this gun will make a hell of a dent in your head. Now let's go upstairs where we can talk quiet."

They closed in on him again. X shook his head. They gave him claustrophobia, like a man might get in a small, tight execution chamber.

As they went up in the elevator, X decided that his best chance would be to send one of his nurses out of the place for help as soon as he could. The thought that he wasn't yet completely isolated from the outside world gave him a little sense of relief. But not much. This was a deadly pair. They were sure he had what they wanted. Money.

Jessie unlocked the door and let them into the apartment. There was an air of quiet in it. X entered the foyer and looked around.

Mike smiled. "No. Your nurses aren't here. We gave them the day off. We told them to come back by tonight. And—if you don't decide to be a nice kid—by tonight you may need them."

X said nothing. He heeled around and walked through the door into the polished black and white living room. He smiled to himself. He didn't like to think about being caught dead in this room.

Mike's yell stopped him. "Hey. Where you think you're going?"

X said, "I need a drink."

They followed him into the front room. He went across to the bar and poured himself a stiff drink. He stood with his back to them, watching them in the tinted wall mirror.

He finished off the drink and turned around.

"All right now," Mike said. "Let's understand each other. We know. This thing is some kind of stall. This business that you don't know who you are. That's for the birds. It's just some more of the tricks you started pulling."

"What tricks?"

Jessie's voice was harsh. "You found out the boys wouldn't back you against Mike. You knew you had to get out. You kept trying to sell out. To Vashney and then to some of the boys themselves. Oh, Mike heard about it. Mike is smart. The way you were always *supposed* to be."

"I was trying to get out?"

Mike's mouth twisted. "Stop stalling. There's no fancy medico around here to be impressed. You moved all your accounts to out-of-town banks. You were ready to clear out. We know. Then Young started his campaign against you— and you knew that you couldn't run. Not as long as they had you framed for Vashney's murder. The FBI would get you for running out from under a murder rap. You never could get away. So now, you kill Ben Young dead in your fishing camp, and turn up—blanko. You don't know who you are. Well, we know who you are. And you know who you are. And you know what we want. We want that money you moved out of town. And before you get out of here, you're going to tell us where it is or wish you had."

Both of them moved forward. *Crowding me again,* he thought.

Mike transferred the small gun he was carrying to Jessie.

"Hold it on him," Mike ordered. "Just so he don't get no ideas."

Now Jessie stood in the center of the room, red hair mussed, too much lipstick, and it had smeared at the corners of her mouth. Her eyes were hard little dots set in her chubby face.

The lines of an old song began to race through X's mind, and he thought how strange it was that he could recall a song, and yet know nothing about his own past: "Baby Face. Baby Face. You got the cutest little baby face, Baby Face." Deadly little baby face.

Mike had moved nearer. X sidled away from the bar and moved toward the divan. That's when Mike jumped him.

X stepped back and Mike missed. X struck with his left and it landed against the side of Mike's face.

It did damage all right. The blood seemed to drop out of X's body. He felt nothing but agony from the top of his head to his feet.

A sound of pain croaked from his face. Mike had heeled around. There hadn't been power enough in that left even to faze the dark little man.

Mike leaped again and this time X was in too much agony to move.

Mike caught the lapels of X's coat, twisting them, jerking X off his feet. He half threw the bigger man to the couch.

X landed hard. Mike didn't release his grip on his coat. Mike shook him. X still couldn't feel the way his head rocked on his shoulders. He was still feeling the agony in his left arm.

"All right now," Mike panted. "I want that money."

"The devil," X whispered. "Go to the devil."

Mike was breathing hard through his open mouth. "This is the last time, Taylor. For the last time. Where is that money?"

"I don't know."

Mike released X's coat with his left hand and brought the hand against the side of X's helmeted head. For a moment the room spun, wheeling and whirling. Mike went flying around out in front of his eyes. Slowly everything settled. Mike was still holding the lapels of his coat.

"See, Taylor. You hurt easy. This is Mike. Mike knows a lot of tricks. Remember that—"

"I don't know—" The frog croak of his voice was gone. Pain had reduced the power of his vocal chords until his yelling answer was only a whisper.

"I think you know. Now listen to me, Taylor. Listen fast. These bandages around your head and face. They have to be applied under pressure, don't they? They have to give you morphine when they change 'em. They have to have all kinds of oils and salves and junk handy. That right, Taylor?"

X tried to twist away from those hands on his coat.

"Is that right?" Mike was yelling at him now. "So if I pulled them bandages off, Taylor, one by one, I'm going to rip every bit of flesh there is left there! You hear me?"

X nodded his head.

"I'm not giving you no dope to make it easy on you, Taylor. There ain't no salves. I'm going to start pulling them off. It's the last chance to save what there is of your face, Taylor!"

X took a deep breath. He lunged upward. The abrupt movement caught the sweating Reglen off balance and they went reeling across the floor. They landed hard on the coffee table. The legs splintered under them and they went down.

X jabbed at Mike's face with his right. He held his left arm at his side like a splintered wing. But the fear and the agony in him gave him strength and speed. His right cracked across Mike's nose and smashed again into his mouth.

He could feel Mike sag under him. Then he was aware of a blur of movement and knew that Jessie had moved in on him. He tried to duck, tried to throw up his arm to ward off the gun she was bringing down across his skull.

He didn't move fast enough or far enough. There was the sharp sound of metal against bone and then his head was alive with brilliant lights. Somebody snapped off the flashing lights and it was dark.

He was on the couch when he came out of it. Sprawled on it with his legs hanging over the side. His hands were tied together in front of him, secured with his own belt.

Jessie was dragging a bottle of spirits of ammonia back and forth under his nose. He awoke stretching his head to escape the pungent fumes.

Mike was standing over him. Mike's nose was bloody and there was a cut on his lip.

"All right. Cut it out," Mike said to Jessie. "He's awake now."

She moved the bottle, stepped back.

X started to sit up. Mike slammed the flat of his hand against X's shoulder, shoving him back against the arm rest.

"Just stay there," Mike snarled.

That was when X saw the strips of gauze in Mike's hand. Long narrow strips of it that they had pulled from his head. He knew they were the outer layers. Some of the strips had faint bloody spots on them.

He shivered. They were down to the last layer. Maybe the doctors could have done something for his face before. But he knew now that they weren't going to be able to do anything. Not when Mike got through. Mike would tear the flesh off in strips. It would take more than plastic surgery to rebuild him then.

He struggled upward.

Mike laughed.

"That's right," Mike said. "We've removed the outer layers, Taylor. Now will you believe us? Now will you see we mean business? Your face is pretty well healed, Taylor. But there are places where it is still caught to the gauze. Nothing is going to help you when I get started. That money ain't going to do you any good when your face is ripped apart, Taylor. Get smart. Tell us where you put that money!"

X shook his head and struggled again, twisting his body and trying to push up from the couch.

Mike's laugh was a snarl. He caught one of the loose ends of the gauze, a strip that began just under X's chin.

Mike jerked the strip. The fire blazed, raging through X's mind as it had that night in the cabin. The agony raced a hundred ways across his face, through his head and along his throat into his body, like the gasoline-soaked paths of flame bursting alive suddenly on a fishing shack floor.

X screamed. But the sound was a whisper. A whisper they barely heard and wouldn't have heeded anyhow. It was as though he spoke a foreign language, and they didn't understand that language.

He writhed up, arching his back. Then the pain was so intense that he slumped to the couch, out cold. The suffocating fumes of the ammonia flooded through the darkness and he stirred. He couldn't see yet. But he began to hear something. The distant whirring of bells, ringing, ringing. They grew louder in his head and he reached for them and they died away. Then the ringing started again. Started and stopped.

But always started again.

15

The ringing was the doorbell.

He swam back through a lake of green to consciousness. They were standing over him. Only a part of the strip of gauze had been ripped from his chin.

Both Mike and Jessie remained as though paralyzed by the incessant clamoring of the doorbell.

Mike snarled over his shoulder. "You better answer it. See who it is. Get rid of them."

"All right," Jessie said. Through the green haze that lifted slowly like wet fog from his eyes, X saw the plush redhead move away from him, across the wide expanse of white carpet, past the faraway black objects that were tables and chairs. She reached the door, but that was too far away for him to see. It was beyond the reach of his blurred vision.

"And you," Mike whispered. "Stay still. Don't try to pull anything, or you'll wish you hadn't."

X was glad for the moment of rest.

From a distant planet, X could hear the muted voices raised against each other in the foyer. Whoever it was, he must have pushed his way in as soon as Jessie cracked the front door.

"Is he here—Taylor, or Young, whatever his name is?"

That was a voice he'd heard somewhere.

And then Jessie's voice, smooth and creamy. "Why shouldn't he be here, Captain Beckart? He lives here, doesn't he?"

"I don't know. Not the way I hear it." The voice was louder. He wished the Captain would come inside—in a hurry.

Then Jessie's voice again.

"No? How do you hear it, Captain?"

"All I know is that Halftime Smith and a girl named Zoe Gardner were out riding together. They got picked up for speeding seventy miles an hour in a twenty-mile zone. When they brought them in, the Gardner girl had a deep welt on her face. They said you and Mike Reglen had taken this Taylor—or Young—at the point of a gun, and brought him here against his will."

"Why, Captain, why should we do that? Jeff is supposed to live here for a week. You know what's the matter with the Gardner dame, don't you?"

"No. I don't. She seems a pretty levelheaded young woman. And she says you struck her across the face with the side of a gun. She says it happened on a lonely road."

"Why, she'd say anything. Anything to hurt me. You know she hates me. And you know why!"

"No. I don't. All I know is that I've talked to Ricey and he feels that perhaps he was wrong. He doesn't want Taylor to spend the rest of the week here. I explained to him that Reglen wasn't above using Taylor's weakness as an excuse to finish him off."

"Why, Captain, what a horrible thing to say. Mike has been Jeff's right hand man for years. Why would he suddenly turn on him? Now is when Jeff needs his friends."

Beckart laughed. "I wouldn't know how minds like Mike's work, sister. All I know is that he took up with you—long before the fire. And that hasn't changed. I know he's an ambitious boy. If the burned man is Jeff Taylor, we want him. For murder. We don't want Mike Reglen to get him first. If he's Ben Young—well, the hospital could be sued for millions for malpractice, for allowing him to be brought here to be manhandled by you and Reglen—"

"A fine way to talk! I'll bet you didn't talk to the high and mighty Youngs that way. Oh, everything was wonderful all during the week they had him there! But you can throw your weight around here. Well, you can't. Suppose you just get out. Jeff is all right. He wants to stay here. With me. His wife."

"Wife?" Beckart's voice made something else out of that word. It hit a new low the way he said it. "I'm not getting out, sister. I've got a warrant right here in my pocket. I intend to get the full benefit from it. Now, turn your fat little tail around and lead me to Jeff Taylor. I want to see him. And I mean right now."

"He's going to stay here!" Jessie's voice was louder. They were coming nearer.

He could see them corning through the living room doorway. Mike just stood there, with the gauze stringing down from both sides of his fist. He didn't make any effort to speak. He couldn't. He just stood as if he'd been suddenly paralyzed.

"We'll just let him decide that," Beckart began. He stopped in the center of the room, staring at the streamers of gauze in Reglen's fist. From the gauze his horrified gaze moved to the single strands remaining wound about X's face. "Name of all that's holy! Never mind. I don't need to see any more."

He strode over, picked up the telephone. First he ordered an ambulance from the hospital. Then he called police headquarters.

"Send three men to Jeff Taylor's apartment. I'm making an arrest. Mike Reglen and Jessie Taylor. I'll hold 'em, but I might need help bringin' em in."

It was gray dusk in the hospital room when X opened his eyes. But gray dusk of what day? The same day? The next day? He didn't know. His head rolled on the pillow. His eyes found Zoe Gardner at the side of his bed. A small strip of adhesive marked the place where Jessie had struck her with the gun.

"Hi," she said.

"Hi."

Brilliant conversation, he thought.

"Are you all right?"

"Me? I'm swell. I'm sorry you got hurt. Thanks for getting to the police."

"It was my idea to speed," Zoe said. "Those two men of Mike's nearly went crazy. They were afraid to let us go, and afraid to try to stop us. Halftime was wonderful. He kept speeding until three cruisers surrounded us. Then they took us to Captain Beckart."

"You really fixed Reglen and Jessie," he said.

She shook her head. Anger made her eyes sparkle. "No. They didn't stay in jail half an hour. Their lawyer was waiting for them. They were taken before some crooked judge. Reglen said you were in pain, they were trying to relieve you by removing the bandages. They were released on bond. You know how much bond? Fifty dollars." Her voice was outraged.

"Have they found Vance Roberts?"

She looked at him.

"They haven't found him," she said. "I don't think they are going to find him. Anyway—not alive."

He looked at her. Her jaw was squared, and her mouth set. There was no use trying to talk to her.

"I talked to Captain Beckart. He thinks that maybe Vance followed you— Jeff Taylor and Ben Young—to the cottage that night. J-Jeff must have heard him outside and—and killed him."

"So if I'm Jeff Taylor there's not one murder charge against me, but two."

She bit her lip. She lowered her head. He looked at the light shining in the blackness of her waved hair. He longed to reach out and touch that sheen. It was as though touching her was going to make him well. His mouth tightened. What right had he?

She nodded. Her voice sounded as though there were tears in it.

Vance Roberts must be some guy, he thought, *to have a girl like this so much in love with him.*

"Captain Beckart says that if they do find Vance Roberts' body—and it will only be a matter of time, he says—they'll have evidence against you. But just now he says he doesn't need it. He says that District Attorney Philip Dickson is taking up the work Ben Young was doing. He is preparing the case against Jeff Taylor. If you are Ben Young, it'll be all ready for you when you are well. And if you are Jeff Taylor—" She shivered. "It will still be all ready for you."

She went away. The nurses came. They went out. The light was snapped off. It was dark in the room. He lay there staring at the darkened ceiling. The hospital grew quiet. Finally there were only the sounds of the dynamo throbbing away in the heart of the building and his own deep breathing.

For hour after hour, he lay there trying to piece together any part of the puzzle that might lead backward into his lost past.

Myra Young. He had known her the first time he saw her. Something about her had stirred him. He would have sworn he knew her somewhere. She had made an impression upon him that had scaled the wall of fire that cut him off from himself.

Halftime. Was the kinship he felt for the big man just a response to the poor fellow's devotion and simple goodness?

Zoe Gardner. Did he know her from the past, or was her beauty just such a spur to his imagination that he liked to think so?

He went back over each moment he had spent in the Young house. He remembered all he had found out. Ben Young was trying to build a career on framed-up evidence against another man. Ben Young had no better taste than to fall for a colorless automaton of a secretary in his office. Ben Young's wife was a cold and scheming woman. He wondered what sort of romance they must have had together. It must have been like two devil fish.

He shook his head. Ben and Myra Young could have looked at Niagara Falls in the moonlight and plotted diverting its course for greater electric power.

Clarinda Young might be his mother. He didn't like to think so.

And that brought him to the hellish nightmare he had walked into as Jeff Taylor. A man hounded by an ambitious Assistant District Attorney, double-crossed by his wife, and betrayed by his partner. What a hell of an existence the top man in Rainier rackets had led! How could he ever trust himself to sleep?

There was nothing about Ben Young that made him wish he was the young lawyer.

Jeff Taylor was only going to live long enough to be tried and shipped off to the execution chamber at Raiford. If he lived that long. Maybe Mike or some of Mike's men would kill him before that. Save the state some money.

He didn't sleep until daylight streaked in through the slits in the venetian blind. All he got out of the sleepless night was the conviction that there was nothing but hell ahead, whether he turned out to be Ben Young—or the doomed Jeff Taylor.

16

When he opened his eyes, the first thing he saw was the blonde hair. As always it made him think of halos and soft lights. And then she lifted her head and their eyes met. Those blue eyes. Scheming. Cold.

"Hello, Myra."

"You feel better now?"

"Sure. I'm swell."

"I hope so. I want to talk to you. We don't have a lot of time. There will be people in and out all the time. Your mother and father will be here soon. So I want you to talk to me and talk straight."

"All right."

"What about this gag—this amnesia business. Hasn't that gone far enough? What more can you gain? You must know that almost no cases of amnesia are truly *complete* losses of memory. They are part lost and part thrown away. Expediently thrown away. A man gets ill and forgets his name. But there are a million other things he remembers. Sounds and smells, familiar sights. Some of them never admit it. They don't want to. They have something to gain. Too many people have faked it. Nobody takes it seriously. I'm not taking it seriously now."

"If I swear to you it's no gag?"

She looked at him.

"I expected you to say that. So we understand each other. You are not going to admit you're Ben. You must have your reasons. One thing I know, you won't admit you're Jeff Taylor. That would be fitting yourself right into the electric chair. So what are you planning to do?"

"I don't know."

"Then listen closely. When your mother and father—when Clarinda and Ben Young, Sr., come in here, I want them to think you are Ben. I want you to tell them that you are." She was leaning close over the bed now; her voice was tense.

"And what will that get me?"

"It will start getting you out of here. Psychiatry is still enough witchcraft so that if you tell them that you remember something of your past they'll accept it."

"Why do you want me to do that?"

"Because you've got to get out of here and start to work. It's getting late. If you're going to be Governor of this state, you've got to get to work, and fast."

He stared at her. "Let's get this straight. You mean you want me to say I'm Ben Young—whether I can prove it or not?"

"I'll help you prove it!"

"You'll help me prove I'm Ben Young?"

"Yes. Yes." Her voice snapped with impatience. "Don't you understand what I'm telling you? I'm sure you are Ben. I want you to get to work. The only way you can do that is to get out of here. I'll tell you a few things out of your past. Enough. You'll get by the psychiatrists."

His eyes widened. "You'll help me because you think I'm Ben Young—but you'll help me anyway, whether I'm Ben Young or not?"

Her face was pale and rigid. Her blue eyes locked with his hazel ones, held. Finally she nodded.

"Yes. Is that too terrible? I can't see that it is."

"I'm nobody. I may not even be a lawyer."

"You don't have to be. There are corps of lawyers working for you. You don't have to be a lawyer. You can be Governor. All you have to do is just what I tell you."

"Has it ever occurred to you that after you make me Governor I might wake up some night knowing who I am—knowing that you've made Jeff Taylor, gambler and murderer, Governor?"

"I'm not worried about that. I'll take a chance on it. Anyhow, I'll tell you this. Jeff Taylor is a gambler. But he isn't a murderer. At least, he never murdered Rick Vashney."

"How can you dare to tell me that?"

"Don't waste my time. It should be obvious. If you are who I *know* you are, then you already know that fact. And even if you're Jeff Taylor you could never prove you're innocent—even if you were fool enough to admit you are Jeff Taylor. Only I know you're not going to do that."

"You've got it all figured out?"

"I haven't thought of anything else. Clarinda Young is convinced you're Ben. I'm very certain. But I'm not a fool. From the first I've had to take into consideration that you might not be. But I've thought it over from every angle. If you're smart enough to listen to me, there's no reason why you cannot fool the whole world—no matter who you are. There's no reason, if you'll do just as I tell you, why you can't be the next Governor!"

"How can people be fooled?"

"They won't be. When it is time for plastic surgery, your face will be rebuilt to resemble Ben Young's. You'll look like Ben Young—as nearly as the best plastic surgeons can make you. I'll coach you. You'll think like Ben Young—and you'll *be* Ben Young!"

"You'll call this irrelevant and foolish as an objection, Myra. But suppose I tell you that no matter who I am—no matter who I was—I don't expect to enter into any bloodless marriage just to fulfill your desire to become the Governor's wife."

"You are wasting time. That doesn't matter."

"Maybe not to Ben Young. But it matters to me. Maybe that's your best proof that I'm not Ben Young."

She laughed. A cold sound. "You're proving to me with every word that I am right. You are Ben Young! Of course, you're ill, and you may be trying to change things. But I want them just the way they were."

"Oh? How were they?"

She had the grace to blush, at least slightly. "The way they should be in every sensible marriage. I didn't care what you did, Ben. I let you understand that. Even that little June Mason in your office. I knew about her. I never said anything. And that's the way it will be from now on. I don't care what you do, Ben, as long as you are discreet."

"Good lord! What a marriage! What a lot to look forward to!"

"Don't be a fool. You've everything to look forward to. Money. Plenty of it. Position. Impregnable position. Well, they looked down their noses at me when my father lost his money. I had to leave the fine school I went to, and some of our best friends dropped us. But I got even. I married Ben Young. And I've had everything. I've rubbed their noses in it. And I'm not through with them."

X stared at her. So that was the driving force behind Myra Young. Slights and hurts in her girlhood. An overwhelming desire to look down on and snub all the people who had snubbed her.

She was willing to do anything to get where she wanted to go. The Young money and influence hadn't proved to be enough. Apparently she was sure that as the Governor's wife she would be where she wanted to go. She wasn't going to stop until she got what she wanted. Whether he was Ben Young or not, she was willing to accept him and remake him into Ben Young's image just so nothing would keep her from the goal she had set for them.

"Now, listen to me. There isn't much time. There should just be a few things at first. So it will look right. So it will appear to the fools that your memory is actually returning slowly. Do you understand?"

"Yes."

"All right. When Clarinda Young arrives, she'll be wearing a blue lace dress. I know. I suggested she wear it. But in the excitement she'll forget all about that."

"The excitement?"

"Certainly. You and I brought her that dress. We bought it in London when we were over there last year. When she comes in, I want you to look at that blue lace dress and sort of choke up—tell her that she's wearing your dress—the one you picked for her in London."

He stared at her. You could forget the cold blue eyes. You had to admire her. He knew that she was right. Just the little things at first. Remembering a dress. The whole hospital would be in an uproar. Probably the *News* would get out an extra. BEN YOUNG REMEMBERS MOTHER'S DRESS.

He nodded. "You're smart, baby. I'll give you that."

Her laugh was colder than ever. "You just don't know how smart I am. And remember, you don't have to do anything except what I tell you. I'll coach you on the people you know, how well you know them, and how warmly you greet them."

He studied her high-cheeked face for a moment. "You'll tell me all I need to know about all of the people I know?"

"Yes."

"Even my mistresses, I suppose?"

Her eyes flashed and she lifted her head, meeting his gaze evenly. She nodded.

"Even your mistresses."

17

Myra was just standing up, ready to leave, when a nurse came into the room.

"An urgent call for you, Mrs. Young. There's a telephone at the day-nurse desk in the corridor."

Myra thanked her and went out of the room.

X lay there. He felt more physically exhausted after listening to Myra than he had when Mike Reglen had pummeled him all over the couch.

So she was going to make him Governor. She didn't care who he really was. When her surgeons got through with him he would look like Ben Young. When she had coached him, he would sound like Ben Young. And finally, one horrible day, he would begin to think like Ben Young.

He shivered.

He wondered where Zoe was. Was she out looking for Vance Roberts? The lucky devil. At least he had had a girl like Zoe in love with him.

Myra came back into the room. She dismissed the nurse curtly. She came back to the edge of the bed and stood by it. He saw that her face was chalky white.

"What's the matter?"

"Nothing."

"You look scared."

"Well, I'm not. At least not for myself. I can face anything. But I want to be sure if you can. That was Philip Dickson on the telephone—"

"My revered boss, the District Attorney?"

She didn't think him amusing. "Yes. He said not to let anyone into this room until after he'd been here and gone. He wants to talk to both of us."

"What about?"

"Of course he didn't say over the telephone. But it has him jittery. He's an old maid anyhow. So don't say anything when he gets here—"

"You've told him that you're sure I'm Ben Young?"

"Yes. I talked to him last week. I convinced him. He has decided to go ahead and build up the case against the gamblers in this town just as you—as Ben—had planned. He also agreed when I talked to him about it that he would continue with the case against Jeff Taylor—"

"Just in case I had any ideas about stepping out of line?"

Her eyes held his levelly. She said, "Perhaps."

"You don't take any chances with your husbands, do you?"

"I don't take chances with anything."

He nodded. "I believe that."

The door was pushed open. Philip Dickson came in. He looked disheveled, sweaty and frightened.

"Myra," he panted. "I've got to talk to you."

Her voice was cool. "Go ahead, Philip."

"Privately."

"This is my husband, Philip. Anything you can say to, me can be said before him."

Philip's mouth whitened. "I tell you this is important. Urgent."

"And I tell you that Ben can listen—"

"But—"

"It is Ben, Philip. I've already told you."

The harassed man stared at the gauze-covered head. He sighed. "If only I could be sure."

"Oh, I'm Ben," X said.

Philip was so startled he almost jumped. "You are?"

"I swear. By my mother's blue lace gown!"

He felt Myra's cold hand against his, restrainingly. He was sorry he'd been a wise guy. It was one thing to make a stupid joke. But this woman was smart. There was no percentage in being a jokester at the expense of a woman as intelligent as Myra.

"I'm sorry," he said. "Myra is sure I'm Ben. She's made me almost sure. She's made me certain I can remember—"

Her tense grip on his hand relaxed. He didn't look at her but he sensed that she sighed.

"You see, Philip," Myra said. "I told you. He's on his way to recovery. Ben's going to be all right."

"I hope so."

"Now then. Tell us, what was it you had to say?" Myra's voice was still cold but there was a tinge of worry in it.

"Well, I had some of my younger men go to work on the Jeff Taylor case. I tell you, Myra that thing is falling apart in our hands. Worse than that, it may explode—and ruin us all. I'm sick that I promised you I'd touch it."

"Don't be hysterical, Philip. What's the matter? What happened?"

Philip Dickson paced the room. "You may as well know. Since the accident, Myra—that is, since the fire—there has been a change of feeling. People feel that whoever the man who lived through that fire was, he is now the product of a miracle. And two witnesses in the Vashney case think that the man might be Jeff Taylor. Both of them say they lied about him—for money."

"The fools!" The words cracked across Myra's lips.

"Fools or not, they refuse to go into court and perjure themselves. Both say they could not possibly have seen *anyone* enter or leave Rick Vashney's secluded apartment at that hour of the night!"

"And that's the only reason they changed their minds? Because of the fire?"

"It must be. We haven't talked to any of the others. Frankly, we've been afraid to. I can tell you one thing, if this thing gets out, Ben Young is going to be disbarred for malpractice!"

Philip Dickson was striding up and down the room. He stopped beside the bed and stared at X's gauze-covered face.

"Because I've talked like this before you, I hope you are Ben Young. But I can tell you this—if you are Ben Young, I'd hate to be in your shoes when the state Bar Association gets through with you. Framed-up evidence to convict a man of murder! They're going to crucify you, Young. That's the best I can see for you."

"Well, you picked a real bright view all right."

"It's no joke, man. You are my assistant in this district. You are sworn to uphold the laws of this state. You have taken an oath. You've flouted it. You've used your office as a means to work a crime of the blackest sort. I-I'm sorry, but I cannot offer any assistance."

Myra was deflated. She looked suddenly old, haggard. She sank to a chair. She stared up at Philip Dickson.

"What are you going to do?"

"Do?" Both of Philip Dickson's chins trembled. "I'll tell you what I'm going to do. I'm going to bury this Jeff Taylor mess so deep in the files it will take six months to dig it out. In the meantime, I want just one thing from you, Young. I want your letter of resignation."

"Resignation?" Myra whispered.

"Yes!" Dickson's voice snapped. "It's the only way we can save the party. If he resigns now it'll save my office when disbarment proceedings start. And I may as well tell you, Young, I'm not asking for your resignation. I'm demanding it. Nothing but my friendship for your father keeps me from ripping this whole mess open now. As it is, I'm giving you a chance to get out."

Myra's mouth curled. "You're giving us a chance to save your fat hide."

"Well, no matter what my motive, I am giving you a chance. I'll have a letter of resignation drawn up. You can sign it. There's no hurry. Any time within the next three hours will be soon enough."

Dickson left. After a moment Myra got up. There should have been something he could say to her but he couldn't think what it might be. She went away.

When he was alone, he lay staring at the ceiling. Now it no longer mattered who he was, Ben Young or Jeff Taylor. He was in trouble up to his teeth, either way.

The more he thought about it, the more he knew that he didn't want to be either of those men, if he could help it.

And then he began to think about Myra. She was going to coach him so that he could have been Ben Young. Back when being Ben Young would have amounted to hitting the jackpot.

First he nodded, then he smiled to himself. And then he was pretty sure that he had found the one way out of this mess, and he couldn't think of anything he wanted more than out.

He pressed the buzzer, sat on it until a nurse came running.

She leaned close to hear him when he whispered.

"Nurse, there's a big barrel-chested guy hangs around out in the corridors. His name is Halftime Smith—"

"Yes. Of course. He's out there now. He's out there every day."

"Good. Send him in here as fast as you can. And, Nurse—I don't want to see anybody but Halftime Smith—and that means nobody!"

Halftime grinned when he came through the door.

"Hi ya, boss," he said. "Hi ya. They said you wanted to see me. Gosh, they said you wanted to see me."

"That's right, Halftime. There's something I want you to do for me. Something that has got to be done—and fast."

"Sure, boss. That's me. Didn't you hear how I got caught speedin'?"

"You're a wonderful guy, Halftime. That's why I'm asking you to do this for me. I want you to find Zoe Gardner for me. Find her. Bring her here. I don't know where she is. But I do know that I got to see her."

18

It was three hours later when Halftime returned with Zoe Gardner. He was clutching her by her elbow and was half-leading her into the room. "Here she is, boss," he said. "I found her. Fast. Like you said."

"You're a wonderful guy, Halftime," X said. "Now will you do me one more favor?"

"Sure, boss. All you got to do is ask me."

"Okay, Halftime. Sit outside this door. Not only don't let anyone in. Don't let them come near enough to hear us talking in here."

Halftime grinned. It pulled his rubbery features into a grotesque caricature of simple happiness. He went outside dragging a straight white chair. He leaned it against the wall and sat there with his arms crossed.

Zoe's eyes were stormy when he faced her.

"You know," she said, "I'll come any time you send for me. You don't have to have me dragged in here."

"Halftime was in a hurry," X said. He tried to show her he was smiling. But that was a hell of a trick when his face was swathed in fresh white bandages.

"All right," she said. "You were in a hurry. Why didn't you just telephone for me?"

"Sorry. I don't know your number. I didn't even know you had a phone."

Her face darkened. "That's right. I keep forgetting. You don't even know who you are, do you?"

He bit his lip. "Don't you think it might barely be possible, Zoe?"

Her voice cracked. "I'll tell you what I think. I think you are Jeff Taylor. I think you lied to me. You told me you were going to take Ben Young up there to *threaten* him. You said you were going to *frighten* him. What you neglected to tell me was that you really intended to kill him."

"That's what you think?"

"That's part of it."

"No wonder you hate me."

"I don't hate you. That's the terrible part of it. I wish I could. Because like I say, that's just part of it. The other part of it is that I've become more and more sure that Vance Roberts followed you up there and you killed him, too—"

"If that's true, I'm not worth saving. And I wouldn't ask you to do anything for me."

"That's what I think! You asked me. I'm telling you. I wish I felt you weren't worth saving. What I see when I look at you is a poor kid growing up in the wrong part of town, getting somewhere in the only business open to him—the rackets. But getting to the top not by using guns and muscle, but by using his brains. By making a business out of it, until the people he trusted turned on him—"

"That's Jeff Taylor?"

"That's the one I knew—" Her fists were clenched, knuckles white. "But I think he started killing and couldn't stop. He killed Ben Young. Then he had to kill Vance Roberts to hide the first crime. And then when he couldn't face what was ahead for him, he came back here—and faked amnesia!"

"You've got it all figured out."

"I ought to have!" she cried. "I haven't thought about anything else. I've eaten it, dreamed it, slept it for six rough weeks."

"Suppose I tell you the idea that I have."

She faced him, her eyes rimmed with tears. "All right."

"I won't pretend to believe it. I was going to. I planned to bring you here and spring it on you cold. I was going to ask you enough questions so that your answers would help me fake it. But I can't do it. I've listened to you. And whatever I am, whoever I am, I'm not low enough to use you like that."

"What are you talking about?"

He lifted his right hand, regarded it for a long time.

"A doublecross. I was going to doublecross you in order to get out of trouble—"

"Tell me! What are you talking about?"

"All right. Suppose Vance Roberts followed Ben Young and Jeff Taylor up to the fishing cottage on Eaton Lake? Remember, it was a two-room cottage. I had that read to me from the newspaper. I won't lie to you about that. Suppose Vance Roberts hid in that back room to listen to what Young and Taylor were saying?"

"Yes?" She was holding her breath.

"Suppose for some reason he didn't know how to get out of there when the fire exploded? It was practically spontaneous. Maybe he tripped and fell in the dark. Anyhow, the room was on fire before he came to. He couldn't get out. He had to break a window and climb out, wrapped in a grass rug!"

"Vance Roberts!" She screamed the words. And then she clapped her hand over her mouth.

"No," he said. "I'm not. That's what I'm trying to tell you. It's all a lie. It's something I made up."

"You're lying now."

"Am I? I tell you I made it up. I made it all up. I lay here in this bed and realized that Vance Roberts has been missing since the night of the fire. I have too much to lose by being either Jeff Taylor or Ben Young. One a murderer. One about to be disbarred. Listen to me! I made it all up!"

She was leaning over the bed. Her breath was short, sharp. Her fingers were digging into the white covers.

"But it could have happened!"

She didn't say it. She was afraid to say it aloud. She whispered it at him.

"No!" He shook his head. He sat up. "I won't let you drag yourself into this. Do I look like Vance Roberts?"

She shook her head. "No. But you don't definitely look like Jeff Taylor, either."

"There was a huge coincidence at work in Jeff Taylor and Ben Young's being of the same age and general build, the same eyes. What color eyes does Vance Roberts have?"

She whispered again. "Brown."

"There, you see, it would never work. How old is he?"

"Twenty-eight."

"All right, the doctors have set my age at between thirty and thirty-three. I wish now I'd never even told you about it."

"A mistake," she said. "They make them all the time. Vance drank so much, he'd probably test out ten years older than he actually is—" Her voice was almost as harsh as his.

"Drank?" Now he was facing her, his eyes narrowed.

"All the time," she said. "Every time he had a problem to face, he faced it with a bottle in one hand."

"I know who would believe me—"

She came closer. "Who?"

Now he was whispering, keeping his voice lower even than it was. "A guy who hates Jeff Taylor. A guy who nevertheless might be forced to believe it. And if he believed it, everybody else would have to because he has most to lose—"

"Tell me!"

"Mike Reglen. I remember the first night they took me to the apartment, Jessie was going to serve drinks. They were both surprised when I took a double bourbon. Jessie fixed it but Mike kept looking at me like he didn't believe it."

"Jeff Taylor never drank," she breathed. "He hated liquor. His old man died drunk. That was all he could think about. He'd take a drink once in a while, but he never liked it—"

"And I'll bet he never took a double bourbon—"

She shook her head. "Very watered blended whiskey is what he drank!"

He shuddered.

She clutched his arm. "What's the matter?"

"If I'm not Jeff Taylor, there's one guy I must be. I must be Ben Young— and that makes me ill just to think about it."

"You won't be. You can't be!" she cried. "I'll tell you who you are. You're Vance Roberts."

"Now you're believing something because you want to."

"All right. I want to. Why, I remember when Vance graduated from high school, ten years ago. He had a blue Ford convertible. I was just a little girl. It was the first drunk I'd ever seen—"

"You can stop that," he said. "It won't work. You're trying to give me some of my past to remember, aren't you? Something I can tell the doctors so I can convince them. Oh no, baby, I'm not mixing you up in this. Besides that's already been tried today. Myra Young tried it. She wanted me to be Ben Young. She wanted me to remember a blue lace dress—"

"Please," she begged. "You can make it work. It will end your worries. For a while, anyway. If you aren't Jeff Taylor, they don't want you for murder—"

"But I'm not Vance Roberts. Do you think I am?"

She looked at him. Finally she shook her head. "No. All right. I don't think so. I think you are Jeff Taylor. Don't ask me why. That's just my wishing, maybe. Anyway, I don't have any doubt. Jeff Taylor was the most decent guy who ever lived—that's why I want you to be Jeff. But I want you to live. I want you to have a chance. And that's what you can buy by pretending you're Vance Roberts."

"No. You're too swell a little doll for that. If I'm Taylor, then I must have killed Roberts—maybe Young. If I'm a murderer, I deserve to die. You stay out of this."

"Don't you see, if you say you're Vance Roberts, the doctors will release you, the police will stop hounding you, and the Youngs won't have any claim on you. Then you can spend all your time finding Vance Roberts."

He felt a sudden clutch of cold in his chest. "Oh," he said. "So that's it. You want me out—so I can find your Vance Roberts for you."

She straightened him. "It's more than my just wanting you to. You've got to find him."

The doctors were ringed around the bed. Webster, Halligan and the others, each making their tests. Finally Ricey spoke from the foot of the bed.

"Where was it you had this blue convertible?"

"Here in town. Why, it was when I graduated from high school. I don't know why I remembered it, except that when this young lady came in—you see, this is the girl I hired to help me write my political column for a while. Well, sir, when she came in, it was like everything got all hot and funny. She looked like a little ten-year-old, sir. She was having hysterics and pointing at me and saying I was drunk—"

Zoe's voice was very low. "It was the first drunken man I had ever seen, Doctor."

"Remarkable. But it is just fantastic enough to be utterly believable," Ricey said. "A newspaper reporter follows two men to a fishing camp and is himself trapped in the fire that killed one of them. Are you gentlemen willing to accept this fragment of memory as any indication—?"

Halligan said, "He's come a long way since he first woke up in here and tried to tear up the bed. It's the sort of thing that might have made too strong an impression to be literally burned out."

"Yes," Ricey said. "That's the way I feel. A child screaming and pointing. A youth's first drunk. Graduation. A new car."

"A blue Ford," X said. "A convertible."

He wondered if he was overdoing it.

Captain Beckart was a little more stubborn than the doctors had been.

"There is still one man missing," he declared. "If we release this fellow, it may prove to be a trick."

"It isn't that we are releasing him," Ricey assured him. "We are sending him back to his apartment. Miss Gardner has consented to take him there. The scenes in that apartment will surely work on him now that his subconscious has begun to feed his mind chunks of his past—"

"All right," Beckart said at last. He walked over to the chair where X was sitting, fully dressed now. "Remember this, don't try to leave town, Roberts." He shook his head. "Hell, that don't even sound right. The name don't even fit the guy."

X stood up. "Maybe you can think of a name that fits me better?"

"I sure can, Mister. I can look at you and just one name comes right into my mind. Taylor. Jeff Taylor. Gambler and murderer."

X shrugged. "Well," he said, "that just shows you how wrong all of us can be sometimes."

By the time X was released from the hospital, the afternoon paper had hit the streets with the full and remarkable story of the man who was neither Young nor Taylor.

He sat in the car between Zoe and Halftime. All he could think was that he agreed with Captain Beckart. The name was wrong. It didn't fit him. Not at all. But it was a good safe name, at least. It didn't belong to a crooked lawyer. Or a murderer. It was a swell name to hide behind.

Halftime drove with both hands on the wheel, his eyes straight ahead.

"What's the matter with you?" X asked at last.

"Nothing. It's just them newspapers. Them doctors. Calling you Vance Roberts. You ain't no lousy stinking drunken newspaperman, boss."

"I'm alive, though," X said. "And there's nobody after my skin."

It took a long time, but finally Halftime got it. "I got it! Boss, I got it. You're giving them the business! Sure, you're saying you are this Roberts. That way Mike will be off guard and we can get him—"

"Yeah, Halftime. That's it," X said. "That's just about it."

Halftime grinned. "I got to hand it to us, boss. I guess we're about the two smartest guys in America."

"Three guys," Zoe said from beside the window. "I'm here, too."

"Yeah!" Halftime laughed. "Three guys. The three smartest guys in America."

It was no elaborate building that Vance Roberts called home.

Halftime parked the gray car at the curb. He looked around with distaste at the shabby street, the unpainted buildings, the slatternly women hanging over window sills watching.

They crossed the walk, entered the darkened foyer. Cheap mail boxes lined the wall. They found "Vance Roberts" listed on the second floor, 212.

Zoe fumbled in her purse, came up with the key.

"In spite of what you're thinking," she said, "I was never here. Vance gave me this key when I was working with him. He said I might want to come down here to do some work. I knew what he meant so I just took the key to keep him happy."

X looked at her, frowning. What kind of double talk was this? A man she thought about finding for six weeks and she wouldn't go near him when she had a chance? What was she? A younger Myra Young?

The second floor corridor was narrow and really dark. They moved along it single file.

"Huh," Halftime said. "You need a flashlight to find your way home in broad daylight. Huh."

"Here it is," Zoe said. She pushed the key into the lock. The force of her hand against the knob pushed the door open.

She caught her breath.

"It—it wasn't locked," she said.

There was a dim bulb suspended from the center of the ceiling. It was burning, the light from it was feeble. But there was enough glow to show paint-scabbed walls, a tumbled bed, sagging in the middle. A table and a cheap, wavy mirror. And in a chair over by the window, a man.

He stood up when the door was pushed all the way open. He looked at the three of them, staring at him. He smiled.

"Come on in," he said.

Zoe's face was transfixed. She looked as if she were going to scream. But she didn't. Instead, she folded quietly and fainted. X leaped to catch her before she struck the floor.

Holding her body, he looked up and faced the man by the window.

"Who are you?" he said.

"Why, don't you know? I'm the man you've been saying all day *you* are. I've been sitting here waiting for you to come home. My name, my friend, really is Vance Roberts."

19

His first confused reaction was that the whole thing was a nightmare and that it had reached its highest moment of pure horror.

The man in front of him was wearing a five-day growth of beard. His clothes were spotted and rumpled. He'd been sleeping in them, and it looked as though he hadn't been particular where he slept.

There was no doubt that it really was Vance Roberts. Zoe Gardner had taken one look at him and fainted.

He lifted her in his arms and carried her over to the bed. He didn't like to let her even touch it but he laid her down on it. Halftime produced a pint bottle of whiskey. X cradled her head, tilting the bottle against her lips.

She stirred, turning her head from the smell and the taste of it. All this time nobody spoke in the room. Vance Roberts stood in front of his chair, an insolent smile showing through the growth of whiskers on his face.

Zoe sat up. She dragged her hands across her eyes.

X tried to smile at her. "Well, anyway, we found your Vance Roberts," he said.

She glared at him. Her voice was still shaky. "That's the second time you've said that. He isn't my Vance Roberts. I don't want him—I wouldn't have him. If you don't want me, don't try to give me away."

"Me?" He whispered the word at her in stunned disbelief.

"Oh, you've made it clear enough. You don't want me. All right. That isn't important any more. What is important is, what are you going to do now?" Her eyes went back to the bedraggled Vance Roberts.

"Yes," Vance said. "That is so important, isn't it? I don't mind sharing my name with you, except that there isn't enough of it to go around."

Zoe snapped at him. "Oh, stop being so smart. You aren't smart at all, you know. Twice in my life I've been struck with horror—and you caused it both times, Vance Roberts!"

He smiled. Shrugged. "Yes. I remember. I was your first drunk, wasn't I? I'll never forget the way you screamed in terror when you looked at me."

Her voice was cold. "And now it has happened again. I've been looking for you for weeks—I've looked everywhere—and now when I don't want you, when you're the last person I want to see, you turn up."

Roberts smiled. "Don't tell me you're behind this plot to use my name in vain—"

"In vain! For the first time in your worthless life your name was doing some good. It was offering safety to—to this man—"

Roberts looked at X. He closed one eye, squinted. He moved across the room, mouth pursed, surveying X from every angle.

"I'd say his name is Jeff Taylor," Roberts said at last. "I should know. I was around Taylor enough. Viewed him from every angle—even, mind you, from under the table. Purely in the interests of journalism, you understand."

"Oh, rubbish. Wherever you've been, whatever you've been doing, it hasn't changed you. You're still as unbearable as ever. Where have you been?"

"Why don't we sit down?" Vance Roberts inquired. "It's a long story. Amusing. And not without its own little climaxes and surprises. But if you really want to hear it—and I'm sure you do—we might as well be comfortable."

He sat again in his chair and leaned back against the window sill.

His voice went suddenly cold. "Before I start, Taylor, you're not going to get away with trying to hide behind my identity."

"I already know that," X replied. "Suppose you tell Zoe what happened to you."

Vance smiled again. "It seemed quite horrible at the time. But now I look back it was rather fun, and I suppose the farther I get away from the rigors of it, the more amusing it will become. Yes, I may look back on these six weeks as the most pleasant of my life—"

"Stop stalling," Zoe ordered.

He pretended not to hear her. "—Although they weren't very pleasant as they transpired. Often while I was living those weeks, I was pretty sure I wasn't going to survive. But I see you grow restive. Yes, what happened to me?

"First, let's go back to the night that I learned Ben Young and Jeff Taylor were going to get together. I had a great deal of interest in that meeting. So I figured I'd better stick close to it.

"The best way I figured to do that was to shadow Jeff Taylor. I did. I followed him and then the two of them closely until the moment I realized for certain that Taylor was taking Young to Taylor's cabin on Eaton Lake.

"I stopped then for a drink at a bar. I'd had several during the evening—against the night chill, you understand. When I reached the bar, I was in a cheerful, even festive and mellow, mood. There were two young men present. They seemed—under the influence of the alcohol I'd consumed—remarkably pleasant chaps—

"They had a drink with me. Then, before I could leave, I had to have a drink on each of them. By that time—"

"By that time you were high," Zoe said.

"Yes. By that time I was rather drunk. I remember going out to my car. I distinctly remember that. My car. Central Florida. A bar. Two swell drinking companions. That's as far as is clear that night.

"When I woke up I was in southern Tennessee, heading north by west."

"You're lying!" Zoe breathed.

"So help me, I'm not. I was lying in a box car. I was cold. I was hungry. I was hungover out to here. I was sick."

"Those two men," Zoe said. "They had hit you over the head, robbed you and then put you on a passing freight and took off."

"Almost right. But you're guessing. The truth is even better. It seems they didn't have to hit me over the head. Either they put a chloral tablet in one of my drinks, or else my capacity that night was far less than normal. I passed out."

"How did you get on the train?"

"My chaps. My drinking friends. They put me on the train. With them. They hadn't taken off—far from it. They removed my wallet from my inert body, and that was the last I saw of it. But they spent my money freely wherever we went as long as it lasted. They enjoyed watching me bum around. They never gave me more than a dime at a time.

"They watched me all the time. They were perfectly friendly. I don't want you to think they weren't. They shared with me all they had—except my money. That they kept.

"They wouldn't let me go. They called me 'pal,' and 'buddy,' and 'kid.' But they kept their eyes on me. They had robbed me and they were afraid I'd yell for the cops. Besides, it amused them to have me along. Helpless, sick, hungry all the time, and freezing until I learned to pad my coat with old newspapers. It pleased them."

"Why didn't you wire home?"

"To whom would I wire to help me? Especially collect? Do you think Merle Cooper at the *News* would accept a telegram from me, collect? From Chicago?

"I knew I was cooked. I knew I had muffed one of the biggest stories of my life. And I was so far north that I couldn't find out a thing about what had happened to Young or Taylor."

"How did you get away?"

"Finally, in Evanston, we got picked up by the police. For vagrancy. I was so sick and so miserable that the judge for some reason showed me leniency. He put me in the county jail hospital for a week, suspended the rest of my sentence. But he threw the book at my pals, and so far as I know they're in the Cook County jail right this minute—and may they rot there."

"It took you all the rest of the time to get home?"

"I was broke, I had to take odd jobs. And I took some of the oddest jobs you'll ever hear about. But for the moment I won't bore you with a recital of them."

Zoe nodded. "Good. I've heard enough. At least Jeff Taylor didn't kill you. Though he should have."

Vance Roberts stared at her. "Why should he have killed me?"

"Because you sold him out!"

"I sold him out?"

"You knew he hadn't killed Rick Vashney. You got drunk one night and bragged to me that you knew it. It was after I had quit you. You were being the big shot. You knew that I had quit because Jeff and I were going to leave town together—"

"Together?" X whispered. His voice croaked.

She twisted her head, facing him. Her eyes were blurred with tears. The reflection of the dim light flared and drowned in them.

"Yes!" she cried. "Together. Why did you think I wanted to find Vance Roberts? Because he *knew* you were innocent of killing Rick Vashney. And—and as long as Vance was alive—then Jeff Taylor hadn't really killed anyone!"

He was staring at her.

"You did all that for Jeff Taylor?" he whispered. "You loved him that much?"

"All right. With all my heart I loved him. There isn't anything in the world I wouldn't do for him. And he's the only man I ever will love."

"Zoe," he said.

She turned her head away, refusing to look at him any more. She faced Vance Roberts now. "You knew how much I loved Jeff Taylor—"

"A conflagration," Vance admitted. "I never saw anything like it."

"And that was why you were bragging to me while you were drunk. You were telling me that I'd never have Jeff. That he was going to be convicted of murder—"

"It's the sadist in me," Vance Roberts confessed blandly. "I love to see women suffer."

"Well, I've suffered," Zoe said. "But now I've found you. You're going to tell the world what you know about Jeff Taylor. The truth. Whether Jeff is dead or not, Vance Roberts, you're going to clear his name!"

"Zoe," X whispered again.

She wheeled about, facing him, her mouth taut. "All right!" she cried. "What do you want?"

He tried to show her he was smiling. He said, "You love Jeff Taylor?"

"I've said it.... Yes."

He nodded. "Then that's what I want. That's who I want to be. No matter what hell is ahead for him—I want to be Jeff Taylor."

20

There wasn't any sound in the room for a moment. It was silent with the beating of their hearts, and with the way they held their breath. It was as though they were alone in the room, alone on the earth, alone in the universe. Two people in love. The first two.

Zoe's eyes shimmered in tears. She touched his right hand with the cold tips of her fingers.

"I want you to be," she said. "But it isn't that simple."

"I've thought it all out," he said. "It is the only way. And it is as simple as going back to the hospital and telling them that I am Jeff Taylor."

"You mustn't!"

"If I told them that I was Ben Young, they wouldn't believe me. They don't know that Ben Young is going to be disbarred. They do know that Jeff Taylor is wanted for murder—"

"And that's why you can't do it."

"I'm in trouble now, Zoe. I've told them I was Vance Roberts. I made them believe it. I made fools of them. And now Vance Roberts is really here. I dragged you into it. There is only one way out. As long as they think I've nothing to gain by being Jeff Taylor, they'll accept that. They'll believe it. Beckart will want to believe it."

"I've lost you once! I won't lose you again!"

"Maybe. Maybe not. It's a chance we've got to take. This man—Vance Roberts—told you he knew Taylor was not guilty of murder—"

Vance Robert's face was milky white under the shabby growth of beard.

"I was drunk when I said it. I was lying."

"We'll see whether you were lying or not. At least you said it. There's a chance you may have been telling the truth—"

The chair legs came down hard. Vance Roberts leaned forward. His eyes were frightened.

"I'm not admitting anything. So far it's just Zoe Gardner's word against mine. Everybody knows she was crazy about Jeff Taylor. He was willing to quit the rackets for her. He was trying to run away so he could have her. She'd say anything to save him. If I were you, I wouldn't count on anything!"

He started to jump up. But X moved off the bed with the agility of a mountain lion. He caught the front of Robert's filthy coat. "Sit down!" he croaked. He shoved hard.

Roberts sat down. He stared up at the helmeted head, disbelief showing in his eyes.

At that moment there was a knock on the door. The four of them froze, listening.

Finally, Zoe got up. She went to the door.

She shoved the night bolt home.

"Who is it?" she said.

"Let me in." It was a woman's voice. A voice that X had heard before.

Zoe heeled around, looking at him. He nodded.

"Let her in."

Zoe shoved back the bolt, unlocked the door and opened it. Myra Young pushed past her into the room. She was wearing a rain slicker with the collar turned up about her neck. She was wearing a hat with a half-veil. It was pulled low over her face.

"What are you doing here?" X said. "Why did you come?"

Vance Roberts spoke then. Some of his self-confidence had returned. "Maybe you can thank me for that. When I hit town this morning, I still didn't know the score. I knew I was going to need help. So I called my old friend Ben Young. Only I didn't get Ben. I got Mrs. Young instead. Didn't I, Mrs. Young?"

Myra was looking at X. "When I heard what you had done—used the ruse I had suggested—and convinced them that you were Vance, I knew you were headed for trouble. I've been working on it all day. I think I can offer you a way out."

Zoe had locked the door behind Myra. She spoke now, from behind them. "What is it?"

Myra smiled. Her smile was cold. She knew she had them all in the palm of her hand. X felt that stirring again. This woman he knew! The feeling beat at his consciousness, pounding, pounding, pounding. He knew her. He knew her so well.

By the name of everything holy, he thought, *I must be Ben Young. Nothing else could explain why I know Myra when I didn't know anyone or anything.*

He looked beyond Myra. At the soft beauty, the dark eyes, the black hair. Zoe. The kind of woman he'd forsake the world for. He would face the sure prospect of the electric chair just to know that for a little while Zoe would love him.

What else did a man have on earth? To be loved for a little while. To be wanted. Needed. The way Zoe loved Jeff Taylor.

No. He wasn't Jeff. That way he'd be getting everything. But as Ben Young—no matter what he gained—he would be lost.

Zoe spoke again. The soft voice he loved!

"What is the way out, Mrs. Young?"

Myra looked at her, one brow arched slightly. "Well, we know now that he isn't Vance Roberts—as you and I must have known all along. I've talked to a good many brilliant lawyers today. And few of them believe that simply because two witnesses admit they lied Ben Young can be ruined, or even touched at all. Whom did they lie to? To Ben Young. To the Assistant District Attorney."

X shook his head. His whisper was hoarse. "But that's what Philip Dickson told you! Those witnesses had been paid to lie!"

She smiled, nodding. "Yes. But not by Ben Young. There's no proof in the world to show that my husband had anything to do with offering those people money. If they lied—they lied to him. If he was counting on the evidence of liars, he was innocently involved."

"And so?" Zoe's voice was empty.

"And so, what I have felt all along is true. This man is Ben Young. He's Assistant District Attorney. He will be the next Governor."

"As I remember it," X said, "Dickson was having resignation papers drawn up."

"An hysterical old maid, Philip Dickson," Myra said. "As you must know, Ben. He ran screaming at the first scent of trouble. But we won't do that— you and I. Philip has agreed to kill the resignation thing. He wants to see you tomorrow. To apologize."

X shook his head. "I'm sorry, Myra. But whoever I am—and I may be Ben Young—I can't go on with that. I know it for a frame-up now."

"You can still be Governor. You need never mention the murder of Rick Vashney again. If you clean up the vice in this town, it will be enough. As one who came back from the dead, you'll be swept into office. I tell you I've talked to important men. They're anxious to have you. Anxious to back you."

Myra glanced at Zoe. Her smile was disdainful. "Must we discuss this in public, Ben? I think you already understand my position toward your—your friends."

X shook his head. "No. I'm afraid we'll have to discuss it. Zoe might not like living in the shadows just so I could be Governor. Just so I could appear respectable. Just so you could have what you want."

"Unless you're both fools, you must know that I'm offering you the only possible solution!" Myra snapped. "I've told you—as long as you're discreet, this girl will be all right. Surely, if she loves you, she's willing to be discreet. Or would she rather see you go to your death—as Jeff Taylor?"

"Since you're discussing me," Zoe said. "May I say something?"

"Please," X said. "Tell her, Zoe. Tell her why we've got to work this thing out—you and I."

Zoe smiled at him. But it was only a fleeting smile. "I'm sorry, Ben. But I can't tell her that—"

"*Ben!*"

"Aren't you Ben Young?" Zoe's eyes were filled with tears, but she held her head high. Her voice was choked, but she spoke clearly. "You can't be Jeff Taylor. As long as there is a chance that Jeff Taylor may go to prison, or worse, I wouldn't want you to be Jeff Taylor. Myra is right. I can see it as she can. *You are Ben* Young—"

"Don't be a fool!" he croaked. "You're only saying that because you think you can save my life. Well, I'm willing to take a chance—"

She shook her head. "But I'm not. As far as I know, you—you are Ben Young. You're right, I don't agree with the things Ben Young did—before the fire. But now—he might be different. Decent and good and strong. There are wonderful things that Ben Young could do—if he were the right man—"

"I don't want to be Governor. I don't want to take this way just because it's easy—"

"But it won't be easy. It will be long and hard—and arduous—for both of us. And lonely."

Myra's voice had the crack of a lash in it. "It needn't be lonely—for either of you. As long as you're smart."

Zoe shook her head. "But that's it. You see, I guess I'm just not smart. I couldn't do the thing you suggest. I couldn't. Maybe it's because I loved Jeff Taylor too much. But—I couldn't."

X's voice was stronger now, louder. "Then don't ask me to do it."

"I'm not asking you, my darl— Ben. I'm telling you, you must. There's the great good that you can do. Whatever bad there was before, you'll wipe that all out. You'll be strong and fine and clean. And whatever you do—you'll be doing it for Jeff Taylor—and for me."

21

"That's all very wonderful," X said. "All very noble. But there's just one thing wrong with it. And I'll tell you what it is."

"There's nothing wrong with it," Myra said. "It's your only way out."

"Not quite. Wonderful as it would be for you. It wouldn't do for me. Whoever I am, I was somebody else before that fire. I'm going to get well. Even Dr. Ricey said that time alone would clear the effects of shock away. And as it clears up, Myra, and you, too, Zoe, what then?"

Myra shrugged, "What then?"

Zoe said, "You'll still be all right."

"Will I? You said I'd be good and strong. All right, maybe I would, remembering you, Zoe, knowing what you want done. But you've both overlooked something. Right now I'm ill. When I'm ill, I have no memory of any promise or bargains I made when I was well. What about when I'm cured? And I'm going to be."

"You still will do as you started," Zoe said. Her voice was level.

"Will I? Or will I forget these bargains and promises you two want me to make? Suppose I am Ben Young. As I hear it, Ben Young was crooked, scheming and vicious when he was well. When I get well—if I'm Ben Young—baby, I'm very likely to be crooked, scheming and vicious.

"And if I am Jeff Taylor, I won't want to live like Ben Young. I wouldn't be able to stand it.

"No. I'm going to get well first. I'm going to find out who I am."

Now Vance Roberts stood up. "I'll tell you who you better be, Mister. You better be Ben Young. Ben Young owes me plenty. And I expect to collect."

"What are you talking about?" Myra said.

"Just this," Vance said. "Why do you think I called your place first when I got back to town? Ben Young promised to protect me. But now, since I've seen all these new developments, why, maybe I don't want just protection, I want riches. And I don't see how you can refuse me."

Myra's voice was cold. "Go on."

"Before it was just a simple matter of knowing that Jeff Taylor was innocent. But now it's really big. Ben Young may not even be Ben Young—"

X's voice was very soft. "And how do you figure to make that pay off?"

Vance's mouth twisted. "When Ben Young wasn't home, I called Jeff Taylor's apartment. I talked to his wife—"

"Jessie," X whispered.

Vance laughed. "That's right. And so now Mike Reglen knows that I'm alive and back in Rainier—"

"You really snarled things up, didn't you?" X said.

"No. I only feathered my nest, old boy. I'm just telling you that you can be Ben Young and Mike Reglen won't even touch you. But try to be Jeff Taylor and Reglen will get you before you could get out of town."

"He's right," Zoe said. Her voice was tense. "You are Ben Young. You've got to be."

Vance regarded his nails. "Of course he is. And since you are Ben Young, I think we had better come to terms before you leave here."

"Terms?" Myra said. "What kind of terms?"

"As I said, before it was just a matter of knowing Ben Young framed Jeff Taylor. I did Ben Young a favor, and he promised to pay off—as long as I forgot what I knew. He promised to pay me twenty thousand dollars."

They heard Myra's sharp intake of breath. "You're lying."

"No, m'am, I'm not. And whether they could prove bribery of witnesses or not, I can prove he agreed to pay me twenty grand. I got his promise in writing."

Myra's mouth became a scarlet sneering line. "How low, how despicable can you get?" she said.

"Well, about as low as your husband, Mrs. Young. That's how low you get dealing with men like he—is—" He turned insolent eyes upon X.

X looked toward Zoe. "You see," he said to her. "That's what it would be all the way. Ben Young's whole life was smeared up. No matter what you wanted to do, you couldn't do it. There are too many Vance Roberts in his life."

Vance bowed. His voice was mocking. "But you haven't heard all of it. You see, now that I know an additional secret, it will cost you an additional twenty thousand to buy my silence."

He turned his arrogant smile upon each of them. Myra's gaze fell under his. Zoe didn't lift her head. Halftime Smith shifted his weight from one leg to the other.

X said, "Now *I've* got a surprise for *you*. I think you've talked too much. I think if you know a secret worth twenty thousand dollars, it's too good for you to keep. We're going to help you keep it. You're going to share it with us."

He took a step forward. Vance backed away. He threw up his hand. "Stay away from me, I warn you!"

"Oh, no. If Ben Young let himself owe you twenty thousand it must have been a pretty dirty secret. He must have known he would be paying for your silence all the rest of your lives. So if I'm paying, Roberts, I got to know what I'm buying!"

He leaped forward suddenly. With a scream of terror Vance jumped backward, upsetting the chair. He heeled around and started across the room. He was fighting his hand into his coat pocket.

Spreading both arms like a huge grizzly, Halftime Smith gathered him in.

Vance was screaming and swearing as those big arms tightened around him like a vise.

"Tell the boss," Halftime said. "What do you know? Or I crack your spine, like a match—"

Vance moaned. He tried to twist away from those arms. They were closing like the coils of a giant boa. He could hardly breathe now. His face was becoming discolored.

"All right!" he gasped. "I did it. I killed Rick. I—I knew how to get in—and out. Young planned it. Promised to pay me—all my life—if I framed Jeff Taylor. I—I stole Taylor's gun from Taylor's office—"

His hand was fighting free of his coat. Halftime had loosened his strangling body hold so Vance could talk.

Zoe saw the gun in Vance's hand first.

She screamed.

X yelled at Halftime. Halftime closed his arms in one mighty crunch. They heard something snap in Vance's back.

At that moment the gun held against Halftime's chest exploded. They didn't fall. They crumpled. It was in slow motion. To X, standing there, it seemed to take forever. Halftime's stranglehold relaxed and Vance slid backward away from him, still clutching the gun in inert fingers.

For a moment longer Halftime stood there. His eyes had glazed over. He was already dead. But for the space of another ten seconds the giant tottered there. Then he staggered and fell across Vance Roberts' body.

The door of the room was smashed in.

They moved in fast. Mike Reglen and his two thugs, Phil and Jersey.

One of the thugs, the bigger one, leaped at X. X hit at him with his right fist. The thug's arms closed on him. They spun around, with X fighting to free his arms.

He saw Mike's arms upraised. And then he felt the intense pain as the gun butt struck his head. It had all Mike's strength behind it. It made the other time X was hit by Jessie Taylor seem like nothing at all. That was a sharp little tap. This was a clubbing. Mike beat him to his knees, and then he fell senseless across Halftime's thick body....

...He remembered waking up with his clothes on fire. He fought to roll himself in the grass rug. He ducked his head, ran across the room. He smashed out the back window with his free left hand. He felt the bone snap, felt the pain all through his body. But there wasn't time to worry about a broken arm, this house was on fire. He had meant to threaten Young, frighten him. But the fool had started fighting, knocked over the lamp. The gasoline had exploded. All he knew was he had to get out of that burning cabin.

It took forever. And all that time he was burning. The grass rug was afire. The window wouldn't give. The trousers were afire, and he could feel the fire in his legs. His head was flaming inside and out.

And all he was thinking was, *I've got to get out. Zoe is waiting for me. We're going to clear out. We're going to be free of the whole dirty mess.*

He couldn't die. Zoe was waiting for him....

22

For a moment, waking up, Jeff didn't know where he was. Why was Halftime sprawled on the floor like that? And why had he landed on top of him?

From a great distance he heard voices. Then they grew stronger, more distinct.

Jeff lay silent, listening.

"All right," Mike Reglen was saying. "I'm giving you dames about two minutes to make up your minds. Who is he? I'm puffin' a bullet through him."

"He is my husband," Myra said. "Pretending to be Vance Roberts was all part of a plan. Vance Roberts was trying to blackmail my husband. Ben chose this way to bring him out of hiding." She had convinced herself that it was the truth.

"Yeah?" But the word wavered. Reglen was almost convinced. He spoke to Zoe. "How about you, sister? You got anything to say? Who is that guy?"

Jeff heard the catch in Zoe's voice. The hurt.

Lying there, he wanted her. It seemed a hundred years since he'd held Zoe in his arms. He couldn't stay there like this. Zoe was waiting for him.

"It's—Ben Young—" Zoe said. "Mrs. Young is telling you the truth, Mike."

Jeff couldn't believe his ears. She was saying that he was Ben Young. How could she say a thing like that? How could she pretend to believe it? And then he remembered why he was here, and he remembered that Halftime was dead. And he knew that under Halftime's body Vance Roberts was dead.

"I'm going to be top dog in this town," Mike was saying. "And I ain't taking any chances. That guy might be Young—and he might carry out the promises he made to me about protection. But there's a chance it's Jeff Taylor. And that's a chance I ain't taking—a chance I can't afford to take."

"You'll never get away with murdering him!" Zoe cried. The pain in her voice stabbed at Jeff's heart.

"Murder? Me? Oh, no. These three boys got in a fight. Vance killed both of them before they got him. And if either of you girls don't feel like agreein' to that—why, I can mighty easy add to the list of Vance Roberts' victims—"

Jeff was thinking. *Under Vance Roberts' right hand is a gun. If I can get my fingers on it before Mike gets up his nerve to shoot me....*

"He is Ben Young!" Zoe cried. "Please! It is! Don't shoot. I tell you it is Ben Young!"

Jeff's inching fingers closed over the gun, moved it. He closed his hand over it and whirled over suddenly on his back.

The bigger thug yelled. Mike wheeled around, and found himself facing the yawning mouth of Vance Roberts' automatic, nestling in Jeff's hand.

"She's wrong, Mike. It's me. Jeff Taylor. This is the chance you've been asking for. You better pull that trigger."

Mike threw his gun around, pressing the trigger.

Jeff fired. The man who wanted to be top dog sideslipped, stepping backward under the force of the bullet in his chest.

The gun slid from Mike's fingers. It fell hard to the bare floor of the cheap room. Mike followed it. The gun didn't move and Mike didn't move, either.

Jeff moved the gun in his hand a little. "All right, Jersey, how about you? And you, Phil?"

"Naw, boss. Naw!" Jersey shouted. "It's like you say, boss. Anything you say."

"Then drop your guns."

They dropped them.

Jeff stood up. Zoe was staring at him. "You're all right?" she whispered.

"Sure, baby, I'm wonderful."

"Let's go," Myra Young said. "We'll go back to the hospital. We'll tell them that you're Ben Young—that these men attacked you—that it was self-defense."

Jeff looked at her. "Myra Young," he said. Contempt made his voice cold. "Now I know why your memory stayed with me through shock and hellfire. I used to think you were perfect. The lovely wife of the young Assistant D.A. Then you began sneaking into my gambling clubs, drinking, gambling and a lot of worse things—and offering me money not to tell your husband. That was when I knew I couldn't do business with Ben Young. The rackets were too dirty for me when women like you turned out to look like angels—and to live like dogs in a gutter."

Myra was staring at him. Her mouth dropped open. All the hope went out of her eyes.

"Jeff Taylor," she whispered. "You are Jeff Taylor." There was a deadness in her voice.

"That's right, Myra. It was your idea for me to remember something that would convince people I was Ben. Well, I remember you in my gambling rooms. So there's no doubt, is there, Myra? You know who I am, don't you?"

She just said his name again, without inflection. "Jeff Taylor." She was the picture of utter dejection.

Captain Beckart and his men took over in Vance Roberts' cheap room. There were no charges. There were too many witnesses to unprovoked attack and killing in self-defense. Mrs. Myra Young. Zoe Gardner. Jersey and Phil. And X, the man who didn't know his own past.

Myra remained staring at the floor until her father-in-law came and led her away.

At last, the Captain told Jeff and Zoe they were free to go. He looked at Jeff.

"I don't suppose you want to take another guess as to who you are?" he asked unenthusiastically.

Jeff looked at Zoe. The Captain wasn't anxious to know. He had believed him once. He wasn't going to believe him again.

"Doctor Ricey says time will wash away this shock you're suffering from," Beckart told the man in the bandages. "Maybe time will clear it all up."

"I hope so," Jeff said. He put his arm about Zoe and they went out of the room and down the dark stairs.

Zoe didn't speak until they were in the clean fresh air of the street.

"What are we going to do?" she said.

"Get out of town, find a job. Be happy."

"That money. You can never dare to claim it. They'd know who you were, then—and there'd be trouble."

"Money? Who needs it? I've got you. I can make plenty of money. I'm a pretty smart guy."

"You're wonderful. But—but aren't you going to tell them who you are?"

He shook his head. "No. They wouldn't ever believe me, really. Not any more." He smiled. "It doesn't matter. I got what I really wanted. I wanted to be free of the whole mess so I could have you. I'm free of it, and I've got you."

"What about a name?" she said. "What will you call yourself—us?"

He looked at her, but he was remembering the good and simple man who had died for him back it that dirty room up there. He sighed heavily.

"Smith," he said. "I can't think of a better one. Halftime Smith. I'll have to live a hell of a good life to be worthy of that name."

"Smith," she said, sounding it, tasting the name on her lips, savoring it, and finding it goon. "Mrs. H. T. Smith." She laughed suddenly, and they walked faster into the darkness. "Hello, World," Zoo said. "Here we come. Meet the Smiths."

THE END

HARRY WHITTINGTON BIBLIOGRAPHY

Vengeance Valley (1946)
Her Sin (1946)
Slay Ride for a Lady (1950)
The Brass Monkey (1951)
Call Me Killer (1951)
Fires That Destroy (1951)
The Lady Was a Tramp (1951)
Satan's Widow (1951)
Forever Evil (1952)
Married to Murder (1951; reprinted 1959)
Murder is My Mistress (1951)
Drawn to Evil (1952)
Mourn the Hangman (1952)
Prime Sucker (1952)
Cracker Girl (1953)
So Dead My Love! (1953)
Vengeful Sinner (1953; reprinted as Nightclub Sinner, 1954; abridged as Die, Lover, 1960)
Saddle the Storm (1954)
Wild Oats (1954)
The Woman is Mine (1954)
You'll Die Next! (1954)
The Naked Jungle (1955)
One Got Away (1955)
Across That River (1956)
Desire in the Dust (1956)
Brute in Brass (1956; reprinted as Forgive Me, Killer, 1987)
The Humming Box (1956)
Saturday Night Town (1956)
Sinner's Club (1956; reprinted as Teenage Jungle, 1958)
A Woman on the Place (1956)
Man in the Shadow (1957) [screenplay novelization]
T'as des Visions! (1957, France)
One Deadly Dawn (1957)
Play for Keeps (1957)

Temptations of Valerie (1957) [screenplay novelization]
Trouble Rides Tall (1958)
Web of Murder (1958)
Backwoods Tramp (1959; reprinted as A Moment to Prey, 1987)
Halfway to Hell (1959)
Lust for Love (1959)
Strictly for the Boys (1959)
Strange Bargain (1959)
Strangers on Friday (1959)
A Ticket to Hell (1959)
Connolly's Woman (1960)
The Devil Wears Wings (1960)
Heat of Night (1960)
Hell Can Wait (1960)
A Night for Screaming (1960)
Nita's Place (1960)
Rebel Woman (1960)
Trouble Rides Tall (1960)
Vengeance is the Spur (1960)
Desert Stake-Out (1961)
God's Back Was Turned (1961)
Guerilla Girls (1961)
Journey Into Violence (1961)
The Searching Rider (1961)
A Trap for Sam Dodge (1961)
The Young Nurses (1961)
A Haven for the Damned (1962)
Hot as Fire Cold as Ice (1962)
69 Babylon Park (1962)
Wild Sky (1962)
Cora is a Nympho (1963)
Don't Speak to Strange Girls (1963)
Drygulch Town (1963)
Prairie Raiders (1963; reprinted as by Hondo Wells, 1977)
Cross the Red Creek (1964)
Fall of the Roman Empire (1964) [screenplay novelization]

High Fury (1964)
Hangrope Town (1964)
The Man from U.N.C.L.E #2:
   The Doomsday Affair (1965)
Valley of Savage Men (1965)
Wild Lonesome (1965)
Doomsday Mission (1967)
Bonanza: Treachery Trail
   (1968; pub in Germany as
   Ponderosa in Gefahr)
Burden's Mission (1968)
Charro! (1969)
Rampage (1978)
Sicilian Woman (1979)

As Ashley Carter

Master of Blackoaks (1976)
Sword of the Golden Stud (1977)
Panama (1978)
Secret of Blackoaks (1978)
Taproots of Falconhurst (1978)
Scandal of Falconhurst (1980)
Heritage of Blackoaks (1981)
Rogue of Falconhurst (1983)
Against All Gods (1983, UK)
A Darkling Moon (1985, UK)
Embrace the Wind (1985, UK; pub
   in the US as by Blaine Stevens)
A Farewell to Blackoaks (1986, UK)
Miz Lucretia of Falconhurst (1986)
Mandingo Mansa (1986, UK; pub
   in the US as Mandingo Master)
Strange Harvest (1986, UK)
Falconhurst Fugitive (1988)

As Curt Colman

Flesh Mother (1965)
Flamingo Terrace (1965)
Hell Bait (1966)
Sinsurance (1966)

The Taste of Desire (1966)
Sin Deep (1966)
Latent Lovers (1966)
Sinners After Six (1966)
Balcony of Shame (1967)
Mask of Lust (1967)
The Grim Peeper (1967)

As John Dexter:

Saddle Sinners (1964)
Lust Dupe (1964)
Pushover (1964)
Sin Psycho (1964)
Flesh Curse (1964)
Sharing Sharon (1965)
Shame Union (1965)
The Wedding Affair (1965)
Baptism in Shame (1965)
Sin Fishers (1966)
Passion Burned (1966)
Remembered Sin (1966)
The Sinning Room (1966)
Blood Lust Orgy (1966)
The Abortionists (1966)

As Tabor Evans

Longarm on the Humboldt (1981)
Longarm and the Golden Lady
   (1981)
Longarm and the Blue Norther
   (1981)
Longarm in Silver City (1982)
Longarm in Boulder Canyon
   (1982)
Longarm in the Big Thicket (1982)

As Whit Harrison

Body and Passion (1952)
Girl on Parole (1952; reprinted
  as Man Crazy, 1960)
Sailor's Weekend (1952)
Savage Love (1952; reprinted as by
  Harry Whittington as Native Girl,
  1959)
Swamp Kill (1952)
Violent Night (1952)
Army Girl (1953)
Rapture Alley (1953)
Strip the Town Naked (1960)
Any Woman He Wanted (1961)
A Woman Possessed (1961)

As Kel Holland

Strange Young Wife (1963)
The Tempted (1964)

As Lance Horner

Golden Stud (1975)

As Harriet Kathryn Meyers

Small Town Nurse (1962)
Prodigal Nurse (1963)

As Blaine Stevens

The Outlanders (1979)
Embrace the Wind (1982)
Island of Kings (1989)

As Clay Stuart

His Brother's Wife (1964)

As Harry White

Shadow at Noon (1955; reprinted
  as by Hondo Wells, 1977)

As Hallam Whitney

Backwoods Hussy
  (1952; reprinted as Lisa, 1965)
Shack Road (1953)
Backwoods Shack (1954)
City Girl (1954)
Shanty Road (1954; reprinted
  as by Whit Harrison, 1956)
The Wild Seed (1956)

As Henry Whittier/
Henri Whittier

Nightmare Alibi (1972)
Another Man's Claim (1973)

As J. X. Williams

Lust Farm (1964)
Flesh Avenger (1964)
The Shame Hiders (1964)
Lust Buyer (1965)
Passion Flayed (1965)
Man Hater (1965)
Passion Hangover (1965)
Passion Cache (1966)
Baby Face (1966)
Flesh Snare (1966)

As Howard Winslow

The Mexican Connection (1972)